HOW TO SUCCEED IN WITCHCRAFT

HOW TO SUCCEED IN WITCHCRAFT

AISLINN BROPHY

putnam

G. P. PUTNAM'S SONS

G. P. PUTNAM'S SONS

An imprint of Penguin Random House LLC, New York

First published in the United States of America by G. P. Putnam's Sons,
an imprint of Penguin Random House LLC, 2022

G. P. Putnam's Sons is a registered trademark of Penguin Random House LLC.
The Penguin colophon is a registered trademark of Penguin Books Limited.

Visit us online at penguinrandomhouse.com

Library of Congress Cataloging-in-Publication Data
Names: Brophy, Aislinn, author.
Title: How to succeed in witchcraft / Aislinn Brophy.
Description: New York: G. P. Putnam's Sons, [2022] | Summary: Half-Black witch Shay Johnson is cast as the lead in her school musical and must decide between exposing her predatory drama teacher and getting the scholarship she desperately needs.
Identifiers: LCCN 2021059587 | ISBN 9780593354520 (hardcover) |
ISBN 9780593354537 (ebook)
Subjects: CYAC: Magic—Fiction. | Musicals—Fiction. |
Teacher-student relationships—Fiction. | Dating (Social customs)—Fiction. |
Lesbians—Fiction. | African Americans—Fiction. |
Hispanic Americans—Fiction. | LCGFT: Novels.
Classification: LCC PZ7.1.B78 Ho 2022 | DDC [Fic]—dc23
LC record available at https://lccn.loc.gov/2021059587

Book manufactured in Canada

ISBN 9780593354520

FRI

Text set in Calisto MT Std

For my parents.
This book wouldn't exist without you.

Chapter 1

Each year, T. K. Anderson Magical Magnet School brings together a class of highly motivated and magically talented students from Palm Beach County. Students are selectively admitted based upon prior school record, magic level, and a rigorous admissions test.

On our campus, we prepare students for the world of higher education by encouraging an atmosphere of healthy competition.

—**T. K. Anderson promotional brochure**

I STARE AT THE CURLICUES OF MAGIC SWIRLING THROUGH THE brown liquid in my Port-a-Cauldron. The stupid piece of equipment should be heating faster. This Flora-Grow potion is due tomorrow, so I have to finish enough to turn in, or my grade in AP Potions will take a serious hit. Probably not a good look for a girl trying to go to college for potionwork.

The numbers on my alarm clock glow from my bedside table—2:32 a.m. It's only two weeks after winter break, and my sleep schedule is already shot. That's cool. Who needs rest anyway? I was stuck singing in a choir performance at our school's Salute to America concert until eight, so I probably shouldn't have decided to pick an extra-complicated brewing project for tonight's assignment. I could have just done a simple cold-curing potion instead, but I couldn't resist brewing something new.

I stick my temperature gauge into the liquid. It beeps loudly, the sound piercing the quiet of our apartment. I wince. Hopefully Mom is sleeping deeply enough to not have heard that. Sometimes she has insomnia, so she'll sit awake doing sudoku puzzles, but I checked before I started brewing, and the lights were off in my parents' room.

The temperature gauge shows that the potion is done heating, so I turn down the burner and focus on the liquid. I concentrate to activate my magic sight, which allows me to see the web of invisible magical energy that exists in every physical object. The thin, silvery filaments of magic come into view, twisting and turning within the liquid. The shape and movements of magic reflect an object's physical properties, and speed correlates to heat, so the magic in this heated potion moves quickly.

I mentally reach for the magic, bending it to my will. The strands vibrate, still holding to their natural patterning, then begin to weave themselves into the lattice framework I have in mind. Once the lattice is complete, the liquid thickens and turns from brown to a brilliant emerald green.

I reach for the magic one last time to seal my intention into the potion. Growth. Life. Green, natural things. I hold those thoughts in mind and push them toward the potion. A thread of my magic wisps out of my head. In it, I see flashes of the images I held in my mind. Once it sinks into the cauldron, the liquid shivers, and then the potion is done.

Nice. Time to test this bad boy out. Thankfully, Dad approved me testing this Flora-Grow on one of his beloved plant babies yesterday.

Dad is a total herbology nerd. He works for Green Witch, that big eco-management company that hires herbologists to maintain Florida's natural landscape. Caring for plants isn't just a job for him, though. Our apartment is stuffed full of useful herbs, miniaturized trees, and flowers he's magically adjusted to smell stronger. He's even got a collection of magic-hybrid plants. There are ghost palms that are invisible except for a faint blue-green glow, midair plants that float through our apartment in search of patches of sun, frost ferns that emit tiny puffs of cold air to chill their surroundings, and several others that have come in handy for my more ambitious brewing projects.

I grab one of Dad's ghost palm seedlings from the corner in our kitchen and bring it back to my room. Okay. Moment of truth. I measure out ten milliliters of the Flora-Grow, pour it into the palm's pot, and stand back. It shouldn't take too long for the potion to take effect.

The seedling vibrates slightly, then shoots upward at warp speed. It looks like one of those plant-growth time-lapse videos, except sped up a thousand times over. New fronds burst out at the top, and the trunk thickens to the size of my leg. Or at least I think that's how large it is. It's kind of hard to tell with a mostly invisible tree. By the time it stops growing, the tallest fronds hang more than a foot over my head. So this potion was definitely a success.

I can still turn out a quality potion while half-asleep. Awesome. My grin stretches so wide that my cheeks hurt, and I do a little happy dance. There's nothing better than brewing a potion that works just right.

I love potionworking. Potions let people do complicated things they might not be able to achieve with just their innate magic abilities. Which is *amazing*. Especially when you're a kid and your powers aren't that strong. I mean, would I be able to do complex transfiguration on this tree to change it into its adult form? Definitely not. But I don't need to, because I can brew a Flora-Grow potion.

A jaw-splitting yawn interrupts my train of thought. Right. Definitely time for bed. I cast one last satisfied look at the ghost palm before turning away to start cleaning up my supplies.

Then everything goes wrong. I grossly miscalculated how well this pot of dirt would hold up a seven-foot tree.

By the time I notice the pot tipping over, it's too late. The whole thing falls to the floor with a massive crash. I let out a startled yelp as dirt and pieces of glowing palm tree fly across my room. A chunk of bark hits me in the face, which feels like a personal eff-you.

Once the chaos subsides, I snatch up a bottle of cleaning potion from my shelf and sprinkle it liberally across my floor. Piles of dirt disintegrate as the liquid hits them, leaving behind a faint scent of lemon. Maybe I can get this cleaned up before Mom busts me.

It takes me a few tries, but I manage to hoist the ghost palm back upright. I prop it against the wall and pray that it won't tip over again. This would be way easier if I had some Light as a Feather potion on hand. I guess I *could* levitate the tree myself, but at my level, magically messing with living things without prior planning is a recipe for disaster.

The floorboards in the hallway creak, and I tense. Time's up.

"Shay? Shay, are you awake?" Mom calls. Her heavy steps echo through the apartment as she approaches my room.

Ooh, I'm dead. I am so incredibly deceased. I'm not actually supposed to brew potions in my room. Ugh, I should have done the easy potion and gone to bed on time.

Mom whips open the door and strides into the room. She's wearing her black bonnet—I definitely woke her up. Damn.

"You okay?" she says as she turns the lights on. "Did something happen?"

I freeze, one hand still resting guiltily on the stupid ghost palm. "Um. One of Dad's trees fell over."

"You good?" She comes over and looks me up and down. "It didn't hit you?"

"I'm fine."

She takes another few seconds to confirm that I'm actually all right. Then she turns her attention to the tree. "Why'd you have that in here?" she says, her eyes narrowing.

"He said I could test my Flora-Grow on it."

She sniffs, catching the scent of my potion, and her eyes flick to the cauldron. "Were you brewing in here?" she says, her hands flying to her hips. "Shayna, you know better than that. While you live in my house, you follow my rules."

I nod obediently, looking as apologetic as possible. "Yes, ma'am."

"You don't need to be working on your li'l potion projects in the middle of the night."

"It's homework. For AP Potions."

Her expression softens, and I sense that I could get out of this without serious consequences. Maybe.

"I had to finish this tonight," I continue. "It's due tomorrow."

"There is no reason to be up all hours doing homework," she says, launching into the lecture I've heard a million times before. "You go to bed at a reasonable hour, and you wake up in the morning to finish things up. You need sleep to do your best work."

"Sleep is for the weak," I deadpan. She quirks an eyebrow at me, unamused.

"Brockton Scholars are well-rested," she says. That, of course, is complete and utter Mom Nonsense. You have to be many things to win the Brockton Scholarship—magically brilliant, academically perfect, chronically overcommitted—but well-rested is not a required quality. She sighs, shaking her head. "Bed. Now." She turns the lights off and leaves, as if I'm going to immediately throw myself into my bed smelling of potion with arrowroot residue all over my hands.

My mom's parenting style is 25 percent "you stress yourself out too much" and 75 percent "be the best that ever was." She doesn't see the contradiction there and doesn't appreciate when I've tried to point it out.

When I look at myself in the mirror the next morning, I want to crawl back into bed. The bags under my eyes could be checked as flight luggage. My brown hair looks greasy as hell too. I need to restraighten it soon.

I tie my hair up, slap on some Face Awake potion to shrink the bags under my eyes, and put on mascara. By the time I walk into the kitchen, I look a little tired instead of like a corpse.

"You okay there?" Dad says, eyeing me over his oat-meal. He's dressed in his Green Witch work T-shirt, ready to head out after breakfast. He hunches in his seat, because he always sits in the chair under the low-hanging light, even though he's so tall that he's in real danger of whack-ing his pale, bald head on it.

"I'm tired," I say, sitting across the table from him. Mom slides a bowl of oatmeal and a mug of coffee onto my place setting. "Thanks."

Dad's blue eyes twinkle. "Hi, Tired, I'm Dad."

I boo him and make a face. "It's too early for dad jokes."

"It's never too early for dad jokes," he quips.

"Little miss was up at all hours of the night brewing a potion in her room," Mom tells Dad. She purses her lips and aggressively refills his coffee cup.

"I had a lot of homework," I mumble into my mug, breathing in the scent of Mom's coffee. I swear she does something to the magic in it, because it's way more effec-tive than any other coffee, but I can't get her to admit it.

"Oh, you think you're grown now? You can just be up all hours?" Mom says.

There's only one answer to that. "No, ma'am." Now seems like the moment to change the subject. I take a sip of coffee and smile at Mom winningly. "You're going to MarTech today, right?"

Mom works at a magitech factory that manufactures fancy televisions. It's the best job in magical technology she can get with her transfiguration degree, since she doesn't have a magical license. She spends her days trouble-shooting problems with the magic encoded in the TVs and transfiguring broken machinery so it works.

"Yeah," Mom says. Her eyes slide over to Dad. "Did I tell you I'm training the new girl this afternoon?"

"Hm." Dad takes a long drink from his coffee cup and raises his eyebrows. "Sounds like manager work."

Mom lets out a little snort. "I know."

"They giving you a raise?"

"What do you think?" Mom says, and they both chuckle quietly.

Mom's job isn't the best. She makes half as much as her manager but does twice the work, because he has a magical license from an accredited university. He likes to remind her that, without him, the unlicensed members of their team wouldn't be legally allowed to do any transfiguration because it's higher-level work. Mom is literally better at transfiguration than him. And even though she basically does his job for him too, she'll never get to be a manager without a license.

"What time do you start work?" I ask.

"One," Mom says. She sinks into her seat at our kitchen table and starts in on her own breakfast. Before she takes a bite, I activate my magic sight and nudge at the magic in her oatmeal to warm it up for her. It's been sitting there awhile, if the slow magic flows in it are anything to go off of.

"Bus day?" I say sympathetically.

"Bus day." She sighs.

Boca Raton is a driving town. Mostly rich retirees live here, and walking definitely isn't their primary way of getting anywhere. The network of floating roads is basically the only way to get around, unless you have a broom and can fly off-road. We only have one car, and Dad drives it to work, so when Mom is scheduled for shifts in the middle of the day, she has to struggle through Boca's depressing public transport situation.

"You know . . ." I drag out the words and grin at Mom mischievously. "If you got a broom, you wouldn't have to take the bus anymore."

"What would I look like on a broom?" She snorts. "Midlife-Crisis Mom? That's what you want your mother to look like?"

"You would look very cool on a broom, honey," Dad says, as cheesy as anything.

"I would look very dead on a broom," she shoots back, which doesn't even make sense. Like, okay, they're slightly dangerous. But she's not going to spontaneously die while riding one.

"I'm just saying it's cheaper than a car," I say.

"Nice try," Mom says. "But nobody in this household is getting a broom anytime soon."

"Better luck next time, kiddo," Dad says.

I sigh and abandon my broom crusade for today. "Lex

said she could drive me to work, so you don't have to pick me up after school," I tell Dad. Lex is my best friend. She, thank god, has her own car.

"Are you two going to *hang out* after work?" Mom asks. She puts a weird emphasis on *hang out*.

"I don't know. We haven't made plans. I'll text you if we do."

Mom definitely thinks Lex and I are secretly dating. When I told her and Dad I was a lesbian, that was her second question after "Are you sure?" (I was sure.) She keeps dropping hints that it would be fine with her if I were dating Lex.

"How's Lex doing?" Mom asks, her face creased with concern.

From the way Mom talks about her, you would think Lex was dying or something. "She's fine. Studying to take the MATs again." I shrug. Plenty of people don't get into a licensing university their first time applying. I wish Lex was still in school with me, because sometimes it's lonely without my bestie, but she seems fine with her involuntary gap year.

"Another group of boys from Pompano ran off to some Midwest commune," Mom says, shaking her head. "They had only been trying to get into school for two years, you know."

I frown into my oatmeal. She's been watching too many news exposés about society dropouts. I think she's secretly afraid I'm never going to get into a licensing college and will end up running away to one of those communes. Which is ridiculous. I would never abandon my parents like that.

"Lex isn't going to become some dropout witch," Dad says. Mom opens her mouth, but he continues before she can get a word in. "She works too hard. She'll get into a licensing college."

"Mm. I just worry." Mom turns her attention to me, tapping her lip thoughtfully. "The Brockton Scholarship info meeting is today, right?"

My stomach flips. It took longer than I thought it would for her to mention it. "Yeah."

She pauses, giving me a once-over. "Is that what you're wearing to school?"

"Yeah," I say sharply. I'm wearing my Willington University hoodie and jeans. I look fine. "It's not like an interview or something. I don't have to dress up."

She lifts her brown hands in surrender. "Okay. I'm just saying that you shouldn't give up the chance to make a good impression on Mr. B."

Now I'm second-guessing my outfit. Maybe I should change. Maybe it's too on the nose to wear a Willington hoodie to a meeting for a scholarship I'll use to go to Willington.

"You should do the chant," Mom says, smiling at me.

"Today is a day for affirmation. And a little extra magic won't hurt."

I visibly cringe. "No way."

Her smile grows a hard edge. "Shayna, if you don't believe in yourself, nobody else will."

I can't believe she won't let go of this tradition. "I believe in myself. I just don't want to do the chant. It's embarrassing."

"Embarrassing?" She shakes her head. "Child, the only people in this room are me, you, and your dad."

"Can we just share magic like normal people?" I say. "Without the weird chanting?"

"What is this 'normal people' you're talking about? You want to be like everybody else? If everybody starts huffing potion fumes, are you going to do that too?"

"Okay, let's—" Dad starts to say, but Mom continues over him.

"Now we're going to do the chant, and you're going to go wow them in that scholarship meeting today. Okay?" The look in her eyes tells me I'm not getting out of this one. I nod grudgingly. "Shayna is a . . . ?"

"Winner," I mumble. She gives me a look.

"Shayna is a . . . ?" she repeats, louder this time. Her magic emerges from her skin in tendrils and drifts toward me in a burgundy haze. It mixes midair with the rich brown of Dad's magic.

"Winner!" I say just as the magical strands sink into my skin. My heartbeat immediately quickens, and a burst of energy hits me. I become more and more conscious of how they're feeling—I can sense Dad's gentle contentedness and Mom's fierce pride and the slight undercurrent of exhaustion that's always there whenever we share magic. Soon their emotions fill my body, as strong and real as my own.

Mom locks eyes with me, and her pride echoes between us. "Shayna is a . . . ?"

"WINNER!" I shout.

"SHAYNA IS A WINNER!" all three of us yell together. The sound reverberates through our apartment. No matter how corny that chant is, it does hype me up.

"Now go get that scholarship, baby," Mom says, her brown face crinkling into a smile.

Chapter 2

The average high school senior has a magic level of 27.
Our seniors have an average magic level of 38.

—T. K. Anderson website

T. K. ANDERSON MAGICAL MAGNET SCHOOL IS KNOWN FOR two things. First, it's ridiculously hard to get in. Even if you live in the school zone and get preferred application status, you only have a 10 percent chance of acceptance. If you live outside the zone, your chance of acceptance shrinks to 1 percent. Mom rerouted all our mail to my rich auntie's house for a few months so she could pretend we lived nearby. She would have moved us near the school, but we couldn't afford any of the expensive properties in the area.

The other thing T. K. Anderson is known for is the Brockton Scholarship. The scholarship is awarded in junior year, and it gives one student a full ride to whatever licensing university they're accepted to. That's why most people are so desperate to get into T. K. Anderson.

Dad drives me to school, which is in West Palm Beach, a whole forty-five minutes away from our apartment. The opportunity is worth the commute. Sometimes it's hard to remember that when I have to wake up at the ass-crack of dawn to get there, but it is.

When I get to campus, I stop by the nurse's office for magic-level testing. T. K. Anderson is intense about tracking student progress, so we all get tested four times a year. I practice generating electricity at my fingertips while I wait in line. Any downtime is a good time to practice basic magic skills. Just as I get to the front, a group of other juniors joins the line. They clock me, then immediately turn in to discuss me. Typical. Their voices are quiet, but I can still hear most of what they're saying.

"Do you think she's going to win the scholarship?"

"It's either her or Ana. And Ana's grades are better."

Electricity crackles at my fingertips. Ana freaking Álvarez. She's not even here, and she's annoying me.

"But Shay's magic level is higher. If it went up any more—"

"Her magic level *can't* go up anymore. It was already thirty-eight last time. Nobody gets over forty as a junior."

"She has a big family, though, so it doesn't really count."

That is completely false. My family does share magic with me for these tests—everyone does that—but there are only three of us, so the effect isn't huge. I could take more from my parents, I guess. Even now, I can feel the connection to their magic, and it would be easy enough to pull on that connection for more power. But I wouldn't want to take anything they hadn't planned to give me and exhaust them at work.

The other students' voices dip, and I don't hear the next part of their conversation. I concentrate on shooting out sparks of electricity from my palm. Maybe if they focused on practicing their magic in their free time instead of gossiping about me, these people would have a magic level like mine.

I make it to the front of the line and head into the office. One last bit of their conversation drifts my way before I'm out of earshot.

"Plus, she's, like, part Black. They're stronger."

Just a little bit of casual racism to brighten up my morning. Love it. Black people literally have the same exact capacity for magic as anybody else. The only things that make you have a higher density of magic in your body are studying and practicing. Somebody made up this idea that Black people are naturally magically stronger, but that we have less control. All brute magical force, no finesse. I wish that kind of no-thinking nonsense had been left behind in the Civil War era, but it very much was not.

I grimace to myself and keep walking. Part of me wants to give them a piece of my mind, but a larger part of me knows that I'll probably freeze up if I try to say anything.

It only takes a few minutes for the nurse to draw my blood. I cross my fingers for luck as she labels my sample. Hopefully, the density of magic in my blood has gone up since last time. When the test results come back in a few weeks, I want to beat everybody in my class by such a large margin that nobody can say it's because of a boost from my family. Success is the best way to spite racists.

Normally I work as a peer tutor before school, but today I head over to the arts building for the Brockton Scholarship meeting. It's the nicest building on campus, because the Brockton Foundation gave a bunch of money to redo it. The tall stone facade sticks out like a sore thumb from the squat stucco buildings around it.

The school ranking board sits smack in the center of campus because T. K. Anderson wants to make sure you never have to go too far out of your way to check which of your classmates have better GPAs than you. The info they have up is a little out-of-date right now—the results are all from before winter break—but I still can't resist looking at it. I pause under the section of the board that lists the members of the junior class and stare up at the words that make my stomach churn.

1. Ana Álvarez—GPA: 4.78, Magic Level: 35
2. Shayna Johnson—GPA: 4.67, Magic Level: 38

Ugh. Stupid weighted GPAs. Her extra AP class really put her over the edge.

By the time I get to the auditorium, about fifteen people are already there. Everyone has crammed themselves into the first two rows. The room smells faintly of desperation—like fancy magical clothing trying to mask people's sweat with floral scents.

I want to sit in the front row, but the only seat left is by Ana Álvarez. I would rather sit on a bed of needles than attend this meeting with her next to me. But I also want to be right in the front so Mr. B can see I'm here.

As if she can sense me thinking about her, Ana tosses her stupidly perfect curls behind her shoulders, making eye contact with me in the process. I realize I've been standing at the end of the aisle staring at her, and my face gets hot.

This is stupid. Ana Álvarez is not going to keep me from making a good impression at this meeting. Mustering up my most confident air, I plop myself down in the seat beside her.

She makes direct eye contact with me before she says anything, which is a weird habit of hers. "Nice hoodie," she says. Her expression stays blank, so I can't tell if she's being sarcastic. "I hear obvious is the new subtle."

Cool. Definitely sarcasm. "Whatever. At least I don't look like I'm going for an interview at Ann Taylor."

It's a weak comeback. Actually, I'm not even sure it was an insult. She looks great. She's wearing these fitted dress pants and a blue-and-white-striped button-down with suspenders. Even the black loafers she wears most days work with her androgynous business casual look. I look like a true plebian in my jeans and orange Willington hoodie next to her. Maybe Mom was right about dressing nicely for this meeting.

Ana Álvarez has been my nemesis since freshman year. People used to get us confused because we're both smart brown girls in choir and the potions club. Sometimes they still make jokes that we're the same person or that we're related, which pisses me off. We don't look alike. We're not even the same type of brown. I'm half-Black, and she's Cuban.

Our body types are different—she's slender, while I'm on the stockier side. She also has long dark curls, which contrast with my stick-straight do, and thick eyebrows that she always raises condescendingly. She does that now. Then she smirks at me, which shows off the dimple on her left cheek. That dimple always throws me off. It's totally at odds with her harsh attitude.

"There are freshmen at this meeting," Ana says, rolling her eyes. "I don't know why they bother coming."

She's right. There's a gaggle of girls filing in four rows behind us, and there are a few other fresh-faced people sprinkled throughout the crowd.

Ana eyes me critically, then shakes her head. "I bet you went when you were a freshman."

I totally did. I went to the meeting last year too. My face must make it obvious that she's right, because she laughs. "You did, didn't you?"

"So what?" I splutter.

"I bet you sat in the front row and wore that old sweatshirt," she says, her expression inexcusably smug.

I rub the hem of my sleeve between my thumb and forefinger, frowning. "There's nothing wrong with my sweatshirt."

"Of course not. You look good in it." She pauses, her brown eyes fixed on mine. For a moment, I almost believe she's going to leave the compliment there, intact. She licks her lips, amusement flickering in her eyes. "Like a little pumpkin."

My eyes narrow. "For the last time—"

"It's like Halloween came early."

"I did not pick the Willington school colors," I snap.

"I seriously hope you wouldn't have picked orange and purple."

She's not wrong, but I'm still offended on Willington's behalf. "If you hate the colors so much, I hope you never have to wear them," I say, giving her a cloyingly sweet smile to punctuate the insult.

"Sick burn." Her flat affect is comically at odds with the words coming out of her mouth. I almost laugh, but that would be what she wants.

"I'm very witty," I say, imitating her tone.

She's still staring me down. She must have missed the memo as a child that staring is rude. "If Willington doesn't work," she says, "you should try comedy."

"Oh yeah?" I say. "What's your backup plan? Since you're not funny."

She settles back in her seat and shrugs lazily. "I don't need one."

I harrumph, which isn't the most intelligent response, but it's the only thing I can come up with. Ugh. She's really the worst. But whatever. I'm sure I can make it through this meeting without rage-throwing one of the potions in my backpack at her face.

Probably.

⋄ Chapter 3

T. K. Anderson boasts the highest rate of acceptance into
magical-licensing colleges of any school in Florida. 30% of
our students are accepted into a magical-licensing college
during their senior year, and 68% are accepted within
five years of graduating.

—**T. K. Anderson promotional brochure**

BRITTANY COHEN, THE BROCKTON SCHOLAR FROM LAST
year, walks onto the auditorium stage, and everyone falls
silent. She has that effect on a room. Maybe it's all the years
she's spent starring in every show T. K. Anderson's drama
department puts on. Or maybe it's because she's tall and
has the bone structure of a Greek statue. She floats above
the rest of us mere mortals because her future is certain. All
she has to do now is spend her senior year doing charity

events for the Brockton Foundation before heading off to college, free of charge.

Brittany sits in an empty chair on the stage and stares off into the distance with a bored expression. A weird few minutes of silence pass. I pull out my magic practice cube, a common tool for doing exercises that work on basic magic skills. After placing it on my lap, I activate my magic sight and mentally reach for the threads of magic in the small metal cube. Okay. Weight drill one. I push on the magic strands with my mind, willing them to expand. As the strands grow larger, the cube grows heavier in my lap.

Out of the corner of my eye, I notice Ana tapping her toes rhythmically on the carpet. Electricity sparks at the tips of her fingers as she does this, each spark lining up with a toe tap. Eight taps with the right foot. Eight taps with the left. Four with the right. Four with the left. Two right. Two left. One. One. One. One. Then she starts over with her heels.

It's not an exercise I recognize. Maybe she has a tutor who is giving her practice drills you can't find in the MAT prep books? The idea of her having a tutor makes me sick with envy. Getting a good score on the standardized test requires hard-core magical training, which is much easier to get through if you have someone helping you.

"We really are nerds, huh," Ana says.

"What?" I say, pulling my gaze away from her feet.

She gestures at my practice cube. "We have five seconds to ourselves, and we're both practicing," she says. "What are you doing? Weight drills?"

"Yeah. Any downtime is good practice time."

Electricity crackles at her fingertips, and a little smirk tugs at the corner of her mouth. "Spoken like a true nerd."

"Whatever," I say, rolling my eyes. "You're a nerd too."

"Oh yeah." She nods solemnly. "A big one." Then she goes back to her foot-tapping exercise, whatever it is.

Finally, Mr. B walks onstage to start the meeting. He's a youngish white man with some light beard scruff in a checkered button-down. From a distance, you wouldn't be able to pick him out of a crowd. Yet every eye in the auditorium is laser-focused on him once he steps out of the wings. Everyone knows he holds the key to their future. Brittany breaks into a radiant smile when he appears. She's been one of his favorites since she was a freshman, so it wasn't a big shock when she won the scholarship last year.

He goes by Mr. B, as if anybody is going to forget the B is short for Brockton. His family of real-estate tycoons runs the foundation that gives the money for the scholarship. He's the head of the committee that picks the Brockton Scholars. He's also the drama teacher.

Mr. B places something small on the floor center stage, then gives it a little nod. The object grows in size, revealing a tall wooden podium. After the podium is set up, he pulls a green-and-black DictaFire ball from his pocket.

"Hi, everyone. Hope you're all having a great day so far," Mr. B says, flashing an easy smile out at the audience. The DictaFire flies through the air, leaving behind a trail of floating green fire that spells out the word *Welcome* in six-foot-tall letters. "Glad you were willing get to school early for this lame old meeting."

I would do anything to win this scholarship. Showing up to school early is nothing. If I don't win, my chances of getting into Willington will be slim to none. I might not get in anywhere I apply next year and have to apply again. And again. And again. If it takes too long for me to be admitted to a licensing college, I might have to consider a non-licensing one. Which means the chances of me making real money and paying back my parents for everything they've done for me are small. All their sacrifices will be for nothing.

I give myself a tiny shake. Stop spiraling, Shay. Pay attention.

"Every year the committee for the Brockton Scholarship gets together and selects one of T. K. Anderson's most promising students to be the recipient of this incredible opportunity," he says. "Now, we're not looking for a candidate who just has good grades. We're looking for a well-rounded candidate. One who truly exemplifies all that T. K. Anderson has to offer. One who embodies the pillars of the Brockton Scholarship."

I could name all of these pillars in my sleep. It takes

true self-control for me to not mouth along with Mr. B as he lists them.

"Dedication, Academic Excellence—" The DictaFire spells out each of the pillars in the air as he says them. "Magical Excellence, Service, and Falcon Spirit." Some joker cacaws from behind me, and Mr. B smiles in amusement. "Exactly," he says. "That's what we're looking for right there."

The falcon is T. K. Anderson's mascot, so what he means is that they're looking for someone who is involved in activities at school.

Even before this meeting started, I knew I wasn't going to get much new information from my third time around, but as Mr. B continues talking, I realize that I could probably give the presentation myself. After I went to the meeting my freshman year, I brought home copious notes, and Mom sat me down to figure out a plan for the next three years. Everything I've done since then has been planned to make my application perfect.

Well, everything except my job at Pilar's Potions, which Mom wasn't a big fan of me spending my time on. But I wanted to save to get my own car sometime before I died, and I felt guilty always asking my parents for money for new potionworking supplies. That stuff is expensive.

Just when I'm about to give up on learning anything real from this meeting, Mr. B pauses, and his tone shifts. I sit up straighter in my seat. This is something new, something he's never said before.

"This year, we want to stress the need for diversity in our applicant pool. Brockton Scholars should represent the true diversity of T. K. Anderson."

That almost pulls a laugh from me. The true diversity of T. K. Anderson has been fairly well represented by the series of middle-class white girls who have won the scholarship. There are about five non-white faces in the auditorium, including me and Ana. I watch as the DictaFire adds *Diversity* underneath the pillars of the Brockton Scholarship.

I just can't get over how people randomly started caring about race last year. There was a big article published in *The New York Times* about how, even counting the three HBCUs, only 4 percent of graduates from licensing colleges were Black. Which, you know, didn't surprise me at all. What did surprise me was how the article went viral. Then this anti-racism organization that I had only vaguely heard of—Don't Hate, Educate—blew up.

Suddenly, people who had never cared about racism were talking about going to local rallies. Students who had made jokes about me and Ana being identical posted Don't Hate, Educate slogans on their WizConnect profile pages. Schools were scared they would get protested, so they started saying things about reconsidering their affirmative action policies to be more effective. And now I guess that's trickled down to the Brockton Scholarship.

Mr. B gives us all a serious nod. "The committee would like to encourage a wide range of applicants to join the competition this year," he finishes. Then he looks right at me.

I stop breathing.

Mr. B is otherwise pretty nondescript, but he has thick dark eyelashes and eerily blue eyes. When you're as close to him as I am, they bore into your soul. I stare up at him, feeling the possibility of the scholarship hurtling toward me in his gaze. Then he starts talking about the due dates for the application materials, and the moment is gone.

Maybe it was all in my head. Mr. B could have been staring at nothing. Or maybe he was looking at Ana. Oh god, please don't let him have been looking at Ana. I sneak a glance at her, and she's sitting ramrod straight in her seat, as unperturbed as usual.

Part of me hates that I could be the "diversity" applicant they're looking for. I've worked my butt off for this scholarship for years. I don't want anybody to tell me I'm just in the running because I happen to be Black. On the other hand, I would sell my soul to have a better shot at the scholarship. I can swallow my pride and sell myself with my race as a bigger part of the package if that will help me get into a licensing college quickly and not have to burden my parents for another few years.

Onstage, Mr. B beams out at all of us. "I can't wait to see which one of you heads off to Willington—or some other college"—he winks, and everyone chuckles dutifully—"in two years."

The Brockton family historically has gone to Willington University, which is the third-best licensing university in the country, so most students who get the scholarship end up going there. The scholarship doesn't officially mean that you're definitely going to get in, but every person who has ever gotten the scholarship has been admitted. Guaranteed admission to a licensing college *and* a free ride? That's life changing.

Willington is my dream college. I mean, any licensing college would be fine, because I don't want to be forced to work under people with magical licenses forever just so I can legally do higher-level magic work. But I've wanted to go to Willington since fifth grade. I wear this Willington hoodie so much that parts of the neckline are tragically starting to fray.

Mr. B claps decisively. "So let's open this up to questions," he says. "You can ask me or Brittany anything you want. And if you don't feel comfortable asking something with me here, I totally get that. Brittany will be sticking around afterward to chat with people, so you can get all the dirty details from her then." He grins.

Ana raises her hand, and I regret not having a question prepared with the fire of a thousand suns. He calls on her first because the universe hates me.

"How much value do out-of-school activities hold

compared to extracurriculars at school when you're making decisions?" she asks.

Damn, I wish I had asked that. I glare at her fiercely, then remember that Mr. B can still see me and rearrange my face into a pleasant smile.

"Good question," he says.

Rage burns quietly in my heart.

"There's no exact formula that we use to determine that. We do tend to more strongly consider candidates who are engaged with a variety of activities here on campus, but we also appreciate that you all have lives beyond this school." He frowns thoughtfully before continuing. "So we want to hear about your achievements outside of here in your application, but if it comes down to two similar candidates, we'll pick the one who is more involved on campus. It ends up being a tiebreaker category most of the time."

Ana's brow wrinkles and smoothens out so quickly that it's almost unnoticeable. Is she bothered by that answer? I think through what I know she does on campus. It's mostly the same as what I do. Potions club. Choir. National Honor Society. She's vice president of the Spanish club, which I'm not in. I'm the potions club vice president, though, so it's not like she's really one-upping me there. I also play terraball in the fall, and I've volunteered for the homecoming committee for the past two years. If we're comparing the two of us, I think I come out ahead in sheer number of T. K. Anderson activities. Plus, I'm more well-rounded, because she doesn't do anything athletic as far as I know.

Still, it's not clear to me which one of us will win. For every achievement I have, she has a roughly equivalent one. I won the Most Magically Promising Student award last year, but she won the Student Philanthropist prize. Her GPA is better than mine—ugh—but my magic level is higher. Every time I think I'm pulling ahead, I learn about some new, infuriatingly amazing accomplishment of hers.

Brittany takes the next few questions, which tell me nothing I don't already know. I don't end up thinking of a question to ask. But some other witch asks a stupid, rambling one about the average SAT score for applicants, and I, like an asshole, feel better about myself.

Once the meeting wraps up, Ana stands and leans idly against the edge of the stage in front of us, staring directly into my eyes as she does so. I wait for the inevitable dig. She crosses her arms over her chest and cocks her head slowly to the side. "So you're the face of diversity at T. K. Anderson, huh?"

I guess that moment with Mr. B wasn't all in my head. "Jealous?" I shoot back.

"Maybe," she says noncommittally. She turns and saunters away, because she's too cool to end a conversation like a normal person.

Chapter 4

And that was the moment I knew—magic is the way
to the American Dream!

—*We the People: Patriotic Monologues for High School Students*

THE MOMENT WHEN MR. B STARED AT ME KEEPS PLAYING IN
my mind as I walk out of the auditorium. He's never paid
me special attention before. I've tried to make a good
impression by saying hi at arts performances and volunteering for any events he would be at, but I'm far from
being one of his favorites. I didn't feel bad about it, though,
because he doesn't have a clear favorite in my grade. It
always felt weird to suck up to him too obviously for the
scholarship. I would rather just be the best candidate. I

know that's naive, but I'm pulling it off so far. Besides, there's a whole scholarship committee, so Mr. B's opinion isn't the only one that matters.

It's just the one that matters most.

"Shay?"

I whip around, startled, and Mr. B stands behind me, as if my thoughts summoned him.

"Do you have a sec?" he asks.

"Um. Yeah," I say. Obviously, I have a second for him. Anybody with even a slight aspiration for the scholarship has a second for him.

"Great, thanks. Let's go in my classroom."

I follow him around the corner to the drama classroom, my heart beating wildly in my chest. What could he possibly want to talk to me about? I rack my brain but come up empty besides a fantasy scenario where he sings my praises and offers me the scholarship on the spot.

He holds the door to the classroom open for me to enter. "Nice hoodie," he says as I pass him.

"Thanks," I say, smiling self-consciously. "It's my dream school."

"It's a great place." He follows me in and leans against his desk. "Any particular reason you want to go there?"

I shrug as I sit on one of the black cubes strewn around the small room. "I mean, it's a great school." I pause. Mom's voice echoes in the back of my brain, telling me not to sell myself short, so I jump to explain further. "I want to work in a magilab, and Willington has one of the best pro-grams for getting into that."

He nods slowly, looking impressed. "So you're into transfiguration? Potionwork? Or . . . magical theory?"

"Potionwork. I want to develop new potions to help with magical diseases. But honestly any potion-development job would be good."

"Oh yeah!" His face lights up with recognition. "You're the potions genius. I had heard about that."

My cheeks warm. I didn't think Mr. B knew much about me. I've briefly spoken to him at fine arts events a few times, but I never got the impression that I particularly interested him before today. "I, um, I've just been super into potionworking since I was little. I was always begging my mom to let me make little kiddy potions in our kitchen."

"Did you ever go to those apothecary summer camps?" Mr. B asks. "I know lots of T. K. Anderson kids went to those in middle school."

"No." I let out an awkward little laugh. "They're kind of . . . expensive? I don't know, I was pretty DIY as a kid."

Great job, Shay. Way to be weird as hell about being poorer than other people at this school.

Mr. B, thank god, flashes me this super-genuine smile that makes me feel better. "That's cool," he says. "DIY all the way. What kinds of things did you like to make when you were younger?"

"I used to make a lot of joke potions. Like, Sonic

Sneeze, you know?" I say, laughing a little. "But eventually I got really into making stuff that my parents could use around the apartment. Cleaning potions, basic healing stuff. Honestly, I'm amazed my parents let me try so many recipes when I was that young. A lot of them didn't work right, but it was still fun for me."

Potionworking is an upper-level magic skill, but it's definitely the most accessible one. Unlike transfiguration or herbology, if you stick to doing easy stuff, you probably won't kill anybody or anything. Still, my parents let me try a lot of things most people wouldn't let their child do.

"How old were you when you got started?" he asks. "Eleven? Twelve?"

"Seven," I say sheepishly, and I brace myself for the inevitable response.

He goes a little slack-jawed. "Seven?" he repeats. "You started brewing potions when you were *seven*?"

"I had been obsessed with potions since I was, like, five," I say. "I begged my parents nonstop to let me make them. I'm pretty sure I was really annoying." I chuckle and send up a silent thank-you to my parents for encouraging my early potions fixation. "My mom vetted everything I did a lot when I started, so we only had a few disasters."

I hadn't mastered the basic magical skills—manipulating magic flows to adjust physical properties of objects like temperature, texture, weight, and density. I couldn't generate electricity or fire, and my magic level was only around five.

But Mom and Dad helped me with anything I couldn't do yet, and it just made me more determined to figure out those skills for myself.

"No wonder your magic level is so high," he says. "I don't know anybody who started potionworking that early."

Oh my god. I've impressed him. I've impressed Mr. B. This is the best moment of my whole life. Ana Álvarez can suck it.

"Yeah," I say, trying to sound humble. I really hope he can't tell that I'm running victory laps in my mind. "It's been my thing for a long time."

"That's awesome. You've had it all figured out for a while." He shakes his head wryly. "I only stumbled into what I wanted to do after college, so you're way ahead of me."

I wonder briefly how he got into Willington. Did he just get in because of his family's money? Or was he an incredible student in high school?

"I was glad to see you at the meeting today," he says. A little thrill runs through me. "We need more people like you applying."

I smile uncertainly. Is he talking about me being Black? Or something else? I decide to go with a safe response. "I would be really honored to have such an amazing opportunity."

He laughs and pushes himself back to sit on his desk. A few wayward papers crinkle under his khakis. "You don't have to be so formal, Shay. This isn't official Brockton Scholarship business. I promise I'm not judging you right now. Relax."

I force a laugh and swing my legs up to sit cross-legged on the block. Hopefully that makes me look more relaxed. God, there's nothing less relaxing than being told to relax.

"Congrats on the concert last night," he says. "Your solo was incredible."

"Thanks."

"Your technique is great," he continues. "Not many high schoolers have that kind of breath control."

"Thank you," I say again, beaming. "I had a good time at the concert. The stuff we sang last night was . . ." I pause, because I've dug myself into a hole. Our Salute to America concert is always pretty mediocre. It's so soon after winter break that we only have a week and a half to properly rehearse. "It was nice to sing 'America the Magical' again," I finish awkwardly.

Mr. B snorts quietly. "Ms. Mooney loves having you guys sing that."

Ms. Mooney, our choir director, whips that song out every time we have to do something on short notice. "All of us have sung it before except for the freshmen, so it's easy to put together."

He leans slightly toward me, lowering his voice. "Just between you and me, if I hear that song again, I'm going to rip off my own ears." A full-blown cackle escapes me in my surprise at hearing him say that. He grins mischievously. "Just keeping it real."

"I mean, you're right." I shrug. "She has truly beaten that song to death."

"I shouldn't make fun of it too much, though. The drama club performances at that concert aren't much better," he says. "I have students perform those same monologues about the 'value of hard work' and how 'magic is the great American equalizer' every year." He does a spot-on impression of the painfully earnest student performances as he quotes the monologues. I laugh. Those monologues are just so cringe.

"All of that aside, though, it was good to hear you sing last night," he says. "I was wondering why you haven't done any theater yet."

Oh. Ohhhh. Is this what he wanted to talk about? "I used to do the musicals at my middle school," I say. "But I switched to choir once I started high school."

He lights up. "I knew it! You've got stage presence."

That is a blatant lie. Ms. Mooney is always telling me to stop looking pained whenever I feel like people are watching me. Which is, you know, what audiences do.

"This year I wanted to branch out a bit from our usual fare when I was picking a musical, and I think you would be perfect for the show!" he continues. "We're doing *Bronxtown Brooms*."

I don't know what that is, but I'll look it up it as soon

as I leave the room. "That sounds cool," I say, pasting on a smile.

"I wanted to personally ask you to audition," he says, dropping his voice into a more serious tone. He leans forward, resting his elbows on his knees. "I know you would be incredible as one of the leads, and it would look *really good* on your Brockton Scholarship application." He stares at me meaningfully for a moment.

What? I swallow hard, meeting his stare. Is he saying what I think he's saying? Oh my god. I've made it. Except . . . this is also kind of icky.

"The committee loves seeing candidates that are willing to jump into activities here at T. K. Anderson," he continues, suddenly affecting such a light tone that it's like the previous moment didn't happen. He smiles. "So I hope you'll come audition on Monday. I would love to have you."

"Yeah, um," I say, grasping for something coherent. "I'll definitely think about it."

"Cool," he says. "I'm glad. I need more students like you."

Still not sure if "like you" is code for "Black," but I don't think he's going to say that outright anytime soon. It's time for me to get out of here. "Okay, Mr. B, I'm going to go to class." I'm already inching toward the door.

"Great," he says, beaming a megawatt smile at me. "See you soon."

Chapter 5

Analyze similarities and differences in the revolutionary roots of the following national slogans.

Liberté, égalité, fraternité
(The national motto of the French Empire)

Hard work, magical power, educational excellence
(The American Magical Way)

—**AP World History exam sample question**

AFTER SCHOOL, I STAND IN THE PICKUP AREA, WAITING FOR Lex to pick me up. I'm itching to talk to her about my conversation with Mr. B. I looked up the musical he mentioned—*Bronxtown Brooms*. It's a retelling of Jane Austen's *Pride and Prejudice* set in a mostly Latinx neighborhood in New York City in the nineties. Based on what I read about the show, I'm 98 percent sure now that Mr. B was trying to talk about race without talking about race.

Also, he might think I'm Latina. So that's a major factor in the Reasons Not to Audition for This Musical list.

On the other hand, there's the whole *"wink, wink, nudge, nudge,* audition for this show and I'll consider you for the scholarship" thing. Which, now that I've had some time to think about it, I'm not sure was as shady as I initially thought. It's not like he promised to give me the scholarship. This is just one more opportunity to impress him.

Lex's blue car flies up to the curb, then settles gracefully onto the ground. Her car is painfully nice compared to the one my family has. It has that new aerodynamic bullet shape, and the propulsion engines at the front and back are near silent. I ache with jealousy every time I see it.

"Hey girl hey!" Lex screams through the open passenger window. Her aggressive EDM blasts out into the parking lot, and she dances in her seat, waving her arms wildly toward me. The few people in the parking lot turn to see who this screaming Asian girl is, which is a common side effect of hanging out with Lex. "You look tired!"

I hit a pose with my hands framing my face. "I am."

"She is beauty, she is grace!" Lex yells. "She is late for work! Get in the car."

"You're the one who's late," I yell back. Once I'm settled in the passenger seat, I turn off her music so we can talk. "I've been waiting for you since I left potions club."

She hands me a Starbucks latte and steps on the

accelerator. The car glides away from the curb, lifting smoothly into the air as we go. "I stopped for coffee."

"Of course you did." I throw her a withering look before sipping my latte. *Mm.* Not as good as Mom's, but still necessary to get me through the rest of this day.

"Hey, we deserve it today. We have to finish filling all the weekend orders before we leave tonight." She stomps on the accelerator and sends the car flying onto the floating road. We glide upward, following the road over the swamp outside the school property.

Her car really is an incredibly fancy piece of magitech. It glides effortlessly through the air. My dream is to buy my parents a car this nice one day.

"How was your day, lady?" Lex asks.

"It was . . . a lot."

"What did Ana do this time?"

"Plenty of annoying ish, but that's not what I want to talk about."

I've always been able to tell Lex anything. She was the first one I came out to—the only person at our school I bothered to tell I was a lesbian. She's easy to talk to, but not because she's the type who listens quietly. It's because she's aggressively supportive. Emphasis on *aggressively*.

"What the hell!" she yells once I finish filling her in on my day. "I knew that the Brockton Scholarship was kind of about favoritism a lot of the time, but that's so shady."

"I don't think it was that bad," I say.

"What?" she says. "You literally just described, like, some weird, backdoor bullshit."

"No—I mean—" I sigh and fidget with my hands in my lap for a few seconds. "I was just saying that's what I thought at first. I'm pretty sure I read too much into it. He didn't actually say he would give me the scholarship if I auditioned for the show."

"He doesn't have to say that. He totally knows that everyone is desperate to do stuff for him." Lex shakes her head, wrinkling up her nose like she smells something bad. "Plus, there's no way he doesn't know that you and Ana are the top picks for Brockton Scholar. You would be, like, the *most* desperate to do whatever he wants."

"You're making it seem super evil," I say. My voice comes out louder than I meant it to. "This is a good thing! He finally noticed me, and he wants to get to know me better."

Lex looks like she's about to say something else, but she swallows it after giving me a sidelong glance. We lapse into silence. I lean toward my window and watch the landscape go by. You can see the cypress swamp beneath us through the floating network of roads. There's a Green Witch van on the ground off to our right. I peer at it as we pass, wondering if it's my dad's crew. The Green Witch employees are tiny green and brown dots below us, barely distinguishable from the landscape around them. A tree bursts from the ground beside their group and grows into a full-grown cypress before they disappear into the distance.

"Mr. B definitely thinks you're Latina," Lex says suddenly.

"Yeah, maybe," I say. "I mean, I think there's one part for a girl who's Black and not Latina? He could be thinking of me for that."

"I guess. So . . ." She pauses, frowning. "You're going to audition?"

"I feel like I have to," I say, shrugging. If I don't audition for the show, that might give him a bad impression of me, which would ruin my chance of getting the scholarship. I'm so close to being a Brockton Scholar. I can't blow it now.

"Girl, you can't act," she says, her eyebrows hovering up by her hairline.

"I'm . . . okay at acting."

She fully cackles at that, which is great for my self-esteem. "You look like you're being tortured when you're onstage. Seriously. Like, you're a beautiful singer. Facts." She smacks me lovingly on the shoulder.

"Thanks."

"But watching you act is painful."

Oh god. I hadn't considered that part of it. What if I suck so bad at my audition that Mr. B never wants to see my face again?

We drive into the parking lot of the strip mall where we work, chug the rest of our coffees, and run into Pilar's

Potions. The jangling bell on the door announces our presence. Pilar eyes us with amusement from where she stands at the counter.

"Aprons on, mijas," she says.

Pilar is one of my favorite people in the whole world. She's a short, middle-aged Afro-Cuban woman who's always wearing the most colorful head wraps and outfits you've ever seen. I've never met anybody with such a calming presence. Just being around her makes me feel more relaxed. She's also a master apothecary with a magical license, so as long as she's in the building, Lex and I can legally make potions for the public.

Pilar's place is one of the last few hole-in-the-wall potion stores left in town after the Super Walmart opened nearby. That Walmart sells ridiculously cheap potions, but they're less effective than fresher-brewed ones. We brew all of our potions in-house at Pilar's.

Lex and I tie on our brown aprons, take turns washing our hands in the big sink in the prep section, and then wait for Pilar's instructions. I breathe in the scent of patchouli and smile, feeling calmer already.

"Lex, you're on the counter today," Pilar says. "Grind the sage and the fennel seeds when there aren't customers. Shay, we'll start the prep for tomorrow together."

Lex swaps places with Pilar behind the counter. "Lucky," she mouths at me over her shoulder.

"We're going to need a big batch of Awakening potions

for this weekend, so you should get started on that," Pilar says to me.

I smile. Making Awakening potions always feels special to me. It was the very first potion ever discovered. It lets people see and manipulate the magical currents in everything. We brew it all the time because every baby is given a dose soon after birth. But every time I brew it, I feel this connection to potions history that's kind of cool.

"I have some specialty orders for Sunday and a few prescriptions to bottle," Pilar continues. "So once you've set that to simmer, you can come help me."

I nod, and we all set to work.

Pilar's prep room is stuffed with every herb, spice, oil, and mineral you could think of. Huge dark wood shelves line the back of the room, each one covered in jars and baskets and cracked Tupperwares filled with supplies for potionworking. There's a whole wall taken up by shelves of the beautiful curved glassware Pilar sells her potions in. When the light hits the glass, it throws kaleidoscopes of colors all over the piles of herbs waiting on the table that fills the center of the room.

I pull an extra-large cauldron from under the prep table, fill it with water, and set it up on one of the copper stoves lining the walls. While the water heats, I grab ingredients from around the room. Angelica roots. Fennel bulbs. Apple cider vinegar. A few magically charged crystals. Echinacea leaves.

Once the water in the cauldron begins to simmer, I pour in a cup of apple cider vinegar and focus on the liquid, activating my magic sight. The currents of magic in the vinegar and the water swirl around each other, each a slightly different shade of glowing amber. I will the magic to wind together, speeding up the process of the two liquids combining.

As I look at the potion, it occurs to me that if I end up doing the musical, I won't be able to work here as much this semester. My connection to the magic in the potion abruptly breaks as my concentration wavers.

"What's wrong, Shay?" Pilar asks, not looking up from the partridge feathers she's sorting at the center table.

I pull myself out of my thoughts and place the crystals I grabbed earlier in a circle around the cauldron. "Just stressed out with school and stuff."

"The drama teacher who runs the scholarship Shay wants is forcing her to audition for the musical," Lex calls into the pass-through window between the prep room and the main store.

"He's not forcing me!" I protest. Lex is making it seem way more terrible than it is.

"He held the scholarship over your head to get you to audition," Lex says. She purses her lips and aggressively grinds fennel seeds with the pestle in her hand. "That's forcing."

Lex and her big mouth. I shake my head and focus on

the magic in my crystals, pulling the magical currents into a latticework that amplifies their energy. Once the magical energy field glows a bright silver, I draw the lattice up and fold the extra magic deftly into the potion.

Pilar gives my work an approving nod as she breezes past me. "What are you going to do?"

"About the audition?" I ask, grabbing a knife and cutting board. "I'm going to do it, I guess. I'm not that good, so he'll probably just put me in the ensemble. Or he might not want me to be in the show at all."

"Is that what you want to do?" Pilar asks.

I line up my knife and cut the stalk away from a fennel bulb. "I mean, not really."

Lex makes a sound as if she's about to interject, but the bell on the door rings. "Hi, welcome to Pilar's," she calls, turning away to go to the counter.

"There are always more options in every choice than you first think," Pilar says to me. "Try to find all of them before you make your decision."

"I can audition for the show. Or I don't audition for the show, and I ruin my chances of getting the scholarship." I aggressively cut another fennel stalk. "That's basically it."

"You could tell someone what happened," Pilar says. "Another teacher? One that you trust?"

I shake my head. "That won't do anything. Nothing really happened anyway."

"It sounds like something happened."

"Lex is exaggerating." What does Pilar expect me to do? Go to the principal to tell him that Mr. B looked at me during a meeting and then told me to audition for the musical? Yeah right. "Anyway, that scholarship is the whole point of me going to this school," I say. "I've worked so hard for it. I don't want everything to be ruined because some teacher decides he doesn't like me."

"Protect yourself, Shay," Pilar says. "Men with power over you are dangerous." She raises her eyebrows and gives me a knowing look.

I let out a short laugh. "It's not like *that*."

She hums quietly, tilting her head to the side. "You are a very powerful person," she says eventually. "Never forget that."

"Yeah," I say, and then I turn my attention back to my potion.

Chapter 6

Young Americans fed up with the rat race are protesting by moving to large communes in Kansas and Nebraska, where residents engage in collective farming. This form of social protest is meant to express their disillusionment with the promises of the American Magical Way and reject the culture of overwork that pushes American youth to struggle for years in a grueling education system, often with little economic benefit.

—"Disenchanted American Youth Join a Mass Communal-Living Movement," *The New York Times*

OVER THE WEEKEND, I WORK TWO SHIFTS AT PILAR'S AND practice for the audition. I have to sing a section from "My Soft Place to Land," which is this song from *Bronxtown Brooms*. The song is sung by Valeria, one of the leads. She's the second oldest in a family with five daughters, and her mom is obsessed with marrying off her daughters to rich men so they won't have financial problems like she does. The family owns a struggling store called Bronxtown Brooms in a neighborhood that lots of people are leaving because the rent is going up. The song is about how much she loves the neighborhood, and how devastated she is that all these rich white people are replacing the people who used to live there.

Because Lex is loyal as hell, she's been trying all weekend to coach me into not sucking even though she doesn't think I should audition. But after we finish working the Sunday shift at Pilar's, she puts her foot down.

"No more practicing," she says as she walks across the parking lot. "Your audition will be fine. You can sing. All you have to do is not look like you want to die while you're doing it."

"But that's so hard," I whine, trailing after her. "Because I do want to die."

She laughs. "You keep, like, staring sadly at the ground. Just stand still and look forward."

I sigh. Easier said than done.

Once we're both in the car, she sticks her thumb into a hole beside the steering wheel. Her car has one of those fancy magical thumbprint ignitions. "Do you want to go to the gym?" she asks as she starts the car.

I almost say no—I have some homework left to finish—but playing a game of terraball with Lex would be stress relieving. And I really need that right now. "Yeah, sure," I say.

"Yeeeeees!" Lex shouts, pounding her hands on the

steering wheel. "Oh my god, we haven't played in forever. I'm going to kick your ass."

"No you're not," I say, giving her a withering look.

"Heh. Keep telling yourself that."

Forty minutes later, I'm panting on the foam floor of the terraball court, clutching the rubber ball to my chest. Lex is, of course, kicking my ass.

"Suck on that!" she yells. "Don't just lie there—gimme the ball!"

"Fuck you," I say, slinging the ball her way. She's so damn fast, it's impossible to catch her. When we were on the T. K. Anderson terraball team together, she was always one of the faster players.

She snatches the ball out of the air, flashing me a cheeky grin. "I love you too." Then she jumps on a foam cube, magically enlarges it, and uses it as a launch pad to get away from me.

Terraball is, at its core, a deeply silly game. You're trying to run across a court littered with foam cubes and throw the ball into the opposite team's goal. Except while you're doing that, the other team is magically changing the size of the foam cubes in your way to mess with you. If you fall while holding the ball, you have to turn it over to the other team.

So essentially, terraball is basketball, football, and those gymnastics foam pits fused into one ridiculous, awesome sport.

I pelt after Lex, shrinking the foam cubes in my way as I go. Once she's about halfway across the court, I wrench at the magic in the red cube in front of her. It explodes outward, growing to be about six feet tall. Lex cuts left to avoid it, and then disappears around the obstacle so I can no longer see her.

"Nice try," she shouts back at me.

But that's not the end of my plan. I hurl several small blocks in Lex's direction, enlarging them once they're almost out of my sight. I'm rewarded with a small *oof* from Lex.

"Oh, you're the *worst*," she says as I come around the side of the red cube. She's on the floor, taken down by my now-giant projectiles.

"Thank you," I say, holding my hand out toward her. "Ball, please."

She tosses it to me and shimmies out from under the pile of foam. "Do you want to come over for cultural-dinner night after this?"

Lex's mom and dad cook Filipino food every Sunday to make Lex feel closer to her heritage. Lex is adopted, so her parents, who are both white, make a big effort to help her connect to her culture. It's a really sweet tradition. Plus, Filipino food is delicious.

I shake my head. "Not tonight. I'm volunteering, and then my mom and I are going to watch *Potion Wars*."

"Oh my god, that show is still running?" Lex says.

"Yeah, but we're just going to watch reruns."

"Okay. You have to come over soon, though."

"I will," I say, and then I take off running toward her goal. This time I manage to score, even though she pulls off an impressive maneuver where she rapidly shrinks and enlarges all the cubes in my path at random. That point takes the score to six for me, and eight for Lex.

On the next play, she immediately pays me back by side-slamming me with a block and sinking the ball into the goal from the two-point line. Then she flops onto the floor. "Okay, I need a break from kicking your ass," she announces, splaying her limbs out like a starfish.

"You're on a roll today," I say as I come to sit next to her.

She flashes me double victory signs. "You know it."

Honestly, Lex is always better than me at terraball. And any other athletic activity she convinces me to do. She's the kind of person who kills it in sports based on her sheer athleticism. Terraball, soccer, cross-country, flame archery—she's good at everything.

I snag a mangled piece of foam and lie down with it propped under my head as a pillow. We both rest there in silence for a minute, taking a moment to catch our breath.

"Do you have MAT prep this week?" I ask.

"No, I convinced the magimeds that I can prep on my own for the last week before the test," Lex says, her expression clouding.

Lex's parents are both magimeds. Seriously. I think they met in medical school. Her mom helps older people whose magical abilities have started to degenerate, and her dad is a heart surgeon.

"My tutor was seriously stressing me out," Lexi says after a pause.

My heart clenches when she talks about her private MAT tutor. I shouldn't still feel this way, because Lex isn't ever trying to throw it in my face that her family can afford stuff that mine can't, but it doesn't make me want that stuff any less.

"She acted like I was stupid every time we met," Lex continues.

"You're not stupid," I say immediately. Lex is self-conscious about that. As far as schoolwork goes, Lex is incredible at things she's passionate about and mediocre at doing work she's not interested in, so her high school GPA wasn't high enough for her parents' standards.

"Thanks."

"Do you want to do practice tests with me this week?"

She pulls a face. "No, thanks. I think I'll be fine."

"Come on," I say, grinning at her. "You can come over to my place. My mom will feed you."

"It's fine, Shay. Don't worry about it," she snaps.

I stare at her, wondering what made her mad. Did she think I was being condescending?

She sits up and rubs a hand over her face, then pushes it back through her black hair. "Sorry. I'm just stressed."

"About what?" I say, sitting up as well.

"My parents are on my back to do all this stuff so I can get into college. I'm already taking that online class, *and* working at Pilar's, *and* doing extra volunteering, *and* studying to take the MATs and the SATs again." She frowns. "It's too late for this year anyway. I've already submitted most of my applications. It just feels like they're planning for me to fail at this point."

I didn't think Lex was bothered by her gap year, but I guess I was wrong. She's always so high energy that it can take a while to find out when something is upsetting her. Not my finest moment as her best friend. "I'm sorry, Lex," I say. "I'm sure you'll get into a great college this year, though. Then it'll all be worth it."

She purses her lips. "Yeah," she says unenthusiastically. "My parents are just, like, convinced I'm going to become some dropout witch and move to a commune or something. They've been watching the news too much recently, and now they're all freaked out."

"Yeah, my mom's been doing that too."

"It's kind of annoying. I'm just tired of people telling me that I need to work harder so things will work out for me. There's this guy at the soup kitchen I'm volunteering at that really thinks I need to hear his opinions about how to be the right kind of hardworking American witch." She rolls her eyes. "But he's also convinced that I'm a Chinese spy here to steal American magical secrets and that Don't Hate, Educate is part of a big Chinese plot to ruin the American educational system, so . . ."

"Um." I blink, taking a moment to absorb that. "Does he know you're Filipino?"

"I mean, no, but I don't think that really matters to him."

"What the hell," I say. "That guy is a straight-up conspiracy theorist."

"I know!" Lex shouts. "And he's young too! He's not, like, some weird old wizard that's stuck in the past. He's just on his third gap year, and he's decided that he's not getting into a licensing college because people 'hate white dudes now.'" She huffs loudly and shakes her shoulders. "Okay, I'm over this. You want to get Starbucks?"

I have no money. Don't even have to check my wallet. "Um . . ." I say awkwardly.

"Pleeease?" she wheedles. She leans over and puts her head on my shoulder. "My treat?"

"Ugh, no. I feel like such a bum making you pay for me."

"No stress, lady. The magimeds are paying for it."

Lex's parents make so much money that Lex could

buy the whole Starbucks menu on her credit card and they wouldn't notice.

We end up going to the Starbucks drive-through on the way home, because Lex is persistent, and she buys me a latte against my will. "I already paid for it, so you have to drink it," she says when she hands it to me.

"It's not like I'm going to throw it away," I say, rolling my eyes. "Anyway, would you want some Night Vision potion? I made too much."

"For what? My career as a spy?" Lex snickers.

"It's useful! I've been taking it so my parents don't realize how late I'm staying awake."

Lex side-eyes me. "Are you using it to do homework?"

". . . Maybe."

The sound of her cackling fills the car. "I feel like other people would use it to, like, sneak out or something," she manages to say.

"Well, I'm a huge dork, so . . ." I throw my hands in the air helplessly. "Do you want the potion or not?"

"I'll take it," she says, still shaking with laughter.

I transfer the vials of Night Vision from one of my wooden transport boxes into her spare leather pouch. I made a new batch of the tanning potion Lex likes last weekend, so I put a few vials of that in too.

We spend the rest of the drive bopping to her earth-shakingly loud EDM. When she drops me off at home,

I hop out and lean against the open car door. "You really should come over this week to study. We can make it low stress! We can even practice drills." I flash her a grin. "I know you love drills."

She snickers, shaking her head. "Girl, you know I love a good drill."

Lex is way better at the practical section of the MATs than the written one. She's in the top percentile for all the drills—temperature changes, change of state, texture adjustment, scentwork, electricity generation, weight and density changes. She doesn't need drill practice, but that might be the confidence boost she needs.

"And I'm sure you don't want to miss my mom's cooking." I dance away from the car, pointing at Lex with my free hand. "Or her weird comments implying that we're dating."

She pumps her shoulders, pointing back at me. "Mm, I can never skip Mama Johnson comments."

"Slightly insensitive, but meant with love." I shrug. "Okay, byeeeeee!"

"Byeeeeee!"

I close the door and head up to my apartment. Dad immediately shushes me from the kitchen as I run in the door.

"Mom's sleeping," he says when I enter the kitchen.

This early? Weird.

"MarTech was really tough today. They had her

checking scentwork patches for eight hours straight," Dad says. He takes the open package of cookies in front of him and holds it out to me. I take two. "I'll drive you to the old folks later," he says, turning to fuss over one of his midair plants that has floated past the side of his head. "I need to pick up groceries at Publix, so I'll drop you off on my way."

"Okay." I sit at the kitchen table, sucking down the last of my latte. Volunteering at the retirement home will be hard tonight, since my voice is tired from practicing so much this weekend. I go to the home during their Sunday dinners and sing jazz standards while one of the residents plays the piano. Thankfully, nobody pays much attention to me while I'm doing it.

Dad squints at his midair plant, his brow furrowing with concentration. One of the spiky leaves shakes, and then a brown spot near the tip slowly disappears. He turns his attention to me as the plant drifts away toward the kitchen window. "Kiddo, I know your mom asked you about this already, but if you want to take the SATs again in March, we can make that happen," he says, sitting in the seat across from me. "No pressure. We don't want you to feel like you shouldn't take it just because it costs money."

But it does cost money. Him reassuring me doesn't make that fact any less true. I already paid for my MAT registration out of my savings, which I only got away with because I secretly registered myself and hoped Mom wouldn't notice. So far she hasn't.

"Your mom said that taking the SATs again could help you with the Brockton Scholarship application. We just want to make sure that you have every opportunity, okay?"

"Thanks, Dad," I say. "But I don't want to do it because I'm probably going to be super busy this semester." Be a big girl, Shay. Spit it out. I take a small bite of cookie for fortitude. "I'm auditioning for the musical at school."

His eyebrows shoot up, and he blinks too much. "You're doing the musical?"

"Yeah."

"But you . . ." He pauses. "Hate acting."

I'm not a mind reader, but I'm pretty sure that wasn't what he wanted to say originally. "You mean I'm bad, right?"

"You have many other talents, Shay," he says tentatively. He runs a hand over his bald head.

"Oh my god, please just lie to me."

"What's this about a musical?" Mom walks into the kitchen, still wearing her sleep-rumpled work clothes. Dad rubs the small of her back when she joins us.

"You're up already?" he asks.

She waves him off, keeping her attention on me. "I was only resting my eyes." Dad snorts quietly at that.

"Mr. B asked me to audition for the spring musical," I

say hesitantly. I watch Mom closely for her reaction. This is going to be a big deviation from our plan, and it'll be a lot harder if she's not on board. "He heard my solo at the concert, and he really liked my singing," I add. "He thinks I would be a good fit for the show."

"Okay," she says, nodding slowly. "This is good, right? You've said before that he has a lot of pull on the scholarship committee."

"Yeah, he does. We actually had a great conversation on Friday," I say, grinning as I remember how I impressed him when I talked about myself. "I think he's interested in getting to know me better before I apply."

"Perfect," Dad says. "If he gets to spend time with you, he'll figure out pretty quick that there's nobody else they could possibly give the scholarship to."

As I look at my parents' faces, any last doubts I have evaporate. Lex really was overreacting. If Mom and Dad don't think this is weird, it definitely isn't.

Mom's expression is thoughtful. "This isn't exactly the plan, but . . ." She shakes her head. "It's too good an opportunity to pass up. You think you'll be able to balance that with all the other stuff you have going on?"

"I'll be fine," I say. "Besides, I can't exactly say no after Mr. B specifically asked me to audition."

"He would understand," Dad says confidently.

But what if he doesn't? Then I'm just fucked.

"Seriously, I'll be fine. I'm not playing terraball right now, so I have plenty of time."

"You'll have to cut down on how much you're working at Pilar's," Mom says.

"I know."

"Okay," she says. "Well, good luck at the audition."

"They say 'break a leg' in the *theater*, honey," Dad interjects. He puts a fancy accent on the word *theater.*

I kind of wish I would break my leg. Then I would have a good excuse not to do this show. If I'm being honest, I don't want to be in a musical. Acting is pretty excruciating. But when I look at my parents, I'm reminded why I'm doing this. They've put so much work into me preparing to get this scholarship. This is the first step toward the life they want for me.

Maybe the American Magical Way didn't exactly work for them—they haven't gotten the perfect, American Dream lifestyle that it promises—but they've put everything they have into making sure it will work for me. I can't let them down now, even if it means doing something I don't want to do.

Chapter 7

Don't Hate, Educate is a grassroots movement dedicated to advancing racial equity in education. We fight to eradicate racism in our schools and elect leaders who are committed to reforming the magical-licensing system. Click below to find a local action near you.

—-**Don't Hate, Educate website**

AFTER SCHOOL ENDS ON MONDAY, I HEAD TO THE AUDITO-rium, going through the lyrics to "My Soft Place to Land" in my head. I can do this. I will sing adequately enough that Mr. B will cast me as a minor part that nobody pays much attention to. I'll be good enough that he'll be impressed with my commitment and willingness to try new things, but not good enough that he'll expect me to ever do a show again.

There's a loud group of students in the hallway outside

the auditorium entrance. People yell across the hall at each other, raucously laughing and swapping nonsensical inside jokes. A group of girls shrieks some musical theater song at high volume, each one of them posing and pouting at nobody in particular. Another group of people sings a different song while doing some intense-looking choreography that involves them shooting flames out of their hands. I lean over the sign-in sheet sitting on a small folding table and scrawl my name on the last line. Another name on the list catches my eye.

Oh no. You have to be kidding me.

I glance behind me and, sure enough, there's Ana Álvarez sitting cross-legged against a wall. She makes eye contact and considers me for a moment. I frown. She stands and saunters toward me.

Why is she here? She doesn't even do theater. Plus, she's the least expressive person I've ever met—as far as I've seen in the two years I've known Ana, her emotions range from smug to serious and back again. She stops in front of me and lifts her chin in greeting. Tilting her head to the side, she considers me, her dark eyes unreadable.

"You're auditioning?" I blurt out.

"No, I just like hanging out in this hallway."

"Ha ha." I purse my lips and flip my hair over my shoulder. She's not going to rattle me.

"Did Mr. B get to you too?"

Just kidding, I'm already rattled. "Um." I open and close my mouth wordlessly.

She raises her eyebrows. "So . . . yes?"

Oh my god, get it together, Shay. I cross my arms over my chest. "He said I should audition, if that's what you mean."

"Guess he was desperate for brown people," she says, grinning smugly at me. Her dimple deepens on her cheek. A rush of annoyance fills me. I don't like her writing me off like that, even though it's probably true.

"I bet he was scared Don't Hate, Educate would protest the performance if he did a mostly white *Bronxtown Brooms*," she continues.

I snort. "They don't care about T. K. Anderson." The closest Don't Hate, Educate chapter is in Miami, more than an hour away, and they spend all their time picketing our senators' Miami offices.

"Obviously not," she says. "Anyway, I don't know why he picked this musical when there's, like, two Latino kids and one Black kid who do drama."

"That's not true. There are . . ." My eyes skim the people sitting in the hallway. She's not wrong. "More than that. Anyway, it's nice that he wants to do a show like *Bronxtown Brooms*."

Her smug grin fades away. "Don't tell me you drank the Mr. B potion."

"Whatever. You're here too."

"Can't let you be the only one getting the diversity brownie points," she says, rolling her eyes.

The door to the auditorium opens, and Mr. B bounds out. Brittany follows close behind him. "All right, people!" he says excitedly, clapping his hands. "Let's get this party started. We're going to do the singing auditions first, and then the wonderful Brittany"—Brittany does jazz hands, and sparks shoot theatrically off her fingers—"is going to lead you all through some choreography for our dance call. Brittany is going to be your student choreographer for this show, so make some noise for her real quick."

Everyone whoops and claps on cue. Brittany curtsies, then dramatically tosses her blond hair over her shoulders. "Thank you, thank you," she says, as if she's accepting an award.

Mr. B laughs indulgently at her, then turns his attention back to us. "I'm excited to tackle this show with all of you this semester. This is a very *important* show. Gets into a lot of issues." He nods at us seriously. "We're going to be learning a lot about gentrification with this one."

I hadn't really thought of this musical as being a deep discussion of social issues. Based on the Wikipedia summary I read, it's mostly a comedic love story about two sisters falling for two guys who move into their neighborhood. I mean, the gentrification stuff is definitely there, but it didn't seem like this big, deep thing. From his tone of voice, you would think the show was a tragedy about the AIDS crisis or the Sino-American Magitech Wars or something.

· "I'll be holding callbacks immediately following the auditions tonight, but don't worry too much about those," Mr. B continues. "You all know the drill. If I need to see more, I'll call you back. If not, still make sure you check the cast lists when I post them tomorrow at four."

Ugh. I have work after school tomorrow, so I won't be able to check right away. I'll have to get someone to tell me what the list says.

"Okay. I'm hoping to get you all out of here by six thirty—"

"So eight?" someone calls out from the back of the group. There's a general rumble of laughter.

Mr. B narrows his eyes, giving all of us an exaggerated glare. "My inability to run anything on time is a charming defect, and anybody that says differently is not getting cast."

More people snicker, and Mr. B throws up his hands dramatically. "I'm feeling attacked here, people."

"Maybe we'll finish on time, then," Brittany says, smiling at him sweetly.

"I hear your complaints, and I'm going to ignore them." He pulls open the door to the auditorium. "Let me get all the witches inside. Wizards, hang tight for now. Don't complain about me too much while I'm gone."

We all end up huddling in a backstage area waiting for our turn to sing. Ana goes out first. The rest of us sit on the floor in a heavy silence.

I can hear her audition clearly, since the door to the wings isn't soundproof. As much as I hate to admit it, she has a beautiful voice. There's an interesting edge to it—slightly raspy, but not in a bad way. Her singing is expressive too. Listening to her sing "My Soft Place to Land" makes me feel like I understand what Valeria is talking about. A sinking feeling fills my gut. I didn't think it was possible to feel more inadequate about my skills, but here we are.

Ana's singing is still playing in my head as I go to do my audition. The stage feels huge when I step out of the wings. I walk past the accompanist and stand in the center. Mr. B sits in the audience a few rows back from the front, lounging lazily against the armrest of his seat. He perks up when he sees me.

"Shay!" he exclaims, gesturing enthusiastically. The pen he's holding goes flying and clatters against a seat before disappearing. He chuckles. "Whoops. Just too excited to see you, I guess." He winks at me. From anybody else that would be creepy, but his friendly older-brother vibe is too strong.

Once he retrieves his pen, Mr. B settles back into his seat. "Whenever you're ready."

I take a deep breath, lock eyes with the accompanist,

and give him the tiniest of nods. He plunks out the first chord, and then I begin.

When I sing, it's . . . not bad. I hit all the notes, and I look fairly relaxed. I chalk that up as a win. The piano plays the final chord, and I force a smile at Mr. B.

"Thank you, Shay," he says, nodding to himself while he scribbles on his legal pad.

I flee the stage, pick my way through the few witches still sitting in the backstage hallway, and go back outside the auditorium. I sit against the wall, and Ed Ferrero scoots his lanky body across the floor to sit beside me.

"Haven't seen you around these parts before, Shay," he says, affecting some sort of weird cowboy voice.

I shrug. "I'm trying something new."

Ed Ferrero is this stoner theater kid who sells his sketchy homemade energy potions to tired students in the back parking lot. The concentration he sells them at is totally illegal. You have to get a prescription to use an energy potion that strong. Everyone who uses them looks wired as hell, and I've heard that their magic currents get all jumpy. But hey, they're awake, which is all that Ed promises.

"Trying to get that last minute in with Mr. B?" Ed asks. "You and Ana really waited to the very last second for this."

I let out a weird chortling laugh. "Mr. B actually asked us to audition. I think he, um, wanted more choir people."

"Ahhhh," Ed says, like everything makes sense to him now. "Yes, yes, more diverse singers for our foray out of white-person theater. Got it. What part are you gunning for?"

"I'd be cool with a small part."

He nods sagely. "There are no small parts, Shay. Only small actors."

Okay, Ed. That would probably be encouraging to someone who liked theater more, but I honestly want to have as little stage time as possible. I give him a tight-lipped smile anyway.

"I'm hoping for Hector," he says quietly. Hector, if I'm remembering my Wikipedia skim correctly, is the Puerto Rican male lead.

Ed is white—his dark hair and patchy stubble mostly make him look like his Italian dad. But I've passed him talking on the phone to his mom after school in Spanish enough times to know he's Latino.

"You'll be fine," I say. "I don't think you have much competition."

"I heard Brittany say that Mr. B was thinking about doing color-blind casting, though," he says mournfully.

"Color-blind casting?" I repeat. "Like . . . Kevin Cho playing Hector?"

"Or our fearless leader, Brittany Cohen, playing Valeria," he says, smiling serenely.

"Huh."

"Yup." He stretches his arms up, then folds them behind his head and leans back against the wall. "Who knows, though. Mr. B picked this musical because he could cast Mikey as Oscar." Mikey is the one Black senior who does drama. It makes sense that Mr. B would have him in mind for Oscar, the Black male lead. "And then there's me and Mateo. One of us could play Hector."

That's where Ed ends his list of all the Black and Latinx people in drama. Literally three people.

Mr. B leans out of the auditorium doors. "Men, you're up. Come on backstage."

Ed bounds to his feet, gives me a little salute, and strolls off to follow Mr. B.

No wonder Mr. B was out trying to drag in every brown person he could find. If he was planning to go with that color-blind casting idea, it would be an awfully pale production of *Bronxtown Brooms*.

The whole thing gives me a bad taste in my mouth. I don't want to be brown window dressing on white *Bronxtown Brooms*. If I get a small part like I'm hoping for, that's what it's going to feel like.

Think of the scholarship, Shay. Think of the scholarship.

Chapter 8

VALERIA:

The neighborhood's changing so much every day

Prices are rising, so no one can stay

And I am just watching the place that I love

Slowly, slowly slipping away

—Lyrics to "My Soft Place to Land" from *Bronxtown Brooms*

ONCE THE GUYS ARE DONE SINGING, BRITTANY ANNOUNCES that we should all meet onstage in five minutes for the dance call. My stomach flips. I'm reasonably coordinated, but I haven't danced in front of anybody since I was in a musical in middle school. And I would prefer to keep it that way.

We slowly make our way into the auditorium, and Ed appears beside me out of nowhere. "Ask me how my audition went," he says, throwing his arm around me.

I push off his arm. We are not friends—we have one class together, and that's the extent of our interactions—so that's way too much Ed in my personal-space bubble for my liking.

"Sorry, dude, boundaries, I get it," he says, giving me finger guns. "Ask me how it went."

"How'd your audition go?" I say unenthusiastically.

"Crushed it," he whispers, grinning. His attention flicks away from me. "Yo, Mikey!" He lopes down the aisle, leaving me Ed-free for a few moments. I slip off my shoes and make my way onto the stage. Once there, I linger on my own while other people chat in groups.

This is one of those moments when I wish Lex was still at school. I don't need lots of close friends, but it would be nice to have her around more.

Ana strides onstage wearing these little black dance heels with leggings and a red leotard. Her dark curls swing behind her, bouncing in time with her steps. I do a literal double take, then promptly feel like a fool and stare down at my socks. She looks like she's here to audition for Broadway, while the rest of us are screwing around onstage like we're toddlers at our first dance class. To make things worse—and I hate that I'm even thinking this—she looks hot as hell.

"Hellooooo, Dolly," Ed says, appearing beside me. He eyes Ana and flashes a grin at me like he said something funny, but I don't get what the joke was.

Ana takes a spot just in front of me, then sits on the floor with her legs in a straddle. She's hot *and* flexible? Her legs are basically in a full split. She stretches over to both sides, then flattens her torso to the floor in front of her.

How is she good at everything? It's like she's a robot or something. A high-achieving robot with a bad grasp of human emotions.

She stands up, spreads her legs apart, and rolls down slowly to touch the floor. As her head hangs between her legs, she catches me staring at her and holds eye contact with me for a few seconds. "What?"

"You look . . . intense," I blurt out. "Your outfit, I mean."

"I like to do things right." She closes her eyes and continues to hang there, bending one knee and then the other.

A stab of irritation hits me. What a condescending response. "Yeah, I totally get that," I say, giving her a tight smile. "It doesn't look like you're trying too hard at all."

She snorts. "Great. I feel much better now that I have your opinion on my outfit."

"You're welcome," I say as snottily as I can manage.

"Do you have any other brilliant opinions to offer?" She straightens. "Or can I go back to stretching?"

"Carry on." I turn away and pointedly ignore her.

"Okay, let's do a quick warm-up before we get started," Brittany says, bouncing to the front of the crowd. "We're going to be learning a little bit of the choreography from the block party number, but let's make sure we're all nice and warm first. Starting with your feet apart in a nice wide second . . ."

I mirror Brittany as she leads us through a warm-up, feeling pretty good about myself. I'm fairly athletic and in better shape than a lot of the other people here. Once Brittany starts teaching the dance, however, my confidence evaporates.

Not only is the choreography fast, but she teaches it in long sections that are impossible to remember. I can't recall any dance terminology I learned from middle-school theater either, so I have no idea what she's talking about half the time. As she starts drilling us on the moves, she yells at us in some nonsense language that's a mixture of the song lyrics, the dance moves we're supposed to be doing, and random sounds that go with the movements or the beat of the song.

"Mm, gah kah, shimmy . . . kah kah. Spin yourself around and step ball change. Gabriela, I can—kah kah kah kah." Brittany eyes us critically. "Let's go over that last part slowly before adding the magic in. You need to make sure your weight is on your left foot."

No, what I actually need is to be able to remember the combination. That would probably assist me in executing it.

Everything only gets worse when Brittany hands us all lighting orbs to use as props. We're supposed to run electricity through them at specific moments to light them up. Electricity generation is a basic magic skill—anybody with a magic level over 20 can do it. But the problem isn't lighting up the orb. It's that I can't manage to coordinate the electricity with everything else. Every time I light it up, I lose track of where I am in the choreography. I keep dropping the stupid thing too.

Of course freaking Ana does the choreography flawlessly. Wearing a pleased smile I've never seen on her before, she spins and shimmies and salsas, her hair whipping around her. Her orb flicks on at all the right moments, and she deftly catches it every time she tosses it into the air. I hate myself for doing it, but I watch her so I can remember what to do once Brittany stops dancing with us.

Where was Ana hiding this secret talent? I thought I knew her fairly well. I know which types of potions she's good at brewing. I know what classes she takes—she likes to make fun of me for taking one less AP class than she does. (Stupid language requirement.) I know what part she sings in choir, and how many solos she's had since freshman year. But I apparently didn't know that she was a trained dancer.

Brittany puts us in small groups to perform, and Ana and I end up together. By this point, I'm so mad that I'm actively glaring at everything in sight.

"Smile!" Brittany calls, tapping the corners of her mouth.

That was definitely directed at me. Or maybe it wasn't, and I'm being too self-absorbed about all of this. Glancing at Ana standing gracefully in front of me, I grit my teeth and smile. Brittany presses play on the boom box, and my group launches into the dance. I manage to drag my body through the moves, though I think it's obvious that I'm watching Ana to do it. When we finish, I leave the stage with my group, my face burning with embarrassment.

"Okay, thanks so much, everyone!" Brittany says once every group has gone. "That's just a little taste of what the choreography is going to look like for the show. Mr. B and I have some cool stuff planned for manipulating the set during that number too, so look forward to that." She giggles and tucks a loose strand of blond hair behind her ear, turning to glance out at where Mr. B sits in the audience. Everyone claps for her. I join in, though I have no idea why we're applauding her. I feel personally traumatized by her right now.

"Take a fifteen-minute break, everyone. Grab some water, cool down," Mr. B says from the audience. "I'll put up a callback list after that. If you're not called back, you can head home."

We all wander out of the auditorium and sit in the hallway. Tension fills the air. Nobody talks much except for Ed and his friend Mikey, who have a loud, weirdly performative argument about what local Mexican place has the best burrito.

I stink of sweat, so I reach for the magic in my clothes and will it to release the lavender fragrance woven into it. The shirt is old, so the magic of the lavender is faint, but it works okay as long as I redo the scentwork on it every few weeks. It's embarrassing to smell like sweat when everyone else at this school can afford clothes with automatic scent magic sewn in.

After way more than fifteen minutes, Mr. B comes outside and tapes a printed piece of paper to the auditorium doors. Everyone immediately swarms the list. I hang back until the first rush is over and I can easily get to the front. I skim the list quickly. Surprisingly, I don't see Mikey's name. But there's Ana, of course, and Ed and Mateo . . .

My name isn't there.

Dismay washes over me. I must have flubbed the dance audition even worse than I thought. Maybe my acting was so embarrassing that Mr. B wants to save me the humiliation. There's no way I'm going to be cast.

"Hey," Ana says, appearing beside me.

She can't bring me down with one of her sarcastic comments. Not right now. I meet her gaze, raising my chin defiantly.

"Don't worry—" she begins to say.

"Good luck with your callback," I cut her off, flashing her a tight-lipped smile. Then I turn on my heel and walk away.

Chapter 9

If you plan to pursue a career that significantly involves magic, you should attend an educational institution that offers higher-level magical training. Students can choose to apply to magical community colleges or non-licensing magical universities, which have less competitive admissions rates than universities that offer magical licenses. Only the most rigorous institutions are accredited by the US government to issue magical licenses.

—*Magical Licenses and You* career pamphlet

PILAR'S IS SLAMMED THE NEXT EVENING, SO I DON'T HAVE time to think about the cast list that my name won't be listed on. Both Lex and I are working the front while Pilar does the prep for tomorrow. Unfortunately for me, Mrs. Morris, one of our more frustrating regulars, comes in near closing and traps me in an obnoxious, never-ending conversation. She's this retired old white lady who refuses to believe that me or Lex are ever telling her the truth.

"What about the 0.5 concentration? Can I get that?"

Mrs. Morris asks. She smooths a strand of silver hair behind her ear and gives me a kindly smile, as if we haven't been having this same conversation for ten minutes.

I smile back, because screaming in frustration isn't a viable option. "Unfortunately, no. You can't get anything besides the 0.01 concentration of the pain potion without a prescription from your magimed."

She pauses, pressing her thin lips together. She's wearing this sickly pink lipstick that bleeds outside her lip line onto her skin. "What about the 0.2 concentration?"

"I'm sorry, but we do need a prescription from your magimed for that." Which I literally just said. Multiple times. Ugh, I wish she would stop coming here and just go to the Walmart apothecary instead. "I'm happy to ring up the Aqualung potion and the Strength potion, though."

"Can I talk to Pilar, young lady?"

She's going to tell you exactly the same thing I said. But whatever. "Sure," I say. I go to the back room and find Pilar slowly stirring a cauldron on the stove.

"Mrs. Morris wants to talk to you," I say flatly. "She thinks I'm lying to her because I won't sell her a stronger pain reducer without a prescription."

Pilar wipes her hands on a dish towel. "I'll deal with her."

"Thanks," I say, taking her place in front of the stove. I spend the rest of my shift tending to the hair-growth potion. When I start bottling the liquid, Lex flies into the prep room.

"Closing time!" she sings tunelessly.

"Do you want to come over for a little and do MAT practice?" I ask.

She groans theatrically and hops up to sit beside me on the prep table. "I think we should go play terraball instead."

"Aw, come on," I cajole, flashing her a winning smile. "Drill practice. Just for like an hour."

"Did you get someone to check the cast list for you?" she says abruptly.

I throw her a disparaging look. "Subtle change in subject there."

"Subtlety is my middle name. Did you get someone to check?"

Shaking my head, I funnel the hair-growth potion from the cauldron into a lilac glass bottle. "My audition sucked. I definitely didn't get a part."

"Shay, it's a high school musical. Everyone gets a part, even if they sucked. You'll just be, like, tree number three or something." She pats me on the back, which doesn't help with my funneling. "Don't worry—you can still impress Mr. B in the ensemble." There's an edge to her voice when she mentions Mr. B. "Besides, there's no way he's not going to cast you after he threatened you to be in the show."

"Oh my god, Lex, he didn't threaten me," I say,

putting down the cauldron. "I definitely read too much into what he was saying. Plus, he asked other people to audition too."

"Other people?" Lex says, raising her eyebrows. "Like who?"

"Ana."

"So one other person? Who he definitely could have threatened with the scholarship too?"

What a horrifying idea. It's not that I think he threatened her. It's just that this turned into yet another round of Ana vs. Shay. Except competing to see who can make a teacher like them more is a new low, even for us.

"Girl, I'm sorry. Didn't mean to upset you," Lex says, her expression softening. She runs her fingers back through her hair, which she does sometimes when she's stressed. "Let's go to your place and do MAT drills," she announces. It's a peace offering for bothering me about Mr. B and Ana. If it gets her to practice for the test, I'll take it.

"Awesome," I say. "My mom hasn't seen you in a while. She's worried we've broken up."

After I finish bottling the potion, we wipe down the prep room and say goodbye to Pilar. I pull out my phone on the way to the car to text Mom about Lex coming over. There's an email waiting when I unlock the phone.

I stop dead in my tracks when I see the sender's name. Why is Mr. B emailing me? I quickly swipe the screen to open the email.

"What's up?" Lex calls, because I'm just standing stock-still in the middle of the parking lot.

The email reads:

Hey Shay,

You didn't come by to pick up your cast packet, so I've attached it here. Get your parents to sign the permission form for the potion use in the show ASAP. See you in rehearsal!

Shit.

Lex was right. Does that mean I'm in the ensemble? I should have gotten someone to check the list for me.

"Shaaaaay, what's up?" Lex repeats.

"I got cast in the show," I say, still staring at the email.

"Oh my god. As what?"

"I don't know." Who can I text to ask? I don't think I have anybody's number who was at the audition. Maybe I could message someone on WizConnect?

"Can you text Ana?" Lex says, bobbing up and down on her heels excitedly. I give her a disparaging look. "I mean, ew, no, we hate her."

As if the universe is taking pity on me, I get a text from someone marked "Chem Project Ed."

CHEM PROJECT ED: yo, my man Mikey
is pumped to be your Oscar

"Who's Chem Project Ed?" Lex asks, peering at my screen.

"Ed Ferrero," I say, already typing my response.

SHAY: lol this is kind of embarrassing, but what part did I get? didn't get to check the list before I left school.

A loud honk pierces the parking lot, and I just about jump out of my skin. When I look up from my phone, there's a large car hovering ten feet from us. Lex waves cheerily at the driver as we run out of its way. I get into the passenger seat of her car and stare anxiously at my screen. A photo comes through from Ed. I open it and find a picture of the cast list. And there, right at the top, is my name.

Oh my god. This can't be happening. I zoom in on my name to confirm I'm not seeing things.

"I'm the lead. Mr. B cast me as Valeria."

"What?" Lex screeches, yanking the phone from my hands. She stares at the screen as if it's going to tell her I was joking.

"But I didn't get a callback," I say numbly.

"I guess Mr. B had already decided to cast you," Lex says, fiddling with the screen. "Wow, Ana is playing Gabriela."

Of course Ana is playing the other female lead. That's

just my luck. There is something deeply ironic about the two of us being cast to play sisters who love each other unconditionally.

I take back the phone and scan the rest of the list. Ed is playing Hector, one of the two male leads. Mikey, even though he didn't get a callback either, is playing the other male lead, Valeria's love interest, Oscar. Mateo is playing Miguel, the creep who tries to run away with Valeria and Gabriela's little sister. And that's the end of the Black and Latinx people in the cast. Brittany is playing Oscar's sister, who has a big number in the second act. I didn't think Brittany would be in the show since she was choreographing it. Also, since Oscar's sister is the only role in the show specifically written for a Black woman, that could have been a nice, smallish part for me.

"I guess you better learn how to act," Lex says.

I sigh and slump in my seat. "I feel like I was affirmative actioned. In a bad way."

Lex gives me an "are you kidding" look. "That's stupid. Mr. B has cast plenty of bad white actors. Remember *Wizards of Brooklyn*?"

Unfortunately, I do remember seeing that heinous piece of theater last year. The two seniors playing the main guys were such mediocre singers, dancers, and actors that I fell asleep out of self-defense.

"Those two wizards were totally cast as the gangsters because they were tall white dudes who looked kind of menacing. How is that different from him casting you because he thinks you're Latina?"

"I guess you're right."

"I am right," she says, starting the car. "Music?"

"Yeah." I don't feel like talking. I need to sit in a horrified stupor for a while.

When Lex and I get to my apartment, my parents are sitting on the couch in the main room. They're drinking cheap wine and talking over the cooking show they have on, which is their favorite thing to do together. I breathe in, and the scent of freshly baked bread fills my nose. We got a super-fancy TV for free from Mom's job, so the scentwork patch on the TV generates the scents from the food on-screen.

"Haven't seen you in a while, Lex," Mom says. She lifts her feet off Dad's lap and turns to face us. "Thought that maybe Shay was hiding you from us."

"Nope, I'm just busy," Lex says cheerily. "Don't have as much time to hang out."

"Well, we always like having you around," Mom says, her tone pregnant with meaning. "So you come over any night of the week, and I'll make you dinner. Anybody special to Shay is special to us too."

Dad takes a sip of his wine, his eyes sparkling with amusement. I think he finds Mom's insinuations about me and Lex funny, even though he's never said anything about them.

Mom looks like she's going to say something else, but

I start backing away from her. "Lex and I are going to go practice for the MATs in my room."

Dad raises his glass to us. "You two are some hard-working witches."

Mom's eyebrows scrunch together. "Leave the door open."

Lex snickers so quietly that only I can hear it. "Will do," I say.

We retreat to my room, stopping on the way to grab supplies for drill practice in the kitchen. I leave the door to my room open. It's ridiculous that I can't be alone with friends of any gender. She's been like this with the few boys that have come over to do school projects too.

"Do you want to start with change of state?" I say, placing the full water glass I grabbed from the kitchen on my dresser.

"Sure," Lex says lazily, barely lifting her head from where she lies on my bed. She goes hazy-eyed, and the magic flows in the water arrange themselves swiftly into a lattice framework.

"Hey, let me time you!" I protest as the water begins to freeze. "And don't break my mom's glass."

"Roger that," she says, her lips curving into a devilish smirk. The lattice of magic unwinds, then spirals faster and faster in the center of the water.

"Lex!" I snatch the glass away before she can send the ice straight into gas state. "Come on, be serious."

A flash of annoyance passes over her face, but then she rolls her eyes and laughs. "You're *too* serious, lady."

"I'm trying to pay you back in advance for all the help you'll have to give me with acting," I say. "Want to do texture-adjustment practice instead? You're too good at change-of-state drills."

"Whatever's fine," she says unenthusiastically.

Ugh, she's right. I'm being too serious. The point of this was to make her feel more confident about the test on Saturday. She doesn't need to practice practical magic anyway.

"Hey, I'm going to miss you when you're all busy with drama shit," she says suddenly, sitting up in the bed. "What am I going to do without my main squeeze?"

"I'm not going to, like, disappear. I've been busy before," I point out.

She ducks her head and runs her hands back through her hair. "Sure, but I barely saw you last semester."

"Yeah, but . . ." I trail off, because she's right. We don't hang out as much anymore. We used to go to the gym to play one-on-one terraball all the time—that was how we became friends in the first place. Our terraball coach at school recommended the gym as a way for our team to get extra practice in, and Lex and I were the only ones who liked going enough to do it more than once. It became our thing. But we barely played together last semester. I think last weekend was the first time we had gone in months.

"I'm sorry," I say. "It really sucks. I mean, you're super busy with your application stuff too. I felt like our schedules never lined up last semester outside of work."

She rolls her eyes. "Yeah, I was locked up in my house writing supplemental essays for my college apps."

I wince. That was a bad time. Lex is applying to all of the top fifteen ranked licensing universities, and they each have different essay requirements.

"At least Galpert doesn't require an additional essay," Lex says.

I raise my eyebrows. "Galpert? You're applying there?"

She plays with my comforter, bunching it up between her fingers. "I added a few non-licensing colleges to my list."

"Why?" I ask, my brow furrowing with confusion.

Her hand tightens into a fist around the fabric of the comforter. "I want to go to college this year," she says. "And I don't even know what I want to study. I know my parents want me to be a magimed like them, but I can try to transfer to a licensing college if I decide to do that."

I blink at her, unsure of how to respond. Giving up on the idea of going to a licensing college after only one gap year makes no sense. I would understand if she was on her third or fourth try, but giving up at this point feels like such a waste after working so hard at T. K. Anderson. And if she doesn't eventually transfer to a licensing college, her career options will be seriously limited.

"Non-licensing colleges aren't bad schools," she says. "You know the whole licensing system is total bullshit. The licensing colleges are so rich they just, like, pay off the government to make sure it's hard for new schools to get licensed."

"Maybe it's bullshit, but that's how it is," I say helplessly. "You just have to work really hard. You can't go all dropout witch and give up."

"You're so black-and-white, lady. Like, my only options are going off the grid and living in a commune or killing myself to get into a licensing college?" She laughs, but it sounds forced. I open my mouth to protest, but she suddenly jumps to her feet. "Let's do change-of-state drills again." She cracks her knuckles and rolls out her shoulders. "I'm feeling good. I think I can beat my best time."

I feel the moment dissolving, and I hope I didn't upset Lex. "You sure?"

"Yup," she says, turning her attention to the water again. "Ready, set, go!"

Chapter 10

Though modern stereotypes tell us that women's contributions to the potionworking field are limited to the brewing of "frivolous" housework and beauty potions, the practice of crafting potions in the United States was pioneered by women during the Civil War. For example, Clara Barton was a prominent early witch who invented many potions to care for soldiers during wartime.

—"**Women in Potionworking**" **essay by Shayna Johnson**

THE FIRST DAY OF REHEARSAL COMES SOONER THAN I WANT IT to. When I get to the auditorium, Ed, Mikey, and Mateo are playing a game of stinkball onstage. Stinkball is a game where you work scent magic on balled-up pieces of paper to make them smell as horrific as possible. Then you throw them at each other. The goal is to magically incinerate the paper balls midair before they can hit you with their stink.

I thought stinkball was something we all collectively decided to leave behind in middle school. But here we are.

"Hey," Ana says, sliding into the aisle beside me.

Hello, Satan. Fancy meeting you here.

Ana nods at the stage, her nose wrinkling up in disgust. "This is . . ."

"Embarrassing?" I finish.

"I was going to go with *disgusting*, but *embarrassing* works too." She sits in the seat next to me, because she's obviously not picking up on the anti-Ana vibes I'm sending out with every fiber of my being. Or maybe she's ignoring them because she likes messing with me.

"How's your APUSH essay going?" she asks.

I scrutinize that question for a hidden snarky meaning but don't find one. Is she going to follow up by telling me how much better she is in APUSH than me? "Fine," I say.

"I'm writing mine on the spread of magical training during the Civil War," she says. "I'm assuming you're writing about potions again?"

"Maybe," I say stonily. "So what if I am?"

She chuckles. "How many of your essays can you write about potions?"

I give her my best glare. "Okay, there are a lot of interesting historical topics about potions."

"I'm aware," she says. "You've written papers on all of them."

I don't dignify that with a response. Instead, I fantasize

briefly about how I'm going to absolutely destroy her when the magic-level test results are released this week. Maybe she'll be less smug once it's clear that she can never compare to me magically.

"Do you dance?" Ana asks. "You were surprisingly good at the dance call."

Surprisingly good? Wow, she didn't waste any time reminding me why I was horrified to do this show with her. Also, were we at the same dance call? I was terrible.

"No, I don't dance," I say stiffly.

"Mm, of course not. My bad."

"What do you mean 'of course not'?"

"I just remembered the Great Sophomore Choir Choreography Crisis." She arches an eyebrow. "'If you're blue and you don't know where to go to, why don't you go where fashion sits,'" she sings. Then she waits a few seconds and awkwardly flails her arms from side to side. "'Puttin' on the Ritz.'"

"I did not look like that!" I protest, heat rising in my cheeks. I hope she can't see me blushing. Brown skin, don't fail me now.

"Mm-hmm, no, definitely not," she says, mock serious.

I suck my teeth, crossing my arms over my chest. "And we're not a show choir. I don't know why Ms. Mooney insisted on us doing choreography."

She snickers, a smirk ghosting her lips. "Yeah, not exactly our strength as a group."

"I'm fine at dancing. Just because you're, like, freak-ishly good at it—"

"Thanks?" she says, her dimple deepening as her smirk gets even smugger.

"No—yeah, I mean—whatever." I huff angrily and stomp away, because I've definitively lost this round of Ana vs. Shay. Better to cut my losses and retreat.

"Shay!"

I turn to see Mr. B ambling down the aisle, holding a box piled high with scripts in one arm. Once he reaches me, he claps me on the arm cheerfully, then leans in toward me. "I'm pumped to have you as part of the team." His hand feels hot on my bare skin. Why is everyone in theater so touchy-feely?

Even though I'm uncomfortable, I smile back at him. His grin is so genuine that it's impossible not to. Also, it's easier to swallow my discomfort when I remember that I only have a month and a half to make a good impression on him before submitting my scholarship application.

"I've got a good feeling about this show," he says, let-ting go of my shoulder to readjust the box in his arms. "I think it's going to be something great."

"Yeah," I say.

"I really appreciate that you auditioned, Shay," he says, fixing me with the piercing blue-eyed stare that so many of the other junior witches are in love with. I never got why everyone thinks he's the hottest teacher, because I honestly think he's kind of average-looking, but now that he's staring me down, I realize it's probably the eyes. Then again, who am I to judge male hotness?

"I'm glad I could try something new," I say, which is a complete lie, but whatever.

His face lights up. "That's—wow, you don't know how great that is to hear. There are so many kids here who are so focused on following that great American Magical Way, you know. They work hard, pull themselves up by their bootstraps, yada yada yada. But they never try anything new."

I am one of those kids. Following the American Magical Way—working as hard as I can, developing my magic skills, getting the best education—is the best chance I have at success. That's how you get into a licensing college and get a job that pays real money so you can buy your parents a house in a gated community when you're older. But sucking up to the right people is also how you get those things, so I smile at him and mm-hmm my agreement.

"I swear there's some potion in the water here making the kids into little genius robots," he says conspiratorially. "Makes slackers like me feel bad."

"You went to Willington," I say. "I seriously doubt you're a slacker."

He chuckles. "Flattery will get you everywhere, young thespian," he says grandly. "But trust-fund tragedies like me get into school by greasing the palm, not by getting the grade."

Oh. It's depressing to remember that even my dream school works that way.

"Don't look so tragic. I'm here atoning for my sins and helping the more deserving get into college." He turns away, giving me one last million-dollar smile, and strides down the aisle toward the stage. "Bring it in, people. Let's make some art!" he yells, pumping his fist in the air. Everyone cheers in response. Is this part of some drama ritual I don't know?

I follow him to join the larger group at the front of the auditorium and catch Brittany glaring daggers at me. Wondering if there's somebody else she could be stankeyeing like that, I glance surreptitiously behind me. There isn't anybody there. She tosses her blond hair emphatically over her shoulder and turns away from me.

Ed's friend Mikey appears in front of me suddenly. I don't notice him coming until I nearly run into him. He's, like, three inches shorter than me, even counting his big Afro.

"I'm Mikey," he says, shoving his hand out abruptly to shake. I'm taken aback at first, and then he looks like he regrets offering the handshake. He starts to slowly jellyfish it back toward himself before I take pity on him and shake it.

"I'm Shay."

"Yeah! You're my Valeria." His brow furrows, and he shoves his hands in his pockets. "I mean, you're not mine. Sorry, that was weird. I'm playing Oscar. So we're playing love interests. That's what I meant. Sorry."

Oh my god, how does this guy have conversations with people? "Don't worry about it," I say, smiling at him in the hope that he'll calm down. He doesn't. Instead, he lingers in front of me, shifting awkwardly from side to side, until Mr. B hands out the scripts. I take mine and grab a seat far from Mikey.

"Before we get started, I want to address something that will shape how we approach this musical," Mr. B says when we're all settled in. "I know that some of you are playing characters who aren't exactly like you, whether that's because they're a different race or they speak a different language or they grew up somewhere you've never been."

I'm not sure all those things are equivalent? I'm okay with pretending I'm from New York. I have a bigger problem with pretending I'm Latina.

"But, guys, that's what acting is," Mr. B continues. "Not every character is going to be just like you. That's part of the fun. I'm not a murderer, but I've played the lead in the Scottish play. You've got to find what's essential about the character and play that. Not their race, not their gender, not their political beliefs . . ." He taps at his chest, over his heart. "But who they are inside."

What is he talking about? First of all, I don't know what "the Scottish play" is. More importantly, I'm baffled by this point he's making about race and acting. Does this mean that the white people in the show are pretending to be Latinx or not? And what about me? Am I pretending I'm Dominican like my character? These characters talk about their identities all the time. But I guess Mr. B just wants us to ignore that.

When I look around the table, most people are nodding fervently. I glance over at the other leads to gauge their responses—Mikey and Ed are cheerfully ignoring Mr. B in favor of transfiguring bits of paper into tiny Poké-mon figurines, while Ana is staring at her script with a blank expression on her face. If I had to guess, I would say she's not into what Mr. B is saying either.

"All right, let's get this party started," Mr. B says, flipping his script open with a flourish. "From the top, people."

We start our read-through of the whole show, which people don't take too seriously. Everyone is free to sing along to all of the songs, and people ham it up for laughs during their scenes as much as they can. There are, unsurprisingly, a few weird moments where people have lines in Spanish that they can't pronounce correctly.

Almost nobody sings along to "Sueños," Ana's song in the first act. It becomes very clear why as we hit the first verse. "'Ya sabes, el que no se puede tirar, se jondea,'"

Ana sings along with the cast recording. "'Where there's a will, there's a way. Keep pushing forward.'"

Luckily, I don't have any of the songs with lots of Spanish lyrics. Ana and Ed have most of those.

We take a quick break between acts, and I text Lex to tell her it's going okay. I send her several funny GIFs for good measure, because she's been down ever since she took the MATs on Saturday. She won't talk about it, but I don't think it went well.

LEX: glad rehearsal is going good

Then she sends me a selfie where she's grinning at the camera, a sheen of sweat on her forehead. Based on the background and her bright pink sports bra, I would guess that she's on a run in her neighborhood.

LEX: missing my running buddy!

> **SHAY: lol when have I ever been your running buddy? you're the only one who likes running like that**

LEX: if I say it enough, that'll make it true

> **SHAY: yeah good luck with that**

"Pizza!" Ed yells, jumping up from his seat and throwing his hands in the air. I flinch, surprised by his sudden outburst, and turn to see what he's yelling about. Mr. B raises his armful of pizzas up victoriously and does a little dance down the aisle toward us. Brittany trails behind him carrying two liters of soda.

No wonder Mr. B is the most popular teacher on campus. The way to high schoolers' hearts is pizza. Proven fact.

We start Act Two while we're still stuffing our faces. Ana looks annoyed for most of the second act, which might have something to do with the cartoonishly bad Hispanic accent that Brittany suddenly puts on for her big song. For once, I'm on Ana's side. The accent is both offensive and confusing, since Brittany's character is one of the few in the script that is explicitly not Latinx.

When we finish the read-through, Ana immediately throws her stuff in her bag and heads out. Everyone else lingers, gathering around Mr. B to make überspecific inside jokes and talk about how excited they are to do the show.

Nerves bubble in the pit of my stomach as I join the group. I don't want to look pathetic, like I'm dying for Mr. B's attention, but I also shouldn't seem standoffish. In the end, I settle on lingering at the edge of the group with a vaguely pleasant look on my face. Eventually the conversation shifts, and I have to listen to one of my castmates complain about the immersion trip she went on over winter break to the French Empire.

"They're just really convinced that the French way is the only way to do magic," she says. "I dunno, I felt, like, profiled for being American. Okay, we get it—you invented magic. But we're better at it, so. Whatever."

What is she even talking about? That's rude *and* inaccurate. The French didn't invent magic, just Awakening potions. Magic always existed, even before many people could manipulate it.

Mr. B laughs. "I hope you didn't say that to any of your new French friends."

There's a brief pause where it becomes clear to everyone that she definitely did tell her French friends that.

"I'm sure they very much appreciated being educated on their country's inferiority," Mr. B says, chuckling. "Maybe we should send you to China next. You can tell them that they only have a stronger economy than us because they stole America's magitech secrets."

The whole group starts to giggle. Mr. B gives her a cheeky grin that asks her forgiveness for poking fun at her. She smiles back and laughs along with everyone else, though her cheeks have gone a little pink.

"So how're you feeling about your first day with these clowns, Shay?" Mr. B says, looking to me. "Have we scared you off yet?"

Suddenly the whole group is staring at me. "Not yet," I say, feeling unexpectedly important now that I have his attention.

"Watch out—we'll convert you to be a theater kid by the time this show is over," he says.

"One of us! One of us!" Ed chants, waving his fists in the air. Mikey starts chanting along with him, and then a few other voices join in.

"We'll see," I say, even though there is absolutely no chance of that happening. It doesn't matter. Saying that was the right move. Mr. B grins at me, and I know, deep in my bones, that doing this show was a good idea.

Chapter 11

As the practice of magic spread across America in the early 1800s, it became common practice for slave owners to Awaken the magic power of their slaves in order to feed off their slaves' magic and increase their own power. The slaves themselves were forbidden from using magic and received no instruction on how to use it.

—United States history textbook, Advanced Placement edition

THE NEXT DAY, THE RESULTS OF OUR MOST RECENT MAGIC-level test are released. I can't check them when they go up. Neither can Ana. The results are posted during the first lunch block, and neither of us have a lunch period. We got approval to take eight classes this year instead of the regular load of seven, so we just eat our packed lunches during the second lunch block while we're in precalc.

I'm starting the process of brewing a Magnetizing potion when there's a sudden outbreak of whispering from my classmates. Several people turn to stare at Ana and me. Dr. Davidson, our potions teacher, remains focused on whatever he's doing on his laptop. As usual. He's always about five minutes late to noticing what's happening in our class once he's sent us off on our brewing labs.

After a few minutes of this, Ana holds out her hand expectantly to the guy at the lab table behind us, and he silently passes her his phone. The moment she looks at the screen, her face goes completely blank. Then she nods and hands me the phone. "Congrats," she says as she turns back to her cauldron.

When I look at the screen, I find a picture of the updated school ranking board that's zoomed in on the top two names.

1. Ana Álvarez—GPA: 4.78, Magic Level: 37
2. Shayna Johnson—GPA: 4.67, Magic Level: 41

Holy shit. Holy freaking shit. I broke forty. Lots of seniors don't even get to forty by the time they graduate. And I'm at forty-one as a junior. A disbelieving laugh escapes my lips, and I hand the phone back to its owner in a daze.

I widened the gap between me and Ana too. It's not the full six-point difference I had hoped for, which would have shut up everybody who says my magic level is only this high because I'm getting help from my family. But still, this is incredible.

When I turn to Ana, she's pulling on the magic in a lump of nickel and kneading it on the surface of the table. I'm so giddy that it feels like my whole body is buzzing. I take a step closer to her.

"I guess I won this round," I say. "Sucks to suck."

"Yeah," she says. "I definitely sucked this time around." She looks down, not meeting my eyes. Is she sad? My gut clenches. Great, now I feel like a complete jerk. She leans over her cauldron, and her expression disappears in the steam.

Gloating doesn't feel as good as I wanted it to. I scramble for something I can say to fix this conversation. "It's just embarrassing at this point that my GPA is lower than yours," I say, offering her an opening into the exchange we've had many times before.

She looks at me, and her face softens. "Yeah, too bad ranking is done by GPA," she says, her mouth quirked in this tiny almost smile. "How does it feel to know that I'm smarter than you?"

"I wouldn't know," I say. And then the balance is restored—I no longer feel like a total asshole, and we both go about our business with our potions. Except things are also obviously different because, for once, I feel like I'm pulling ahead in our competition.

I get a few other congratulations, mostly from the seniors in our class. The juniors are all salty that I have them beat so badly. Which is nothing new.

Eli, one of the junior wizards in the class, leans across my lab table, eyeing me skeptically. I try to pretend that I'm too into brewing my potion to see him, because I don't see this interaction going anywhere good. He's giving off majorly sketchy vibes. "Hey, Shay," he says. "I was just wondering . . . does your family have a magic-sharing pool?"

I suppress my need to scream with frustration. This again. People are so deeply convinced that there's no way I could be this powerful naturally. This clown literally has class with me every day and hasn't noticed that I'm—gasp—better at magic than him. And how rich does he think I am to suggest that I have a magic-sharing pool?

Sharing magic is invasive by nature—it creates a connection between people that lets you use their magical energy and gives you a window into how they're feeling. If you're significantly more powerful than the person you're sharing with, you can actually use that connection to influence their feelings. Most people only do it with their families, since you want to be sure that someone won't use that connection to manipulate you.

Because of all the associated risks, it's incredibly expensive to hire someone to share magic with you. Families that have whole groups of people they've hired to make a magic-sharing pool for themselves? They're rich beyond belief.

I unclench my jaw to speak. "No, I don't have a magic-sharing pool."

"Yeah, yeah. I got it—you don't want to say." He laughs, and it's so condescending that I can feel my blood pressure rising.

"No. I don't have one. And I don't have a big family, and Black people aren't naturally stronger magic users." I give him my most venomous smile. "Any other questions?"

He scoffs at me. "I didn't say all that. Why are you getting so mad?"

I'm so angry I can't even look at him. This is why I don't fight back when people are assholes to me. Even if I think of something to say fast enough, I somehow always end up on the losing side. I'm the one who's crazy, or too angry, or seeing racism where there isn't any.

"Whoa, buddy." Ana slides up next to me, wearing her frostiest expression. Her eyes are practically ice chips. "I think you should go before you *really* piss off the strongest witch in our grade." She shrugs. "Just a suggestion. She could probably brew a Death by a Thousand Cuts potion and poison you before you figured out how to pull your head out of your ass."

I'm a little pissed that Ana thinks I need her help. And I'm surprised she's offering it. But mostly I'm just tired, and she's way better at this kind of thing than I am.

Eli gapes at her like a perplexed goldfish. "I didn't—"

"I think the word you're looking for is *congratulations*," Ana says. A few seconds pass, and he doesn't move. She raises her eyebrows like she's confused about why he's still standing there. "Bye."

That finally gets rid of him. I sigh as I reach for my softened lump of nickel and drop it in my cauldron. The taste of victory has gone sour in my mouth.

"You can't murder him on school grounds," Ana whispers. "So maybe just beat his ass at potionworking?"

I snort. "That's the plan," I mutter. Mom always told me that success is the best revenge.

At the end of class, we all gather to test our potions. When I apply my Magnetizing potion to one of the magic practice cubes Dr. Davidson has given us, every metal object in a five-foot radius flies toward the cube. Only a few other people brew potions that work. Ana, of course, is one of them, though her magnet ends up being slightly weaker than mine. When I look over at Eli, his practice cube is lightly smoking with no metal objects attached. He refuses to meet my eyes.

I'm back in the auditorium in the afternoon because the schedule for this show was designed specifically to torture me. I have rehearsal every day after school except for

Fridays. I don't even get Friday nights off to relax, because I have potions club, and I refuse to give up my shift at Pilar's that night. I'm already losing enough money because of this show.

It turns out that we're going to be front-loading learning the choreography, so Brittany will be teaching us all the big dance numbers for the first two weeks. After Brittany leads us in some stretches, Mr. B takes Mateo to learn his music in his classroom, leaving Brittany in charge. I didn't think this was possible, but the rehearsal is worse than the dance call. Because I'm a lead, I'm in the front of all the formations, which means I can't watch anybody. Which means I forget the moves the second Brittany stops doing them with us.

"No no no, stop," Brittany yells after I spin the wrong way and body slam Mikey. Telling us to stop is unnecessary. Mikey is on the floor, his stocky body sprawled out uncomfortably, and everyone has stopped dancing to gawk. "You turn to the right, Shay. The right. Got it?"

"Yeah," I mumble, offering Mikey a hand to get up. He takes it and hops back to his feet. "You okay?"

"I'm cool!" he says, giving me a thumbs-up. "It'll take more than that to take me out!"

I make eye contact with Ana, who smirks and hums "Puttin' on the Ritz" under her breath.

"Shut up," I mutter at her. She's vastly exaggerating how bad I was at that choir choreography anyway.

Things don't get better from there. After we stumble through the first thirty seconds of the dance a few more times, Brittany cuts our final attempt off with a dissatisfied wave of her hand. "Okay, enough. We'll have to come back to that. Let's practice stage slides. Give me space so I can show you how to do one." She flaps her hand again, waving people out of the way. She runs a few paces, then puts her feet down flat and slides across the whole width of the stage at high speed.

"So you need to adjust the texture of the floor ahead of you at the right moment, or else it doesn't work," Brittany calls back to us. "It takes some coordination to get, so make sure you think of the magic you're doing at least a few seconds before you try the slide."

You have to be kidding me. She wants us to adjust, like, twenty feet of the floor to be smooth enough to slide on while maintaining our balance and basically ice-skating across it?

"Do you guys need to see it again?" Brittany says impatiently.

There are a few nods from the group. Out of the corner of my eye, I see Ana tentatively slide a few feet. There's no way I'm going to let her get it before me, so I move to the side and try it for myself.

I sink my awareness into the magical currents in the floor. They swim into sharper focus, brown-green and tightly coiled together. I'm going to need to unravel these coils of magic to make this work. Not too much, though, or I'll ruin the structural integrity of the floor. I jog a few steps and hope for the best. When I put my foot down to slide, I haven't finished smoothing out my path, so I fall and smack my elbow in the process. I stay down for a moment, rubbing my elbow. Brittany slides past me, mid-demonstration. "You should probably be watching," she says snidely as she passes.

Who peed in her orange juice this morning?

"Try it slower," Ana says, sliding up next to me. Of course she's already figured it out. "If you try from a walk a few times, it's easier to—"

"I got it," I snap.

Her brow furrows. "Um. Okay."

Turns out, I don't got it. In fact, I never get it. By the end of rehearsal, I'm part of the small, shameful group of people who can't do a stage slide without falling on their face. Or their ass, depending on momentum.

Mr. B comes back right before we finish up and watches us run through what we've learned so far. When we get to the part where I'm supposed to do a stage slide, I run to my next spot instead, my face burning with embarrassment. He gives us a slow clap when we finish the section we know, and I want to tell him not to.

As everyone disperses, Brittany stands squarely in my path and stares at me like I'm a particularly gross bug. "Do I need to change the choreography?" she says disdainfully.

"I can move you to the back so you don't need to do the stage slide if it's too hard for you."

"I'll figure it out." I narrow my eyes and raise my chin to meet her stare. Ugh, why is she so tall?

"Don't make Mr. B regret picking you, okay?" Brittany says. "I know you don't have much experience with theater—"

My face twists with irritation.

"But I wouldn't want people to think you're in the play because he wanted to go with *authentic* casting or whatever." With that, she flips her hair over her shoulder and strides away.

What. The. Hell. I'm so mad that I'm momentarily frozen. My brain somehow feels fuzzy and laser-focused at the same time. I can't believe she said that to me. I can't believe I *let* her say that to me. Why didn't I tell her where she could shove her racist self?

Do other people think that's why I was cast? Honestly, they probably do. I mean, that's why I think I was cast. I'm not exactly good at acting or dancing.

Lex. I have to tell Lex. I grab my stuff from where it's piled in one of the aisles and stomp out of the auditorium, already punching Lex's speed dial on my phone. I call her a few times before she answers, by which time I'm pacing back and forth by the parking lot and sweating my ass off in the Florida heat.

"OH HELL NO!" Lex shrieks after I explain what

happened. "She's just salty because she doesn't get to be the lead for once."

"I didn't say anything to her, Lex!" A few people look at me weirdly on the way to their cars, which is probably because I'm yelling furiously into the phone. I'm also definitely sweating out my blowout, but I couldn't give less of a shit right now. "I just stood there like a dumbass, and she, like, strutted away flipping her stupid hair in the wind!"

Lex emits this rage-filled scream, and I have to hold my phone away from my ear. "Fuck her."

"Yeah, for real."

"Don't let her get to you, lady. It's high school theater. It's not that serious." She huffs angrily, and I can practically feel her rolling her eyes through the phone. "You're a gorgeous singer, and you work harder than anybody I know. You deserve to be there just as much as she does."

"Thanks, friend," I say, wiping sweat off my forehead.

"Anytime. Let me know if you want me to set her hair on fire. I'll make it look like an accident."

"Will do."

"Okay, I have to go," she says reluctantly. "I'm actually at the soup kitchen volunteering right now, and I can't hide in the bathroom forever."

"Okay. Have fun."

"I'll try. Byeeeee." She hangs up.

Even after talking to Lex, I don't feel much better. I

can't fail like I did during this rehearsal when people like Brittany think I'm a diversity casting choice. People already think I'm cheating to be good at the things I'm good at. I *can't* be bad at stuff. I have to be the best a million times over so people will acknowledge me.

I practice the choreography in my room every night after rehearsal that week, which does not help me finish my ever-growing piles of homework. It's fine, though. I just sleep less. More importantly, I need to stop sucking at these dances, pronto. Nobody is going to be able to say I got this part just because I'm brown by the time the show comes around.

Chapter 12

Some of the slaves evidently did use their newfound magic, as their masters noted that their magical reserves grew significantly over time. As the correlation between magical power and frequency of use had not yet been established, their masters instead came to the conclusion that Africans were predisposed as a race to be magically powerful.

—United States history textbook, Advanced Placement edition

ON SATURDAY, I FINALLY GET TO WORK ON MY OWN PERsonal brewing projects. It's the first day I've had time to do that in a while. I feel a little guilty ignoring my homework and self-imposed dance-practice schedule, but I can't pass up the opportunity to make the Eagle Eye potion I saw on my favorite potionworking blog. It ends up being a superfun project. There are lots of interesting lattice patterns to twist the magic into and a nice relaxing bit where I get to blend the potion into a cream.

I finish the potion by sealing my intention into it. Staring at the blue cream in my cauldron, I imagine the image in front of me getting bigger and bigger, as if my eyes are zooming in on it. I hold that idea in my mind for a moment, then mentally push it toward the magic of the potion. The strand of magic containing my intention sails out of my head and into the cream.

Once that's done, I grab my potionworking journal, which floats conveniently at eye level while I work. I note down my observations about how I could potentially improve the brewing process for this potion underneath the recipe I wrote down. Then I carefully scrape the cream into jars and clean up the kitchen.

"How's it going in there?" Mom calls from the living room. Dad's been called into work today—something about an emergency soil-pollution cleanup that they needed all hands on deck for—so Mom and I are the only ones at home.

"I'm done," I call back as I slide my cauldron into the cabinet. Once everything is all cleared up, I go join Mom in the living room.

She's sitting on the couch, watching the news on TV while she folds clothes. I settle down beside her and grab some pants to fold. We watch the news in silence for a few minutes. They're covering a new scandal I haven't heard about before. Apparently, the CEO of a big magitech corporation was recently busted for forcing witches at his company to share magic with him so they could get promotions. It's majorly messed up. What does he even need extra magical power for? He's a CEO. He doesn't work on making or developing products himself. It's obviously just a power trip.

"Never share magic with someone to get something, Shay," Mom says. Her face has a hard set to it. "Never ever."

"I won't," I say, wondering why she's being so intense about this.

"White men in this country think that they can still take our magic to use whenever they want. Like it's a gift they gave us that they have some right to." She pulls me over and kisses me roughly on the top of the head. "They don't own you, baby."

"Yeah," I say awkwardly, because this is happening out of nowhere. She always gets so riled up about the news. To make things worse, they're introducing a new segment about communes. I only make it through a few minutes of them interviewing some semi-hysterical wizard about his daughter going to a commune after her fourth gap year. "Can we watch something else?"

"Sure," Mom says, grabbing the remote. "*Potion Wars*?"

"Yes, please."

She finds a rerun of *Potion Wars* that's playing. The show is almost over, but it's from a season that we've seen before anyway.

"Fatima should have won this round," Mom says, shaking her head. Fatima was her favorite competitor in this group of apothecaries.

"That's true," I say. "She makes better potions. She only lost because Lisa took some of the supplies she needed."

We watch the rest of the episode, and even though we knew what was going to happen, Mom still looks personally offended when Fatima loses. She clicks the TV off with a disapproving sniff.

"Did you see the email I sent you about the big broom sale?" I ask. "The dealership is really close to our apartment."

"Shay, enough with the broom stuff."

"I don't need one that goes fast or anything, just something to get me around."

She purses her lips. "You know how many people die on brooms every year?"

Yes. I looked it up, hoping that I could prove her wrong next time we had this argument. The number was bleak. "I could get a slow one with lots of safety magic built in. Plus, I'll carry healing potions and Light as a Feather potion with me whenever I ride it."

"No. I'm not talking about this anymore," she says, and I can tell from her tone that I need to give up my broom crusade for today. She shakes out a particularly wrinkled shirt, then takes a handful of LaundrEase potion dust from the little bucket by her feet. When she sprinkles it on the shirt, the wrinkles disappear. "How's school going?" she asks. "Your magic level is so high now that everything should be pretty comfortable for you."

"I mean, it's fine," I say, picking up a pair of my leggings from the unfolded pile. I fold it and start a new pile by my feet. "I should feel good about the whole magic-level thing, but some people were jerks about it, and that kind of ruined it for me."

She sits up. "Who was a jerk about it?"

"Just some guy in my class," I say, shrugging. "Nobody really thinks I could actually be as strong as I am. Other people have said stuff before too."

"Stuff? What kind of stuff?"

Suddenly, I regret bringing this up. "Just stuff." She gives me this expectant look when I try to leave it at that, so I reluctantly continue. "Like, I'm only strong because I have a big family . . . or because I'm Black."

I tried to say that in a super-casual tone, but when I glance at Mom, I think she's about to bust a blood vessel. Her eyes have gone wide with fury. "I'll go talk to the school, see what they have to say about their students saying things like that."

"No, you don't have to do that!" I shake my head furiously. The last thing I need is Hurricane Mom descending on the school. What will it even do? Nothing. People will keep saying the same stuff, but then I'll be the weird kid whose mom made a big fuss. "It doesn't matter. I have them all beat anyway."

"Shay, you've got to use me. I don't mind looking like the crazy mom for you."

"I know," I say. My mind flashes through all the other times she's gone to fight for me at school or at other activities that I've done. It's not that I don't appreciate it. I do. It's just that it doesn't always work.

When I was in middle school, I told her about people making fun of me for being a lesbian. I hadn't come out at that point, so I was pretty upset about it. She went to the school and chewed them out for not teaching their students to not bully others. Then we had a whole antibullying assembly that focused on how "gay was okay." Everybody knew it was about me. It didn't make things better. Eventually I graduated and went to T. K. Anderson for high school, where I wasn't the kid whose mom made the whole school have an antibullying assembly. Moral of the story: Sometimes you just have to endure the shitty stuff and wait until you can leave.

Mom stares at me intently. "Baby, you've got to tell me how you're feeling."

"I'm fine," I say. "I know you'll help me if I need it, but I'm good. Seriously. People are annoying sometimes, but I'll prove them wrong."

"You don't have to prove anything to them anymore," she says. "You're one of the top students in your class."

This comment rankles. Despite all my efforts, I'm not *the* top student in my class—I'm just one of them. That's the only part of our plan for me to get the scholarship that I haven't been able to execute. Maybe if I was the undisputed top student, people wouldn't doubt my skills. And maybe if I was good at dancing, people wouldn't think I was a diversity casting choice. I stifle a sigh. I should have practiced my choreography instead of brewing the Eagle Eye potion.

But none of those thoughts are helpful for this conversation. I shake off my doubts and nod at Mom. "You're right." I smile at her. "Can you test my potion for me later?"

"Yeah," Mom says. "Are you sure you're okay?"

"I'm sure," I say, standing up. "Thanks for watching *Potion Wars* with me."

"Of course. We can watch more tomorrow if you want."

"Yeah, if I have time," I say, heading back to my room. I need to practice this *Bronxtown Brooms* choreography before my shift at Pilar's. There's no need to call in the mom cavalry. I've got this all on my own.

Chapter 13

HECTOR:

It's the Bronxtown Broom Race, baby!

I've picked my partner, placed my bets

And now it's time to see who's best

—**Lyrics to "Bronxtown Broom Race" from *Bronxtown Brooms***

BRITTANY CLICKS OFF THE MUSIC, ENDING OUR LATEST attempt at the broom-race choreography. Most of the cast immediately floats to the floor, panting with effort. I drape myself over one of the broom props that's suspended in midair and wait for the inevitable judgment. Brittany stands up from her seat in the audience and clicks her nails on the hard plastic top of the seat in front of her. "That was . . ." she says. "Okay."

"Well, fuck you too," Ed mutters. He tries to stand up

from where he's sitting on the stage, but the Light as a Feather potion we all took mid-scene is still in effect. He ends up floating slowly into the air instead.

The premise for the song we're rehearsing is that Valeria and Gabriela's family broom store is holding their annual broom race. So far, we haven't been able to execute the intense midair choreography or pretend that we're flying on these broom props to Brittany's satisfaction.

"Let's take five, and then we'll keep working!" Brittany says.

A collective groan rises from the group. Nobody is a big fan of Brittany right now, which suits me fine. I'm currently the president of the anti-Brittany club.

Ana flies up to me, using her arms to sort of swim through the air. I hate that she looks so coordinated, even while levitating. When she gets to me, she floats silently for a moment, making her usual weirdly direct eye contact. "You're getting better. I was starting to think your performance in the audition was a fluke, but that last run was almost good."

"Thank you," I say with as much obviously fake sincerity as I can muster.

"Seriously. You didn't take anybody out this time. That's a big improvement."

"You almost kicked me in the face just now, so I guess the tables have turned." If I'm being honest, that wasn't her fault. It only happened because Mikey, my dance partner for the song, accidentally threw me off our broom in the wrong direction.

"If you want, I can help you with the choreography," she says. "I have a lot of dance experience."

Oh god no. I would rather die than accept her pity offer. "Don't worry about me." I drop off the back side of the fake broom and air-swim away from the stage.

I need more caffeine, or else I'm not going to make it through this rehearsal. There should be a few sips left of the coffee Lex brought me. As I float toward the aisle where I've left my stuff, I hear a warning cry from behind me. I half turn and see Ed hurtling toward me at high speed. I barely have time to get out of his way before he flies past.

"This potion is no joke," he says, grabbing hold of a seat a few paces down the aisle. Then he launches himself back into the air, and I have to move out of his way again. He catches himself on the opposite bank of seats.

My brow furrows. I still can't figure out how to make the Light as a Feather potion, and it's really bothering me. I tried to research it last week, but the recipe is under copyright.

"I think you took the wrong concentration for your size," I say, pulling myself down to sit in one of the audience seats. I can feel the sense of weight returning to my body as I slowly sink farther into the seat. "You're floating, like, two feet higher than everyone during the song."

"I guess you're the expert on recreational potions, huh?" Ed says, waggling his eyebrows.

I snort. "Not like you." I don't mess with brewing potions that are classified as controlled substances. Not unless I have permission to brew them legally at Pilar's.

He nods sagely. "Well, if you're ever in need, I'm your man."

"Oh, I know," I say dryly. "Everyone knows."

"What can I say?" He raises his arms in an exaggerated shrug. "My services are widely talked about."

"I'm not into that. I'm too brown to be messing with that stuff."

"I get that. My mom would kick a fit if she knew. But I've got that white privilege, so it's not as big an issue for me," he says. "I'm just out here doing the Lord's work, scamming white kids into overpaying for potions." He pounds his chest, which sends him flying backward.

"Okay, Ed." I laugh.

"It's easy money. This is how I pay for comics."

"Hey. Tell me when that wears off," Brittany calls from a few aisles over. Her lip curls scornfully. "You obviously didn't take the right amount, so I guess we'll have to wait for you."

"Yes, Your Majesty," Ed says, sweeping into a dramatic bow as he propels himself up into the air. Brittany rolls her eyes and goes back to examining her nails. Ed throws her a withering look. "Dude, she needs to get that stick out of her butt."

"Seriously," I say.

"Your parents getting divorced doesn't give you the right to be an asshole forever. No-ope." He makes the word two syllables. I would make fun of it, but Ed is confident enough in his brand of weird that he somehow pulls it off. I nod instead, filing away this new Brittany fact. "She keeps ragging on you too, which is bullshit. Don't let her get to you."

"I guess I'm, like, threatening her queen-bee status or something," I say.

"Queen-bee status?" Ed lets out a loud bray of laughter. "No, she's just naturally weird and uptight. She barely talks to anyone that isn't Mr. B if she doesn't have to."

Huh. I assumed she was popular. It's true that I've never seen her talking with anybody during any of our breaks. Maybe I just assumed that because she's tall, blond, white, and thin. Basically, she looks like what every teen movie says the popular witch looks like.

"Guess I don't have to worry about her sending minions after me, then." I say that like it's a joke, but I would be lying if I said the possibility hadn't been a legitimate worry of mine.

"Minions? Who do you think she is?" He lands on the floor with a weighty thump. After he bounces up and down a few more times, it becomes clear that the potion has finally worn off. "Damn. I was into that antigravity shit," he says, settling into a disappointed stillness. "Well, I gotta take a leak before Her Majesty starts rehearsal again. Later, skater." He salutes me and jogs away.

A wave of exhaustion passes over me. Coffee. I still need coffee. My parents shared magic with me this morning so I had a little extra for my AP Transfiguration test, but the energy boost isn't lasting enough to erase the fatigue I'm feeling right now.

A few minutes later, Mr. B, who has returned from the smaller music rehearsal he was running in his classroom, calls us all to gather at the front of the auditorium.

"Brittany tells me that you guys have been kicking this choreography's butt," Mr. B says, glancing around the circle of students.

Brittany harrumphs. "I definitely didn't say that."

"Yeah, she thinks we suck," Ed calls from the seat he's slumped into sideways. Mikey guffaws, then covers his face with his hand to hide it.

"Dang, Brittany, lower your standards," Mr. B says, tapping her playfully on the shoulder with the back of his hand. "As for the rest of you, suck less. Sound good?"

Someone boos quietly from the other side of the group, and everyone chuckles, including Mr. B.

"Okay, so in the pursuit of you all sucking less," Mr. B

says, "we're going to take some time to demonstrate parts of the choreography Brittany thinks people are confused about. Ana, can we borrow you for a minute?"

"Sure." Ana hops up onstage, and then she and Mr. B demonstrate several chunks of the partnered choreography from "The Block Party." Meanwhile, Brittany shouts commentary at the rest of the cast.

"See how her leg is straight there?" Brittany says, giving us all an accusatory glare. "*That's* what I want."

While I watch them dance, all I can think is that I would be so uncomfortable if I had to partner up with Mr. B. I guess physical contact is a normal part of theater. People are much more comfortable with touching each other than I am. But dancing with a teacher? That's a no from me. To make this weirder, some of the junior witches in the row behind me keep whispering about how hot Mr. B looks while he's dancing.

"Can you guys hold there?" Brittany says. Mr. B and Ana freeze midway through a dip. "This is the shape we're going for. You see how he's supporting her back?"

"Lucky," one of the witches behind me mutters. A shudder goes through me. God, the way some of them thirst after Mr. B is so creepy.

Once they finish the demonstration, we all get back onstage. The rest of rehearsal is a struggle, since I'm too exhausted to be doing all this physical activity. To make things worse, Mr. B loses track of time and keeps us fifteen minutes late. As per usual. All the jokes about him never ending on time annoy me now, because it's like the jokes make it okay for him to keep doing it.

Once we're finally released for the day, I unlock my phone to a text from Dad saying that he's running late. I glance over at the group. They're all clustered around Mr. B, who sits on the edge of the stage with his legs dangling off into the aisle. I consider sticking around to hang out with the Mr. B fan club, but then Brittany laughs hysterically at something he says, practically doubling over as she cackles, and I remember that I would rather pluck out my own eyes than spend more time with her right now. I shoulder my backpack and head out to wait in the Florida heat

Chapter 14

All T. K. Anderson teachers have magical licenses and magic levels over 60.

—T. K. Anderson website

I TEXT DAD ASKING WHAT HIS ETA IS, BUT I DON'T GET A response. Twenty-five minutes pass, and still nothing from him. When I call, it goes to voicemail.

Then it starts to rain.

I run for cover, evaporating the water from my hair as I go. Once I'm inside the closest building, I call Dad again. My phone, because it's an old piece of shit, dies mid-ring. Now I'm worried. Why didn't he respond? I generate a spark of electricity and send it through my phone's charging port, but the screen just flashes with a message that says CONNECT TO CONSISTENT POWER SOURCE before going dark again.

I need a phone charger, and the only person who I can think of who might still be on campus this late is Mr. B.

I head back to the arts building. Everyone else should be gone by now. Probably. People hang out with him for so long after rehearsal ends that I wonder if Mr. B has a life outside school.

Crossing my fingers, I walk through the auditorium and over to Mr. B's classroom. The light is still on inside, thank god, so I go in.

Mr. B sits at his desk, phone pressed to his ear. "Yes, sir," he says, his shoulders hunching until he's a shadow of his usual self. I stop in my tracks, still in the doorway. "I'll be at the groundbreaking for the new property, and I do appreciate how generous—" He pauses, clearly having been interrupted by the person on the phone. "This is not a hobby, it's my career, so please—" He pauses again. Closing his eyes wearily, he rubs a hand over his brow. Seeing him like this feels like an invasion. It's so far from the confident teacher that everyone knows. "I'm not trying to relive anything, Dad. And calling them my glory days . . ." A bitter laugh escapes his lips. "Well, you're vastly overestimating how cool I was in high school."

Oof. I definitely shouldn't be hearing this. I scuff my sneaker loudly on the floor and lift my hand in greeting.

Mr. B looks my way, startled. A ghost of a frown passes over his face. Then he pulls himself up, flashing me a boyish grin, and he's once again the Mr. B I'm used to seeing.

"Give me a sec," he mouths, holding up a finger. I nod and flee back into the hallway.

After a few minutes, he pulls open the door and beckons for me to come in.

"Sorry about that," he says as I follow him into the room. He settles into the chair behind his desk and rolls it back and forth absently. "Parents, man," he says, shaking his head good-naturedly. "They don't get any easier."

"That's . . . depressing," I say. Thinking about him having parents is weird to me. "Um, my phone died. I was wondering if you had a charger?"

"Yeah, somewhere around here." He starts riffling through his drawers.

The photos sitting on his desk catch my eye. There are seven of them, and each one shows him and one of the Brockton Scholars. I don't see a photo of any of the wizards who have won, but the witches are well represented. Seven beautiful white girls hold framed certificates and smile like they just got everything they've ever dreamed of. Their names are inscribed on plaques at the bottom of the frames. Meredith. Lydia. Heather. Ericka. Wendy. Sarah. And at the center of his desk, Brittany. She beams out at me from the photo, her teeth perfectly white and her hair impeccably curled. I stare at her, wondering what it feels like to not worry about your future.

"Got it," Mr. B says triumphantly, pulling a phone charger out of his bottom drawer. "Can I have your phone?" I hand it over, and he plugs it into the wall behind his chair. "It's getting late. Where's your ride?"

"I don't know. My dad said he was running late, but I haven't heard anything else from him for a while."

"I can give you a ride home if you need one," he offers.

That would be so much time stuck in the car with him, and I would be worried about impressing him the entire time. Hard pass. "Don't worry about it," I say. "My dad will be here soon."

"I thought you said you didn't know where he was?"

Ooh, he really just called me out. I blink and change tactics. "I mean, he'll be worried if I'm not here when he gets here."

"Shay, I'm being selfish, okay? I want you to get home earlier so you can get some sleep tonight and not be exhausted in rehearsal," he says. "Sorry, I'm a jerk, I know. But let me help you." He pauses and grins. "For me."

His eyes crinkle as he smiles, and a few tiny crow's-feet crease at the corners. He seems not that much older than us when he's joking around with students, but sometimes he shifts into adult mode, and I realize that he has to be at least thirty.

"Well . . . I really don't want to bother you," I say hesitantly. "I live kind of far away."

"I don't want a young, pretty girl like you stuck outside so late." He leans forward, propping his elbows up on his desk. "Makes me nervous."

The word *pretty* feels weird coming out of Mr. B's mouth. I mean, he's my teacher—I don't want him to comment on how I look. But his expression is so earnest. It feels like he's a concerned older brother more than anything else.

I wave away my discomfort before I start overthinking this. Still, I don't really know how to respond. "Um." Out of the corner of my eye, I see the light from my phone screen turning on. "Oh, my phone is on. Can I . . . ?"

"Go ahead," he says, scooting his chair out of the way. He gestures for me to come over to the other side of the desk.

I'm hunched over where my phone sits on the floor and am checking for new messages from Dad when the door to the classroom opens. "Hey, are you—"

I turn and see Brittany stop in her tracks. "Oh," she says, narrowing her eyes. "What are you doing here?"

The real question is, what is *she* doing here? It's super late for her to still be hanging around campus.

"Brittany," Mr. B says, giving her a look of weary amusement. "Come on. Be a little nicer."

"Sorry," she says, rolling her eyes. "Hi, Shay." She

immediately turns back to Mr. B. "I thought we were going to go over the rehearsal schedule for next week."

"Yeah," Mr. B says. "Mm-hmm, yeah."

"You forgot," she says, putting her hands on her hips.

He laughs. "I forgot."

"You're killing me here." She saunters over to his desk, pointedly ignoring me. "Did you figure out how much time you're going to need to block the opening for Act Two?"

Blessedly, a phone call from Dad comes through at that moment. I answer immediately. "Hello?" I gesture an apology to Mr. B and retreat toward the door.

"Take the charger," he says, pulling it out of the wall and pushing it toward me.

"Thanks," I say, and hurry out of the room with Brittany glaring after me.

It doesn't take Dad long to break the bad news. Soon after I hang up, Mr. B sticks his head out of his classroom door. "Any updates?" he asks.

"Our car broke down," I say. Dad just got towed to the mechanic, so he won't be able to pick me up anytime soon.

"Is someone coming to get you?" Mr. B asks.

"Um," I say, glancing awkwardly back at my phone. Dad said he was going to figure something out, but there definitely wasn't a plan in place yet.

That seems to be all the answer Mr. B needs. "I'll drive you, then."

"You really don't have to do that," I protest. "I live, like, forty-five minutes away."

He smiles at me kindly. "How about this? We compromise. I'll take you to the SkyRail station instead of all the way home. Do you have a stop near your place?"

The SkyRail is a high-speed bullet train that flies along most of the eastern coast of Florida. It's only useful for going long distances, because the stops are really far apart, but there is a stop close-ish to my apartment. "Yeah," I say, doing a quick mental calculation to make sure I have enough money to pay for a SkyRail ticket.

"Sounds good. I'll pack up and we'll go." As he disappears into his room, I get a quick glimpse of the absolutely murderous glare Brittany is sending my way through the open doorway. Dang, why is this girl holding such a huge grudge about me having a lead role instead of her? She doesn't seem to hate Ana the same way she hates me, so the whole thing is just strange.

"But I thought we were going to—" The door closes on Brittany's words, leaving me to wonder what plans she could possibly have had with Mr. B this late in the evening. They're way too intense about the musical.

So that's how I end up in the passenger seat of Mr. B's shiny black sedan as he flies us toward the local SkyRail station.

"I never got to congratulate you on the magic-level results," Mr. B says. "I'm not exactly surprised now that I know you started potionworking so early, but it's still amazing. Nice job."

"Oh. Um, thanks!" I say.

"How did your classmates take it when you totally blew them out of the water?" He laughs heartily. I can't bring myself to laugh along. He glances at me, then sobers abruptly. "So . . . not good?"

"Well . . ." I look out the window at the tangle of greenery below the road. "Not really, no."

"Makes sense. They're jealous." He sneaks a quick glance over at me, giving me a flash of the sincerity in his blue eyes. "Want to tell me about it?"

God no. I should have just laughed along with his joke and pretended everything was fine. Now I'm going to sound like I'm complaining. "It's not really a big deal."

"If you're upset about it, it's a big deal." A few moments of silence go by. "Come on," he wheedles. "Talk to me."

He's impossible to ignore. I suck my bottom lip into my mouth and chew on it for a second, trying to come up with something to say that doesn't sound whiny. "It's nothing new, honestly. People are just saying I only have a high magic level because I have a big family, or because I have access to a magic-sharing pool." It occurs to me too late that his family is ridiculously rich and probably does have a magic-sharing pool. Whoops. "Not that there's anything wrong with that," I add quickly. "But it feels like people just want to invalidate me all the time. Like, no matter what I manage to achieve, I must have cheated or gotten extra help somehow."

He lets out a thoughtful hum and then goes quiet for a minute. His fingers tap at the steering wheel. "You know, my family never thought I would amount to anything," he says. "I was always the family fuckup growing up."

Um. Okay. That's personal. Where's he going with this?

"But you know, I'm here now," he continues. "I do something I'm really proud of. I started the scholarship at T. K. Anderson, and I run a pretty successful theater program, if I do say so myself. And I think next year is finally the year we're going to be able to expand the scholarship program to some other schools."

My eyes widen. "Oh. Wow, that's amazing."

He waves away my admiration. "Yeah. Anyway, all that's to say, it's not always easy when people don't believe in you. I get it. But all you need is one really big win to show them that they're wrong."

I nod slowly, letting his words sink in. That's what I always thought, so it's nice to hear my own feelings reflected back to me.

"I guess you've got to become a Brockton Scholar," he says in this devastatingly casual tone. He says it like Brockton isn't his last name, like he isn't one of the people who makes that happen.

"I guess I do." I address that to the glove compartment

in front of me because I can't pretend to be relaxed about this and look at him at the same time.

A few minutes pass where Mr. B drives without saying anything. I see two witches on matching brooms zoom above us, hair streaming behind them as they fly. They have those classic Ford brooms, the ones with the old-school brush tails that look like they're straight out of a vintage broom show. The handlebars and shafts are a brilliant gold with crimson accents, and the seats attached to the shafts are leather. If only I had a broom. I could be flying myself home right now and looking cool as hell doing it.

Mr. B's gaze flashes toward them as they go by, and then his face lights up. "I've been thinking about the award ceremony night, trying to figure out what would be the best numbers for us to do," he says. "We usually do two, a group number and a solo."

Oof. I have actively been avoiding thinking about the Brockton Scholarship award ceremony. When I heard that the drama department does a selection from the spring show at the ceremony, my blood curdled. On the most nerve-racking night of my life, I'll have to suffer through the embarrassment of musical theater performance? No fucking thank you.

"I'm considering doing 'Bronxtown Broom Race' for the group number," Mr. B says. "What do you think?"

He wants my opinion? Wow. "That's probably our

most impressive song," I say. "The choreography looks cool."

"Good point. We'll have to make sure we whip that one into shape." He checks over his shoulder and shifts the car into the next lane. "I think we'll do 'My Soft Place to Land' as the other song."

My solo? He wants me to do my solo at the award ceremony? "Okay," I say, pretending that my soul didn't vacate my body when he said that.

It really hits me then that I've done it. He likes me. And if I win the scholarship, some people might say that I only won because I was one of his favorites. My gut twists at the idea, but it's too late to stop now. I can't go back to the time before I auditioned, before he noticed me at that info meeting. The only thing I can do at this point is move forward.

I can see the SkyRail station coming up on our right. It's a massive coral-and-white structure floating hundreds of feet in the air. The SkyRail trains shoot through the sky and dock on the electric rails at the center of the station.

Mr. B pulls off the road and brings the car to a stop on the northbound side of the SkyRail station. "Here we are," he announces in a dorky voice that kind of reminds me of my dad.

I pull my backpack onto my lap from where it rests by my feet. "Thanks for driving me. I really appreciate it."

"All in a day's work," he says. "You ever need anything, don't hesitate to ask, okay?"

"Okay. Bye!" I slip out of the car, tugging my heavy backpack along with me, and hike up the stairs to the platform to buy my ticket.

Mom insists that we sit down and eat a family dinner once Dad and I are both home. Even though I'm sweating bullets thinking about all the homework I have, I don't protest. You don't fight with Mom about family dinner. You will lose and come out worse for the wear.

"How's the car?" Mom says, sliding into her seat at the table. She smiles at Dad, though her hazel eyes still look worried.

"It's seen better days," Dad says. "The flight fail-safes are the fritz again. I flew it off the highway exit, and it just fell straight down onto the road below like a hunk of scrap metal. Bob said he would do his best."

Bob is the mechanic we go to. I think he's basically holding our car together with sheer force of will at this point. The magic in car engines is incredibly complicated and, therefore, incredibly expensive to fix. We can't afford a new car, so Bob keeps repairing the same problems in our engine over and over again.

"Did he give you a quote?" Mom says.

"Yes." Dad leaves it at that and starts eating the catfish Mom fried up. Mom doesn't ask anything more.

"That was nice of Mr. B to give you a ride to the station," she says eventually.

"He really insisted on doing it," I say. "I know you and Dad would have figured out a way to get me, but I guess he thought it would be faster if he just drove me."

"Thank him for me." She looks tired. Exhausted, really. The circles under her eyes have deepened.

"I will," I say.

After dinner, I linger in the kitchen, setting up my potionworking supplies for my AP Potions project. Luckily, Mom leaves the kitchen first, so I leap at my chance to interrogate Dad. "How much is the car going to cost to fix this time?"

He sighs, pulling a box of cookies from the cabinet. "Don't worry about it, Shay. We'll figure it out."

"I have money saved," I blurt out. "If you need it. It's not, like, a lot, but . . ."

"Don't be silly."

"I'm serious."

He smiles at me sadly and reaches out to pat my shoulder. "You put too much pressure on yourself, kiddo." He holds out the box of cookies. "Want one?"

"No thanks."

"More for me, then." He takes the cookies and heads over to the living room.

I don't finish my homework until after two in the morning, which is mostly because I keep losing focus and staring blankly into space. The potion for my AP Potions homework should be a breeze to brew, but I'm just too tired.

I'm starting to think that no amount of coffee is going to get me through my current workload. At this point, I'm jittery all the time, and even though I'm technically awake, my brain is basically asleep. I'm sort of alert on the days I get to share magic with Mom and Dad, but they usually only offer on days when I have important tests in my magic classes.

But oh well. I brought this on myself, and it's all in the name of the scholarship, so there's not much I can do but suck it up and run with my four hours of sleep. Huzzah.

Chapter 15

At magic levels between 25 and 50, you will develop more control over the building blocks of physical magic. It is also possible to begin training in higher-level magic skills, such as transfiguration, molecular magic, and herbology.

—*Your Magical Body: A Health Textbook for the Magical Teen*

Lex, because she's true blue, drives me to school in the morning. Mom and Dad take the bus to the mechanic to deal with the car.

"You look like shit," Lex says when I get in her car. She's wearing the Victoria's Secret sweats she sleeps in, and her hair is in a messy bun. "I love you, but you really do."

"I got rained on yesterday," I say, gesturing to my frizzy ponytail. "Didn't have time to restraighten it this morning."

"No, you look tired. You've got dark circles like nobody's business."

Dang. I forgot to put on Face Awake potion.

"Here." She hands me a small Starbucks cup.

"Aw, you got me coffee," I say, clutching the warm cup.

"No, I got *myself* coffee. Because I woke up at six in the morning for you. Because I'm the best friend ever."

"True. You are the best friend ever."

"You need the coffee more than me, though," she says, turning around to check her blind spot. She reverses out of the parking spot at a breakneck speed.

Even with the coffee, I have a hard time staying awake in my classes. Every time I sit still, my brain force quits, and I nod off violently.

Ana pokes me in the side during AP Transfiguration just as I've fallen asleep again. "You alive there?" she whispers, raising a single eyebrow.

"Yes. Yes, I am very alive," I snap.

"Someone's cranky." She pushes her curls out of her face and continues to take notes.

I tune back in to the lecture. It seems like our teacher, Mrs. Lee, is on another one of her tangents about safety.

"I've been looking at the proposals some of you have submitted for your upcoming project, and I would like to once again remind you that transfiguration at your level is *permanent*. You do not have the skills to return things to their original forms without degrading the molecules."

Mrs. Lee presses her mouth into a very thin line. "I refuse to be the teacher with a death toll because you insisted on de-transfiguring as a beginner and spontaneously created carbon monoxide. I don't care how impressive you think it will look on your college resume."

When I glance at the board, I realize I've missed a good chunk of the material for today. My notes so far have weird scribbles where I fell asleep mid-word, and there are all these gaps in what I've written. I rub my hand across my face tiredly.

Ana slides her notebook across the lab table toward me. "You can copy mine."

I shake my head and push the notebook back.

She pushes it toward me again, locking eyes with me. "Don't worry—even if you copy my notes, I'll still do better than you on the test."

I scoff and yank the notebook from her. No matter how much she annoys me, her notes are excellent. Mrs. Lee's eyes land on me, and I try to look like I'm paying attention.

"And no, you cannot transfigure anything alive for your project," Mrs. Lee says. "Or anything adjacent to being alive. If you are questioning whether it counts as being alive, it's not an option. You won't be trying that kind of thing until your magic level is over seventy. Remember, you signed a waiver to be in this class." Mrs. Lee gives us all an ominous look. "If something goes wrong, I will be fine. You will be dead."

And on that cheery note, I scribble down the missing sections into my notes and return Ana's notebook to her.

"You're welcome," Ana says, smirking at me.

I roll my eyes at her and return to the important task of desperately trying to stay conscious. I do pretty well for a bit, but then I blink for too long and Ana has to poke me awake again.

"We're moving on with our metals unit, since you all have mastered the aluminum-to-silicon transfiguration," Mrs. Lee says. I see that she set up a new demo at the front of the classroom while I was asleep. "This time we're going to be transfiguring copper . . ." She pauses and waves a hand at the reddish-brown block of metal. The metal shrinks slightly and flashes brightly before turning a silvery-white color. "Into nickel."

She turns to write on the ElectroBoard, sparks of electricity leaping from her outstretched finger to the board. The sparks sink into the board, and letters form in their wake. She writes out instructions for the basic steps of the transfiguration: reach for the magic in the metal, picture the end product, and push that mental image into the magical threads.

"Who's going to be able to transfigure this first? You or me?" Ana whispers.

"Is that even a real question?" I say. "Obviously me."

"I doubt it," she says, amusement shimmering in her eyes. "But I'd love to see you try."

In an infuriating turn of events, she does a partial transfiguration first. But by the end of class, I've managed to transfigure more of my lump of copper into nickel. When I point that out, she smirks at me. "I thought we were competing to see who could do it first," she says breezily. "But if you want to change the rules so you can win, go right ahead."

I don't respond. Instead, I scowl at her lump of copper and nickel.

Despite Ana's relentless sarcasm and Brittany's torturous choreography, I drag myself through another week and a half of school and rehearsal. I start the free MAT prep class at the library that Saturday, so I wake up early despite my body's protests. Between MAT prep, work, volunteering, and studying for my precalc test on Monday, I won't have much time to relax this weekend.

Mom drops me off at the library on her way to Publix for groceries. When I get to the activity room where the class is being held, it's empty except for a single person, who sits at the front table with her familiar curls draped over one shoulder.

"You have to be kidding me." Ana turns around in her seat, and my jaw drops like I'm in a Saturday-morning cartoon. It actually hangs open for a second.

She makes long, slow eye contact, then lifts her hand and gives me a single wave. I stand there stupidly. Despite my frantic mental pleas for her to spontaneously disappear, she saunters over to me.

"Are you stalking me?" Ana asks.

"Um, no," I say, still reeling from her existence in this room.

"Very believable. I think you need to work on your acting skills."

"Why are you here?"

"I'm pretty sure you can figure that one out." She flashes me that smug grin I hate so much.

Apparently, it isn't enough that we do almost all of the same extracurriculars and take most of the same classes. Now we have to spend our Saturday mornings together as well.

"Do you live near here too?" Ana asks.

Too? We're multiple cities away from school. "Yeah," I say.

"Cool. I live behind the Publix off 441."

That's literally where Mom just went to grocery shop. How have I spent so much time with Ana over the last two years and never known that she lived less than ten minutes away?

"That's . . . close," I say.

Silence falls. She stares at me expectantly. "This is the part where you say where you live."

"So you can stalk me?"

"I'm pretty sure we established that you're the one stalking me." Her dimple deepens.

I huff and walk around her to put my backpack down at the table farthest from where she's sitting. "I live by Lyons and Southwest Eighteenth Street."

"Cool," she says, following behind me. She leans against the front edge of the table, looking at me over her shoulder. "Are you really going to sit back here?"

"Yeah," I say, studiously unpacking my bag. I place my electrical meter, temperature gauge, and practice cube on the table without meeting her eyes. Maybe she'll get the hint and go away if I ice her out. Of course, that tactic has never worked before.

"Did you see Mr. B's email?"

I tense. Somehow, I doubt this is going to be good news. "No."

"He changed the rehearsal schedule for next week, so we'll be reviewing the big dance numbers again before we start doing scene work."

Oh god, what fresh hell is this? I suppress a groan.

She chuckles. "You don't have to look so horrified."

"Easy for you to say," I mutter.

"Everyone is having a hard time with the choreography, Shay."

"You're not," I shoot back.

She flips around to face me head-on. "I spend, like, four

hours dancing most days. If I couldn't do Brittany's fake salsa choreo, that would be embarrassing."

"Four hours?" I repeat, staring at her incredulously.

She smiles. Not a smirk, a real smile. One that makes her dark eyes crinkle until they're almost closed. It lights up her face in a way I've never seen before. For a moment, the only thing I can think about is how pretty she looks like this, all happy and unaffected. I quickly shut that thought down, of course.

"Well, I'm not dancing that much right now because of the show." She tucks a stray curl behind her ear, still beaming. "I'm a student teacher at my dance studio."

Who is this person, and where has Ana Álvarez gone? She looks . . . genuinely excited. I think I've entered an alternate universe.

"I help teach the little-kid classes, so I get my classes for free," she continues. "That's where I go after rehearsals."

I'm sorry, what? She leaves our rehearsals and goes to dance more? Has she replaced her body with magitech parts?

"That's . . . a lot of dancing," I say.

She glances down at her feet, and her face rearranges itself back into the sardonic expression I'm used to. "Yeah."

We hang in an awkward silence for a few seconds. After it becomes clear that the conversation is finally over, I turn my attention to my magic practice tools. I might as well get a head start on practicing drills so I'll be warmed up for class.

I activate my magic sight, focusing on the magic flows in my practice cube. Okay. Density drill two. Let's start there. I shove the threads of magic together, making sure to preserve their general shape, and the cube shrinks down to half its original size.

"My offer to help you with the *Bronxtown Brooms* choreography still stands," Ana says. She turns and heads back to her seat, smirking at me over her shoulder as she goes. "If I can teach three-year-olds ballet, I can definitely help you with the stuff Brittany is teaching."

"Are you comparing my dancing ability to a toddler's?" I say, frowning at my practice cube.

"You're right—I shouldn't do that. It's insulting to toddlers."

"Yeah, I'm good," I say, tugging on the magic in the cube to bring it back to its original size. "I prefer teachers that don't insult me."

"You might have to stop learning from Brittany, then."

I frown, because unfortunately Ana's right about that. She leans over and riffles through her backpack, apparently finished torturing me with her conversation. I inspect my practice cube, making sure that I haven't accidentally destroyed its structural integrity, then reach for the magic to repeat the drill again.

Chapter 16

Answer all parts of the question that follows.

Explain ONE similarity and ONE difference between magical developments in Europe and the United States in the first half of the eighteenth century.

Explain ONE political or social response to the discovery of magic in Europe in 1788.

—AP World History exam sample question

I PULL AN ALL-NIGHTER ON SUNDAY NIGHT TO STUDY FOR MY precalc test, so my sanity is wearing thin before school even starts on Monday. Peer tutoring turns into a real struggle. The sophomore who shows up wants me to help her outline an AP World History essay, and I can't remember any relevant information about the topic. I also can't stop yawning, which doesn't exactly inspire confidence in me as a tutor.

After school, I get to the auditorium early for rehearsal

and fall asleep in the back corner. Using my backpack as a pillow, I curl up as inconspicuously as possible on the floor. It isn't comfortable—I'm pretty sure my graphing calculator is making a permanent indentation in my cheek—but at this point it doesn't even matter.

Someone shakes me awake before my phone alarm goes off. I open my eyes and stare blearily up at Ed, who squats beside me. "This is sad, dude," he says.

I sit up, rubbing my face sleepily. "Mm. Yeah. Needed sleep."

He glances around, then slips a small vial into my hand. "Here. On the house."

My face screws up in confusion.

"You should take, like . . ." He considers me, scratching his beard scruff. "Half of it, I think."

Oh. It's an energy potion. Obviously. Wake up, Shay. I try to push the vial back into his hands, but he shakes his head.

"I know you're not into it, but keep it just in case," he says, standing. "Also, get some real sleep. It's not even tech week. You can't be exhausted yet."

Oh god, tech week. For the week before we open, we'll be rehearsing the show with all the technical elements every night until eleven. The thought makes me want to cry. "Right," I say vaguely, wondering if I'll make it to opening night. Ed shoves his hands into the pockets of his basketball shorts and walks away, leaving me to consider the illegal substance he's given me.

Even though all the practical parts of my brain say I should throw it out, a small part of me wants to try a little of the potion. I stare at the vial, twisting it back and forth between my fingers so the brown liquid swishes around inside. I've always wondered about energy potions. From an apothecary's perspective, I mean. Besides, this dance rehearsal is going to be a disaster if I keep feeling as tired as I do now. My phone alarm blares, interrupting my train of thought, and I scramble to turn it off.

What am I doing? I can't believe I'm considering this. I'm not one of those rich kids swigging illegal energy potions in the library after partying in Miami all weekend. I can do this on my own. I'll just keep the potion so I can analyze its magic for fun later.

"Okay, people, let's get started," Mr. B calls, striding into the auditorium with Brittany at his side. I shove the potion in my backpack and hurry to join the rest of the cast onstage. "We're going to run through all the choreography we've learned so far and see where we are. I'll be running all the major magical effects from now on, so you guys can get used to that. I know we've been a little ambitious with the choreography for this show—"

"A little?" Ed says dryly. A few people give him snaps for that comment.

"Okay, you goons. We wouldn't have given you this

choreography if we didn't think you could do it," Mr. B says. He looks to Brittany, who nods like an overenthusiastic bobblehead. "So suck it up, and get your butts over to the piano."

Mr. B leads us in a short vocal warm-up, then tells us to go to places for the opening of the show. Thank god this is the first thing we're doing. I'm in less than half of this song.

I stand in the wings as the rehearsal track for the opening, "Neighbors," begins to play. The run-through gets off to a rough start. An air of general bewilderment hangs over the group as they attempt to sing the harmonies while doing the intense, slow-motion choreography. The people in charge of freezing the water gushing out of the fire hydrant props aren't hitting their cues, so Ed keeps getting sprayed in the face. He valiantly keeps singing about how excited he is to move to a new neighborhood but looks like he's about to break down laughing.

Meanwhile, Mr. B is manipulating magic left and right. He transfigures whole live trees into existence, electrifies streetlight props to light up, and starts a fire in the grill prop. I watch, mouth slightly ajar, as a whole massive piece of our set—the house my character lives in—grows from a tiny square to an almost-life-size facade. He basically creates the entire setting of the neighborhood onstage during the song, and he does all of it on cue with the music. It's a ridiculous display of power and control. I knew that our school's musicals had really intense magical effects, but I didn't know that almost all of them were run by Mr. B. I assumed he had people helping him.

We only get through half the song before the track clicks off. I stick my head out of the wings, wondering what happened.

"I think we can all agree that sucked," Mr. B says genially. "Everyone needs to be downstage by the end of the first verse. If you're still upstage, you're going to get hit by the house. Reset for the top."

We start again. And again. And again. Once I finally get to enter, I feel as lost as everyone has looked since we started rehearsing this. All the music on the rehearsal track sounds the same, and not everyone is singing their harmonies. It's all just sonic mush at this point.

Mikey comes to lift me. I realize belatedly that I'm standing too close to the person next to me to execute this fancy lift Brittany has us doing. I jerk my head at him and take a step forward, but he doesn't get the memo. He goes straight for the lift, wrapping his arm around my waist and bending his knees.

"Mikey, no," I whisper, but it's too late. Because I don't jump, he essentially throws me to the floor. I land flat on my face out next to where Ed is singing in the front, and the dance grinds to a halt.

"I'm so sorry!" Mikey yelps, rushing over to me. He reaches out to help me get up, but Ed has already offered his hand. I almost regret taking Ed's help getting up, since Mikey stands there wringing his hands uncertainly. "Sorry!" he says again.

"Shay, are you okay?" Mr. B says, bounding onstage. "Did you hit your head?"

"I'm fine," I say, wiping my hands on my damp shirt. I landed in one of the puddles from the fire hydrants, so now I'm wet as well as bruised.

Mr. B's gaze flashes quickly over the floor, and the puddles evaporate. "You're bleeding," he says, pointing at my knees.

That would explain the pain. It doesn't look bad, though. They're just skinned.

"Take ten, everyone," he says. "Let's get you cleaned up."

I follow Mr. B off the stage and into the dressing room backstage, trying not to visibly limp as we walk. Now that the adrenaline from my fall has worn off, it turns out that my knees hurt more than I initially thought.

He grabs a first aid kit from a side cabinet while I sit in front of one of the mirrors. My hair is a mess. I retie my ponytail and flip the chair around so I don't have to look at my tired reflection. Mr. B hands me an antiseptic wipe and a vial of Minor Wound Healing potion.

"Thanks," I say, taking a look at my knees.

"Are you sure you're okay? You went down pretty hard," he says.

"I'm fine. Seriously." I wince as I clean my right knee

160

with the wipe, which probably doesn't help me make my point. But still, I have a skinned knee. I'm not exactly dying.

"Okay," he says, giving me a skeptical look. "But you can go home if it's too much."

"Thanks. I'm good, though."

"You're a trooper." He pulls a chair over from another mirror station and sits across from me. Now that I get a good look at him, I can see a sheen of sweat on his forehead, and his breathing is ragged. All of that coordinated, high-level magic he's been doing for the last half hour must be taking its toll. "I wanted to ask if everything is okay with you," he says. He pauses briefly but continues off my blank look. "You're looking a little . . ." He flaps his hand vaguely.

"Dead tired?" I supply for him. He nods. I shrug and dab some potion onto my knee. The skin tightens, then itches as the raw skin scabs over. "I'm just stressed with school and stuff."

"You're a special kid, Shay," he says, patting my hand. "There aren't a lot of students at this school like you."

I smile. "Thanks."

"You know, I started the scholarship because I wanted to give people who've been overlooked the attention they deserve," he says thoughtfully.

My heart flutters at the mention of the scholarship.

"Sometimes I wonder if I'm having the kind of impact

I want, because so many of our applicants are just . . ." He waves a hand in the air. "Middle-class kids who've had every opportunity handed to them. But then candidates like you come along. Students who've really struggled, you know. You guys make it all worth it."

"Thank you," I say, ignoring the knot of irritation in my chest. He's not totally wrong. My family makes less money than most people at this school. I'm not sure I would describe myself as having "struggled" in life, but I can suck it up and ignore that.

"I'm lucky to have you and Ana doing the show." He says Ana's name wrong, giving the first *A* in her name a super-nasal sound. I don't correct him. If he can't even say her name right at this point, I've really got her beat as far as making a good impression on him goes. "This show would have been a snowstorm without you."

I blink at him. "What?"

"A snowstorm?" he repeats. "Like . . . very white?"

"Oh," I say, not sure how else to respond.

"Is that not a thing the cool kids are saying nowadays?" He puts on a dorky voice and does the super-cringey hand motions white people think all rappers make.

I laugh, trying to pretend away my discomfort. "No."

"Great," he says, chuckling. "Good to know I'm officially out of touch. Anyway, I'm glad to have you in the show." He puts his hand on my thigh and leans forward to inspect the newly formed scab on my knee. I go completely stiff. When I look at his face, his expression is one of concern. His thumb strokes the top of my kneecap once, twice. Then he pulls his hand away.

With his hand gone, I feel silly for overreacting. He was just looking at my injury. "You're working really hard," he says. "I know you don't have tons of experience with dance—well, you look great during the salsa sections, but that's more natural for you. Don't beat yourself up about the other stuff. Just, you know, do your best and all that jazz."

I've never felt less encouraged by a pep talk in my life. What the hell was that salsa comment? I swear he's seen my mom at fine arts events—how has he not figured out I'm not Latina? I highly doubt he thinks I'm Afro-Latina either.

"Okay, heart-to-heart over," he says, slapping his hands to his knees. He pushes himself to his feet and strides toward the door. "Thanks, Shay."

"Yeah." I nod at him as he leaves even though I have no idea what he's thanking me for.

That was my chance to finally explain to him that I'm not Latina, and I totally missed it. Mr. B gets a four out of ten for racial sensitivity. Good intentions, bad execution. But I don't want to be the one who calls him out on that.

After the last few weeks, I thought Mr. B understood me, at least a little, and was on my side. Now I'm almost positive he just thinks I'm special because I'm some poor, brown charity case. I finally have his attention, but I'm just mad. I guess this is what I have to deal with until this year's Brockton Scholar is chosen. If he wants to think I'm an underprivileged Latina girl who desperately needs his help, that's his problem. I'll ride his assumptions all the way to the scholarship, even though the idea makes me sick to my stomach.

Besides, if I were white, I wouldn't be worried about this at all. Mr. B favors white kids all the time, and they go on to win the scholarship, go to Willington, and have the perfect lives the American Magical Way promises. The game has always been rigged in their favor—why shouldn't it be rigged in mine for once?

I finish cleaning my other knee in a huff and go back onstage. We're still on a break.

Mikey rushes over to me right away. "Hey, I'm so, *so* sorry about that," he says. "I should have checked to see if you were ready."

"It's fine," I say.

"We're supposed to . . . breathe together? And make eye contact? Before we . . . do it?" He punches a fist into his palm awkwardly, looking like he doesn't know what he should be doing with his hands. "Yeah. I'm sorry. I'll do that. Next time."

"Seriously, Mikey, I'm good," I say, already edging away from him. "Don't worry about it, okay?" Before he can continue with the most awkward apology of all time, I leave to go sit in the audience.

Ugh, this sucks. I'm working so hard on this show, but Brittany and Mr. B are both, in their own way, making me feel like I don't belong. This is high school theater, not Broadway. I'm doing fine.

If I weren't so tired, I would be much better at this choreography. I make a lot of mistakes because my tired brain blanks out on me. My eye lands on my backpack.

Maybe I was too harsh about the energy potion before. If I take it, I can show Mr. B that I'm a kick-ass witch who can conquer anything through sheer force of will.

I crouch down beside my backpack and pull out the vial. Remembering Ed's instructions from earlier, I suck down half the potion. Then I shove the vial in the front of my bag just as Mr. B calls us back to the stage.

I jog to join the group onstage, feeling more energetic already. It definitely hasn't kicked in yet, but I still feel pumped.

"So we can avoid any more of you being maimed, we're going to move on to rehearse 'The Block Party' now," Mr. B says. He props his legs up on the audience seat in front of him, which doesn't look like a comfortable sitting position at all. Brittany gives his legs a disparaging look, but he just grins and links his hands behind his head. "All right, from the top. You can mark the singing."

Great, I don't even have to sing full out. I'm going to

crush this. I run offstage to wait for my entrance. The rehearsal track starts, blaring out a tinny horn melody.

When my entrance finally comes, I sail onstage, projecting as much confidence as I can muster. Shimmy. Arm flail. Spin. Step ball change. I know this. I've practiced this dance so much I could do it in my sleep. I grin out at the spot in the audience where Mr. B and Brittany are sitting. This has never gone so well before. I even remember where my spot in the next formation is, *and* I get there on time.

Suddenly, the world blazes with color and light. I flinch, missing my next step, and blink hard. All the magic threads in the room shine in my vision, creating a blinding, kaleidoscopic effect.

What's happening to my magic sight? I'm not purposefully using it. I stumble away from the group, trying to pull my focus off the magic in the room. Nothing happens. My magic flows churn and shake inside me, and I feel like I'm going to throw up. I try again to pull my focus from the magic, but the threads just shine brighter as if to taunt me.

It's the energy potion. I must have taken too much.

"Shay?" Mikey whispers.

Shit. I'm supposed to be moving right now. The music kicks up again, and I run to my spot at the back of the stage. My hands shake, and my heart beats too fast. I focus on what I have to do next in the dance, trying to shut out the blinding magic around me.

Ed does a stage slide past me, and I want to wring his scrawny neck for giving me this horrifying potion. Okay, Shay. Breathe. Dancing requires breathing. I sing a bit of my part quietly and go for my stage slide.

As I do the run-up to the slide, I reach for the magic in the floor. It's right there for me, closer and easier to tap into than it's ever been before. I can feel the brown-green coils of magic rotating around each other so slowly that it's like they're not moving. With the smallest nudge, I flatten a few of the coils and step onto the smooth floor in front of me. My hair whips out behind me as I glide across the runway I've created.

Then everything goes incredibly wrong.

What I thought was the smallest magical adjustment ripples outward, flattening the magical coils in the entire stage floor. Ana is the first to go down. In any other situation, I would derive some sort of pleasure from that, but all I feel is horror.

"'Gabriela, can I have'—*hngk!*" Ed hits the floor mid-lyric. Other people fall around him, crying out in pain and confusion as they slip on the smooth floor.

I hurtle across the stage toward the wings. When I try to stop myself, I trip full force into the black curtain at the side of the stage.

"What the hell?" Brittany shouts from the audience.

How am I going to explain this? I scramble farther offstage on my hands and knees, panic pounding in my chest.

Brown-green magic threads shine under my palms in smooth waves. I'm too afraid to try to fix them. Who knows what would happen?

I glance back at the stage as Mikey unsuccessfully attempts to get up from where he's fallen. I'm totally screwed. What is Mr. B going to think? I can't breathe. Oh my god, I feel like my heart is going to explode. I crawl to the backstage door, slip into the hallway, and run full tilt to the closest bathroom. Then I lock myself in the middle stall and hunch on the toilet, ready to burst into tears.

Chapter 17

OSCAR:

As time goes on, I've developed an unfortunate condition

And believe me, I have tried to beat it back into submission

A situation that is somewhat less than ideal

But now I see you I'm compelled to tell you how I feel

Valeria, I love you

—Lyrics to **"My Unfortunate Condition"** from *Bronxtown Brooms*

THIS IS A TOTAL DISASTER. FORGET THE SCHOLARSHIP; I could probably be expelled for this. I could end up in jail. White kids don't get busted for using illegal potions, but brown kids do all the time. This is definitely one of the top five most foolish things I've ever done.

I close my eyes, because even the magic in the plastic stall dividers is dazzlingly bright. What a terrible side effect. It's like I can't turn off the part of my brain that controls my magic sight. What is Ed messing up in these potions to make the batches so wonky? Ugh, if I was going to be stupid and use an illegal energy potion, I should have at least used one I made myself.

The door to the bathroom makes a quiet whoosh of air, and someone walks into the bathroom.

"Shay?" Ana calls.

There is nobody I want to talk to less right now than Ana. I stay quiet, hoping she'll go away, but her feet stop outside my stall.

"Shay, I know you're in there."

"Did you come to gloat?" I snap.

"Um, no. Are you okay?"

"I'm fine," I say, though my voice quavers and sounds very not fine.

She crouches, peering under the stall door. "That's a lie."

"Oh my god, what if I was peeing in here?"

"You're not peeing; you're hiding," she says sensibly. "Will you open the door, or do I have to crawl in?"

"Go *away*." I press my hands to my face, wishing she would disappear.

"I fixed most of the floor pretty fast, so people didn't really figure out what happened. I'm assuming that was you?" I don't answer, so she continues. "They're all working on redoing the spacing for the stage slides now because Brittany thinks that people's pathways got crossed and messed their magic up."

I relax slightly. Maybe this will be okay.

"I said you were feeling sick, and Ed looked kind of guilty," Ana says. "Did you take one of his stupid energy potions?"

"No," I say vehemently. She lied for me? I don't understand why she went so far out of her way to cover up what I did out there.

"Right," she says, and I can practically hear her raising her eyebrows at me in her voice. "You know those things are dangerous, yeah? He's not a good apothecary."

"Yeah, I know," I snap.

"Okay," she says, and I'm lost for a moment. Where's the classic Ana Álvarez sarcastic remark?

A sharp pain lances through my brain. I hiss audibly, my body tensing against this sudden-onset headache.

"You okay?" Ana asks.

"Why are you being nice to me?" I ask, opening my eyes slightly. The tile floor shines with a multicolored latticework. I keep my gaze trained there, with Ana's scuffed black loafers in the corner of my vision.

"Um, something bad happened to you?" she says, a note of amusement entering her voice. She shifts, and I see a little more of her crossed legs peeking under the stall door.

"No, I'm serious," I say loudly. My heart is still pounding too quickly. I wish it would calm down, because it's making me even more anxious than I already am.

"Okay?"

"Why? We're, like, nemesises," I blurt out.

She snickers. "Nemesises?"

"Nemeses. Whatever."

"Literally what are you talking about?"

"We're enemies! We compete for the same stuff all the time, and you're always making fun of me, and we both want the scholarship, and—and—" I've run out of stuff to say, but now I'm breathing hard and raring to unleash hell. "You're my nemesis, okay? You're mean to me, and I'm mean to you. So why are you being nice to me?"

We sit there in silence. My head throbs. I glance at her foot, wondering what she's thinking. Will she leave me alone now?

A quiet sound comes from the other side of the door. My brow furrows in confusion. And then she bursts into hysterical laughter, cackling so hard that she gasps for breath.

"Why are you laughing at me?" I yelp, so enraged that I stomp my foot like an angry toddler.

"I'm s-such an idiot," she hiccups out through her laughter. "I th-thought we were friends."

"What?" I say incredulously.

She gets her laughter under control and sighs. "Or, like, friendly rivals?"

"How?" I say, my jaw hanging to the floor. "We fight all the time."

"I thought it was banter?"

"Banter? You're mean to me."

"I dunno—l thought it was, like, our thing." A small giggle breaks out of her. "I can't believe you actually hated me all this time."

"Why are you laughing? I'm serious about this."

There's silence from the other side of the stall door. "It just doesn't feel real, Shay," she says finally. "People don't go around professing their undying hatred for me all the time, you know. Maybe I'll be upset about it tomorrow, but for now I'm just going to try to be really nice to you so we can be actual friends."

Just as another sharp pain goes through my head, she peeks under the door, her expression calm and assessing. I wince visibly. Then her eyes narrow with concentration, and the air around my head cools. It almost feels like there's a cold compress against my forehead. "Does that help at all?"

"Yeah," I say grudgingly. The cold feels nice on my head.

"Is your magic still feeling weird?"

My first instinct is to lie to her. But that seems pointless now, because I doubt I'm getting rid of her, and I don't think she'll believe me anyway. "Yeah."

"Okay. Can I drive you home now?"

My face screws up into an expression of distaste. "No."

"Rehearsal doesn't end for another hour, so I doubt

your ride is going to be here anytime soon, and I'm going the same way anyway," she says, and I hate her for being right.

"Just bring me my backpack," I say. "I have a magic stabilizer in there."

"Why do you have . . . ?" She trails off. "Never mind, I don't know why I'm asking that. Of course you just happen to have the potion you need in your backpack."

"I test a lot of potions on myself." It's not a normal thing to carry around, I know, but Mom makes me do it.

"Right," she says, sounding amused. "Do you think that's enough to fix this?"

I frown, considering my response. It will definitely help, but I highly doubt the magic stabilizer will fix this enough for me to be able to show my face in rehearsal again.

She clearly reads the answer in my silence. "Okay. So step one is getting the potion. After that, do you want me to drive you home, or no?"

"I don't know."

"Come on," she says. "Let me make up for my unintentional assholery. You can pick the music in the car."

"Ana—"

"You totally don't have to," she says smoothly. "I just thought you probably didn't want to deal with your parents."

Oh god, she got me there. I don't want to wait an hour

for Dad to come after work, and I definitely can't call him and tell him to pick me up early. He would want to know why.

"Fine," I say unwillingly.

"Great. I'll tell Mr. B I'm taking you home," she says. "Thanks for getting me out of this rehearsal."

Chapter 18

VALERIA:

I would not love you if you dosed me with love potion

I would not love you if you gifted me the ocean

If you saved our store

Or respected my name

I would not love you

I will never feel the same

—Lyrics to "My Unfortunate Condition" from *Bronxtown Brooms*

ANA DRIVES A DILAPIDATED BLUE VAN THAT VIBRATES SOFTLY when she goes above fifty miles per hour. She warns me about that when we first start driving, so I'm expecting it by the time we fly on the highway to leave West Palm Beach. Still, it's jarring when the car starts to shake.

Ana laughs, probably noticing the terror on my face. "Yeah, I wasn't kidding. This thing is a piece of shit. I bought her off my uncle for basically nothing after I got my license."

"At least you have a car," I say grumpily. If I had a car, I wouldn't be in this situation. I could have driven myself home once the potion wore off.

"Are you mad at me for driving you home?" she asks.

Um, what? I rest my elbow on the car door, lean my face into my hand, and stare out the window. I watch the greenery underneath the highway for a while before answering. "I dunno. No," I admit. "I don't know how to act with you now, okay?"

"Okay. I thought I'd ask, since I apparently suck at figuring out how you're feeling."

We lapse into silence. I can't see the magic in faraway objects anymore, thank god, so now the dim glimmers of magic I see in the passing scenery are pretty instead of overwhelming.

"Mr. B was really worried about you being sick. I made up some story about how you hadn't been feeling well for most of the rehearsal, and I thought he was going to ditch everyone to come help you for a second," Ana says, sounding amused.

"Great," I say flatly. More reasons for him to pity me. Love it.

"Do you not like him?" Ana asks. "You're, like, his new favorite. I thought you were all *rah-rah* Mr. B now."

"I don't hate him or anything," I say. That salsa comment he made pops into my head, but I shove the thought away before I can dwell on it too much.

"He loves you, though. He stopped our rehearsal for, like, fifteen minutes because you skinned your knee. When Ed fell doing a stage slide last week, Mr. B tossed him an ice pack and told him to 'suffer for his craft.'" She does a startlingly accurate Mr. B impression on the last bit. It's that tone of voice he always uses when he's making a joke he knows is a little mean but is still going to get a laugh. I snicker, despite myself. I'm not sold on me and Ana being friends. She's not going to win me over with a few good jokes. But still, that comment was funny.

"He's just happy I did the show because he wanted to have a racially accurate cast," I say, barely suppressing an eye roll.

"Racially accurate?" she scoffs. "Please. You're not even Latina."

"He hasn't figured that out," I say dryly. I shouldn't complain about this to her, not when I'm reaping the benefits of his misunderstanding. It's not like I've corrected him. I'm just trying to minimize my offensiveness in this show by not doing an accent. Still, it feels nice to talk about this with someone who gets it.

"The guy is so not woke that he's basically asleep." She puts on her turn signal, which makes an aggressively loud ticking noise, and shifts lanes. "He's acting like he's going to get an award from Don't Hate, Educate for doing this show, but he still doesn't know how to say my name right," she says matter-of-factly. "And he's totally fine with all the terrible accents people are doing in the show. Brittany is rolling her *r*s so hard in her song that she sounds like a lawn mower starting up. Which doesn't even make sense because that character is not supposed to be Latina."

I don't want to give her the satisfaction of laughing, but that really cracks me up. I end up guffawing into my shoulder like a weirdo, trying to stifle the sound.

"You okay over there?" she asks.

"Yup. Yeah. Just . . . you know . . ."

"Laughing at my incredibly brilliant sense of humor?"

"Marveling at your wildly inflated ego?" I shoot back.

"Hey, be nice to me. I'm trying to win you over with my hilarious jokes. Here." She holds one end of an aux cord in front of me. When I don't take it immediately, she waves the cord back and forth until I grab it so she doesn't crash the car. "I promised you could pick the music."

"The stereo works in this thing?" I say, staring at the antiquated sound system skeptically. Like the rest of the car, it seems janky as hell. There's a big knob missing, and it looks like a dog chewed on it at some point.

"Sometimes," she says. "Whenever it cuts out, I just fiddle with the magic and whack it a few times. That usually fixes it."

I plug in my phone and sort through my music. Mostly I have Lex's playlists on here, which are filled with music that would make my headache worse.

"The fact that I don't like him as much as everyone else does is making it really hard to suck up to him," Ana says.

"What?" I say, still sorting through music on my phone.

"Sorry, I'm on Mr. B again."

"Oh. Yeah," I say haltingly. A little part of me is glad she's not successfully sucking up to him. Even if we weren't on the same page about being enemies, she's definitely my rival for the scholarship.

"He tries way too hard. I'm like, why do you care so much if a bunch of teenagers like you? And—dude, what the fuck? Don't cut me off." She says all of this in the same measured tone, so I don't realize that she's talking about another driver for a second. She slaps her turn signal loudly and then shifts into a different lane.

"Whoa, road rage much?" I say, shooting her a look.

She shrugs, a half smirk tugging at one side of her mouth. "That's not helping me win you over, huh?"

"I mean, I was kidding," I say, suddenly feeling self-conscious.

"Yeah, I know," she says, a full grin spreading across her face. She glances at me out of the corner of her eye, but I pretend to be too engrossed in my phone to notice her.

I finally pick some music, and Witch Rebellion plays quietly through the stereo. Ana taps her hand absently to the beat on the steering wheel.

"Nice choice," she says mildly. I can't tell if she's being sarcastic or not.

"I don't have a lot of music on here," I say. Besides Lex's playlists, I have a few things on my phone that I listen to, but they're these relentlessly gay pop songs. Normally, listening to pop divas sing about kissing witches pumps me up, but playing that in Ana's car when we're alone felt weird. Not that I think she's homophobic, but still.

My heart rate spikes, and I jiggle my knee distractedly, wishing the effects of this potion would disappear already. I want to get up and burn off some of this extra energy, but I'm trapped in this car for at least another twenty minutes.

"How're you feeling?" Ana asks.

"Meh."

She purses her lips thoughtfully. "Would food help?"

"Um, I don't know," I say, not wanting to prolong this car ride.

"Oh, there's a McDonald's off the next exit." Her face lights up with a genuine joy I've almost never seen from her.

"McDonald's?" I repeat, confused by the level of rapture she's experiencing right now.

She makes direct eye contact with me for a moment, her expression dead serious. "It's a sign. We can't skip out on McDonald's."

She takes the next exit while I stare at her in bewilderment. "You're really serious about McDonald's," I say.

"Oh yeah. Top three food options." She lifts one hand and counts them off on her fingers. "Pastelitos. McDonald's. Rice and beans." She grins at me, tucking a dark curl behind her right ear. "Are you writing this down? Once I convince you to be friends with me, that info might be useful."

"Shut up," I say, my mouth wrinkling up as I suppress a smile. Was she always funny? I mostly remember her being annoying and sarcastic.

She takes us into the drive-through and orders two cheeseburgers and a large fries for us to share. When I try to take out my wallet, she waves me off. "My treat. It was my idea anyway." She whips a pile of bills out of her wallet and fans them out in front of her face. They're mostly singles, with a few fives thrown in there. "Plus, I'm still rolling in dough from my job this summer." She fans herself with the money for emphasis.

"Were you a stripper?" I say before my brain catches up. Oh no, Shay. That's not a funny joke. Why did you say that? Why why why? "Because . . . all the ones," I add limply.

She snickers, sticking the money back into her wallet. "Waitress."

Great. I'm going to go crawl into a hole and live there forever. She pulls up to the second window and pays for the food while I wallow in acute embarrassment. Glad to know Ana still makes me infinitely stupider with her presence, even when she's being nice to me.

We demolish the food in record time, and I feel better after eating. By the time we pull into the parking lot of my apartment complex, I'm pleasantly energetic instead of jittery, and my headache has mostly gone away.

Ana glances at the clock display on the radio as she puts the car in park. "We got here pretty fast. I'm going to be super early to the studio today."

"You're going to dance tonight?" I ask.

She shrugs and opens the storage compartment between our seats. "Gotta keep in shape for my stripping career," she says, bending over the compartment to dig through it.

I flush. "Oh. Yeah."

Pausing her search, she lifts her head slightly and glances up at me through her dark eyelashes. Her face fills with wry amusement as she stares at me for a few seconds. I look down at my lap. Why does she have this weird habit of staring at people without saying anything?

When I glance back at her, she's digging through the storage box again. "Um, thanks for the ride," I say, pulling my backpack up onto my lap.

She makes a quiet cry of triumph, pulling a hair elastic from the box. "Yeah, of course," she says, gathering her hair up into a bun. "Let me know if you ever need a ride home again after rehearsal."

Yeah, that's not happening. I make a noncommittal noise and get out of the car. "Bye."

"See you tomorrow."

Chapter 19

The concept of a magical license, which would create a uniform standard for magical training, first entered the public consciousness in the 1910s. The idea did not become popular until 1964, when a series of high-profile magical accidents in new magitech factories caused widespread destruction in surrounding areas.

—**United States history textbook, Advanced Placement edition**

WHEN I FACETIME LEX TO DO A DEBRIEF OF MY DAY, SHE'S at the gym doing flame archery. My phone projects a tiny illusion of Lex's face and upper body above the screen as she answers the call. A black metallic bow dangles loosely in her gloved hands.

"Wanna see me shoot?" she says immediately.

"Obviously," I say, rolling up to sit cross-legged on my bed.

She fiddles with her phone, and the illusion of her side

grows more detailed. Red spheres appear, suspended in the air around her head, and I can see the target she's shooting at in the background.

"When did you get back into archery?" I ask.

"Today," she says breezily, bringing the bow up into shooting position. One of the red spheres flies toward her bow. It flattens and stretches midair, turning into a long arrow that nocks itself against the bowstring. With a little grin, she lights the arrow on fire and lets it fly. It hits the target pretty darn close to the center.

"How? *How?*" I gesture wordlessly at my phone. "How are you so good at that?"

She does a little victory shimmy. "I've still got it."

"You're ridiculous. When was the last time you even did archery?"

"Like, two years ago? I dunno." She shrugs. "Did you call for something?"

"Yeah." I rub my temples. My head still hurts a bit. "I have to tell you about my day."

I barely get through an explanation of what happened before she launches into a tirade.

"Oh my god, did you leave your brains at home this morning?" she shouts exasperatedly. "You know those energy potions are bad news. Everyone knows that!"

"Yeah," I mumble, rolling over on my bed to bury my face in my pillow.

"I can't believe you got your panties all in a twist

because Mr. B said something annoying," Lex says. She's waving her bow wildly in the air for emphasis. "I love you, but what the hell, Shay! You're lucky Ana covered for you, or else you would have been totally screwed."

I lift my head from the pillow and prop my chin in my hand. "I still can't believe she did that. Like, why?"

"Probably because she's a nice, normal human being," Lex says. "You act like she's the human equivalent of a dumpster fire."

"Well, she kind of is," I mutter, even though I'm not so sure about that fact anymore.

"You know you hate her totally irrationally, right?"

I glare at her illusion. "It's not *totally* irrational."

"Um, hello, yes it is. Do you remember how you decided you didn't like her?"

I let out an angry huff. "Um, yeah. Because all the seniors in choir freshman year called me Ana Two." I sit up and scooch myself backward to sit cross-legged at the head of my bed. "It was so annoying. They all said we were the same person. And she made that comment about how it made sense that we were both called Ana instead of Shay, because I was just copying her."

"I kind of thought that was funny in context."

Ugh, it still makes me mad to think about it. The choir seniors all liked Ana more than me too. They used to joke around with her about how serious she was all the time.

"So you decided to not like Ana because *other people*

said stuff about you guys, and then she made one comment you didn't like." That's a radically oversimplified version of what happened, but Lex continues on before I can protest. "Are you guys going to be friends now?"

I groan, slumping against the wall. "I don't know. We're still, like, rivals for the scholarship."

"Oh my god, Shay, that's not a good reason to hate her. Give her a chance. Maybe she'll be cool," Lex says. She's gone back to waving her bow for emphasis.

"Why are you on her side? You don't even like her," I say indignantly.

"Lady, I've, like, never even talked to her. I only hated her because you did," Lex says. "Anyway, you should probably have more friends besides me. I won't be around forever."

My heart sinks at her words, but I put on a light, joking tone. "Right. You're so desperate to leave me that you're applying to non-licensing colleges!"

There's silence from her end, and she turns away from her phone. I watch her fiddle with her ponytail, wishing I could see her face. "Yup," she says eventually. "Don't turn into a hermit after I'm gone."

My conversation with Lex is still rolling around in my mind the next day when I get to school. Maybe Lex is right, and I was being totally irrational about Ana. But even so, I'm not sure I want to be friends with her.

When Ana walks into our first class, I brace myself. For what, I'm not sure, but I'm positive this can't go well. I watch her out of the corner of my eye as she saunters across the room, passing her usual seat. She slides into a seat on the opposite side of the room from me, takes out a small lump of gray metal, and starts staring at it intently. After a while I notice that spots on the metal have turned a dull gold.

The whole period goes by, and she doesn't look my way once. She leaves the classroom the second the bell rings. I watch her go, convinced she's ignoring me.

The same thing happens in our next class together. And the next. She doesn't even say anything to me in choir when she's standing right next to me.

By the time school ends, I'm steaming mad. Is this all some plot to make me pay more attention to her? If it is, I hate that it's working. Thankfully, she won't be in my rehearsal today, because Mikey and I are working on a scene with Mr. B. Brittany will be rehearsing one of the dance numbers I'm not in with the rest of the cast.

I wander over to Mr. B's classroom and text Lex, complaining about Ana ignoring me. Lex replies almost immediately.

LEX: boooooooo

        SHAY: I know, it's so annoying

LEX: just ask her if she's mad
at you.

There's a brief pause before her next message comes through.

LEX: anyway, I can't really talk much
right now, sorry. my parents are making
me look at internships for this summer.

        SHAY: okay, good luck with that.
        let me know if you want to vent later.
        love youuuuu

I'm so involved in my phone that I nearly run straight into Brittany as she rushes out of Mr. B's classroom. "Sorry!" I say, flinching back.

Brittany's pale face is flushed and twisted with some emotion I can't identify—misery? Anger? Embarrassment? She barely acknowledges my presence before she passes me and disappears around the corner toward the auditorium.

When I go into the classroom, Mr. B is busily re-arranging the black rehearsal cubes in the center of the room. He grins at me, as if an upset student didn't just run out of his classroom. "Hey, Shay. Are you feeling better?"

"Oh, um, yeah. Is Brittany okay?" I ask, shoving my phone in my pocket.

He looks up at the ceiling, pursing his lips. "She's having a bad day," he says finally. "Parents, and . . ." He waves his hand vaguely and bends down to adjust one of the pieces of tape he's laid out on the floor to approximate the shape of the set.

It seems like that's all he's going to say, so I drop my backpack on the side of the room and open Instagram to kill time until we start rehearsing.

"You know, I think she's a little jealous of you."

I glance up from my phone, confused. "What?"

"It's not that crazy," he says, sitting on one of the rehearsal blocks. He fixes me with an ice-blue stare, his expression serious. "You're smart and beautiful, and you give everything a thousand percent. She's threatened."

Why is he talking about my appearance again? Ugh. It's uncomfortable that he's talking about two of his students like this. He tries so hard to vibe with students that sometimes he crosses the line and says something I don't think a teacher should really be saying. It's clear that he doesn't mean anything inappropriate by this. Still, I hate it. "Thanks," I say reluctantly.

"Winning the scholarship has made her pretty used to being the special one. But she's not the first student I've mentored, and she won't be the last." He lifts his hands lazily while shrugging, as if to say "It is what it is."

Is he implying that he wants to mentor me like he mentors Brittany? Dear god, no. I can't deal with any more of his weird, insensitive comments. Ana was right. *He's so not woke that he's basically asleep.* I get why other people like him—he's charming and funny and obviously cares about his students. But I can't be genuinely close to him, since he can't talk about race without making me want to leap out a window. My goal is to maintain a nice, surface-level relationship with him until the scholarship is awarded.

He stares at the photos on his desk, his expression clouding. "She reminds me a little of Meredith sometimes," he says so quietly that I wonder if it's to me at all.

"Meredith?"

He flips around one of the frames, showing me a picture of him with a grinning redheaded witch. "I mentored her a few years ago. She was a great kid—just got too cool for me after she won the scholarship." He chuckles.

I imagine myself standing where Meredith stands, grinning into the camera with Mr. B. Maybe I can do what she did and deal with Mr. B's "mentorship" until I win the scholarship.

"Sorry that Brittany's been getting on your case in rehearsals," he continues, pushing himself to his feet. "She's a lonely person. Plus, her mom is a real . . ." He mouths the word *bitch*, and my heart just about stops. "And sometimes . . ." He grimaces. "Apple. Tree."

"Yikes," I say, which is mostly an automatic response

to suddenly having Brittany's personal information dropped on me. On the bright side, it also works as a response to what Mr. B said about Brittany's mom.

"She just cares a lot about the show." He stares at me thoughtfully for a few beats. "Shay, you don't have a lot of experience with acting, right?"

"No," I say reluctantly.

He gives me a kind smile. "Well, if it would help you to work with me one-on-one, we can schedule some time to do that."

One-on-one? No, thank you. That would be hideously awkward.

"It would help get you comfortable with this material," he adds.

"I think I just need to memorize the lines. It'll be easier without the script," I say, even though that is a total lie. I will probably continue to suck even without a script. I take a step backward and jerk my thumb toward the door. "Do you want me to go look for Mikey? He's running pretty late."

"Maybe in a few minutes," he says. "I had one other thing I wanted to ask. This isn't your hair, right?" He gestures in the general direction of my head. "I mean, naturally. I don't know the words to talk about women's hair, so bear with me here."

"Um, no," I say, tucking my hair behind my ear self-consciously. "It's naturally curlier."

"Great!" he says, giving a big sigh of relief. "You know Valeria is supposed to have curly hair, right? I was really hoping we wouldn't have to transfigure your hair." He leans toward me conspiratorially, his eyes crinkling with amusement. "That always looks terrible."

"Well, my hair—"

He cuts me off before I can explain that my hair can be difficult to handle and probably won't look the way he's imagining. "Can you have it curly for rehearsal on Thursday?"

I want to refuse, but he just keeps staring me down with those eerily blue eyes, and I realize it will sound silly if I say no. "Sure."

"Great!" he says, flashing me a big grin.

Mikey enters the room, saving me from any more awkward moments with Mr. B. "Hey!" I say brightly.

Mikey blinks at me, perplexed. Which makes sense, because I have never been this excited to see him. He lingers in the doorway and lifts his hand to wave at me. I'm confused about why he's waving when he could just say hello out loud, but I return the wave anyway.

"Now that Mikey has deigned to join us, we can get started," Mr. B says. He plops down on one of the rehearsal cubes, and we finally—*finally*—start running our scene.

Chapter 20

Ultimately, the communes are a result of a disenchanted middle class that faces rising student loan debt, increasing competition for magical licenses, and a widening class divide. The social resistance movement is worrying government officials, who see it as a threat to economic prosperity and American magical supremacy.

—"Why America's Youth Are Escaping to Communes,"
The Washington Post

THE NEXT DAY, ANA IS STILL IGNORING ME. I STARE AT HER across the room in our classes, getting more and more frustrated as the day goes on. She was the one who wanted to be friends. I didn't care about whether or not we talked a few days ago. I barely thought about her. Or, well, I only thought about her in a negative way.

Trying to put Ana out of my mind, I hole up in the greenroom behind the stage to work on the *Bronxtown Brooms* choreography until rehearsal starts. I slowly fumble through the section of "The Block Party" that I still can't get down, twisting under and around my imaginary partner. Practicing alone in this small space isn't super helpful, but it's the best I can do. Kevin is also a terrible partner, so running through things with him isn't much help anyway.

My phone dings as a series of texts comes through from Lex. I plop down on the couch to read them, happy to have an excuse to take a break.

LEX: omg lady look at this insanity
the magimeds left in my room

She's sent a photo of a pamphlet next. The title reads *How Communes Are Killing America, and How to Keep Your Kids Out!*

LEX: have they LOST THEIR MINDS
LEX: none of this is even true! there's this
whole section about how everyone in
communes is malnourished, which doesn't
make sense because they definitely have
some herbologists there
　　　　SHAY: oof, I'm sorry
LEX: I kind of made fun of the pamphlet when
they talked to me about it and they got really
mad. like, they alexandra nicole evans-ed me
　　　　SHAY: damn 😣

LEX: UGH I'm so annoyed. maybe I should run
away to a commune just to spite them
            SHAY: ew don't even joke
LEX: brb googling how much flights to the
nearest commune are
            SHAY: LEX
LEX: but seriously, the people in them are
doing fine. it's just meant to be a statement on
how messed up the whole licensing system is.

She follows this up with a link to a *Washington Post*
article called "Why America's Youth Are Escaping to
Communes."

I frown at the screen. She can't be serious.

            SHAY: you can't just abandon everyone you
            know though. that's so lazy and messed up

It takes a while for her to send her next message.

LEX: w/e. I'm not going to actually move
to one. my parents would disown me
            SHAY: phew 😅

I don't get any more texts from her after that. She's
right, I guess. The communes don't seem so bad. The news
on TV makes them out to look like cults, but when you see

photos, it's just a bunch of people living out some crunchy hippie fantasy. But still, I can't believe she would even joke about running away to one of them.

She doesn't reply when I change the subject and tell her about Ana ignoring me either. Eventually I give up and return to practicing the dance.

Shimmy. Stupid arm move. Hate myself. Spin. As I turn, I catch a glimpse of a person standing in the doorway. I stop mid-spin, almost tripping over myself.

It's Ana. Of course. We stand there, silently staring at each other for a few long seconds.

"Can I get to the sink?" she says, her face studiously blank. She lifts the water bottle she's holding, as if to explain her presence.

"Are you ignoring me or something?" I say as she brushes by me.

She stops and looks at me over her shoulder. "Isn't that what you want?"

I open my mouth and close it again wordlessly, which I'm sure makes me look really intelligent. I don't know what I expected her to say, but that wasn't it. "I thought you wanted to be friends?"

"I did, but I realized that you didn't," she says as she goes to the sink.

"Are you mad at me?" I say incredulously. The only response I get is the sound of water filling her bottle. "You're mad at me."

"I woke up yesterday, and it actually sank in that you hated me. Which, you know, didn't feel great."

Okay, she has a point. But I don't understand how she did such a 180 from the way she acted two days ago. "But you said you wanted to be friends," I say, and the words come out with such a bratty tone that I'm embarrassed for myself.

"I'm not super good at figuring out how I feel right away, okay?" She switches off the water and goes to leave.

This can't be it. We're going from enemies to possible friends to just . . . nothing? A knot of frustration grows in my chest, making it hard for me to think. I grab her elbow as she passes me, then immediately let go and step back.

She turns, a single eyebrow arched questioningly. I flush as she meets my eyes.

"Can you help me with the choreography?" I blurt out. Wait, no, that's not what I should say. I drop my gaze to the floor. "I mean, I'm sorry?"

My words hang in the air, and I wish the earth would swallow me up so I wouldn't have to experience this silence. When I glance at Ana, her face remains as serious as usual. The only cue I have that something is going on behind that blank exterior is that she has one hand hooked around the back of her neck. Her fingers play fitfully with the collar of her shirt.

"You sure?" she says.

"Yeah?" I say questioningly, because that seems like a weird response to an apology.

"Don't think I'm, like, desperate to make us friends," she says, staring fixedly at my feet. "I mean, I wanted to be friends—I thought we were friends—but I don't want to be your pity friend. I came on too strong the other day, and I'm cool to just cut my losses if . . . yeah."

Oh my god, I think she's embarrassed. I'm officially living in an alternate universe. She drags her gaze up from the floor, and I realize when she meets my eyes that I'm staring at her. I snap my head around to stare at the wall in a move that definitely looks calm and collected and not twitchy at all. "I think I was maybe being stupid?" I say. "I don't know . . . um . . . can we just start over?"

"Start over?" she echoes, her face unreadable.

"Yeah, like . . ." I trail off. Ugh, I don't know what I'm doing. The idea that this can't be the end of our relationship keeps rolling around my head. These past two days have been lonely, if I'm being honest. Ana used to be the only person I spoke to much in class, even if most of that was us messing with each other. I feel stupid realizing how essential she was to my day-to-day life. No wonder she thought we were friends.

"I'm sorry I made you feel bad," I say finally. "I guess I'm just kind of dense."

There's another long, terrible silence. Her expression is

so damn unreadable that I want to scream. She keeps fiddling with the back of her collar and staring past me as if I'm not here.

Just when I start grasping for something else to say, she steps toward me and holds up her hands. It takes a moment for me to realize that she means for me to take them. When I grab them uncertainly, she begins to lead me in the moves from "The Block Party." Her hands are cool to the touch, and I'm suddenly aware of how warm and sweaty my own hands are. Nerves flutter in my chest inexplicably.

"You're rushing the turns," she says softly. "It's throwing you off balance."

"Okay," I say, biting my lip in concentration. She leads me through one of the turns again, and it goes slightly better.

"Nice," she says. The air around us heats as she summons little bursts of flames. They float around us, looking like hundreds of flickering candles. When she dips me, the tendrils of fire in my way wink out of existence with a small hiss. When Kevin leads me through this part, I always end up a little singed. But with Ana, it's perfect.

A few more steps, and we're done. The floating fires go out all at once. "How do you know Kevin's parts?" I say, stepping away from her. I wipe my sweaty hands on my shorts.

A small smile appears on her face. "I've watched

Brittany go over it a million times with you guys. I can fake it pretty well by now."

"Oh." Ugh, Brittany. I guess, for once, her singling me out in rehearsal all the time has a benefit.

"Rehearsal is starting soon. We should go," she says, but she doesn't move. She smiles at me tentatively, and her dimple deepens on her cheek. "So you do want to be friends? You're not just using me for my dance experience?"

"Well, the dance experience is a big perk," I say. She makes direct eye contact with me, putting her hand on her waist, and I get the sense that she's going to wait for me to say what she wants to hear. "I mean, yeah. We should, um, try the friends thing."

She laughs. "Wow, you're blowing me away with your excitement here."

"I'm—yeah, okay," I say, because my brain has stopped working right when I need it most. "Woo! Friendship!" I shake my hands in a sad imitation of jazz hands.

"Okay, that was extremely convincing," she says dryly. She turns to leave but pauses briefly. "I'm still kind of mad."

"Um, okay," I say.

"Okay." With that, she leaves the room. I stand there after she's gone, staring at the door blankly. I guess we're friends now?

Chapter 21

T. K. Anderson fosters a diverse, equitable, and inclusive
environment where our students are affirmed and respected
in their learning journeys. We believe that true excellence
can only be achieved by embracing diverse perspectives.

—T. K. Anderson website

LOOKING AT MY HAIR IN THE MIRROR THE NEXT MORNING, I'M
embarrassed by my own reflection. I blow-dried it after
washing but gave up when the front section got all frizzy.
Now my hair is five different textures, and none of them
are cute. I doubt Mr. B is going to like this look I have
going on. My lack of knowledge about curly-hair potions
is killing me right now. When I did some research, I realized that the problem wasn't that the potions I found were

difficult to make—it was that I had no idea which one would work for my hair.

I wrinkle up my face in the mirror, groaning under my breath, and reach for the magic in the lights to flick them off. Think about the scholarship, Shay. You can deal with having bird's-nest hair if that's what Mr. B wants.

When I walk into the kitchen, Mom immediately stops scrambling the eggs she has cooking and stares at me critically. She pulls on the magic in the stove, turning down the heat on the burner, and crosses her arms across her chest. "This is new," she says, using the same tone I imagine she would use to say "Your hair looks like shit."

I clench my teeth, swallowing my immediate annoyance, and sit at the table across from Dad. "Yeah," I say. As if to spite me, a clump of my frizz falls into my eyes. I push it back behind my ear violently.

Dad, who has been busy healing some shriveled patches on a potted sparking shrub, looks up at me. "You look nice," he says, smiling at me kindly. The shrub flashes with electricity between us.

"Yeah, sure," I snap.

"Excuse me, Shayna?" Mom says sharply. She takes a threatening step toward the table, her face darkening into an expression that reminds me that I have not—and will never—age out of being whooped.

I drop my gaze to my lap. "Sorry."

After that auspicious beginning to my day, I tie up my hair. It looks more acceptable in a ponytail. Still, I can't help but sigh with jealousy when Ana walks into our first class, her curls looking as impeccable as always.

"Hey," she says, sliding into the desk next to me. "How's my favorite enemy doing today?"

I roll my eyes. "Oh my god, please never call me that again."

"I like it," she says, and I can tell from the devilish glint in her eye that the nickname isn't going anywhere.

"I don't," I grumble.

"Well, you still owe me for your declaration of hatred," she says matter-of-factly. I hate the phrase *declaration of hatred* even more than *my favorite enemy*, but I check my impulse to argue with her about it. We're friends now, or something like it. Still, I give her my most withering stare because she looks so damn smug. She laughs, then narrows her eyes thoughtfully. "So you're going natural?"

"Yeah, I guess," I say, frowning. I pull on the frizzy ends of my ponytail self-consciously. "Mr. B wants me to wear my hair curly for the show."

"I've never seen your hair curly," she says, reaching down to dig in her backpack.

"I haven't worn my hair curly in, like . . ." I pause, watching her pull out a worksheet from her bag, because I can't remember the last time I wore my hair natural. "Like, five years?"

"Damn," she says, turning her attention to the work-sheet. I glance at the paper, and my brow knits together in confusion.

"Is that the potions homework?" I ask.

She writes an answer down. "Yup."

"That's due next period."

"Yup," she says, not looking up from the paper. "I'm busy and I like sleeping. So here we are."

I can't imagine doing that or being so calm about it. I'm getting secondhand stress just watching Ana right now. I lean over to see how far she's gotten, and one of the answers she's written down sticks out to me. "That's not right," I say, reaching over to point at it. "The magic in the system isn't balanced. You have to write out the full state change before you can do the secondary reaction."

"Oh." She taps her pencil thoughtfully to her lips, then erases the incorrect answer. "Thanks."

"No prob."

The bell rings. Ana slides her math notebook to cover the worksheet and continues working on her homework covertly. "Can you help me with this question really quick after class?" she says quietly. "Since you're a potions genius."

"I'm not a genius," I say, feeling like she's making fun of me. Some people call me that, but I think it's an exaggeration. I just started earlier than most people.

"Don't be modest. I know how good you are. You

always have, like, four potions you're testing out in your backpack."

Oh, that was a real compliment. I'm going to need to adjust to this whole friends thing. "Um, thanks," I say. "Yeah, I'll help you later."

"Cool."

Overall, my first official day of friendship with Ana goes okay. Neither of us bites the other person's head off. We chat more than we did before because I'm not trying to find an excuse to end every conversation we have. It all feels familiar, like we've been friends for much longer. I guess I really was wrong about the whole mortal-enemies thing.

After school we head over to rehearsal together because we're working on a scene and song we're both in. It's just us, Brittany, and two other people in this part of the show, so the auditorium is quiet when we walk in. All I hear is the soft sound of Brittany's voice, though I can't make out what she's saying. She stands on the stage with Mr. B, smiling and gesticulating wildly in his direction. He has this oddly pained expression on his face, which reminds me of the time I walked in on him talking to his dad.

Mr. B's face melts into his usual easy smile when he notices me and Ana. "Shay, your hair!" he calls, hopping off the stage into the aisle. As he approaches me, he lifts his hands in an excited motion, and I tense, thinking that he's going to touch my hair. Thankfully, he doesn't. When he lowers his hands, I feel silly for my tiny mental freak-out.

"Can you take it down?" Mr. B says, his blue eyes shining with excitement.

"Um," I say awkwardly, not certain how to refuse him. Ugh, I shouldn't have put it up in the ponytail. After I put my hair up, it holds the shape of the ponytail. I end up with this weird bump in the back if I take it down. "I don't—"

"You don't know how excited I am that your hair is the real deal," he says over me, not noticing my discomfort. "No transfigured white-girl hair in our *Bronxtown Brooms*!"

Ana glances at me and blinks a few times, her whole face stiffening. Even though her change in expression is barely noticeable, I can tell she's sensing how weird this moment is. I've never been so glad to have her with me. I purse my lips and raise my eyebrows slightly back at her.

"How long is it?" Mr. B asks, still on his own planet.

"Like this long," I say, gesturing to my shoulders. "It doesn't look that good today."

"That's okay," he says cheerfully. He continues to stand there, staring at me expectantly.

Realizing that there's no way I'm getting out of this without making a fuss, I reach up and untangle my hair from around the ponytail holder. Though I can't see it as it comes down, I can tell from the way it feels that it does not look good. The frizzy front part of my hair is fully doing its own thing, separate from the rest of my curls. Embarrassment heats my face as Mr. B's expression turns quizzical.

"Hm. It's a bit . . ." He trails off, stroking his beard scruff thoughtfully. "Can you make it . . . bigger?"

"Bigger?" I repeat.

"Curlier?" he says, waving his hands vaguely around his head. "I don't know. Brittany, you know hair. What am I trying to say?"

Brittany barely spares us a look. "I have no idea," she says, picking at her nails with a troubled expression.

"Okay, well, I'll just keep shoving my foot firmly into my mouth, then," he says, laughing good-naturedly.

"More defined?" Ana offers, giving Mr. B a wooden smile.

He looks at her like he's just noticed she's standing there. "Yes, that! Ana gets me. The rest of you are all useless," he says cheerfully. He still pronounces Ana's name wrong. Ana's mouth twitches, then resolves back into that wooden smile.

"I'll make sure I . . . define it for the show," I mumble.

"Yes, define away!" he says. "Thanks for bearing with me on my hair and makeup notes, guys. I've got strong opinions, and absolutely no idea what words to use to explain them."

"You can say that again," Brittany says. And for once, I agree with her.

Chapter 22

If your magic level reaches the 50 to 75 range, you will
experience a great leap forward in your magical abilities.
At that point, you can learn to cause multiple magical
effects at once. You will also be able to store magical
instructions in objects, which is a key skill if you hope
to work in magitech fields.

—Your Magical Body: A Health Textbook for the Magical Teen

WHEN I WAKE UP ON SATURDAY, MY HAIR LOOKS EVEN WORSE
than it has for the past two days. I pull it into a messy bun
and wait for Mom's inevitable side-eye. She doesn't disap-
point. I can tell she thinks my hair is making me look
unkempt, and there's nothing she dislikes more than me
going outside looking like she didn't teach me proper
grooming.

Surprisingly, she doesn't say anything about the sweats

and hoodie I'm wearing when I show up at the kitchen table. She just offers to share magic with me so I'll have some extra power for MAT tutoring that morning. The magic sharing lessens my exhaustion, but it also lets me sense Mom's current frustration, which puts me on edge. The feeling thankfully lessens as we load into the car to go to MAT tutoring. Once I've fastened my seat belt, she hands me a to-go cup of coffee and rubs me comfortingly on the back. "All set?" she asks.

I nod, taking a sip from the cup. The liquid nearly burns my mouth, so I tug lightly on the magic in the coffee to cool it down. My second sip is the perfect temperature. Thank god for Mom's special coffee.

A text comes through on my phone.

LEX: lol Ana's got jokes

For a second, I'm confused as to what she's talking about, but then I see that last night I was texting her a story about something funny Ana said in choir.

SHAY: you're up early

LEX: wanted to go to the gym before work

She sends me a photo of an archery target. There's a flaming arrow stuck in the ring second from the center.

LEX: do you want to go play terraball after our shift?

I sigh and take another sip of my coffee. I'm exhausted, so that doesn't sound fun to me right now. But I haven't gone to play with her in, like, a month. This is exactly what she was worried about—that I would be too busy to hang out with her now that I'm doing the show. I'll just have to rally between now and then.

SHAY: sure!

"I canceled your volunteer shift tomorrow," Mom says as the car flies bumpily out of our parking lot.

A rush of relief hits me. Maybe I can finish my homework before work tomorrow, and then I can go to cultural-dinner night at Lex's house. Or I could watch an episode of *Potion Wars*. Or I could pretend I'm going to do one of those things, and then go to sleep early instead. The possibilities are endless!

"Wait, why did you cancel?" I ask, because I need to look this gift horse in the mouth. Maybe Mom has some other chore she needs me to do, and I won't have extra free time.

"A bag of potionworking supplies came in the mail for you. I thought you'd want to use them right away."

I gasp with excitement. "My new crystals! Yes yes yes yes!" Mom's face crinkles into a smile as I pump my fists in the air and dance in my seat. Her own happiness filters toward me through our magical connection, adding to the joy I feel. "I found this new bulk discount store online. They sell crystals that have the highest magical content you can get for personal use, and they were on *sale*. Oh my god, I totally forgot I ordered those."

"You forgot?" Mom says, giving me a skeptical look out of the corner of her eye.

"Well, they took a long time to ship," I say, shrugging. And I've been busy with a million other things, so it was the last thing on my mind.

"You haven't been making any potions the past few weeks."

"I do my AP Potions homework," I say. "And I make lots of stuff at Pilar's."

"I meant for fun," Mom says, shaking her head. "You still know what fun is, right? It's when you do something you can't put on your resume."

I snort. "Savage, Mom."

"I have eyes, Shayna." I tense when she says my full first name. A spike of her frustration jars me. "You're pushing yourself too hard," she continues. "If you burn yourself out, you won't be able to finish what you started, and then all that hard work you've put in goes to waste."

"I'm doing fine," I say, my voice unintentionally taking

on a slight whine. It annoys me when she tells me off for working too hard, like she didn't push me to be like this.

"Honey, look at yourself," Mom says, her hands gripping the steering wheel tightly as she makes a turn. The car shakes for a moment, since its magic is overdue for a tune-up. "You're not even *dressed*—"

"How is that related—"

"You shuffle around the apartment like a zombie when you're at home, and I know you sure haven't been sleeping enough. Even though you know I want you in bed by midnight," she continues over me. I open my mouth to deny her accusation, but she lifts a hand to silence me. "Don't try and pretend. I was born at night, but it wasn't last night."

At this point, I just wish that we hadn't shared magic before having this argument. Her frustration mixes with my own until I can't tell where her feelings end and mine begin. "You're making this into a big deal, and it's totally not," I say huffily. "It's not the end of the world if I'm a little tired."

"Have you finished your Brockton Scholarship application yet?" she asks, as if my answer is going to prove her point.

"That's not due for weeks, Mom."

"When are you going to work on it?"

"I'll get it done," I say, coming dangerously close to shouting. I slump in my seat and glare out the window.

Her anger changes flavor from red hot to a dangerous iciness. "Don't you raise your voice at me, Shayna Maree," she says in a warning tone.

"Yes, ma'am." I clench my teeth and push down my own anger. Or at least I think it's my own anger.

"You need to quit working at Pilar's."

"What? No!" I yelp, jerking around to face her. She stares at the road ahead, her face set resolutely. "That's not fair—"

"Until the show is over."

"That's not how jobs work—"

"Oh, you know how jobs work better than me?" She sucks her teeth, shaking her head. "Child, you need to focus on what's going to help you get what you want. You can't be wasting your time with extra activities."

"I'm not wasting my time. I love working there! Just because you don't like it—" I cut myself off real quick and look up to the heavens for patience. What I was about to say sure wasn't going to win me any points with Mom, and I can't lose this argument. "I'm doing good, okay? I'm following the plan we made to get the scholarship. I've done everything I'm supposed to do."

"Shayna, I'm telling you to do less. There's no point to any of this if you burn yourself out completely."

"I won't burn out! I'm supposed to work hard. We made a plan—"

"Forget the plan for one minute," she snaps. "Yes, I

want you to work hard. But I won't let you work yourself to death."

Forget the plan? How can she say that? The American Magical Way wasn't originally made with us in mind—that image of the perfect family with great magical jobs and a floating house in a good neighborhood is a white one. But we made the plan so that I could get there too. I would work myself to death if it meant I could give my parents that picture-perfect life.

Looking at the hard expression on Mom's face, however, I know this is a lost cause. I chew on my lip for a minute, stewing on what to say next. Frustration pulses between us. "I can take off volunteering until the show opens," I grit out. "And I'll ask Pilar to cut one of my shifts."

She doesn't respond right away, which I hope is a good sign. At least she didn't say no immediately. "I've already volunteered at the home for more than two years," I add, hoping to win her over. She loves me volunteering at the home—it was her idea originally. But if I'm going to give up anything, that's the thing I care about the least. "I have so many community service hours already that taking a little time off won't affect my application." I watch her drive in silence while she mulls over my suggestion.

"All right," she says finally. Thank god. "But if this schedule is still too much for you, you'll have to quit working," she adds, because she obviously couldn't just agree with me.

"Fine." I give Mom the silent treatment for the rest of the car ride. As we get closer to the library, I sense a flicker of sadness from her, but I ignore it because I'm too annoyed. She can be such a dictator. I know she wishes that I didn't have to work, that I could be like my classmates who get allowances from their parents, but I actually like my job at Pilar's.

When we arrive at the library, I flee the car as quickly as possible. I'm still steaming mad when I slide into the empty seat beside Ana. The activity room, as usual, is empty except for her when I get there. We're both early to everything. After greeting her hastily, I rip open my backpack and dig out my magic practice tools. The potions bottles in my bag clink against each other.

"Having a bad day?" Ana says, watching me grunt in frustration when I can't find my temperature gauge.

I yank out my practice cube instead and drop it loudly on the table. "How could you tell?"

"Lucky guess."

Finally, I find the temperature gauge. I pull it from my backpack forcefully and drop it in front of me.

Ana props her head on her hand, watching me with an amused expression. "Do you want to complain, or do you want to just keep throwing things around?"

"Ugh," I say, slapping down my electrical meter. "Both." She shifts in her chair, as if settling in for a long story, and stares at me expectantly. "It's just my mom.

She's being super controlling because she thinks I'm, like, doing too much."

Ana raises a single eyebrow skeptically. "You *are* doing too much."

"I mean, sure, whatever," I say, throwing my hands in the air exasperatedly. "But let me do too much in peace! And you can't talk. You do too much too."

"Well, yeah." Ana shrugs. "But there are too many of us for my mom to really notice what I'm doing, so I don't have your problem."

"Too many of you?"

"I have four sisters."

"I'm sorry, what?" I say. I had always imagined her as an only child for some reason. Does she share magic with all her siblings?

"Okay, it's not that crazy," she says, pushing my arm playfully. I can feel the faint heat of her fingers against my skin for a few seconds after she pulls her hand back. "You're acting like I said I have nine siblings."

I laugh, and it sounds too loud in my ears. A sudden wave of self-consciousness hits me, though I can't figure out why the hell I'm feeling that way.

"I don't really tell people at school," Ana adds. "People get really weird about that when you have a higher magic level." She frowns. "When I share magic with my sisters, it's always me giving them power anyway. It makes them really tired if we take from them."

I feel a little awkward, because I immediately wondered if she shared magic with her siblings. Which is a real jerk move, considering that people make all kinds of assumptions about me sharing magic for power too. "I get that. I wouldn't tell people either," I say. "We go to school with a lot of assholes."

"Oh yeah, like that dude who asked you if your family had a magic-sharing pool." She rolls her eyes. "I wish our school didn't have such a strict no-fighting policy. I would have loved to watch you electrocute that guy."

"I wish I was badass enough to do that."

She grins at me. "You are, though."

Now I'm just staring at her silently because she apparently thinks I'm much cooler than I am. "Um, my hair," I say, grasping for a change in topic.

"What?"

"It's killing me," I say, gesturing at my unfortunately frizzy bun.

She gives me a faux-serious look. "Literally?"

"No, not literally." I suck my teeth in annoyance, mostly directed at myself. I thought I had at least two working brain cells, but apparently they've both gone on vacation now that I'm talking to Ana.

"I think it's cool that you're going natural," she says. "Screw white beauty ideals."

"Oh. Um, thanks." I hadn't ever thought of my hair as

being a statement on race or something. It just doesn't look good natural, and Mom likes it better straight.

"I thought I was going to, like, spontaneously combust when Mr. B was talking to you about your hair the other day," she says, rolling her eyes. "So annoying."

"For real."

"Sorry I didn't say anything to him," she says, looking down at the tabletop. She hooks her hand behind her neck, rubbing the neckline of her fitted white T-shirt between her thumb and forefinger. I think I'm getting better at figuring out what's going on behind Ana's composed facial expressions because, even though her face is blank, I would guess that she's feeling embarrassed.

"I mean, I didn't say anything either." I shrug. She shouldn't feel bad about that. In the grand scheme of things, so what if we have to suck it up and ignore a few weird comments from a teacher? That's how life works. "I was glad you were there," I add.

"This is all so messed up," she says flatly. "I can't believe I cut back on dancing at my studio to do this annoying school musical." In one smooth motion, she flips her whole body toward me and tilts her head quizzically to the side. "Do you ever wonder how far you would go to get the scholarship?"

"It's kind of hard not to, especially when I'm watching Brittany suck up to Mr. B all the time." I point to my hair and make a face. "Obviously I'm willing to go pretty far to impress him, though, or else I wouldn't be trying to wrangle this disaster."

"It's not a disaster."

"Um, do you need your eyes checked?"

"You've messed with your texture because you straighten it so much, but you just need to learn how to take care of it." She leans toward me, examining my hair thoughtfully.

"Easy for you to say. Your hair is naturally perfect." I catch a whiff of something sweet as she enters my personal space. Is that scentwork on her clothes? Wait, no, that's coming from her curls. Fuck me, her hair even smells great.

"You think my hair just does this?" she says, pointing at her head. "We live in Florida, Shay. It's humid as hell. I use a lot of potions so I don't look like a Chia Pet."

I feel stupid, because I did think her hair just did that. But if she's able to manipulate her hair to look that good, maybe there's hope for mine.

"I could show you how to take care of your hair. If you want," she says, turning away from me. She bends her head, and a thick section of curls falls over her ear to block her face. Since I can't see her expression, I'm not sure if that was a sincere offer. But I'm so desperate to stop struggling with this unruly mop on my head that I immediately nod.

"Yeah, that would be cool."

She lifts her head, and an expression of surprise crosses her face for a moment before she settles back into her customary seriousness. "Great. Maybe on Friday night? I can't do this week, but I could do the week after."

"I have work."

"That's fine," she says. "I have a dance class after potions club anyway, so later is better."

"Okay." I guess I'm going to hang out with Ana. Voluntarily. Wow.

"Want me to time you?" Ana says, gesturing at my magic practice tools. "We can run electricity-generation drills to warm up for class."

"Sure. We were supposed to do the five-volt drill, right?"

"Yup," she says, pulling her stopwatch from her bag. "I can usually hold the current for two minutes." She gives me a smug look, daring me to take the bait.

"Only two minutes?" I say, turning my attention to my electrical meter.

"Let's see you do better."

I reach for the magic in the air, pulling nearby threads to flow in a slow circle through the meter. "Watch me."

Chapter 23

The Brockton Foundation was established through the generosity of Arthur T. Brockton, one of the founding partners of the luxury magical real estate services company Alliance Financial Group. Our mission is to promote the arts, education, and initiatives that bring magical training opportunities to underserved areas.

—The Brockton Foundation website

THE WEEK GOES BY EXCRUCIATINGLY SLOWLY. EVEN THOUGH my workload is lighter now that I'm not volunteering, every day still feels like I've stuffed three days in by the time I go to sleep. It doesn't help that the deadlines for the Brockton Scholarship application are coming up fast.

The deadline for the first part of the application—the intent-to-apply form—is on Thursday. The form takes almost no work to put together. It's a single piece of paper with your basic information and the names of two T. K.

Anderson teachers who have agreed to nominate you. Even so, my stomach is full of butterflies when I go to the main office before rehearsal on Thursday to turn it in. The secretary barely meets my eye before pointing a manicured finger in the direction of a plastic inbox labeled BROCKTON SCHOLARSHIP INTENT FORMS.

I gingerly take the paper out of a folder in my backpack, making sure to not crinkle the edges, and skim it for any last-minute typos. It's not like I have time to reprint it if I find any mistakes, but I can't stop myself. After that, all that's left is to sign it.

I scrawl my signature at the bottom of my form. With a quick tug on the magic in the ink, my signature shifts to a brilliant gold. And then it's official. Shayna Johnson is a Brockton Scholarship applicant.

I drop my form onto the pile, wondering idly if Ana has already turned in hers. She probably has. She wouldn't leave something this important to the last minute. I bet she also got Ms. Mooney to do one of her recommendations. Ms. Mooney loves both of us, and it makes you look well-rounded if you have an arts or athletics teacher do one of your recommendations. It's a mystery to me who her other recommendation could be from, though.

I guess, now that we're friends, I could ask her. But, for some reason, that feels like I would be crossing a line. I don't want to talk about scholarship stuff with her. We joke about it, sure. During AP Potions today, she told me—with comically fake smugness—that I shouldn't be so nervous about turning in the intent form because "it's obvious who the winner will be this year." I rolled my eyes so hard that it hurt a little. Then I told her she needed to deflate her ego before she stopped being my favorite enemy and started being my least favorite enemy again.

When I get to rehearsal, she doesn't ask where I've been, even though I hightailed it out of our last class together instead of walking to rehearsal with her. She's bent over a notebook in the back of the auditorium. When I look closer at what she's doing, I see that she's doodling in the corner of our math homework. "Thought you were going to be late," she says as I sit next to her.

"I'm never late."

"Ninth-grade choir field trip," Ana says immediately, raising a single finger in the air.

I stare at her in disbelief. She's not wrong. I remember it vividly because our car broke down on the way to school. I was stuck on the side of the highway with my parents for almost an hour. "Okay, creeper, that was two years ago. Why do you even remember that?"

She just laughs and gestures at the homework in her notebook. "Have you finished this yet?"

"No, I've only done the first problem." When I look at her paper, the doodle in the corner catches my eye. "What's that?" I say, pointing at it.

"A flower," she says, dead serious, as if *I'm* the strange one for being confused about what that malformed blob is supposed to be.

I snicker. "No it's not."

"Since when are you an art critic?" she says, rolling her eyes.

My snickering turns into a full-on cackle. "Oh my god, I've discovered the one thing you're bad at! I'm documenting this moment," I say, pulling out my phone to take a picture.

Her thick eyebrows beetle together. "It's obviously a flower." I sense a small magical shift, and a light floral scent wafts off the paper. "See, it even smells like one."

"It doesn't look like one, though," I say, busily snapping photos.

"Okay," she says, laughing. "My favorite enemy is bullying me, so I'm going to leave." She closes the notebook and gets up. Before she goes, she pauses for a moment, then leans over me with her arms crossed. My heart stutters for a second.

This isn't a good moment to notice this, and I wish I could erase the thought once it occurs to me, but Ana is . . . gorgeous. My eyes stick on her lips as they curve into a tiny grin. Of course I always knew she was good-looking. The perfect hair, the adorable dimple, the subtle shine in her brown eyes when she's amused at something I've said—I've seen all those things. But it's one thing to know it factually, and another thing completely to be thinking about it while looking at her distressingly attractive face.

"For the record," she says, and I have to mentally shake myself to pay attention. "I'm bad at plenty of things."

With that, she turns on her heel and leaves. I start breathing again. "Want to tell me what they are?" I call after her.

"Nope!" she says, not turning around. Then she goes onstage to stretch before rehearsal starts.

I pointedly don't watch her, since my brain has betrayed me by forcing this awareness of Ana's hotness on me. Instead, I text Lex a photo of Ana's drawing.

SHAY: I've found Ana's weakness

LEX: lol what is that?

SHAY: exactly!!!!

Rehearsal starts soon after that. Brittany—ugh—is reviewing and cleaning the big dance numbers with us today. We start with "The Block Party." As per usual, I manhandle Kevin through all of our parts together so we don't get off the beat.

"Stop trying to lead, Shay," Brittany calls out during our first run-through.

I keep smiling like I'm supposed to, but it definitely looks less like I'm enjoying myself and more like I'm gritting my teeth in frustration. The moment I relax and let Kevin lead, he throws me out for a turn in the wrong direction. Ana smoothly moves out of our way so she can do her jump without kicking me in the process. She flies up in the air, and I can't help but admire how effortlessly beautiful the leap looks, even though I've seen her do it a million times. When she lands, she spins upstage and scrunches her face up at me for a moment before dancing away.

When we finish the number, Mr. B ambles down the aisle, doing a slow clap. I can tell he's sweating all the way from here. He looks permanently tired these days, since he insists on running the magical effects full-out for almost all of our rehearsals. During this number alone, he shrinks all the set pieces and makes several sections of the stage floor permeable, which creates a trapdoor effect that half the cast disappears into.

"Not too shabby," he says, winking at Brittany. "You're whipping these goons into shape, huh?" Her face splits into a wide smile, and she tucks her hair behind her ear shyly. "Shay, can I grab you for a second?"

Brittany's smile dies as quickly as it appeared. I let out a tiny sigh. "Yeah, sure."

I follow him out of the auditorium. We fall in step next to each other in the hallway, and he heads in the direction of his classroom. "Did you turn in your intent form?"

My heart rate speeds up just hearing him mention the application. "Yeah."

"Good," he says, looking pleased. "I'm sure you didn't have any problems finding people to nominate you."

I shrug modestly, but he's right.

"I would have loved to nominate you, but that would be a 'conflict of interest,'" he says, putting air quotes around the phrase. "But you'd better come to me for your college rec letters. I'm a lean, mean, college-recommendation-writing machine." He makes a fist and glares at me with a face I think is meant to look tough. I laugh politely. "Can't wait to see your full application in a couple weeks. I'm sure it'll be killer." He claps me on the back.

"I hope so," I say.

"How's it going so far?"

"Good," I say. "I'm mostly done with the essays and stuff. I just have to take the MATs this weekend."

We arrive at his classroom, and I'm confused about why we had to go all the way here. "Don't psych yourself out comparing yourself to other people," he says sagely, holding the door open for me.

"I'll try," I say wryly as I enter the classroom. All I've done for two years is compare myself to everyone and try to come out on top. But sure, this last-minute advice is definitely going to rock my world.

"I'm serious," he says, following me in. He leans against the wall next to the doorframe. "Some kids here get everything handed to them. Tutors, dance classes, summer programs, MAT prep, blah blah blah." He waves a hand in the air dismissively. "So if your resume doesn't look just like everyone else's, that's cool. Don't get down on yourself."

It feels a little fake to hear this from a rich white dude who went to a top-five licensing college. The man literally has a scholarship fund named after his family. He teaches at a school where his family's foundation redid the building he teaches in to be fancier. So excuse me if I'm not falling over myself to vibe with him about how "different" I am from everyone else at T. K. Anderson.

I take a deep breath. The scholarship application deadline is only two weeks away, and I can't afford to mess this up when I'm so close.

"Thanks," I say, flashing him what I hope is a passably sincere smile. "What did you need me for? I don't want to miss too much of rehearsal, or else Brittany might, like, murder me." I tense. Wrong thing to say. I meant that as a joke, but it's too close to the truth. "I don't want to hold everyone back," I add awkwardly.

"Yeah, she's being a real tight-ass about this show." He chuckles. I try to laugh with him, but it feels so forced that I quickly give up on it. "I thought you could use a break from her torturing you guys. We can work together on your choreography for 'The Block Party.'"

"Oh." I thought I made it clear already that I didn't want special help last time he asked about this, but I guess I suck too much to ignore.

"I hope I'm a better partner than Kevin," he says, stepping toward me with his hands held up. I hesitate, but there's not a polite way out of this situation, so I steel myself and take his hands. His skin feels uncomfortably warm on mine. "From the section after 'You're dancing with the only hot girl here,'" he says, quoting some of the lyrics. I nod, and he counts us off.

I hate every second of us dancing. We're too close. I can smell the light scent of cedar wafting off his clothes. I'm torn between the urge to rip my body away from him and the need to be mature about this. Sometimes, I wish I wasn't so bothered by people being in my personal space.

"You're too tense," he says after we finish running through the section. Even though we're done dancing, he doesn't release me from his grasp. "Loosen up!" He shakes my right wrist so my hand flops around limply.

"Sorry," I say quietly, pulling away from him. I think back to all the times I've seen him dance with Brittany or Ana to demonstrate some piece of choreography. They don't get all weird and uncomfortable. Other witches in the cast have even asked him to help them with choreography. I just need to suck it up.

We run through the section again. He's definitely a better partner than Kevin. He's not as good as Ana, though. Plus, dancing with Ana doesn't make me as horribly uncomfortable, which is an added bonus. I resolve to ask her to help me again so I can avoid this situation ever being repeated.

After several attempts at the choreography, he claps me on the shoulder and nods approvingly. "Better," he says. "Better."

"Thanks," I say, relief flooding through me.

"Anytime. I'm always here to help."

"I should go back to rehearsal before Brittany puts out a hit on me," I say, backing slowly toward the door.

He laughs heartily and waves me off.

When I return to rehearsal, Brittany ignores me, which is honestly the best outcome I could have hoped for. Ana looks at me inquisitively as I move into my place in the number we're rehearsing. But I say nothing.

Chapter 24

Ken Gardener, CEO of the multimillion-dollar magitech corporation PlexMatics, Inc., has been dogged by rumors of abusive workplace dynamics for over twenty years. A recent open letter, signed by six witches who are current or former employees of PlexMatics, Inc., claims that Gardener coerced each of them into sharing magic with him in exchange for promotions or other workplace advancements.

"It made him feel stronger than us," said Rashida Page, one of the witches who signed their names to the searing open letter. "And he liked that."

—**"Ken Gardener's Accusers Tell Their Stories,"**
  The Wizard's Daily Newspaper

ON THE FRIDAY OF THE FOLLOWING WEEK, PILAR PUTS ME ON prep work for the weekend orders in the back while Lex works the counter. Mrs. Morris shows up soon after we arrive, so I set myself up with crystals and an extra-large cauldron as far from the pass-through window as possible. Even at a distance, I can still hear Mrs. Morris's quavery voice drifting through the pass. I can't make out exactly what she's saying, but I'm pretty sure she's arguing with

Lex about collecting a special-order potion that she didn't put in a request for.

After placing my crystals in a circle around the cauldron, I tug on their magic threads and tie them together. Once the latticework is secure, I draw it into the cauldron and fold it into the water inside. Giving the extra strands some time to naturally spread, I head over to the back shelves. Pilar slides past me, grabbing supplies of her own. The soft fabric of her green-and-yellow dress brushes my ankles as she goes by.

"You look more rested, Shay," she says, giving me a once-over.

"Yeah," I say, carefully working a glass bottle of powder out from behind a Tupperware of premixed herbs. "Sorry I had to ask for another day off. I promise I'll come back to my normal schedule as soon as the show is over."

"Don't you worry about that," she says. "Lex and I can manage."

Lex's head appears in the pass-through window as I carry the bottle of blue vervain powder back to my in-progress potion. "Pilar, Mrs. Morris needs your help."

Pilar passes me in a blur of green and yellow, breezing out front to deal with the problem. Moments later, Lex leans against the table next to me as I sift powder into the cauldron.

"Bad luck getting stuck with Mrs. Morris today," I say.

"Seriously." She groans theatrically and sticks out her tongue in Mrs. Morris's direction. I laugh quietly, giving my sieve a particularly hard whack that sends the last flurry of powder falling into the cauldron. "So," Lex says, a playful smile spreading across her face. "Are you excited for your hot date tonight?"

"Hot date?" I repeat. Has Lex lost her mind? All I'm doing tonight is going over to Ana's house so she can help me with my hair.

"With Ana?"

"What?" I say, putting the empty sieve down on the table.

Lex huffs. "Oh my god, lady, why are we still pretending you don't like her?"

My heart just about stops. "I don't—what—why do you—" I sputter, my cheeks flaming. Has Lex been huffing potion vapor or something?

"You're obsessed with her," Lex says, answering the question I never managed to ask. "You talk about her all the time. I mean, you used to complain about her all the time, but now you just straight-up talk about her."

"I do not!"

"Really?" Lex says, her dark eyebrows shooting upward. She whips her phone out of her jeans pocket dramatically and clears her throat. "'Wish my hair was as perfect as Ana's,'" she reads. "'Thank god Ana helped me with this choreo.'" She scrolls down and continues reading my texts aloud. I shrink further into myself with every word she reads. "'Ana called Ms. Mooney the human equivalent of a meerkat and I'm literally peeing myself laughing.'" A snort escapes her. "And then you just kept sending me photos of bad drawings she's done . . ." She pauses and glances up at me, her finger still pressed to the screen. "Do I need to keep going? Trust me, I can."

"No," I mumble.

"I stalked her online to find out if she's gay," Lex says, her lips curling into a catlike smile. "I mean, if you're totally sure that you're not interested in her at all, I won't tell you what I found . . ."

I purse my lips in annoyance. I *don't* like Ana. We were enemies up until two weeks ago. Sure, we get along, and I guess I talk about her a lot. But I would know if I liked her. Still, I am curious. "Tell me what you found," I say reluctantly.

Lex immediately looks so smug that I want to take back my words. "Well, there wasn't anything obvious on her WizConnect or Insta," Lex says. "She mostly retweets dance stuff on Twitter, but I did find her retweeting some stuff about Miranda Martinez."

"Who?"

"Iconic Latina actress," Lex says. "She's bi."

"Okay," I say slowly. That seems like a weak link to hang an argument that Ana's gay on, but it's not nothing.

"But wait!" Lex says, throwing her hands in the air. "Then I found her Finsta."

"Oh, you went deep," I say admiringly.

She flips her ponytail over her shoulder and preens. "Thanks." She leans toward me, lowering her voice for dramatic effect. "Her bio has pink, purple, and blue hearts in it. Like, all in a row."

"Okay?" I say, not picking up what she's putting down.

"Like the bi flag!" Lex slams her hands against the prep table.

"Oh," I say, a little thrill running through me. I don't like her, but it would be nice to have a queer friend. Right now, I'm sorely lacking in that department. I squelch my excitement quickly. "That's not, like, proof, though."

"I know," Lex says sympathetically. "But it's something. I'll keep looking. In the meantime, you should make a move tonight."

"I'm not—I don't—"

Pilar sails into the room, retying her purple apron behind her back. "The coast is clear, mija."

"Thanks," Lex says. She blows me a kiss and bounces away, leaving me behind in the prep room to fuss over our conversation.

Lex is clearly wrong. There's no way I like Ana like that. I'm just intense about my friendships. Right?

Right.

Lex's words stick uncomfortably in my brain while I work on my part of the potion prep for the weekend. I still haven't managed to shake my growing self-consciousness by the time I hop into Ana's car after work.

Ana and I drive mostly in silence for a while. I stare out the window at the passing cars, composing myself. I don't know why Lex's comments are bothering me so much. I don't like Ana. Even if I did, the chances that she likes girls are slim. The chances that she likes girls and specifically likes me are even slimmer.

"How's my favorite enemy doing?" Ana says. I startle, even though her voice wasn't loud. "Wow, you were deep in thought," she says. "Sorry to interrupt."

"I'm just tired from work," I say, realizing that it's probably rude for me to ignore her the entire time we hang out. Get it together, Shay. "Zonked out there for a sec."

"Did you brew anything cool today?"

I sit up straighter in my seat. "Yes! I got to do this new potion today that helps with breastfeeding, and I got to manipulate the magic into all these cool star patterns that were really hard to get right." I give her a full description of how the potion is brewed, complete with enthusiastic hand gestures. By the time I finish the story, I realize that I haven't let her get a word in for at least five minutes.

"You're such a potions nerd," she says, giving me a small smile.

"So are you," I say. She does almost as much potion-working as I do at school.

She makes a noncommittal noise. "I just want to make money when I get older, and if I study potionworking in college, I could work in a magilab or go to medical school."

"Oh." I always thought she was pretty into potions. "Would you do something else? If you didn't have to make money?"

Her face goes blank. She stops the car at a red light, and the silence stretches so long that I wonder if she's going to answer. "Teach dance," she says finally. "Probably."

"You'd be good at that."

"Thanks." She taps her fingers against the steering wheel, staring at the road ahead. I sneak a glance at her every few seconds, wondering what's going on in her head. She doesn't say anything else until the light turns green. "Thanks for not telling me that I should, like, pursue my dreams," she says as she pulls the car into the intersection.

"Oh, um, no problem?" Surreptitiously, I check her expression to see if she's kidding, but she seems completely serious. "I'm lucky because my dream job happens to be something that makes money."

"I mean, I like making potions," Ana says, shrugging.

"But when I see you do it, I realize I don't love it like that. You have this face you make when you talk about potion-working, or when you're brewing something you think is cool. It's like your whole face lights up."

Heat rises in my cheeks. God, she's right. I am such a nerd about potions. "You get that too," I say, looking down at my hands. "When you talk about dancing." The second those words leave my mouth, a wave of self-consciousness washes over me. I just admitted to watching her—well, not watching her, but *noticing* her. I mean, I was just following up on what she said, but still. "And McDonald's," I add, trying to lighten the mood. "You get that face when you talk about McDonald's too."

"Yeah, McDonald's and dancing are my true passions in life." She laughs. "That's the one good thing about *Bronxtown Brooms*. There's plenty of dancing. Not as much McDonald's as I would like, though." I giggle, and she looks pleased. "Honestly, I would've told Mr. B no when he asked me to do the show if it didn't have so many good dance numbers."

"Oh yeah," I say, sobering. "I forgot he forced you to do it too."

"I wouldn't say forced," she says.

Oh shoot. I didn't mean forced. That's Lex's word, not mine.

"He just asked me if I might be interested, and I said I

would do it," she continues. "Wanted to get those brownie points with him before submitting my application, you know?"

"Oh," I say, turning to look out the window so she can't see my face. I guess I was the only person he pushed with the scholarship, then. Good to know.

Chapter 25

Hey Witches! So today I'm going to be sharing my recipe for re-creating one of the most popular potions for Type 3 curls— Coil Care from Madam C. J. Walker Beauty. This recipe does require some pretty subtle manipulation of magical lattices, so be careful when you're brewing.

If you're not comfortable with higher-level potion work, do not try this on your hair. Trust me! Enough of us have accidentally turned our hair to dust with a home-brewed potion. No more hair casualties!

Potion Commotion **blog post**

ANA LIVES IN A SQUAT STUCCO HOUSE PAINTED IN A FADED version of the coral that's so popular in Florida. A pair of scraggly palm trees planted in mulch lines the walkway leading off the driveway to the door. The rest of the lawn is made up of patches of grass and weeds that are in various stages of dying. Dad would have a field day if he ever got the chance to mess with their lawn. Saving neglected plants is his favorite thing.

"Brace yourself," Ana says as we walk up the sidewalk

to her house. Brace myself? What? She opens the door before I can ask what she means.

The first thing I notice when we walk into Ana's home is that there are people everywhere. I count four people who are visible from the front door, and they're all packed into a fairly compact space. The living room and kitchen connect to form one front room, with a half wall in between that has a long table shoved up against it. A middle-aged woman with short dark hair and a distracted expression sits at the table, watching the news in Spanish on a tiny silver TV. I catch a quick mention of Ken Gardener, that wizard who's been on the news a lot recently for making witches at his company share magic with him.

In the living room, two girls who look like ten-year-old versions of Ana—complete with wild curls and the same thick eyebrows—are playing a raucous game of Magic Marbles. They shriek with delight and anger in turn as they freeze and melt the patches of water in the game board, each trying to bounce the marble into the other's goal. Next to them, a man with dark, shiny hair snores loudly on an overstuffed couch.

"That's my dad," Ana says, nodding at the couch. She slips off her loafers into the pile of shoes by the door. I follow suit. "He can sleep through basically anything. He works nights, so he kind of has to. And those are my sisters Isabel and Xiomara."

Isabel and Xiomara scream, as if to prove her point.

One of them jumps up and does a wild victory dance. "¡Tramposa!" the other girl yells repeatedly.

"Ana!" The woman watching TV at the table turns toward us, finally noticing our arrival. "¿Quién es ella?"

"Mi amiga Shay," Ana says, walking over to the table. "Shay, this is my mom."

"Nice to meet you," Mrs. Álvarez says, smiling widely. She has a melodic accent and enunciates each word carefully when she speaks. "Are you hungry?"

"Yes, ma'am." I am sort of hungry, and I get the sense from her tone that, like my mom, this family won't take no for an answer.

"Mami," Mrs. Álvarez calls, leaning out of her seat toward the edge of the wall dividing the living room and kitchen. "Por favor prepara—"

Before she can get the words out, a tiny old lady with spiky silver hair hurries out of the kitchen carrying a bowl of rice and beans. She laughs and speaks effusively in Spanish. Ana and Mrs. Álvarez laugh loudly. I smile politely and take the bowl when the old lady offers it to me.

"Lo siento, no hablo español." This is, unfortunately, the only Spanish phrase I can say.

The woman, who I'm assuming is Ana's grandma, gives me a thumbs-up. "No problem!"

"My grandma doesn't really speak English," Ana says. "You're missing out, though. She's really funny."

Ana's grandma pulls out a chair for me. I smile at her

and sit down, wishing I hadn't taken French as my language requirement. Ana sits beside me, her face set in a serious expression that contrasts with her mom's and grandma's easy smiles. So far, Ana's family couldn't be less like her in terms of mannerisms.

"Hija," Mrs. Álvarez says, reaching over to stroke Ana's shoulder. "Hazme un favor. Llama al plomero, por favor."

"Le llamo mañana," Ana says quietly. She says something else, but I can't hear it because Xiomara and Isabel have started a new game of Magic Marbles and are approaching banshee level with their shrieking.

Once I finish eating, Ana leads me into the hallway behind the living room. I follow her into a small room with vibrant pink walls. The room is split down the middle into two different decorating schemes. On one side, the colors are plain and sensible—black, white, and navy—and there's a massive poster of a Black ballerina hanging on the wall beside the bed. I know this has to be Ana's side of the room even before she drops her bags at the foot of the bed.

The other half of the room is all pinks and purples. Piles of faded stuffed animals are everywhere, and a poster of Einstein dominates the wall, surrounded by printed pictures of constellations and rocket launches. On the floor, almost hidden in a pile of pink and purple pillows, a little girl is reading. She scrunches her brow as she flips a page, her face a tiny mirror of Ana's.

"That's my sister Caro," Ana says. Caro's dark eyes dart toward me briefly before settling back on her book. "She's shy," Ana mouths.

I nod. "So your grandma lives here too?"

"Yeah," Ana says, amusement flickering briefly over her face. "She moved in temporarily to help when Caro was born. That was seven years ago."

So counting Ana, her four sisters, her parents, and her grandma, there are eight people living in this house. But I only saw four doors on this hallway, and one of them was the bathroom. "I better learn some Spanish so I can talk to your grandma," I say, dropping my backpack by the door. "Don't want to miss out on what she's saying if she's so hilarious."

Ana's lips curl into her most genuine smile, the one that makes her eyes scrunch up until they're just lines of long, dark eyelashes. "Yeah, you'd better," she says. "She'll really like you. Just don't bring up any of those 'Jesus was just a wizard' conspiracy theories, okay?"

I snort. "Literally why would I do that?"

"I don't know," she says. "I'm just saying that it's a surefire way to alienate most of my family."

"Okay, I'll make sure not to do that, then." I don't really know much about religion, so it wouldn't have occurred to me to say anything about it to Ana's family. My grandparents on my mom's side were Pentecostal, I think, because a lot of Black magic users in the South are.

But I never met them before they died, and neither of my parents is religious now.

"Um, so how are you going to fix this disaster?" I ask, pointing at my head.

"Well, I have a hair potion that's good at getting rid of frizz," she says. "Which should probably help. What product are you using in your hair right now?"

"Um, gel. And Suave?" I say. "It's, like, their two-in-one shampoo and conditioner?"

She presses her palm to her face and groans softly. "Hearing you say that caused me actual physical pain," she says, her voice muffled by her hand. "Okay, let's go wash the gel out of your hair so it doesn't look so crunchy, and then we'll go from there."

Clearly, I've been doing everything wrong when it comes to my hair. I follow her into the bathroom, which is strangely tidy considering that eight people share it. The countertop around the sink is clear, and all the surfaces are squeaky clean. Ana opens a small closet and retrieves a towel, which she shakes out and lays carefully around my shoulders.

"I'll give you salon service," she says, grinning at me mischievously. "Fancy, huh?"

Once I'm kneeling by the bathtub with my head stuck underneath the running water, I have to laugh. "Oh yeah, this is *just* like a salon. One hundred percent." Water dribbles down my forehead and into my mouth. I sputter, glad that Ana can't see me spitting out water from where she sits on the edge of the tub.

"Shut up," she says playfully. I sense her doing something above me a moment before I'm hit with an icy blast of water from the tap. I jerk back, narrowly avoiding whacking my head on the wall in the process, and Ana laughs shamelessly.

"Hey!" I yelp, glaring at her through a curtain of my dripping hair. I splash my hand under the faucet, flicking water toward her. Ana raises an eyebrow at me, wholly unrepentant, and calmly wipes the droplets off her face.

"Serves you right."

"This salon has terrible service."

She continues washing my hair, her fingertips running along my scalp as she detangles my knotted curls, and a little shiver goes up my spine. This is nice. Soothing. She gives my head one last scrub, then pulls her hands out of my hair. "Okay, that's done. We can put the hair potion in now."

Ana hands me the plastic tub of hair potion. I sniff it before starting to coat my hair with it. The potion smells a little like the shea butter lotion Mom uses, mixed with something else I can't identify that reminds me of Pilar's shop. My curls immediately look more defined, and a haze appears around my head as the water starts to evaporate from my hair faster. I resolve to start brewing curly-hair potions this week.

Ana takes her hair down from its tight bun, sticks her head under the tap, and gives her scalp a quick scrub. "I can't believe you hated me, like, a month ago," Ana says, squeezing the water out of her hair. She holds out a hand, and I pass her the tub of hair potion. After turning off the water, she stands and finger-combs the conditioner into her own hair. "All I could think when you told me you hated me was, wow, that's some *Bronxtown Brooms* level shit right there."

"Yeah, if *Bronxtown Brooms* was about two witches who were . . ." I fumble for how to continue. "Academic rivals turned . . ." I pause again. "Friends?"

She chuckles. "I was wondering where that was going."

There's a moment of silence where I mentally yell at myself for the weirdness that just came out of my mouth.

Ana tilts her head to the side, considering me. "You have something—here." She wipes her hand off on one of the towels, then swipes a finger across my cheek. My heart relocates to somewhere in my throat. She pulls her hand back and shows me a glob of hair potion.

"Um, thanks," I say, and my voice sounds too high in my ears. "Sorry, wow, I'm a mess."

Okay, if this had happened before Lex said all that stuff about Ana possibly being into girls, I wouldn't have thought anything of it. But now my brain is short-circuiting, and all I can think about is how I can still feel the brush of her finger on my cheek.

"Anaaaaaaaaaa!" a voice yells from somewhere else in the house.

I jump, startled. Ana turns toward the door, wearing an expression of weary resolve. Pounding feet run by the bathroom. Ana's name rings through the house again, whinier this time.

"Are you going to—" I start to say.

"Don't worry, she'll find us," Ana says, coming to lean against the countertop next to me. A few quiet seconds tick by, and then the sound of pounding feet returns.

A gangly tween bursts into the bathroom, her round face screwed up into a theatrical pout. "Ana, I need help with my math homework, and Xio and Isabel are fighting over—" She stops in her tracks and blinks uncomprehendingly at me, which looks super dramatic because she's wearing a full face of makeup. I've literally never seen a twelve-year-old with her face this well beat. I was rocking an unfortunate raccoon eyeliner situation until, like, two years ago. "Who are *you*?" she says, arching an eyebrow at me.

"This is my friend Shay," Ana says. "Shay, this is my incredibly rude sister Liliana."

"¿Tu amiga? ¿En serio?" Liliana gasps comically, holding a perfectly manicured hand to her chest. "Not like a study partner? Or like you're working on a project together?"

"Lili, I have friends," Ana says dryly.

"Ha. Qué funny."

Ana stares at her silently until Liliana holds up her hands in surrender. "I'm going, I'm going," she says, heading out of the room. She sticks her head back in the door immediately. "Math homework?"

"Tomorrow," Ana says firmly. Liliana nods, her loose bun bobbling at the crown of her head, and disappears. "Sorry, she has the drama of five people contained in one body," Ana says.

Ana's sisters keep appearing in the bathroom with various questions and problems for Ana to solve. Xiomara and Isabel burst in next, arguing furiously in an incomprehensible mix of Spanish and English about their Magic Marbles game. Or at least, I'm pretty sure it's about their Magic Marbles game, because they mention that several times as they yell over each other. Ana watches them calmly, then silences them with a few short sentences in Spanish.

Liliana reappears several times—once with a frantic question about where her new nail kit is, once with a meandering complaint about something Mrs. Álvarez said, and once to brandish a YouTube video of a makeup artist at us. Even Caro appears eventually. She slips into the bathroom and mumbles something to Ana before leaving quietly.

Every time one of her sisters appears, Ana's incredible calmness makes more sense by contrast. She's the rock her sisters swirl around. No matter how much they yell and argue and shove things at her to look at, she waits them out with that even stare and then helps them.

"You're really patient with your sisters," I say after Caro leaves the bathroom.

Ana shrugs. "They're little monsters, but I love them. Sorry they keep bothering us."

"It's fine," I reassure her. She doesn't look convinced, so I nudge her playfully on the arm with my elbow. I immediately feel horribly self-conscious but soldier on. "Seriously, it's fine."

"I wish we had a bigger house," she says. "They get a little restless sometimes. You can't get away from anyone here."

"Yeah, I feel like that in our apartment sometimes, and there are only three of us."

"I'm hoping I'll get into a licensing college right away so I don't have to stick around here after graduating," she says quietly. "They'll have a lot more room if I'm gone."

For a moment, I wish that both of us could get the scholarship. Ana deserves it. She's doing just as much as I am, without as much help from her parents. And I totally get wanting to succeed and help make things easier for your family.

Ana takes a spray bottle marked HAIR DRYER and spritzes my head a few times. I'm immediately blinded by the fog that forms around my head as all the remaining water evaporates from my hair. Once the fog dissipates, I stare silently at myself in the mirror for a few moments.

"It looks . . . kind of good," I say. My curls are all defined and bouncy. Even the tightly coiled curls near the nape of my neck seem to be behaving somewhat.

"You're welcome," Ana says smugly. "Now you just need to keep using a de-frizzing potion on it regularly and not fry it so much with the flat iron. And don't ever let someone transfigure your hair to be straight, because that will fuck it up forever."

I keep playing with my curls as we return to Ana's room. Caro is gone when we get there. Ana sits cross-legged on her bed, and I hover awkwardly for a second before sitting across from her.

"It's getting kind of late," Ana says, wiping stray drops of water off her neck. She didn't feel like drying her own hair, so her bun is still wet. "You can sleep over if you want," she offers. "You can borrow pajamas and stuff."

I want to say yes, but then I remember how unlikely it is that Mom will let me sleep over. "I don't think so."

"Sick of me?" she says teasingly.

"Duh," I say. "No, my parents—well, my mom . . ." I trail off, not sure how I want to explain this.

"They're strict?" she supplies.

"No. Well, sort of." I look down at my lap, tapping my fingers uncomfortably on my knees. Say something, Shay. Anything. The truth, maybe. "Well, um, so." I glance at her, and she arches an eyebrow at me questioningly. My brain scrambles. "I'm a lesbian," I blurt out.

Okay, I could have introduced that more smoothly.

Ana nods. "Yeah." The utter lack of surprise in her voice throws me for a loop.

"You . . . knew?"

"I mean, yeah," she says, her thick eyebrows drawing together in confusion. "I didn't think it was a secret? You have a rainbow flag in your Twitter bio. And you . . ." She trails off, then switches tactics. "I didn't mean to make you uncomfortable, sorry. I can drive you home now."

Great, I've freaked her out with my weirdness. Amazing end to this night, Shay. "No, it's totally fine that you asked me to stay," I say as she stands up from the bed. "I would stay if I could. Really. It's just my mom is strict about me sleeping over with girls. She makes Lex sleep in the living room when we have sleepovers. I think she's convinced I'm going to, like, have wild sex or something." She stiffens when I say this last part, and I swear her face goes a little pink. "Not that I thought we were going to—" I cut myself off. Okay, kill me now. I wish I could spontaneously combust. "Sorry, I made it weird."

Ana lets out a tiny choked laugh and sits back down on the bed next to me. She's so close that I slide sideways toward her as the bed compresses under her weight. "You did."

"Thanks," I grumble, adjusting myself so I don't fall into her.

"Was I supposed to lie and say you didn't?"

"Yes."

"Sorry," she says, though she doesn't sound very sorry. "You're cute when you're flustered, though." She glances over at me, a smile curling at the edges of her lips, and then down at her lap. My brain and body have simultaneously ceased functioning, so I'm not sure what my face looks like. She stands and shoves her hands into the pockets of her sweatpants. "Come on, I'll drive you home."

Chapter 26

VALERIA:

Back then I said

I will fly so high for you

I'll go to the world and I'll bring back the moon

But now I stand here with my heart in my hand

And I realize this block is my soft place to land

—Lyrics to "My Soft Place to Land" from *Bronxtown Brooms*

"She said *what?*" Lex screeches. Her voice is so loud I have to hold the phone away from my face. "Oh my god, she's gay. She's so gay. What did you say?"

I moan, shoving my head violently into my pillow. "Nothing."

"What?"

I heave a dramatic sigh, not wanting to repeat myself.

"Wait, I'm FaceTiming you. This is a FaceTime-worthy event." The ringtone plays, and I sit up to answer her

FaceTime call. My phone creates a tiny illusion of Lex's face and upper body above the screen. "Oh my god. I'm so excited!" The illusion wavers because she's flailing around so hard the phone is having trouble capturing her. After a moment, the illusion solidifies, and her mouth makes a little O of surprise. "Oh damn, your hair looks good, lady."

That gets a smile out of me. "Thanks."

"So what did you say?"

"Nothing." I stare up at my popcorn ceiling, hoping for divine intervention. Or maybe a time machine so I can go back and make the last several hours less awkward.

"What do you mean nothing?"

"We left right after that. I said bye to her family, and we drove home and talked about other stuff."

"Did you flirt with her then?" Lex says, her eyebrows beetling with confusion.

"No." Or at least, I don't think I did. We talked like we normally do. It was aggressively normal, actually. I think I might have been babbling a little, but Ana made fun of me like she usually does, because, apparently, she thinks it's cute when I'm flustered. She thinks I'm cute, and maybe she's into girls, and she definitely already knew I was a lesbian. Oh my god, I think I'm having a stroke.

"How do you feel?" Lex asks, and I have never felt less prepared to answer a question in my life.

"I don't know," I say helplessly. "Confused?"

"But you like her," Lex says, as if it's an undeniable fact.

"I don't know."

Lex harrumphs as if I'm being stupid, but I'm completely serious. What if I'm reading too much into this? What if Ana doesn't like girls, and I end up heartbroken and even more awkward than I already am around her? I can't avoid her—we do basically everything together.

Lex tries to get more details about how I'm feeling about Ana, but I'm too wound up to talk about it much more. Soon after we hang up, Ana texts me to say that Lili has decided I'm cool. I tap out ten possible replies before settling on **bless** 🙌. I send it, then stare at my screen wondering why I thought that was a sensible response. She doesn't reply, which is definitely proof that she just thinks of me as a friend. After ten minutes of opening and closing apps on my phone and ignoring Lex's texts about letting love into my life, I decide to organize my potion-working supplies. At least that's a productive, relaxing way for me to not get any sleep.

I'm sitting on the floor surrounded by crystals and glassware when my phone buzzes. I don't grab it right away, telling myself that it's not Ana and it doesn't matter even if it is. But then it buzzes again, and again, until I snatch it up from the floor. There's a string of links to magical-makeup tutorial videos from Ana.

SHAY: ???

Since when is Ana super into makeup? I've never seen her wear anything other than ChapStick, which barely even counts. These videos about color-changing eyeshadow don't seem like something she would be interested in at all.

A few minutes pass before my phone buzzes again.

ANA: sorry, Lili hijacked my phone

Ah. The world makes sense again.

SHAY: hi Lili!
ANA: lol don't encourage her
ANA: anyway, what else are you up to this weekend?

So, we text. And we keep texting until my eyes droop and I fall asleep in a lull between her responses.

On Monday, a pit of anxiety bubbles in my gut when I wake up. I try to pretend that it's not related to seeing Ana for the first time since that night at her house, but that level of denial is too hard to maintain. As if I don't have enough reason to be nervous, my Brockton Scholarship application is due on Friday.

"There's my genius child," Mom says when I show up at breakfast. She kisses me hard on the forehead.

I got my MAT results over the weekend: 1320 out of 1400. Even better than I'd hoped. Mom has been overjoyed since I got the news. I wish I could be excited with her, but I'm too distracted by my nerves.

By the time I get to school, I'm ready to fake a serious illness and have Dad drive me back home. I settle into my desk in my first class reluctantly and root around in my bag for my phone, hoping to distract myself.

Ana walks through the door, compulsively early as always. She lingers there for a moment, her brown hands holding loosely onto the ratty straps of her backpack. My heart does this gushy, melty thing that can't possibly be healthy. Which, okay, sounds an awful lot like a thing that happens to you when you like someone.

I yank my hand out of my backpack and wave jerkily at her, like some sort of nervous puppet. I want to rip off my own arms and pretend I didn't do that. Thankfully, the corner of her mouth curls upward slightly, and she comes to sit beside me.

"Help me with the potions homework?" she says. "I couldn't figure out one of the questions."

I laugh, even though that doesn't make sense as a response. "Yeah. Yeah, sure."

"Oh, wait." She pulls out her potions notebook, flips to the back, and rips out a sheet of paper. "Here." Her face remains serious as she presents it to me. It's a large drawing of . . . a rose? Honestly, it's not completely clear. But she's scented the paper so it smells strongly of rose. "Since you're so obsessed with my art skills."

Oh my god, this is adorable. And funny. It smells really good too. "I'll, um, put it up. On my fridge."

What? What am I talking about?

She chuckles. "Sounds good."

After AP Potions, I covertly text Lex while Ana and I walk through the hallway.

SHAY: I think I like her. help.

The response comes right away.

LEX: lololololol DUH
LEX: just be chill and find a good time
to tell her. I'm 100% sure she likes
you too.

> **SHAY: lex I can't be chill. I nearly set**
> **myself on fire in potions class because**
> **she got too close to me. That is literally**
> **the opposite of chill!!!**

LEX: lmao you can do it lady, I believe in you!

I spend the rest of the school day proving that Lex's belief in me is entirely misplaced. By the time we get to rehearsal after school, I need a break from my own nerves.

Ana and I are dropping our backpacks in a side aisle of the auditorium when Mr. B waves us down. "Shay, can I grab you real quick?" he calls.

"Sure," I say, trotting over to him.

"We have some time before rehearsal starts," he says. "I want to work on your solo a bit."

"Oh. Um, okay." I glance back at Ana. I'm not thrilled at his insistence that I need extra help, but at least I can pull myself together without her in the room.

"Great. Let's go to my classroom," he says. "Good thing you're always early, huh?"

He hustles me to his classroom and drags his rolling chair out in front of his desk. As he sinks into the seat, he cues me to sing with a hurried gesture. We've worked on my solo, "My Soft Place to Land," once before. I hated it then, and I hate it now.

I close my eyes, centering myself before I sing. Focus, Shay. Don't let your anxiety about whatever happened with Ana this weekend get in the way.

"How did that feel?" Mr. B says after I sing through it. He leans forward in his chair, resting his tented fingers in front of his mouth.

Pretty mediocre, if I'm being honest. Partway through

the song, the memory of Ana singing it at the audition popped into my head. After that, I couldn't stop wondering why Mr. B decided to cast me as Valeria instead of her. "Okay," I say, because I'm a liar. "Um, should we go back to the auditorium for rehearsal? I think we're supposed to be starting soon."

"We've got plenty of time."

"But—"

"It's fine, Shay." He stands and crosses over to where I stand in the middle of the room, watching me with an air of amusement. "Relax," he says, clapping his hands onto my shoulders. "You're too tense. Shake it out."

Awkwardly flailing my body around doesn't make me less tense. It makes me feel ridiculous, which has the side effect of making me stiffer. Also, I wasn't tense before he touched me. Distracted, maybe. But not tense. I'm tired of him crossing my physical boundaries. When I see him touch one of the witches to correct them on a dance move or clap a wizard on the shoulder when they're joking around, they seem fine with it, which makes me feel trapped into enduring things like this. I don't want to bring it up, because everyone else is cool with it, and I'm scared of him liking me less for being a stick-in-the-mud.

When I don't immediately do what he's asked, he takes a step away from me and wildly shakes his arms. He hops twice, then looks at me expectantly. The image is so absurd that I can't stop a small snicker from escaping.

"Excuse me," he says, holding up a palm. "This is very serious business." He grins boyishly and flails around again. I laugh more openly this time, and he looks pleased. "I will stand here and make a fool of myself until you shake it out."

Humoring him, I shimmy my shoulders slightly.

"Was that so hard?" he says, raising his eyebrows.

"Yeah," I say. The stress of pretending I like being in this musical must be getting to me, because it comes out with more than a hint of sass. On the bright side, Mr. B loves when students sass him. His blue eyes light up with satisfaction.

"Maybe you should sing the whole song like that," he says.

"I think I'm good," I say dryly.

"Well, it's too bad that I'm the one in charge here," he says cheerfully, sauntering back to his seat. "From the top! Forget the blocking and just sing the song. The rules are that you have to keep moving no matter what. You don't have to copy my amazing movement style—" I roll my eyes at that. "But move in a way that feels natural to you. Make sense?"

Yup. Clear as mud. I nod, and he gives me a thumbs-up as he sinks back into his chair.

"'I remember when that was Nino's bodega, where he sold potions and café con leche,'" I sing. "'And he gave you free candy if you got good grades. Those were the days.'"

I sway back and forth, thinking about how to twist my face into the emotions I'm supposed to be conveying. Sadness. Disappointment. Love for her parents. Love for her community. It all seems too big, too hard for me to express in a way that doesn't look stupid and over the top.

"'But the rent went up, and he closed his doors,'" I continue. "'And that was that. The place was no more.'"

"Electricity-generation drill one!" Mr. B shouts suddenly. He grabs one of the lighting orb props off his desk and lobs it at me. I catch it and trail off, startled. "Keep singing! Don't worry about acting, just do the drill and sing."

Tentatively, I pick up where I left off in the song and light up the orb. Five seconds pass, and then I cut out the electricity. Five seconds on, five seconds off. Three on, three off. Two, two. One, one, one, one.

It turns out that it's hard to sing nicely while doing the drill. Soon, all I can focus on is breathing deeply and keeping my voice steady. My self-consciousness lessens—thank god—as my focus shifts.

"Stop there," Mr. B says as I take a huge breath, preparing to belt my face off in the next phrase. The orb goes dark. "What's this song about?"

"Um, I guess it's about how much Valeria loves the place she's from and how she's sad to see it changing," I say.

"That's part of it," he says. "But what about the second half of the song? When she starts talking about her dad?"

I think of the lyrics in the middle of the song. *He told me to take my dreams and leave this place behind / But what can I do when my family needs me?*

"She's talking about how she feels like she can't leave home even though her dad told her to, because she needs to help with her family's store," I say tentatively.

"Right. She thinks that the neighborhood is her safe place, and she's afraid to leave it in case it's not there when she comes back. It's a song about giving up your dreams," he says, his blue eyes boring into me from across the room. "What would you say is your dream?"

My gaze flicks down to the tile floor. Where is he going with this? The answer comes to me easily, but it takes me a moment to decide that I might as well tell the truth. "I want to be rich enough to help out my parents when I'm older."

"Right. So imagine that you have to give that up. It's never going to happen. What does that look like?" He stares at me with an expectant expression. "Describe it to me," he prompts me. "What could happen so that you could never make that dream a reality?"

I tense. The thought of not achieving my goal makes something inside my chest clench up. The air in the room suddenly feels heavy, claustrophobic. I don't want to talk about this with Mr. B. It's too real, makes me look too desperate.

"Shay, you have to be emotionally vulnerable to act,"

Mr. B says gently. "You can't always keep your walls up. Let me in a little so I can help you." He allows the silence to settle, ready to wait me out until I open up.

"Not getting the scholarship," I say quietly. The words scrape at my heart as they come out, leaving me a little bruised inside. I think of my parents, who are stuck in their low-paying jobs even though they're both qualified magic users who went to college. "Not getting into a licensing college. Not getting a good job."

He hums sympathetically. "I'm sure it's not easy for your parents, having you go to school here. They have to drive you all the way down here every day and buy all the extra materials for your magic classes. And that's just the tip of the iceberg."

My chest clenches further. Why is he saying all this?

"How would you deal with knowing that after everything they've sacrificed for you, things just didn't work out? You didn't win the scholarship, you didn't get into a licensing college, and you never get that job in a magilab you're hoping for." His voice is low and soft, and I want to put my hands over my ears so I can't hear him saying these things. "It's not so hard to imagine. Getting the scholarship is a long shot. Do you know how many applications we get?" He pauses, and I'm not sure if that was rhetorical or not. I give him the ghost of a nod, and he continues. "And you know that more than eighty percent of students don't get into a licensing college on their first try?"

I did know that. That fact pounds in the back of my mind constantly, no matter how much I pretend it isn't there. My face crumples. It hurts too much to acknowledge that things might not work out no matter how hard I push myself. He leans back in his chair, lifting a finger to point at me. "Yes. That's it. Now sing the song again."

Singing is the last thing I want to do right now. I would prefer to hide in a hole and delete the last fifteen minutes from my memory. Instead, I take a deep breath and start the song. His words echo in my head, and I focus to keep my breath steady. My eyes feel uncomfortably warm. They start to prickle, and a rush of dread fills me.

No. I am not crying in front of Mr. B. There's no way in hell that's happening.

I blink hard, wrestling down the horrifying swirl of feelings in my gut. But then I get to the final chorus of the song, and I choke on the notes. All I can imagine is a world where I have to live with the fact that I failed my parents, that I took everything they gave me and wasted it. I can feel Mr. B's eyes on me. I look up at the ceiling, hating that he can see me feeling this way.

I pull myself together enough to finish the song, and he stares at me. "That was it," he says reverently. "That was amazing, Shay. You're incredible."

Hearing those words, delivered so genuinely from the person whose opinion means *everything*, breaks me. Tears leak down my cheeks. Lowering my gaze to the floor, I swipe them away viciously. In a flash, Mr. B's in front of me, his warm hand resting on my shoulder. I stiffen. "It's okay," he says softly. "Let it out. That was hard." He stands there, leaving his hand on me until I slowly relax. "This show is going to be great, Shay. Because of you. Don't doubt yourself."

Even though I'm a miserable crying wreck, and I never ever want to do that again, hearing him say that makes me feel the tiniest bit special. I can't help but believe that maybe, with his help, I can learn to act well.

I nod mutely, not trusting my voice to come out steadily. "Let me take a look at your scholarship application before you send it in," he says, leaning in closer. "It'll be our little secret."

My breath catches in my throat. "What?"

He smiles ruefully. "What can I say? I'm a softie." I search his face for even the slightest sign that he's kidding. I don't find one. "I can't let that nightmare of yours come true. The rest of the committee will never know. Just let me help you out."

"Isn't that . . . against the rules?"

He grins. "It's only against the rules if someone finds out."

"Yeah," I say faintly.

I want to say yes. I want it so bad that I can feel how the yes would taste. It would ruin everything if I said no. I went through all this trouble to do this show, and change my hair, and ignore his weird, semi-racist comments. What could it hurt to go along with one more thing Mr. B wants?

But every fiber of my being screams that this is shady. It's unfair to everyone else applying. It's unfair to *Ana*. If I found out that he had helped Ana with her application before she submitted it, I would be furious.

I swipe tears off my face, looking everywhere but at him. "I don't know."

"Shay, you have to take opportunities when they appear," he says, the grin dropping off his face. "If you don't really want the scholarship, I understand, but—"

"No, I want it," I say hurriedly.

"Great," he says, as if the question is settled. He turns on his heel and heads toward the door. "We'd better get to rehearsal," he calls over his shoulder. "Can't wait to see your application. Send it to me tonight."

Of course, we're late getting back to the auditorium for the group rehearsal. We're so late that all the eyes in the room flick questioningly to us as we walk down the aisle. I scurry to where I left my backpack and pretend to search for something in the front pouch. I can feel Brittany glaring at me murderously from across the room.

"Sorry, sorry," Mr. B exclaims, striding past me. He pauses, claps his hands together, and bows his head apologetically. "Time management. Just can't get it down. I promise I didn't forget about you guys."

"Suuuuure," Ed calls from where he lounges on the stage. He gives Mr. B a skeptical look, his eyes flattening into slits as he raises his eyebrows. A ripple of laughter passes through the cast.

Ana squats next to me. I focus on rummaging through the potion bottles in my backpack. "What did Mr. B want you for?"

"He wanted to work on 'My Soft Place to Land' with me," I say, my voice sounding high and fake in my ears. It's not technically a lie. Anyway, I don't know how to wrap my head around everything that just happened, let alone explain it to Ana. What would I tell her? That she's right, that I am Mr. B's new favorite? That I have to take special favors from him so I don't lose everything I've worked for? That I'm going to do whatever it takes to win, even if she deserves it just as much as me?

"You okay?" she asks.

I zip up my backpack, abandoning my fake search. "Yeah." I force a laugh. "You haven't gotten any better at figuring out how I feel, huh?" I leave her crouched in the aisle and walk away to join everyone onstage.

Chapter 27

Many teens are not fully aware of the consequences of sharing magic. It can seem exciting to share magic because of the positive side effects. It is true that sharing magic gives the recipient of extra magic an energy boost, higher stamina, and an increased ability to manipulate magic. Remember, all of these effects are short-term and will last for less than forty-eight hours.

—*Your Magical Body: A Health Textbook for the Magical Teen*

NOW THAT MR. B IS GOING TO BE LOOKING OVER IT, I suddenly realize that my application is nowhere near as good as it should be. In fact, it might be the worst one anybody has ever put together. If I'm going to deal with the guilt from getting help from Mr. B, I should be sending in the best possible version of my application for him to look at. Right? Right.

On Tuesday, after I've spent every spare moment for

the last twenty-four hours putzing around with my essays, Mr. B pulls me backstage while Brittany is helping other people with choreography. He leads me over by a stack of miniaturized set pieces, grabs me by the shoulder, and leans in toward me. His body looms over mine in a way that I find a little menacing even though he's smiling. "Don't forget to send me your application."

The anxiety hits me so hard that I can literally feel sweat coming out of the pores on my palms. "Yeah, I will. It's just not done yet," I say. My eyes dart past him to the ensemble members dancing onstage. We're barely out of earshot here in the wings. "I kind of freaked out about it not being good enough and decided to redo a bunch of it."

"Don't worry about it so much," he says, releasing me. "Send it to me, and we can figure out what needs to change together." I nod, and he walks away, slipping around the black curtain at the side of the stage to head into the audience.

Okay, I might have been stalling a little because I felt guilty about this whole thing. But I need to get over myself. It's not that big of a deal. Mr. B was right—I need to take opportunities when they appear.

That night, I put some quick finishing touches on my application draft and attach it to an email to Mr. B. Just as I'm about to send the email, a text from Lex comes through.

LEX: got another college rejection today

LEX: which brings the grand total up to 15
rejections, 1 waitlist, and 0 acceptances

SHAY: where'd you get waitlisted???

LEX: Bremen State

I've never heard of it, so I assume it's a non-licensing college. A quick Google search confirms that.

SHAY: how many more licensing colleges
are you waiting to hear from?

LEX: one. so this probably isn't my year either.
maybe I'll never get out of here lol

Oof. The surest sign that someone is upset is when they put *lol* after something incredibly sad, as if the *lol* makes their misery less obvious. It takes the message from regular sad to downright depressing.

LEX: I kind of regret not trying harder with
terraball. I know my parents thought it wasn't
worth wasting that much effort on, but if I had
trained harder I could have maybe been
recruited

She isn't wrong. If she had focused on terraball, instead of going for the more well-rounded resume her parents wanted, I think she could have had a shot at being recruited. But sports recruitment for licensing colleges is even more cutthroat than regular admissions, so I get why her parents didn't want her to do that.

> **SHAY: don't stress yourself out thinking about stuff you could have done differently. you will get into college!!! you're the most amazing witch I know**
> **SHAY: these colleges are clearly confused about my bestie. if they were smart they would obviously have let you in already. let me know who I need to talk to so I can fix this mistake**
> **SHAY:** 🔥🔥🔥🔥🔥🔪🔪🔪🔪🔪🔪🔥🔥🔥

LEX: love you

My heart hurts for Lex. Magic is supposed to be the great American equalizer, the thing that makes sure everyone who works hard enough gets to succeed. I know how hard Lex has tried, and she deserves to go to a licensing college. Except it's not working out that way.

This whole conversation with Lex feels like a sign. It's a terrible reminder of what my future could look like without the scholarship. Watching her not get into college last year was devastating. I can't go through that myself. I take a deep breath and press send on the email to Mr. B with my application draft. He responds immediately, even though it's almost midnight. The email reads:

> I'll get this back to you by tomorrow afternoon.
> We're a little under the wire here, but I'm sure we'll
> be able to polish this up in time for Thursday.

As I send him a quick thank-you email, my phone buzzes with another text. I assume it's something from Lex, but when I look, it's a message from Ana. I dismiss the notification.

Spending time with Ana this week has been torturous. That mushy feeling I got from thinking about her before has turned into something jagged and sad. Now I'm stuck in this strange limbo where I can't quite bring myself to avoid her, but I have this sense of doom hovering over me every time we're together. I keep catching her staring at me like I'm a homework problem she can't make sense of. As if things weren't hard enough, I have to keep avoiding Lex's questions about me and Ana, since I don't have the emotional energy to get into this whole thing right now.

During rehearsal on Wednesday, Ana and I sit in the back of the auditorium together. Mr. B is rehearsing a song we're not in, so we're doing homework. Or at least I am. Ana has been staring at me pensively for the last few minutes. "You know you're acting weird, right?" she says finally. "Did I do something?"

"No," I say, tapping my pencil nervously against my potions worksheet.

I want to tell her we shouldn't be friends. Or anything more, if that was something she was interested in. It was never meant to work out between us, because there's only room for one of us to succeed.

I've got to think realistically about this. The odds of us both being accepted to any of the licensing colleges we apply to are abysmally low. As much as I would argue that we're very different people, the fact remains that we're two brown girls from the same high school with similar extracurriculars, GPAs, and career goals. We won't both be accepted to Willington. We can't both win the scholarship. And I don't know if I could watch her succeed while I failed, so I sure as hell can't expect her to not hate me if I take all the opportunities she's worked so hard for.

Ana is still staring at me. When I turn from my worksheet to face her, she meets my eyes boldly. "Are you going to tell me what's up?"

"Nothing's up," I say, the guilt in my chest intensifying as I look into her brown eyes.

"That's bullshit," she says calmly. "But we don't have to talk about it if you don't want to."

"Okay, let's take a quick break, everyone!" Mr. B shouts, his voice echoing through the room. "When we come back, we'll be working on 'Bronxtown Broom Race,' because we've got to get that one perfected for the award ceremony. And then we'll run from the top up until 'My Unfortunate Condition.'"

Ana unfolds her limbs and stands, looking unfairly graceful as she does so. She grabs both of our water bottles from the floor and walks away in the direction of the greenroom. God, she's being so nice. I hate myself. I'm a selfish, ambitious asshole.

I stand so abruptly that I feel a little light-headed and go to the far left aisle to practice my stage slides. All this self-pity is giving me a headache.

In an extraordinary display of bad timing, Ed sidles up to me. He flashes that sheepish grin he's worn around me ever since he poisoned me. "Hey, Shay."

"What's up, Ed?" I arch an eyebrow at him. At this point, I'm mostly over the energy potion disaster, but he still deserves to squirm a bit more for how abysmal his brewing was.

"First of all, I wanted to offer my most sincere apologies about that potion mishap." He slaps his chest emphatically. It doesn't make that loud of a sound, since he has the muscle mass of an overstretched twelve-year-old. "If you ever want any product on the house, just say the word."

"I think I'm good," I say dryly.

He nods, his face twisting into a wry smile. "Makes sense, makes sense," he says. "Just hoping you don't hold it against me or my man Mikey. It was an honest mistake, and I will atone however you would like. Seriously. You can take that to the bank."

"Um, okay," I say, perplexed. Why would I hold that against Mikey? And why is Ed following up on this now? He apologized after it first happened.

"Also, I wanted to ask how you might be feeling about my good friend Mikey," he says, half sitting on the arm of one of the seats at the edge of an aisle. I stare at him in bewilderment.

"What?"

"Mikey. You know. Tall, dark, handsome," he says, waggling his eyebrows.

"Yeah, I'm familiar with him."

"I wanted to put a good word in for him because my man is cool and funny and would totally hold your purse and shit, but he's also shy as hell."

I'm sorry, do I look like someone who needs another person to hold their purse? I don't even own a purse. I would point this out to Ed, but he's on a roll and doesn't seem to need my input to continue this conversation.

"So if you would maybe feel inclined that way, he would definitely be down for a movie, or coffee, or . . ." He pauses, glancing around like the air is going to present his next words to him. "Hanging."

Oh. He's saying that Mikey likes me. Maybe? God, I hope I'm wrong. "Sorry, Ed," I say. "I don't think so."

"The man is a catch!" Ed says, with all the intensity of a stoned used-car salesman. "He calls his grandma all the time. He can name seventy-five Pokémon off the top of his head, so . . ." He taps his temple twice. "Good memory. *And* he has the voice of an angel. What more can you want?"

I really hope Mikey never has Ed write a dating profile for him. Or try to set him up ever again, because this is weird and misguided. "Ed, I—" I start, but Ed continues talking.

"Just consider it," he says, staring at me intently.

"Ed—"

"For real. You don't have to tell me yes or no now, but I hope I'm, you know, planting the seed." He does a hand motion that looks more like throwing a basketball than planting a seed.

"Ed, I'm a lesbian!" I snap, because I clearly said no, and he's pissing me off. Ed's mouth opens and closes once, but no sound emerges. He nods thoughtfully, looking as though he's putting together a difficult puzzle in his head.

The soft sound of someone clearing their throat comes from behind me. I turn, and there's Mr. B, his face stuck in a wooden version of his usual grin. My heart clenches. Did he hear what I said? Who am I kidding, he definitely heard what I said.

Rationally, I know it's unlikely Mr. B is going to secretly be homophobic. I mean, he's the drama teacher. Plus, his whole shtick is that he's the cool teacher.

Still, I would prefer to tell people about my sexuality on my own terms. You don't know how people are going to feel about you being gay, and I don't like things being so far out of my control.

"If you're not too busy coming out, shall we get started with rehearsal?" Mr. B says, the wattage on his smile turning up to blinding levels.

Oh, he's trying too hard to be cool with this. Bad sign. "Um, okay." I take a deep breath as Ed and I follow him down the aisle toward the stage. Calm down, Shay. There's no reason to panic. Mr. B loves you. He's already made that very clear.

Except my panic seems justified when Mr. B starts making fun of me during the rehearsal.

"Get it together, Shay," he calls merrily when I miss an entrance. His blue eyes twinkle as he flashes the grin that always goes with his jokes.

"Sorry," I say, running to my place next to Ana.

"Don't get distracted by your scene partners," he says, still smiling.

All my scene partners are girls. I tense and force a laugh. Out of all the ways that someone could find out I was a lesbian, my least favorite has got to be my drama teacher making a bad joke about it in rehearsal.

Ana meets my eyes, angling her body so Mr. B can't see her face. "What?" she mouths.

I give her the tiniest shrug, hoping the moment will be forgotten by everyone quickly, and run back offstage as I hear the music restart. Unfortunately, the weirdness doesn't end there.

"Okay, Shay. I know you're a magical genius and everything, but this is some sloppy work. All those walls are the wrong size." He's stopped us mid-number to chew me out about how I magically adjusted the prop walls to be slightly too large. Every eye in the cast is trained on me while I shrink into myself in shame. "I can't do that on top of everything else I'm managing, but if you need someone to take that effect from you—"

"No, I've got it!" I say.

"Okay," he says. "Then let's try that again."

We make it all the way through to the end of my duet with Ana before he stops us again. He taps a finger on his bottom lip. "Ana's really got a handle on Gabriela as a character—she needs to exude exactly that kind of quiet power. She needs to be someone who's always been the prettiest, most charismatic person in the room." He turns his attention to me. "That's why Valeria is such a good part for you, Shay."

Ana makes a little strangled noise, so quiet that only I can hear it. I stare at Mr. B, bewildered. Is he saying I'm not pretty or charismatic? Damn. Is this the same guy who's been telling me all semester about how beautiful, special, and hardworking I am?

He continues jumping on my every mistake as we stumble through Act One.

"Let's do this again for Shay," he says for the third time, and I almost burst into tears of rage as I go back to my spot for the top of "What a Witch Should Be." Brittany has this expression of surprised blissfulness, like she just won the lottery. Racist asshole. Of course she's thrilled that Mr. B has turned on me.

"When exactly do you want us to evaporate the water for the fog?" Ana says, hitting Mr. B with her blankest stare. "I think we're all confused, not just Shay. Maybe you should explain what you want?"

"What, you all haven't developed mind reading yet?" he says. A few people giggle, but I can't muster the energy to fake a laugh. "I clearly haven't been doing my job right."

"Yeah," Ana mutters, glancing at me.

With every comment Mr. B makes, I can feel the scholarship slipping out of my fingers. Everything I've done to stay on his good side is suddenly pointless. There's no way he's going to consider my application, let alone want to break the rules for me to give me advice on it ahead of time.

But maybe I'm just being self-conscious. It's getting a little late in the rehearsal process for me to be making so many mistakes. Maybe I'm making this about me being gay, but it's actually just that Mr. B has finally lost patience with my theatrical incompetence.

I hurry out right after rehearsal ends, too angry and embarrassed to face anyone. Ana texts me when I'm in the car on the way home.

ANA: you okay?

      SHAY: just feeling stressed about
      my scholarship app

That isn't technically a lie. Just a gross understatement. She doesn't push me more on the subject.

For the rest of the evening, I refresh my inbox obsessively, wondering if Mr. B will email me like he promised. Around eleven, a message from Mr. B finally arrives. It's only one sentence.

Didn't have time to get to this, sorry.

My heart drops. Shit. The scholarship deadline is tomorrow. I was so close to the finish line. If I had just maintained Mr. B's good opinion until this was all over, I could have won. I always thought I could get the scholarship by pushing myself to be the best version of myself. Maybe I should have just pretended to be someone else.

Chapter 28

OSCAR:

I love you

Even though your family's a mess

Even though your clothes are cheap

Your cousin's a freak

And your mom is just so indiscreet

VALERIA:

Excuse me?

—Lyrics to **"My Unfortunate Condition"** from *Bronxtown Brooms*

I SUBMIT MY FINAL SCHOLARSHIP APPLICATION BEFORE SCHOOL the next day. It should be an earth-shatteringly meaningful moment. Instead, I stare at my gold signature for a few long seconds before shoving the pile of papers into the waiting tray. A sick sense of dread pools in my stomach.

"You'll know by the end of next week if you're a finalist," the secretary drawls, her fingers clacking on her computer keyboard. "Good luck."

The office door opens behind me. I turn, and there's

Ana. Her mouth hitches up in a tentative half smile. The dread in my stomach intensifies. She's going to win. She's going to win, and I'm going to lose, all because I messed everything up.

"Hey," she says. She slips past me and places her own application on top of mine. "Want to walk to class with me?"

I'm already backing toward the door. "Um . . . no. Sorry. I have to go to my locker."

The disappointment that flashes in her eyes haunts me all day.

When I walk into rehearsal that afternoon, Mr. B clocks me, then turns back to his conversation with Brittany. My heart sinks. His expression isn't exactly cold, but it's nowhere near the warm smile I'm used to seeing. Soon after Ana arrives, he makes a beeline for her. Suddenly, the Mr. B charm is switched on again. Even from across the room, I can tell that he's turned the full power of his interest and enthusiasm on her. They stand in the aisle and talk for a while as I watch, feeling like a pile of hot garbage.

Things only gets worse once rehearsal starts. Mr. B singles me out even more obviously today, making me run my solo over and over again while everyone waits impatiently.

"I just need *more* from you," he says. "You've got dead eyes. Lights off, no one's home."

"Right," I say, nodding deferentially. "I'll, um, make them less dead."

His stare is hard and uncompromising. "Do you understand what I'm saying here?"

Not at all. "Yes," I say.

"Okay." He sounds skeptical. "Let's try it again, then."

I bite back my frustration and throw myself into acting, trying to replicate whatever it was I did last week in our private rehearsal. No matter what I do, though, it's not good enough.

We eventually go back and run the section that leads into "My Unfortunate Condition" because Mr. B was so dissatisfied with how it went yesterday. Before we start, I cast a wary eye out at where he sits in the audience, writing idly in his composition notebook. With his legs propped up carelessly on the seats in front of him, he looks relaxed. Once we start the scene, however, he waves a hand for us to stop after only a few lines.

"Shay?" he says, not looking up from his notebook.

"Yeah?" I say with trepidation.

"What?"

"Yeah?" I repeat, louder this time.

He cups a hand to his ear and shouts, over-enunciating each syllable. "I can't hear you. Please say your lines louder!"

Ana goes very still beside me.

"Burn!" someone hollers from offstage. Other people hoot and hiss and laugh. Brittany lets out this obnoxious, simpering cackle right in my ear. I give Mr. B a thumbs-up.

Something touches my arm lightly, and when I look over, I see that it's Ana's hand. She gives me a sidelong look. For a moment, I feel less alone. Then I realize I'm a dick for letting her comfort me when I'm being so weird to her. I take a deep breath, paste on a smile, and go back to my spot to start the scene again.

When we take a break, Ana pulls me aside in the greenroom. "What the hell?" she says, her voice low and angry. "He's being such an asshole to you this week."

"Yeah, well . . ." I lean back against the wall and cross my arms over my chest.

"Did something happen?"

The image of Mr. B talking to her before rehearsal flashes in my mind, and my insides curdle. I bite my lip, not meeting her eyes. "No."

"You're a bad liar," she says softly, and a pang of shame goes through me.

When rehearsal ends, I don't stick around to chat with Mr. B and the rest of the cast. I head right out to the pickup circle to wait for Mom. Thankfully, Mom gets there pretty quickly. She sticks her head out the car window.

"Johnson Taxi Service?" she says. "Are you Shay?"

"Mom, no," I say, shaking my head. I climb in the passenger side and throw my backpack in the back. "Who are you? Dad?"

"He got all his best jokes from me."

"Yeah, sure," I say, but the words come out flat.

She flies the car out of the pickup area and onto the main street. "Did something happen today?" she asks. "Seems like you're in a mood."

I want to tell her everything. To have her reassure me that it'll all be fine and fix everything for me. I open my mouth to spill my guts before I consider it too deeply. "I'm just . . ." I trail off, not sure how to explain what's happening with me. "I'm just having a hard time with Mr. B."

Her eyes narrow. "A hard time?"

Okay, roll back, Shay.

She can't fix this for me. I need to say something that will get her to give me advice but also keep her out of Berserker Mom mode. I can't deal with a repeat of what happened with that horrible assembly back in middle school. If she shows up at the school and makes a big stink, everything will be permanently ruined.

"I think he's just frustrated that I'm not as good of an actor as he wanted me to be," I say eventually. Or maybe he's homophobic, I add in my mind. Honestly, it's probably both.

"He's a teacher," Mom says. "It's his job to help you if you're not doing as well as he wants."

"I guess so," I say. "He's tried to help me out a lot so far, but he probably got annoyed that I'm still messing up so much. It's just so close to the scholarship being awarded. I feel like him being annoyed with me right now will hurt my chances."

"Do you want me to meet with him?"

"That's okay," I say. "That'll seem like I'm making a big deal out of nothing."

"If he's expecting something of you and he hasn't told you what it is, that's not good teaching." Her eyes dart over to look at me for a moment before returning to the floating road ahead of us. "You need to stand up for yourself, Shay."

"I don't need to make a big fuss every time something kind of annoying happens."

"Maybe not, but you can't let people treat you however they want either."

"How do you deal with Travis?" I ask. That's her manager at work, the one who's super annoying and thinks he's better than her because he has a magical license. "I know you don't fight him on everything, even when he's wrong."

She shakes her head. "That's different."

"How is it different?"

"It just is." Her tone is sharp, knifelike.

Great, I guess this conversation is over. I slump in my seat and practice generating sparks of electricity at my fingertips. Pointer finger. Middle finger. Ring finger. Pinkie. Thumb.

A group of broom riders swoop above us, whooping loudly as one of them does tight loop-de-loops in the air. I'm surprised Mom doesn't immediately come out with a biting comment about broom safety.

"I pick my battles at work," she says, looking resigned. "Sometimes I just say what Travis wants to hear and move on with my day. It doesn't feel great, but they fire people who are 'too disruptive.'" She doesn't actually do air quotes when she says those last two words, but I can hear them in her voice. "I want better for you. You are smart and powerful and educated. You deserve to be treated right."

"You're all of that too," I say. "And people still aren't treating you right."

"But you," she says, giving me a little smile, "have me on your side. So tap me in if you need help, okay?"

"Okay, Mom."

How can I possibly tell her that things are the same for me? It's better to pick your battles like she does. One day I'll have my magical license, and I'll be the boss. Then nobody will be able to mess with me. But for now, I need to say what Mr. B wants to hear so I can move on.

Chapter 29

Engaging in magic sharing outside your family poses a risk
to your emotional and physical health. The connection created
by magic sharing will allow people with magic levels more
than fifteen points above your own to magically influence your
emotions. Once the connection has been formed, it is also
possible for connected magic users to draw upon your magical
power at any point until the connection fades.

—*Your Magical Body: A Health Textbook for the Magical Teen*

REHEARSAL ON MONDAY IS EVEN MORE TORTUROUS. MR. B
stops calling me out every five seconds but instead wears
this wearily amused expression whenever I do anything
onstage. I slowly shrink into myself over the course of the
afternoon, watching that amusement shift to flashes of
annoyance. Meanwhile, he throws several effusive com-
pliments Ana's way. Her polite responses are tinged with
confusion. She keeps darting glances at me, but I don't
meet her eyes.

As the end of rehearsal approaches, I steel myself. Today is the day I fix this.

"Okay, everyone," Mr. B says cheerily after we finish our run of "Bronxtown Broom Race." Our rehearsal was supposed to end twenty minutes ago. Ana has gone so stiff that she resembles a statue more than a person. I can tell she's counting down the seconds until she can run to her car and get to her dance studio. "That wasn't our best work, but it wasn't our worst. I'll take it. It's starting to look like we might be making some art." He tilts his head from side to side thoughtfully, a sly grin growing on his face. "Maybe."

With that, we're dismissed. Ana downs the Light as a Feather reversal potion and runs out. I take it as well, then make a beeline for where Mr. B and Brittany stand in the audience. Hopefully, I can pull him aside before the usual Mr. B fan club gathers.

"Mr. B," I say, grabbing hold of a seat back to anchor my still-floating body. The potion kicks in, and my feet land on the floor in the aisle. "Can I talk to you?" Brittany plops down into the seat beside him, leaving her long legs splayed in the narrow aisle to block my path. I pause, casting a disgruntled look at her. Then I compose myself and turn a tentative smile on Mr. B. "Um, privately?"

He gives me a smile that seems tinged with . . . pity? I'm not sure. "Brittany and I have a planning meeting right now."

"It'll only take a second," I insist.

A long moment passes, and I'm not sure if he's going to brush me off. Finally, he gives me the barest hint of a nod. "Okay. Let's go to the greenroom."

Brittany lets out a long-suffering sigh when he gets up, as if him talking with me is some massive inconvenience. Whatever. I follow Mr. B backstage into the greenroom. He closes the door behind us.

The room feels smaller than it should with just the two of us alone in it. Mr. B eyes the gray sofa against the wall but doesn't sit. Instead, he crosses his arms and stares at me. He looks tired. Exhausted, actually. He always looks worn out these days, especially after manipulating magic during rehearsals. Even so, his presence right now is mildly terrifying.

I take a deep breath, forcing myself to meet Mr. B's eyes. "What I said to Ed the other day," I say haltingly. "You know I was joking, yeah?"

God, I hate myself right now. When I'm on the other side of the country at Willington, none of this will matter. If I have to tell a homophobic teacher I'm not gay to get there, so be it.

"What you said to Ed?" he repeats.

Come on. He knows what I'm talking about. "About me being a lesbian." I say *lesbian* quickly, almost tripping over the word. "I was just trying to get him off my back."

Mr. B grins at me, but there's something hard and fake about it. "He can be persistent."

"Yeah," I say, letting out an uncomfortable laugh.

"You don't have to pretend to be something you're not, Shay," he says, still grinning at me. I wish he would stop. "Plenty of people have questions about their sexuality in high school."

"No, seriously. I felt really weird about him trying to set me up with Mikey," I say, feeling worse about myself with every word that comes out of my mouth. "I just said something to make him leave me alone. It was stupid, and I shouldn't have said it."

"Well." His face slips out of the grin and into a neutral expression. "I'm sorry I misread the situation."

"That's okay," I say, struggling to force a smile. Am I out of the woods? I can't tell what his vibe is right now.

"I could have helped you if I knew. Do you want me to talk to Ed and Mikey?"

I shake my head, self-hatred bubbling in my gut.

"Okay," he says. "But if they keep bothering you, tell me. You know, if you're attracted to women, that's fine. Lots of people are bisexual."

But I'm not bisexual. I would say that, but the words stick in my throat. I thought he didn't like that I was gay?

He sits on the couch, then pats the empty space beside him. I sit down as far from him as possible and put my hands on my lap, trying to make myself small and unobtrusive.

"Why did you want to talk to me about this?" he asks.

I shrug, hoping he'll leave the topic alone, but he waits silently for my answer. "No reason," I say.

He raises his eyebrows. "Come on, Shay."

"Um, well," I say. "I thought you were mad at me for some reason? And I wasn't sure . . ."

"Shay, I'm not mad at you," he says tenderly. He closes the distance between us, and I stare up into his face, fear fluttering in my chest. "I'm disappointed."

I freeze, pinned in place by his stare. "Disappointed?"

"You could be really incredible," he says. "But watching your performance in rehearsal recently . . ." He shakes his head. "I'm not convinced you're putting your all into it. I've been trying to offer you some extra support, but you don't seem to want it."

"N-no, I want it," I say. Maybe that's not true, but I would say anything, do anything to get him back on my side.

"Do you?" he asks.

"Yes," I say, with every ounce of sincerity I can muster.

His expression doesn't change, and he continues as if he hasn't heard what I've said. "I want you to live up to your potential. If you can't give everything you've got, you're not going to get the scholarship."

My jaw goes slack with horror, and I stare at him, dumbfounded. He can't be—is he threatening me?

"Do you want the scholarship?" he says.

"I want it, I do. I really do," I babble. "I can work harder! I promise."

He clasps my shoulder in his hand. My first instinct is to shy away from the touch, but I shove down the impulse. "You're a good egg, Shay," he says with a grin, and suddenly the charming teacher I know is back. "I was starting to wonder if we should switch to Ana's solo for the scholarship ceremony performance instead of yours, but now that I know you're willing to put in the work, we don't have to do that."

My stomach ties itself into even more intricate knots. Is that what he was talking to Ana about the other day? Did she know he was thinking of replacing my solo and didn't tell me?

"I'm glad you came to talk to me," he continues. He drops his hand from my shoulder, chuckling a bit to himself. "I should have known you weren't a lesbian. You're too pretty; it would be a waste."

I freeze into a statue of a Shay that isn't offended. Mentally, I am gone, gone, off in another dimension where I can tell Mr. B that he can go fuck himself.

With that comment, he gets off the couch and strolls out of the room. He has a lightness in his step that's so at odds with our conversation.

"Bye," I say weakly, watching his retreating back.

I sit there long after he's left the room. Have I redeemed

myself? I think so. A deep exhaustion sets in as tension leaves my body.

It's time to face the truth. Mr. B is manipulative. He knew how I would respond when he said I wouldn't get the scholarship if I didn't try harder in rehearsal. And why would he tell me that he was thinking of having Ana perform her solo at the scholarship ceremony instead of me?

He keeps using the scholarship to influence me, and I'm tired of it. I made excuses for him before. When he said that auditioning for the show would be good for my scholarship application, I convinced myself that there wasn't anything wrong with it. He scared me with the idea of losing the scholarship to inspire me to perform my solo better, but I told myself that it didn't matter because it worked. Why am I wasting all this mental energy bending over backward to justify his actions?

But acknowledging this changes nothing. I still need to make it through the next two weeks and stay in Mr. B's good graces. I don't need to like him to get this scholarship. I just need to make sure he likes me.

Chapter 30

Over long periods of time, consistent daily magic sharing will make your body used to containing a higher density of magic. If you stop regularly sharing magic, your body will experience a period of acute exhaustion, and you may find it difficult to complete magical tasks that you once found easy.

—Your Magical Body: A Health Textbook for the Magical Teen

EVERYTHING GOES BACK TO NORMAL, MORE OR LESS. FOR THE next few days, I'm pulled into private rehearsals with Mr. B. We go over choreography, all of my scenes, and my solo. It's helpful, but uncomfortable. He's decided we're best friends now and really wants to shoot the shit with me while we're working.

It feels as if I have to pretend to buy into our so-called friendship. Every time I try to get us back on track, he doubles down on our previous conversation by asking me a super-personal question. At this point he knows most of what there is to know about my family and friends, my interests, and my entire (nonexistent) dating history.

In our group rehearsals, I am very noticeably Mr. B's favorite again. My castmates gossip about it endlessly. They don't talk to me about it, of course, but when I pass groups of people on our water breaks, they fall silent. You would think that actors would be better at playing it cool than that. Ed, because he low-key lives for drama, takes it upon himself to appear and confirm that I'm the current hot topic.

"Dude, what did you *do*?" he asks, sidling up to where I sit at the front of the stage. We're essentially on break because Mr. B is busy magically fiddling with the broom props. "Last week you were the second coming of Jesus, then you were suddenly just like the rest of us, and now the sun shines out of your asshole again."

"I didn't do anything," I say.

"I heard that you and Mr. B had a secret conversation in the greenroom." He waggles his eyebrows at me. "With the door closed."

"What?" His last few words echo in my mind. "I talked to him about what I could do to perform better in the show. What are people saying?"

"Just stuff." He shrugs and plops down to sit beside me. "A bunch of them have weird crushes on him, so . . ."

"So they made up a rumor that I'm hooking up with

him?" Ed doesn't deny my guess. I cast a surreptitious glance at where Mr. B hovers in the air, paranoid that he can hear this conversation from across the stage. "What the fuck?"

"I know you don't swing that way, so I told them you wouldn't do shit like that," he says. I make a sort of alarmed choking sound when I process what he's just said. "Don't worry, dude," he continues. "I didn't out you or anything."

"But—but—" I can't get a more coherent thought out for a few seconds. "That's not like a fun rumor. That would be *illegal*. If they think that's true, they're cool with just chatting about it behind my back and doing nothing?"

"It's not that deep," Ed says, flapping a dismissive hand in my direction. "There have always been stupid rumors about him getting with students, but it's just because so many of the witches are into him. Mr. B would never actually do something like that."

There's a moment, just a moment, where I think that Ed is wrong. I could imagine Mr. B doing something like that. But I think better of it before I go too far down that rabbit hole. I don't like Mr. B anymore, sure, but that's not a good reason to imagine that he's guilty of every bad thing in the world.

"Anyway, did you and Ana get in a fight or something?" Ed asks.

My heart decides to relocate from its position in my

body and search for a new owner. It takes me about five seconds too long to regain my chill. "Ed, for real, get out of my business," I say, rolling my eyes. "Did you just come over here to gossip with me about myself?"

"Bruh, no shame in being nosy. That's how I get the good info."

I snicker. "Yeah, okay."

Mikey appears behind Ed and lightly smacks him on the shoulder. "Dude, are you bugging her again?" he says.

"Of course not. Me and Shay are besties," Ed says. He folds his hands on top of his head and grins at me. I shake my head good-naturedly. Even when Ed is being annoying, he's kind of charming about it. Plus, he's one of the few people in the cast who tries to include me in things, which I appreciate.

Mikey's eyes flick over to me. "Is he bothering you?"

These are legitimately the first words Mikey has spoken to me outside of a scene rehearsal in a week. "No, he's fine," I say.

"Okay." Mikey lingers there, digging the toe of his sneaker into the stage floor. He clearly wants to say something, so Ed and I watch him silently. This goes on for so long that I grasp for anything I could say to make this less weird. "Are we cool?" he says finally.

"You and me?" I ask.

He nods.

"Yeah," I say.

"Cool." He smiles, a bit self-consciously. "Cool." And then he walks off without another word.

"That was touching," Ed says, pretending to wipe away a tear.

"Shut up." I laugh. "He's normally less weird than that, right?"

Ed starts laughing as well. "Oh yeah," he says through his laughter. "I'm going to make fun of him for that so hard."

"All right, let's go back to the top," Mr. B announces. He drops down to the stage floor, wiping sweat off his forehead.

"Millionth time's the charm," Ed whispers to me as we get to our feet. I cross my fingers in response. Maybe this will be the time that Mr. B is satisfied with our performance of "Bronxtown Broom Race." As the scholarship ceremony performance gets closer, Mr. B gets more and more anxious about this song being perfect.

We take our doses of the Light as a Feather potion—I swear this production alone is keeping this potion brand in business—and hurry to our places for the beginning of the song. As the music starts, I sneak a glance at Ana. She hasn't talked to me much the last few days. Even in AP Transfiguration, where we've been paired up to work on a project, she doesn't chat with me any more than necessary. I guess she got the memo that I was avoiding her. Which is . . . fine. I miss her, but this is how it has to be.

Ana and I launch ourselves toward the broom props

suspended above us. We meet Ed and Mikey midair and pair off, me with Mikey and Ana with Ed. Even though I've seen this a million times before, my gaze still gets stuck on Ana as we all dance. She looks beautiful in the air.

"Focus, Shay!" Mr. B calls out. When my attention snaps back out to the audience, he gives me a thumbs-up and a wink.

Potions club on Fridays is my safe place. No rehearsal, no Mr. B, no Brittany—just a bunch of nerds brewing potions in Dr. Davidson's classroom. The most stressful thing that happens there is me having to explain for the millionth time that we can't brew More Amore potions on campus illegally and that love potions aren't half as effective as people think they are anyway.

Our president has completely checked out since she got into a licensing college, so most of the club leadership duties have been passed on to me as the vice president. Now I spend less time brewing my own potions and more time making sure freshmen don't set themselves on fire.

This Friday, after setting the club members up to brew Illusion Dust, I hover near Lina Gregory, one of the freshmen. She has an unfortunate habit of accidentally igniting every third potion she makes. To disguise my true purpose for being near Lina, I idly scroll through my favorite potion blogs on my phone, looking for recipes the club could brew in the future.

This requires very little brainpower, so I spend the rest of my energy on my new and definitely not self-destructive habit: pining after Ana.

Out of the corner of my eye, I see her grinding down ingredients with her mortar and pestle. Her arm muscles are super defined. She looks gorgeous, as always. And even if she wasn't incredibly hot, there's something about watching her brew potions that makes my heart go all warm and fluttery. My traitorous heart obviously doesn't understand the current situation. Fuck you, heart.

Suddenly her eyes flick up, and she meets my gaze boldly. "You need something?"

I nearly drop my phone. "Hm?"

"You've been staring at me."

I scoff at that, trying to play it off like I wasn't staring. It comes out way more intense than I mean it to, so I sound like a jerk. She stares at me, blank faced, and I deflate. "Sorry," I say. "I totally was."

A little smile curls at the corner of her mouth. "Creep."

"You stare at me all the time," I retort.

She inclines her head, conceding the point, and the smile disappears. I want it back. Before I can beat that impulse into submission, I take a step toward her lab table. "Want help with that?" I ask, pointing at her mortar and pestle.

She looks at me, cool and distant. "Sure," she says eventually.

What am I doing? If I'm going to avoid her, I can't be all wishy-washy about it. That's not fair to her. Even so, my feet are taking me to the supply closet to grab another mortar and pestle. When I return, I set myself up beside her and start grinding down fennel seeds.

We work in silence. It's not a nice silence, or a comfortable one. It's a silence that crackles awkwardly in the air between us. A silence that tells me that, yes, I have messed things up between us. Of course I have.

"I heard that Mr. B was thinking of swapping my solo for yours at the scholarship ceremony," I say, trying to fill this awful quiet.

She stops grinding. "What?"

This was a bad choice of topic. I shrug. "That's what he said," I say. "I was just wondering if he talked to you about it."

She doesn't reply right away. Instead, she goes back to grinding fennel seeds, with more force than before. A sophomore flags me down from across the room, and I reluctantly leave Ana's side. He wants my feedback on the Chameleon potion he's brewed for his honors potion class, so I inspect it and rub a bit on my hands. While I'm waiting for it to take effect, I return to Ana's lab table.

"He mentioned that he wanted to schedule more time to rehearse my solo. That's it," Ana says when I approach.

Her face has gone blank. I've absolutely pissed her off. "Why'd you ask me about that?"

"I was just wondering."

"Really?" she says, icy cold. "That's the first real thing you've said to me for, like, two weeks, you know."

My shoulders sag. She's not wrong. "Sorry," I say quietly. She keeps looking at me expectantly, but I don't have anything better to say. "Um, you don't have enough wormwood for the recipe. Do you want me to get you some more?"

She tents her hands over her nose, sighs, and stalks off to the supply closet. I follow her because I don't know what else to do. When we get there, I instantly regret following the witch I have a crush on into a small enclosed room. She closes the door to access the shelf with the wormwood, which makes everything worse. I shift awkwardly in place, lamenting the choices that brought me here.

Ana faces the wooden shelf with the wormwood but doesn't move. "Did I do something wrong?"

"No," I say, staring at the back of her head as if it's going to give me answers as to how I should deal with this conversation.

"Then what?" she says, rounding on me. "I can't deal with this, Shay. If you don't want to be friends with me anymore, you have to tell me. Stop doing this shit where you act all angsty and don't tell me what's going on."

Oof. She's absolutely correct, and I am the worst. "I want to be friends with you," I say haltingly. "I just feel like . . . with all the scholarship stuff the way it is, we can't really be close."

She blinks at me. "That's the problem?" she says incredulously. "That doesn't make sense. You knew we were competing for the scholarship when we started being friends. What changed?"

I don't know what to tell her. We stare at each other.

"Forget it," she says eventually. "I'm over this."

She turns away from me, and I know this is it. If I let her go now, we'll never have any kind of relationship again.

"Mr. B was going to replace me with you," I say, the words pouring out of me. "He got annoyed with me, and I wasn't the favorite anymore, and I had to really suck up to him to fix things. It felt gross, Ana." I let out a frustrated sigh. "It made me realize that . . . I don't know. This isn't like a fun competition, you know? This is my whole life. I'm really trying to win. And if I win, you lose."

"You think this isn't hard for me?" she snaps. "Do you think I'm some kind of robot? That I don't have feelings? I've been watching you leave me behind this year, and . . . fuck. You're *winning*, Shay. You're the potions genius. You're the one with the ridiculous magic level. You didn't even need to be Mr. B's favorite to get the scholarship, but you got that too."

Her brown eyes are screwed up with pain and frustration. My heart is breaking. How long has she felt this way?

She exhales, and all the fight goes out of her. Now she just looks sad. "Sometimes I feel like, if you didn't exist, I would have the scholarship in the bag," she says quietly.

My shoulders slump. "I feel like that too sometimes."

"It sucks. Makes me feel like a bad person."

"Yeah."

We hang there in a defeated stillness. Her face has mostly reverted to her usual mask of composure, but there's something tired in her eyes that wasn't there before.

"I'm sorry for trying to ghost you," I say. "That was a shitty thing to do."

She doesn't say anything, which seems about right. She deserves better than a half-assed apology.

"I should have talked to you about what I was thinking. I got really stressed about the stuff with Mr. B and took it out on you, and I shouldn't have done that."

Still nothing. I am literally sweating at this point.

"Okay, I don't know if there's anything I can say that would make this better, but I care about you a lot, and I would be really upset if I fucked this up." I swallow hard. "I've been focused on one thing for, like, as long as I can remember. My whole life has been about trying to be the perfect witch and get this scholarship. And sort of because of the scholarship I spent a really long time thinking that we were enemies. And then we weren't enemies, and I was super into you, and that was confusing, and now I'm kind of feeling like I'm letting the scholarship get in the way of my actual life. So I'm sorry."

Ana's eyes have gone very wide. "Did you just . . . ? Do you like me?"

I replay the word vomit that just came out of my mouth and realize what I've said. Oh no. No no no. "I, um— what? Yes?" I choke out.

Excuse me while I leap into the nearest volcano.

"This was the moment you picked to tell me?" she says, giving me a hard stare.

"No. I'm sorry. This was bad." I close my eyes and bury my face in my hands, praying for imminent death. I thought this interaction was potentially salvageable before, but I've ruined everything.

"Your hands are invisible."

"What?" I take my hands off my face and find that the Chameleon potion I tested has kicked in. They're not actually invisible, but the skin shifts to match whatever background it's against. "Oh my god, kill me."

I hear a little snort of laughter, and before I can confirm that Ana is actually *laughing at me* in what might be the most embarrassing moment of my life, I feel her lips on mine. Her mouth is so soft that I lose all brain function for a second. She bites my bottom lip lightly, and I let out a little gasp. I can feel her smile against my lips.

Even though we're literally kissing right now, I have to

keep checking in to make sure I'm not hallucinating. Yes? She's still there? Beautiful, and gay, and kissing me? She wraps her arms around my waist, pulling me closer. I respond by pushing one of my hands into her hair, because, oh my god, I love her curls.

By the time we break apart, I'm wrecked. My brain has flown into a million scattered pieces, and I have no hope of reassembling it anytime soon. I stare at Ana, barely breathing. Her lips are slightly parted, and I can see the bottom edges of her front teeth.

"We should probably get out of the closet," she says.

She smiles at me—a full, devastatingly dazzling Ana Álvarez smile—and slips out the door, leaving me with the realization that I just had my first kiss in a potion supply closet.

Chapter 31

GABRIELA:

Sueños

I wake up to dream each day

Reaching for a future that I hope will find its way to me

Sueños

People say that I am quiet

But my dreams echo loudly in the spaces in my mind

—**Lyrics to "Sueños" from** *Bronxtown Brooms*

"SO WHAT NOW?" ANA ASKS WHEN I JOIN HER AT HER LAB table. She's gone back to brewing her potion like nothing happened. She even snagged the wormwood we went into the closet for. When she did that, I have no idea.

I, on the other hand, am staring at the other club members and wondering if they know that I'm a big old lesbian who just made out with a mind-bogglingly incredible witch in an *actual closet*. There's a coming-out joke to be made there, but I'm too mentally zonked to put it together.

"Do you want to date me?" I say tentatively.

There is an uncomfortable amount of silence after I suggest this. She meticulously places seven crystals in a perfect circle around her cauldron and starts folding their magic into her potion. I wonder if I'm about to live through a nightmare I didn't know I had until this moment—getting rejected while someone brews a potion. What if she likes me enough to kiss me, but not enough to date me?

"Are you sure?" she says finally.

Did she just ask me if I was sure? Me, the mayor of asshole town? The person who was begging for her forgiveness just a few minutes ago? I stare at her, befuddled. "What?"

"I don't want you to choose me because I'm the easy option," she says quietly. "I know there aren't a lot of queer girls around. I mean, I'm sure you know more than I do. But I don't want you to be with me just because you know I'll say yes."

"What are you talking about?" I say. I notice a pair of sophomores glancing over at us, so I lean in toward her and lower my voice. "I want to go out with you."

The confident Ana from a few minutes ago seems to have disappeared. This new, nervous Ana won't make eye contact with me and keeps moving potionworking supplies around like her sanity depends on it. "I've been pretty obvious about liking you, and you seemed sort of uninterested. So I started to give up."

"So you like me?" I say, focusing on the most important part of what she's saying here.

"Yes!" she says, yanking on the magical threads in the fire under her cauldron. The flame goes out. "I've liked you all year. And probably before that too, but I didn't realize I was bi until this summer."

"Oh my god," I whisper. My grin is so big my cheeks hurt. "Then go out with me."

She's blushing so much that it's obvious even on her brown skin. "Okay." She laughs quietly, like she can't believe what's happening, and gives me a small smile. Her dimple melts my heart. "Okay," she says again, more surely this time.

"Okay," I repeat, grinning at her.

"I'm not out, really," she says shyly.

"That's fine," I say. Nothing else matters besides the fact that she's into me. "So your family doesn't . . . ?"

"No, they don't know," she says. The wattage of her smile dips a little. She glances around the classroom. "They're kind of conservative."

"Oh, gotcha." Not ideal, but I'd be a total asshole if I made a big deal out of that. Coming out was hard even for me, and my parents ended up being fine with it. We'll just have to be private about the two of us. "That sucks," I add.

"Yeah." Her expression goes serious, then determined. "I don't know if this makes sense, but sometimes I feel like I'm putting myself into a box for them. Like, I'm the big sister. I fix things; I always do everything right. But this"—she gestures between us—"is something for me. Does that make sense? I'm not great at talking about my feelings, so . . ."

"No, it does. I get what you mean." We're both putting ourselves in boxes for our families. They're slightly different boxes, but still.

"I'll tell them someday," she says. "Just not right now."

"That's fine."

"You still want to be my girlfriend?"

"Yeah," I say, my grin splitting my face again. "Yes. Definitely. I definitely want to be that." I giggle, for no other reason than that I'm absurdly happy. "Hey, do you remember when we were enemies?"

She laughs, rolling her eyes at me good-naturedly. "No. I do remember when I was really into you and you hated me, though."

"Sorry I'm so dense."

"It's kind of cute," she says. I close my eyes and hide my face in my hands because I think I'll explode if I look at her for one more second. She laughs again, which I'm sure is because I look ridiculous with my camouflage hands. "I think . . ."

Nothing immediately comes after that statement. I slowly drop my hands from my face so I can see her again. "I think we shouldn't talk about scholarship stuff," she says seriously. "Not until after the ceremony."

That brings me back down to earth a bit. "Are you sure?" There's stuff I should tell her. Stuff about Mr. B, and how he's been treating me, and how he's given me special favors. Part of me wants to take this way out, and part of me recognizes that it's a bad idea. "I know I told you a little bit about what's been happening with me—" My throat tightens up so it's hard to even say this. "But I should probably tell you more."

"I don't want to ruin this," she says, and her expression is deadly serious. "We're both trying to win, and if we talk about it, we're only going to hurt each other."

I chew on my bottom lip, contemplating my response. She does seem pretty certain about this. "You're sure?"

She nods. "I'm sure."

Relief washes over me. This will be okay. Future me will explain everything to her once the scholarship has been awarded. I'm wondering whether I can subtly take her hand, since my hands are still chameleon-ing, when Lina Gregory's potion catches fire at the table next to us.

"Shoot." I abandon Ana to help this combustion-prone girl. Even once Dr. Davidson gets up from his desk to intervene, finally roused from his email-induced stupor, I'm pulled away for more club duties. The sophomore I spoke to earlier wants feedback on his Chameleon potion now that it's started working, and there are various people who have questions for me about the Illusion Dust they're brewing. Because of the whole "potions genius" thing, a lot of the club members will ask me for my advice before they ask Dr. Davidson, a man with a literal PhD in potionworking.

While I help them, I can feel Ana watching me; she wears a private little smile that turns my heart into a puddle of sentimental mush. It makes me hopeful that everything, somehow, is going to work out for the two of us.

⋄ Chapter 32

The US Magic Corps. Build a Better Future.

Being a Soldier has its rewards. On top of the unmatched
benefits package and competitive salary, the US Magic Corps
will provide educational and career support both while you
serve and afterward. After five years of service, all Magic Corps
service members are eligible to enroll in the United States Magic
Corps Academy, where they will earn a magical license that will
boost their career to new heights.

—US Magic Corps recruitment pamphlet

WHEN MOM PICKS ME UP AFTER POTIONS CLUB, SHE TAKES
one look at me giggling over a text from Ana and arches
an eyebrow. "Ana?"

A garbled sound of surprise comes out of my mouth. I
blink and try again for a sound that resembles human
speech. "Yeah."

"Are you two together yet, or you going to keep moon-
ing over her until you drop dead?"

I'm so dumbfounded that I actually choke on my own

317

spit. Mom looks up to the sky, as if asking for patience to deal with her foolish daughter. "This child thinks she was being subtle," she says to the heavens. She clicks her tongue and flies the car out of the school lot.

"We're, um, we're dating now," I say, my cheeks flaming.

"Well, you bring her over for dinner soon," Mom says.

"Okay," I say meekly.

Thus begins what is arguably the best week of my life. At first, I tell myself that I'm not going to be one of those people who becomes completely insufferable once they start dating someone. That idea only lasts until the next morning, when I wake up to a text from Ana.

ANA: good morning to my favorite enemy 🖤

At the sight of that little purple heart, I bury my face in my pillow and scream. Then I spend a good five minutes selecting the best color of heart emoji to send with my reply. I settle on red because that's romantic, right?

> **SHAY: good morning 🖤 am I**
> **still your favorite enemy now that**
> **I'm your girlfriend?**

ANA: definitely. you're the best enemy
I've ever had.

**SHAY: do you normally make out
with your enemies?**

ANA: only when they're as cute as you

Oh my god, I can't handle this. I open my text thread with Lex and quickly send her a message.

SHAY: Lex she is so cool wtffffff.

LEX: plz don't live text me your
entire relationship lol

When I look back at our texts over the last twelve hours, I discover that, yes, I have been doing that. But who can blame me? I, Shayna Johnson, have a girlfriend. A hot, scarily competent girlfriend with perfect hair and killer dance skills.

My alarm clock goes off for the second time, and I'm slowly levitated out of my bed. The clock's magic lifts me into the air, then deposits me softly on my feet next to my nightstand. I guess I should probably get ready for work. As I walk to the bathroom, I return to my text thread with Ana.

SHAY: what are you up to today?

ANA: I promised to take Lili, Xio, and Isabel
to the mall

ANA: pray for me

        SHAY: maybe Lili will give you a makeover

ANA: that's what I'm scared of

There isn't a time when both of us are free, so I don't see Ana that weekend. I have to settle for texting all day and FaceTiming late at night. Whenever Lex notices that I'm trying to sneak onto my phone at work, she draws a little heart made of fire in midair with her index finger.

"Shay has a girlfriend," she sings every time. And each time she does it, hearing the word *girlfriend* out loud sends a little rush of warmth through me.

On Monday, Ana shows up at the classroom where I'm finishing peer tutoring. She waves at me through the window, and I ditch the sophomore I'm working with so quickly that I don't think they notice until I'm out of the room.

"Hi," I say, beaming at her.

"Hey." She leans over and kisses me quickly. I'm left with the sweet scent of her hair product in my nose and a growing sense of wonder. I get to just do this all the time now? Incredible.

She hands me a little iridescent box. "I saw this at the mall and thought of you." The colors on the box shimmer for a few moments and then slowly shift until a green-and-pink logo appears. "It's not a big thing, but I thought you might like it."

When I open it, I find a little glass globe with a thick layer of dirt on the bottom. There's a button on the side of the base. I press it, and mist fills the globe. After a few moments, plant seedlings begin to poke their way out of the dirt. Ferns, tiny glowing mushrooms, and a miniaturized weeping willow grow until the globe is filled with plants.

"Oh!" I say, staring intently at the still-growing terrarium. "That has to be Flora-Grow potion. Wow, they've measured it so precisely! Everything grew to exactly the right size. This is genius."

"So you like it?" Ana asks.

"What?" I drag my attention from the terrarium and find her watching me with an amused expression. "Yes! I love it—this is so cool."

"Nerd," she says affectionately. "I made the lady at the kiosk write out how they make them, because I thought you would want to know." She points at a paper lying at the bottom of the box.

"Really? Am I right? Is it Flora-Grow?" I pause in my scramble to pull out the paper when I hear her laugh. I lean over and kiss her on the cheek. "Thank you."

"You're welcome," she says, and I'm blessed with a full-on Ana Álvarez smile. "Glad you like it."

With Ana at my side, rehearsal becomes tolerable. I can't be as close to her as I would like because of Mr. B, but I still get to watch her dance. Plus, when Brittany snipes at me unnecessarily during rehearsal, I can catch Ana's eye and know that I have an ally there with me. On Thursday, however, Ana's not called. Without her, I have to grit my teeth and smile through several hours of Mr. B mining my personal life history to help me find motivation for my acting.

When I check my phone after rehearsal, I have a missed text from Dad.

DAD: car won't start—at the mechanic now

This again? Why did this have to happen on the one day Ana isn't around to drive me home?

Just as I'm lamenting my lack of a ride, another text comes through.

LEX: I GOT INTO COLLEGE!!!!

I sling my backpack onto my shoulder and book it out of the auditorium, pressing the button to FaceTime Lex as I go. Her head and upper body pop up above my phone moments later.

"Congratulations!" I say, throwing my free arm in the air.

"Thank you, thank you." She does two little bows, which makes her ponytail bobble happily back and forth.

"I told you that everything would work out for you," I say, pressing a button on the side of my phone. It floats out of my hand and hovers in front of my face, leaving my hands free to do a little victory dance for Lex. "You worked way too hard not to get into a licensing college."

Her smile dims. "I didn't."

"What?" I say, my excitement faltering.

"I didn't get into a licensing college." She shrugs. "I got rejected from the last one a week ago."

I stop dead in my tracks, alone in the center of the hall-way. "You didn't tell me."

"Sorry. My parents were super upset. It was a whole thing."

"Oh," I say, staring at the little illusion of her. "That sucks."

She looks down, not making eye contact with the phone, and starts twirling the end of her ponytail around her finger. "Yeah, they went off on this weird thing where they thought I should join the Magic Corps because I could get into one of the military colleges that give out licenses later."

I cringe. Magic Corps recruiters come to the T. K. Anderson career fair every year, and one of their major selling points is that you can get a magical license afterward. But you have to serve for *years* before that. Lex obviously had no interest in taking that path. Her parents aren't even very pro-military, so they must have really freaked out to start suggesting that. "That's intense," I say. "I'm really sorry."

"It's whatever," she says, looking resigned. "I got in somewhere, and I'm going to accept it, and they can be disappointed with me from across the country."

My heart sinks. "Across the country?"

"Yeah. I got into Galpert. It's in California."

"That's great," I say, trying to muster up some enthusiasm for my best friend to leave me for a faraway college that doesn't even give out magical licenses. "So what's your plan? Are you going to try and transfer to a licensing college after your freshman year?"

She frowns. "I don't know."

"Okay." I start walking again, pushing myself out the nearest door and into the Florida humidity. My phone bobs along in front of me as I go. "I've heard that going to another school for a year can actually make your application stronger, so this will probably help you when you apply again."

"You know what? Forget it. I shouldn't have talked to you about this." She throws her hands up in exasperation. "I thought you would be happy for me."

My eyebrows scrunch together in confusion. Why is

she upset? "I am happy for you," I say, but it doesn't come out as convincingly as I want it to. Truth be told, I'm only sort of happy for her. She's settling for something less than what I know she deserves.

"No, you're not. You look like I just invited you to my funeral," she says fiercely. "If everybody else judges me for my choices, whatever. But you're my best friend. You're supposed to be on my side!"

"I *am* on your side!"

"But you've been making me feel like shit!"

"What?" I recoil, and my chest tightens with icy dread.

"You act like my life is over because I didn't get into college on my first try, and now I'm going to a non-licensing college," she continues. "I'm going to be fine, Shay. I'm sorry I'm not as smart and perfect as you, but going to a non-licensing college does not make me a failure."

I feel the pain in her voice like a slap to the face. "I never thought you were a failure," I say softly. "I just wanted you to go to a good school. You're really smart. And super good at magic."

Her steely gaze doesn't lighten. "I know you hold yourself to these ridiculously high standards, but not everybody is going to have the same goals as you. Maybe I'll never go to a licensing college."

Ridiculously high standards? My standards for myself might be high, but they're not *ridiculously* high. And what is she saying about never going to a licensing college?

That's a massive change from what her goals were before. "But you probably won't get as good of a job without a license," I say hesitantly.

At that, she softens slightly. "I know that's a really big deal for you, but it's not the same for me," she says. "If I don't make a lot of money, it's not the end of the world. I just want to have a job I like."

"Oh," I say, and it sounds like the air has been knocked out of me. I suddenly realize that there's a fundamental difference in our thinking here. A licensing college is my ticket to a better life for me and my family. But Lex and her family already have that better life.

The little illusion of Lex, somehow imposing despite its size, stares me down. "You know it's fine to go to a regular college, right?"

I gape at her, baffled. No, I don't know that. What has my time at T. K. Anderson taught me if not that there is only one path to success? If you get into a licensing college, they put you on the school website as a success story. If you don't, you might as well be dead.

"Okay," she says, and her disappointment cuts through me. "So you think that all the people who don't get into licensing colleges are stupid and lazy."

"No!" I protest.

"Oh, so it's fine for other people to go, but if I go, then I'm not living up to my potential?" she snaps, her eyes flashing dangerously. In those words, I hear an echo of what I'm sure her parents are saying to her. I feel small and horribly mean.

"I'm sorry," I say. "I really didn't mean to make you feel bad."

She sighs, crossing her arms over her chest. "Yeah, I know." A few beats of silence go by. Clearly, neither of us knows what else to say. "Okay, I'm gonna go."

"Okay," I say reluctantly.

She hangs up.

I stand alone outside the fine arts building, feeling heavy and frustrated. I'm filled with a need to smash, burn, *destroy* something. Anything to make myself feel better.

With a grunt of frustration, I summon a burst of fire to my hands and hurl it off into the distance. It flies along the sidewalk, hurtling past the edge of the building before fizzling out midair. I don't feel any better.

"Fuck," I say limply. God, I can't believe I made Lex feel bad about going to a non-licensing college. What kind of shitty best friend does that?

I grab my phone out of the air, turn off float mode, and shove it in the pocket of my backpack. Then I start to walk across the campus, aimless. Dad hasn't heard back from my auntie who lives near T. K. Anderson about whether she can pick me up, so I am well and truly stuck here, alone on this mostly deserted campus with only my thoughts for company. I *could* ask Mr. B for a ride. He's probably still here having one of his oh-so-important planning sessions with Brittany. But I would rather not spend more time with him.

Instead, I pace the length of the sidewalk that runs alongside the back parking lot, absently tugging on the magic in the air around me to cool things down while I mull over my conversation with Lex. Her words ring in my head. *So you think that all the people who don't get into licensing colleges are stupid and lazy.* Of course I don't think that. But then again, I can't conceive of someone I care about being cool with going to a regular college. They should keep trying to go for that magical license; it's a cop-out to go for anything less.

I reach the end of the sidewalk and continue off in the direction of the back faculty parking lot. Under my feet, the ground changes from asphalt to the dirt and dusty white stones that line the parking lot. I kick some of the stones as I walk.

So I guess I've been thinking about college like this: It's fine for *other* people to go to regular colleges, but not me or my friends. That thought kind of makes me sound like an elitist asshole. Is that how I act?

I gather my hair up into a bun, wiping sweat off my neck as I do so. Out of the corner of my eye, I catch a flicker of movement and light coming from a car at the far end of the lot. It's the only car around this late in the evening. Wondering who's still on campus, I walk closer to the car, squinting against the flickering light coming through the windows.

The two figures in the car are pushed up against each other, hands grasping at each other desperately. Their magic glimmers, silver and red streams twisting across their bodies. I realize, belatedly, that they're sharing magic. The girl tosses her blond hair out of her face, sliding her fingers reverently over the stubble on the man's chin. There's something familiar about . . .

Holy shit.

It's Mr. B and Brittany.

I duck instinctively so they don't see me. Mr. B leans away from Brittany and bumps his head back against the window. His eyes stay fixed on her, not noticing my presence. He looks . . . sad? Frustrated? The expression wrinkles his brow, and I can almost see the lines that appear on his forehead, the ones that remind you he's older than he acts.

Brittany leans into him, bringing her lips to his, and my stomach twists. Then I'm running, running who knows where. The potions bottles in my backpack clink wildly against each other with each step I take. I run out of the faculty parking lot, through the main lot, and past the fine arts building. I only stop once I'm off campus, panting on the sidewalk underneath the wide road floating alongside our school.

I pull my phone out from my backpack. Should I call Ana? She's at dance, so she won't answer. Still breathing hard, I punch Lex's speed dial. It rings, and I wait with my heart in my throat for her to answer.

329

The phone rings, and rings, and keeps ringing. My heart sinks. There's no way she's going to answer. But just as I'm about to hang up, the miracle of miracles occurs, and she answers the phone.

"What's up?" she says flatly. I can hear the sound of her EDM playing in the background.

"Lex," I say, my voice crackly with emotion. "Thank god. I—thank god."

"What happened?" she says, confused. The volume of the music dramatically decreases. "Are you okay?"

"Yeah. No. Mr. B, he—I saw him and Brittany. I didn't mean to, but the car broke down, and my dad couldn't come pick me up . . ." I can't get my thoughts together. "Nobody noticed, but they were so close. Like, weirdly close. How did nobody see it? And the scholarship—"

"Okay, calm down," Lex says. "What's going on?"

A car honks at me as it passes by, and I yelp with fear. My breathing goes all hiccuppy, and before I know it, I'm sobbing into the phone. "I'm s-sorry," I manage to gasp out with difficulty.

"It's fine. You don't need to apologize for crying, just . . . Where are you?"

"Um, on the s-street," I say, trying to get my crying under control. "Outside school."

"I'll be there in fifteen minutes."

Chapter 33

You can be a positive influence on your friends' well-being by encouraging them to also not share magic.

Your Magical Body: A Health Textbook for the Magical Teen

WHEN LEX PICKS ME UP, SHE IMMEDIATELY HANDS ME THE half-drunk Starbucks drink in her cupholder. I cradle the cup in my hands, letting the cold seep into my skin and ground me before I drink any. When I take a sip, the flavor of toffee nut hits my tongue.

"Thanks," I say.

Lex gives me an expectant look. "So what happened?"

I lean my head against the window, exhausted. "Mr. B

and Brittany. I, um, saw them together. In the faculty parking lot."

"What? Like . . ."

"Like they were making out. And sharing magic."

"What the actual fuck!" Lex shouts. She slaps a hand violently against the steering wheel. "That's so creepy! At school?"

"Yeah," I say. There's an air of unreality around me right now, like none of this is actually happening. I feel strangely disconnected from myself. My brain keeps circling back to the image of Mr. B and Brittany kissing, but it's like something I saw in a movie somewhere. Not something that happened in real life.

"I knew he was a creep, Shay!" Lex says. She jerks the wheel to the right, flying us into the nearest plaza. "I knew it. It always felt weird that he forced you to audition by threatening you with the scholarship. That's why I told you not to do the show."

"Yeah," I say dully. Belatedly, I notice that I'm still clutching the coffee cup. I relax my grip on it and place it back in the center cupholder.

Lex glances over at me as the car settles onto the ground in a parking space. "Did Mr. B ever . . . do anything to you?"

I rear back from her, shaking my head definitively. "No." But as I say that, a sour taste fills my mouth. "I mean, he was kind of touchy-feely."

"Touchy-feely?" she echoes.

Memories flash in my mind, suddenly invested with new meaning.

There's Mr. B pulling me out of rehearsal to practice partner dancing alone with him.

And there's Mr. B telling me that I'm too pretty to be a lesbian.

And there's Mr. B touching my thigh when I scraped my knee in rehearsal.

And there he is grabbing my shoulder, leaning too close, telling me to relax.

Suddenly it seems obvious—sickeningly, horrifyingly obvious—that he was much sketchier than I ever admitted to myself. I explain just a few of these memories to Lex, and she goes positively incandescent with rage. "He *what*?" she barks, fury contorting her features. "You never mentioned anything like that to me. Why were you okay with that?"

"I didn't have a choice," I say. "I need the scholarship."

"You *did* have a choice!" Lex practically shouts. "This is exactly what I was talking about earlier. Shay, you're so obsessed with this, like, really specific idea of success. It kind of bothered me before, but this is ridiculous."

"What?" I say, staring at her. "How is this related to what we talked about earlier?"

"It's like you think that if you don't get the scholarship and get into Willington and get rich from working in a magilab, you're a failure. Yeah, okay, I get that it would be expensive for your family if you didn't get into college right away. But still. It's a fucking scholarship, Shay. You almost got molested."

There's silence. Lex pushes a hand back through her hair, scowling. When she puts it like that, I feel like I've been acting like a whole fool. I've been killing myself for this one thing for so long that I can't imagine any other path. Maybe I wouldn't have been in this situation if I'd been just a little bit less obsessed.

"Sorry," Lex mumbles, rubbing her face tiredly. "I just—I'm so mad."

"At me?" I say in a small voice.

"Oh my god, no! I'm mad at Mr. B for being a manipulative creep." She taps her orange nails on the steering wheel and shakes her head slightly. "You have to report him to the school."

I'm hit with a wave of panic just hearing those words. "Nobody would believe me, Lex. Everybody loves him. Like, they *really* love him."

"Yeah, but—"

"This is not going to work out for me!" I snap. This kind of thing happens. You see it on the news: Powerful, rich wizard makes his problems go away with his influence. But the second part of that is that the witch always gets fucked over. Always. "If I report him, there's no way I'm getting the scholarship."

She groans with frustration. "Forget the scholarship!"

"I can't!" My voice breaks a little as I say that. "I get that I'm obsessed with it, but I can't give it up because Mr. B did something wrong."

My words linger in the air between us.

"Okay," she says, her tone softening. "I'm sorry."

"What if I don't tell anyone?" I say. "I guess it's not really illegal. She's eighteen already. And age-gap magic sharing is fine in Florida."

Even as I say this, I know I'm making excuses. I want things to work out easily, but we're past that point now.

"Fucking Florida," Lex mutters.

"Yeah." Florida has startlingly few laws about magic sharing. The state is all about personal freedom and not letting the government interfere with citizens' rights.

"Even if it's technically legal, it's definitely still against school rules," Lex says. Her gaze is hard and flinty when she looks at me. "You know, this could be like the witches at that company."

"What company?"

She waves a hand vaguely in the air. "The one with the CEO that made witches share magic with him for promotions."

"Oh," I say. "You think Brittany got with Mr. B just for the scholarship?"

Lex shrugs. "I mean, I know she's been kind of an asshole to you, but that could have been like a cry for help or something."

"But then why would she still be with him?" I ask.

"Maybe she feels like she can't ditch him while she's a Brockton Scholar."

My heart drops when she says this. I don't like Brittany, sure. But I shouldn't leave her to be manipulated by Mr. B. No matter how annoying and racist she is, she doesn't deserve that.

The image of Brittany running out of Mr. B's classroom, clearly upset, replays in my mind. I should have seen this coming. There were so many signs: all the extra hours they spent together, Brittany's obsession with following him around, his weird lack of boundaries with students.

"You're right," I say. "I'll talk to her tomorrow. Maybe I can convince her to tell the school."

"Yeah, that's a good idea." She nods encouragingly, looks me straight in the eyes, and then reaches over to grab my hand from my lap. "I'm sorry all of this happened to you; it really sucks."

I chuckle, and it comes out sounding a bit delirious. "It really does."

She gives my hand a squeeze, and then we sit there in a companionable silence. "Can you drive me home?" I ask after a bit. "Our car broke down again, so I'm sort of stranded."

"Of course," she says.

As she's moving to put the car in gear, I realize there's

one important thing I still haven't addressed. "Hey." I turn in my seat to face her fully. "I'm really sorry I've been making you feel bad about your college stuff."

Lex pulls her hand off the gear shift. She flips her hair to the opposite side, then flips it again moments later. "I know you don't mean to do it," she says after a few seconds. "You're just always trying to encourage me to, like, study for the SATs, or do MAT drills with you, or work on my college essays. And I know you're trying to be helpful, but it makes me feel like you think I'm not working hard enough."

"I don't think that," I say firmly. "At all. And you going to a non-licensing college is great. I'm sorry I was such a jerk about it."

"Okay," Lex says. "You're forgiven. You have to come to cultural-dinner night soon though and tell my parents how great you think Galpert is. They love you, so maybe they'll listen when you tell them."

"Done," I say, and I hold out my pinkie. She links her pinkie with mine, sealing the promise, and I feel like I've made a small step toward redemption in this area.

When I get home, Mom takes one look at me and frowns. "What's wrong, Shay? Did something happen with that Ana girl?"

That's so far off base that I let out a laugh, but it sounds more like a sob. "No. I just feel kind of sick."

"I'll make you an immune booster," Mom says, already moving toward the kitchen. I suppress a groan. Her immune-system-boosting potion is, hands down, the worst-tasting potion of all time. It's just a bunch of boiled garlic with honey, lemon, and an extra infusion of magic from her amethyst crystals. Mom will shove it down your throat to cure you of any and all health problems.

I follow her into the kitchen reluctantly. Dad sits at the table in his usual spot, slumped over. He straightens when he notices me enter. "Sorry about stranding you at school, kiddo."

"It's fine. I, um, got a lot of work done. It was relaxing." I have literally never told a bigger lie in my life, but he doesn't seem to notice.

He nods slowly. "Well, I'm glad Lex was free to drive you home."

Mom clears her throat, and they exchange a quick look before she goes back to pulling the skins off cloves of garlic. "Shay, the problems with the car are turning out . . . more expensive than we thought," he says.

"Yeah?" I say, coming to sit at the table across from him. A sense of foreboding fills the room. I glance between him and Mom, who continues peeling with single-minded focus.

"We would like to ask if we can borrow a thousand

dollars from your savings." Dad looks so guilty I want to cry.

My answer flies out of my mouth. "Of course!" I smile, though my heart is breaking. That's almost all the money I have saved. What if something else happens, and we need more money?

This is why I have to get on the fast track to making money. My parents deserve a car that works and regular vacations in foreign countries and a house with magitech security so they don't have to worry about people breaking in. This is why I need the scholarship.

"We'll pay you back," Mom says fiercely.

"You don't have to," I say.

"We will." She throws garlic into the pot of water on the stove and then glares at the mixture like it personally offended her in some way. When I drink the immune booster with my dinner, it tastes like an apology. I want to tell her she has nothing to be sorry for, but I know she won't listen.

This convinces me that talking to Brittany is the right move. If I can get her to come forward on her own, there's a better chance this will all work out okay. I could get out of this without losing my shot at the scholarship. There's still a chance that I won't have to ruin everything I have to achieve.

Chapter 34

T. K. Anderson Magical Magnet School is proud
to announce its nominees for this year's Brockton
Scholarship Award:

Ana Álvarez

Rebecca Callahan

Jacob Greenberg

Liam Hollowell

Shayna Johnson

The Brockton Scholar will be selected by
a panel of judges and announced at the
scholarship ceremony next week.

—Email from T. K. Anderson

THE NOMINEE ANNOUNCEMENT FEELS LIKE A SICK JOKE. I should be happy. This is it, the moment I've been working for all this time. But instead I stare at the email, wondering if I only got this because Mr. B thinks I'm pretty. My parents freak out over the announcement, of course, and I have to fake some enthusiasm to celebrate with them.

Thankfully, I don't have to pretend for too long because Ana picks me up soon after to drive me to school. Liliana, Xiomara, and Isabel are raising hell in the back seat, so

Ana doesn't kiss me hello, even though I can tell that she wants to from the look in her eye.

"She made me sit in the back for you," Liliana informs me as I slide into the front seat. "I usually get to sit there, but I gave it up because you're cool."

"Thanks," I say, craning my neck to smile half-heartedly at her. She grins in response, and the highlight on her cheeks changes color from silver to an iridescent purple. Xiomara and Isabel mumble indecipherable greetings at me. The two of them are engrossed in playing that weird kid's game where you zap electricity at each other until someone cries uncle. They're young enough that they can't generate much power, but it still hurts after a while.

"I have to drop them at Boca Middle," Ana says. Her dark eyes lock on mine. "Congratulations."

"Thanks." I'm itching to hold her hand, but I keep that impulse in check. "You too."

The moment is bittersweet. It reminds me that I have to tell her what's going on. Forget what we agreed about not talking about scholarship stuff—this is bigger than that.

"Hey, I need to talk to you about something," I say quietly. "Later. Maybe after school?"

As the words come out of my mouth, I realize that giving advance notice of a serious conversation this early is a terrible, horrible, asshole move. It forces the other person to worry about what the content of said serious conversation is going to be for hours beforehand.

Or at least that's what I do. I think Ana might be slightly less anxious than me.

"Sure," Ana says, her face unreadable. She puts the van in reverse, and it levitates unsteadily before gliding out of the parking spot in front of my apartment. "Is something wrong?"

"I mean, don't worry about it," I say. "We should just talk later."

"Okay." She laughs affectionately. "You're being weird, Shay."

"I'm frequently weird."

"That's true," she says, nodding gravely.

After school, I post up behind the cafeteria, which has the perk of being both pretty private and not too bizarre of a place for me to ask Brittany to meet me. I sent her a Wiz-Connect message saying that I had a thing about the show I wanted to discuss with her. I'm not sure why, but she agreed to come talk without too much fuss.

I pace the sidewalk, watching the cracks in the cement. My head feels thick with nerves. I don't want to do this. I've made a terrible mistake.

Of course, the moment I start to spiral into self-doubt is when Brittany shows up. She comes around the corner wearing her most dismissive expression. Once she catches sight of me, she twirls the tip of her ponytail around her finger and shoots me a stony glare.

"So, what's your problem?" she says. "Do you need extra help with the choreography or something? I know dancing isn't exactly your thing."

A stab of irritation goes through my chest. This is off to a great start.

"Um, that's not actually what I wanted to talk about."

"Okay?"

I hook my thumbs into the pockets of my shorts, looking for something to do with my hands to make me feel less awkward. "It's not actually about the show."

We stand there staring at each other. The distant sounds of soccer practice come floating from beyond the cafeteria. I can't anticipate how she's going to respond here, and it's psyching me out.

"Oh my god, spit it out," she says.

I shift from side to side uncomfortably, gathering my nerve. "I saw you . . . and Mr. B . . . together."

Her breath catches in her throat. Then she clenches her jaw into a steely smile. "What?" she says, twisting her face into an expression of confusion. Those years of acting are really helping her right now. If I hadn't seen the split second of terror on her face, I would believe she had no idea what I was talking about.

"Yesterday. After rehearsal. In his car." I swallow hard, forcing myself to continue looking at her. I reach for the cooling magic in my T-shirt to deal with the nervous sweat beading on my skin.

"And? He gave me a ride home after rehearsal because my car was at the shop," she says, glaring down her nose at me. "Not that it's any of your business."

"You were . . . sharing magic. And kissing."

Her eyes widen minutely, then settle into furious slits. "What do you want?"

"What?"

"You're trying to threaten me with this crazy story, so you have to want something."

"N-no," I stutter, baffled by the turn this conversation has taken. "I want to help you. You should tell people about what he's doing to you."

"Don't try this goody-two-shoes act on me," she snaps. "You're just jealous. You've been throwing yourself at him since you started this show, and you don't even care about him. You just want the scholarship."

She's not exactly wrong, but I have no idea how she's come to the conclusion that I'm trying to blackmail her. What would I even want from her? "He's taking advantage of you," I say, using the kindest tone I can muster. "You know he can manipulate your emotions right now because you've shared magic. You have to say something."

Her hands are shaking at her sides. The fingernails are bitten down to the quick, and the skin around one of her pointer fingers is ragged and scabbed. She notices me staring at her hands and folds her arms sharply across her chest. The movement curves her in on herself, as if she's protecting herself from me. "He would never take advantage of me. He wouldn't."

"Brittany, he's, like, thirty—"

"I'm eighteen," she snaps. She pauses, looking like she regrets saying that. "He's never—he doesn't think of me like that. He just wants what's best for me."

"I saw you together," I say softly.

"Are you trying to ruin his life?" Her blue eyes flash dangerously as she advances on me, drawing herself up to her full height. "You can't just make accusations like this. Jeff is a good teacher. A really, really good teacher. He helps lots of people."

"Jeff?" I repeat, but she continues over me like she can't hear me.

"He writes letters of rec for, like, all the seniors, and he coaches people for their college auditions for free, and he got his dad to give the theater program all this extra money, even though his dad's a total bastard. He even spent all that extra time on *you*. Why would you want to do this to him?"

"I'm not, like, targeting him," I say. "I didn't make this up. You know I'm not making this up."

"Well, good luck convincing anybody of that," she says nastily. "If you say anything, I'll tell them just how full of shit you are."

With that, she turns away from me. "Brittany," I call, grabbing her wrist desperately. "Just—" Before I manage to say anything else, she throws out her other hand, generating sparks of electricity that shoot painfully through my bicep. "Ow!" I yelp, shaking out my arm. I can't believe she would attack me. If a teacher saw her, she would get at least suspended for that.

"Don't fucking touch me," she says, and the air above her hands lights up with flame. She swings at me, and I flinch away, grabbing her forearms to keep her flaming hands away from me.

I frantically reach for the crimson strands of magic in the fire, trying to put it out. She resists me. I know with a chilling certainty that I'm destined to lose this fight because she's older and just slightly stronger than me. Still, I push on the magical threads with as much mental force as I can muster. My head starts to hurt with the pressure, and I clench my jaw against the pain.

"What are you *doing*?"

Brittany and I both flip to face this voice, and there's Ana, running around the corner of the building.

"Whatever," Brittany says, pulling her arms out of my grasp. The flames go out. "Stop spreading lies about me." She points at me threateningly. With that, she hightails it into the cafeteria, leaving me to massage my tingling arm.

Ana's eyes flick back and forth between me and where Brittany disappeared to before finally settling on me. "Are you okay?" she says, coming over to me. She grabs both my hands, examining me for any injuries.

"I'm fine," I say.

She takes my face in her hands. "You sure?"

"Yeah."

Then she kisses me, and it's a tiny respite from the shit-storm of awfulness that I've been living in for the last twenty-four hours. "I'm glad I found you," she says when we break apart. Her face is creased with a concern that I find both adorable and touching. "I was looking for you to see if you wanted to go to potions club with me."

"I'm glad you found me too," I say, my insides still gooey from the kiss.

"Do you want to find a teacher? We can tell them what happened."

That brings me back down to earth quickly. "No, I don't think so," I say, sighing. "Can we talk about the thing now?"

She quirks an eyebrow. "The big mysterious thing?"

"Yeah, that."

We sit on the ground, our backs leaning against the outside wall of the cafeteria, and I muster up the courage to start my story. It's just as difficult to tell her as I imagined. I explain everything—all the strange interactions I had with Mr. B, what I saw yesterday, the conversation I just had with Brittany. I'm so nervous that I keep tripping over my words.

At first Ana's nodding along, and her brow is creased with sympathy. But when I get to the part about Mr. B offering to look at my application, all emotion drains from her face. I keep watching her for a reaction, but there is none. Once I finish, she just sits there, so still and silent that it's like she's turned to stone.

"Okay," I say tentatively. "That's everything. Any thoughts . . . or . . . ?"

"I don't know," she says, shaking her head slowly. "I think I need time to process this."

"Yeah, I get that," I say, even though I'm dying inside. What if she processes this and decides she hates me? What if she's so freaked out that she never wants to speak to me again?

"I think—maybe—I'm a little mad at you," she says, and my heart tumbles down a flight of stairs never to be seen again. "For doing all that shit to be his favorite. But I also feel like you're a victim, and I'm not really allowed to be mad at you." A flicker of frustration appears on her face. "Damn, he really knew how to press your buttons."

I swallow hard. "Do you want to break up with me?"

"No," she says vehemently. "It was so hard to date you in the first place, I'm not letting Mr. B and his bullshit ruin it."

"Oh, thank god," I say. Relief washes over me. "I was so nervous I thought I was going to die."

She grabs me by the hand and squeezes hard. "He's

such a fucking creep," she says. "I feel like I've been living in an alternate dimension. It was so obvious something was up when he ditched you and switched over to pay attention to me, but nobody thought that was strange." Her lip curls in disgust. "Everybody knows he has his favorites and that his favorites always win. Nobody cares about that. Everyone just accepts that's how it is."

"And then there's that rumor going around the cast that I, like, hooked up with him or something," I say, and a shiver goes up my spine.

"Yeah, and nobody thinks that's weird. They just think *I'm* weird when I tell them they shouldn't say that because it's not funny." She huffs and starts gently interlacing our fingers. "So what are you going to do about all of this?"

I stare at our hands, frowning. "I don't know. I was hoping I could convince Brittany to tell the school."

"Yeah, the chances of that don't seem good, considering that she just tried to fire-punch you," Ana says drolly. "Are you going to report them?"

I consider her question. That seems like the right thing to do now that I know Brittany won't come forward. Even though it will ruin everything for me. "I have to." I look at her pleadingly, wishing I could steal some of her incredible composure. "Right?"

"If you report them to the school, he'll deny it," she says. "It's not exactly great for Brittany either. She would probably lose the scholarship, and it would be a big scandal." Her dark eyes narrow. "He's popular too. Everyone loves him. And the school loves the money his family gives them."

"Are you saying I shouldn't report them?"

"No, I'm just trying to be realistic about this." Ana's expression goes thoughtful. "This thing with Brittany kind of reminds me of my cousin. She was in this really bad relationship with a wizard who had a much higher magic level than her."

"Really?"

"Everyone told her he was bad news and that she shouldn't keep sharing magic with him, but she didn't believe them," Ana says. "She basically turned into a zombie. Every time they had an argument, he could mess with her emotions to make her agree with him."

Oh god. How long has this been happening to Brittany? Maybe that's why she's so messed up about him. Some of my horror must show on my face, because Ana reaches over and wraps her arms around me, pulling me in for a hug.

I tuck my head into her shoulder, burrowing into her warmth. Her soft skin and sharp, muscular angles press against my body, filling me with a much-needed sense of comfort. We stay like that for a while, me listening to her breathing until I can almost pretend that everything is okay. "You're so bony," I say, adjusting my head on her shoulder.

"Excuse me," she says dryly. "I can take back this comforting hug anytime."

"No, that's okay." My voice is slightly muffled in her shoulder. "Ana?"

"Yeah?"

"Is it wrong that I still want to win the scholarship?"

She doesn't say anything right away. When her answer finally does come, her voice is sad. "I still want it too. So I guess we're both wrong."

Chapter 35

AFTER MY DISASTROUS ENCOUNTER WITH BRITTANY, I'M NOT sure what to do next. I feel even more lost and uncertain than I did before. At work that evening, Lex and I end up in the back brewing the weekend orders while Pilar helps customers out front.

"So Brittany's definitely not going to tell the school," Lex says, leaning across the worktable toward me.

"I don't think so," I say. "He's really got her brainwashed. She bit my head off right away."

Lex groans, long and loud. I focus on my Nap in a Bottle potion, tuning her out for a moment while I think of the intention I'm going to use to seal the potion. The mood I conjure is the way it felt when I was little to wake up from my afternoon nap, sunlight streaming onto my face. Warm and rested. Happy. I send that intention into the potion. Once the liquid settles, I let out a long breath. Imagining that was a stretch, considering that it is the exact opposite of my current state of being.

"I've been thinking . . ." Lex says, her lip curling. "I bet Mr. B's done this before." With more force than is truly necessary, she pops a cork into the top of the bottle of stomach-soothing potion she's just filled.

My heart stops. An image of all the picture frames on his desk flashes through my mind.

The other scholarship winners. They've mostly been women.

"Oh my god," I murmur numbly. "The other witches."

"I remember the one who won my freshman year. Lydia Sackett. She was one of his, like, special favorites." She pops a cork into another bottle emphatically. "She didn't even do drama, and she spent all this time in his classroom."

I gasp. "What if we talk to them? If Brittany won't admit anything happened, maybe one of them will."

"I can do it," Lex says immediately.

"Okay. Thanks," I say, feeling a renewed sense of hope.

Maybe there's still a way to solve this without it becoming a huge mess.

My phone vibrates in my pocket. I pull it out to silence it and see that I have notifications for a series of Wiz-Connect messages from Brittany.

I really need to talk to you.

Just the two of us.

Come to my house tomorrow.

Please.

"Oh my god," I say, slumping over the prep table.

"What's up?" Lex asks.

I stare at the messages from Brittany, letting out a long breath. If I have another chance to talk to her, I should take it. I might still be able to convince her to come forward.

"Brittany just messaged me. I think . . . I think I'm going to go meet her tomorrow," I say, hoping that saying it out loud will make me more confident about the idea. Instead I'm hit with a whole new wave of doubts. "What do you think she wants?"

Lex leans over my shoulder to read the texts. "I don't know," she says, shaking her head. "I can't tell the vibe from these messages."

"Yeah, me neither," I say, tapping out my response. I message Brittany to tell her that I can talk to her tomorrow. She replies right away, and we arrange to meet in the afternoon. It's the most civil interaction I've ever had with Brittany. I can only hope that tomorrow goes similarly.

I sleep deeply that night, which is entirely because of the sleep potion I dab under my nose before going to bed. When Lex picks me up to drive me to Brittany's house, she's on speakerphone with one of the previous scholarship winners, Sarah Newkirk. Sarah seems to be . . . talkative.

"We weren't that close, but I always wished we were!" Sarah says. "He was such a nice guy. He wrote one of my friends a recommendation letter that she *swears* was the reason she got into such good colleges. I mean, I wasn't one of his favorites. But whatever. Turned out okay for me!"

"Who do you—" Lex starts to say, but Sarah keeps talking over her. Lex shakes her head resignedly, and I get the sense that this has happened several times already. I click my seat belt in as quietly as I can.

"I still got to go to Willington, so it's all worth it. You know, there are four of us here right now. The Brockton Scholarship witches!"

"Who—" Lex tries again.

"I was thinking that we should all get together or something—" Sarah continues.

"Who were his favorites when you were in high school?" Lex says firmly.

"Who? Mr. B's?"

"Yeah."

"Oh, Lydia Sackett for sure. She didn't do drama, but her friends did, so she spent a bunch of time in his classroom. I think he liked her because she was such a suck-up."

Lex gives me a look and shakes her head. "I talked to her," she whispers in my ear. "Nothing there."

"And that freshman. What was her name? Brittany?" Sarah continues. "Her parents were getting a super-nasty divorce, and they would leave her at school for *hours*. I used to go home late after cheer practice, and she would still be there, just sitting in the parking lot. She would glare at you as you walked by, like you were being mean just by looking at her. Anyway, I think she started hanging out in his room after school when she got the lead in the spring musical, and then everyone knew she was *set* for the scholarship."

Lex thanks her for chatting with her, which is when I learn that she apparently told Sarah she was doing interviews about the Brockton Scholarship for some sort of T. K. Anderson alumni newsletter. They hang up soon after that. "Okay, I've got bad news, and I've got more bad news," she says, reversing the car out of the parking space.

"What other kind is there these days?" I say.

"So I've talked to most of the witches who've won the scholarship—"

"How?" I say incredulously. "It's barely been a day."

Lex flips her hair over her shoulder. "I'm very persistent and good at stalking people online." She sobers abruptly.

"So the bad news is that I found someone who was also groomed by Mr. B. Her name is Meredith. She graduated five years ago."

"Okay," I say, sighing. I have a dim memory of him mentioning her for some reason.

"The worse news is that she told the school about what happened years ago, and they didn't do anything about it."

I feel like I've been punched in the gut. "Shit."

"Yeah, I know." Lex slaps her turn signal violently. "Apparently the principal told her they were investigating for a while, but then it just never really went anywhere."

"Oh my god, it feels like this is all totally pointless," I say, putting my head in my hands.

"Maybe it'll be different if multiple people come forward?" Lex says, but it doesn't sound like she fully believes that. "We'll figure something out."

"Yeah," I say, even though I'm not sure we will. I glance down at my phone, where there's a text from Ana waiting on the screen. A little rush of warmth fills me as I read it.

ANA: let me know how it goes with Brittany 🖤

The drive to Brittany's house takes a while, so I have plenty of time to contemplate possible horror scenarios for this visit. Maybe Brittany will slip a potion in my drink and poison me while I'm there. Or maybe she'll try to fire-punch me again. Or maybe Mr. B will pop out of a closet in her house and transfigure me into stone.

I text my fears to Ana. Even though she's busy at her dance studio today, she responds to reassure me that several of those things are unrealistic. And what's not unrealistic, she's certain I can handle. I'm not so sure, but it's too late to turn back now. We're already pulling into Brittany's neighborhood.

Brittany lives in a beige house with impeccable landscaping at the end of a cul-de-sac. There are two cars in the driveway. I recognize one of them as being Brittany's.

"Do you want me to come in with you?" Lex says as her car settles down onto the driveway.

"I think I have to do this alone," I say, even though I wish she could be there. Brittany probably wouldn't be happy if I brought along a random extra person. "Thanks, though."

"Okay, I'll wait for you out here," she says.

After walking up the front path, I stand in front of the white front door and work up the courage to ring the doorbell. This feels like my last chance. If I can't convince Brittany to come forward with me, it's my word against Mr. B's. And I'm not sure the school will even care about what I have to say alone. Gathering all my courage, I summon a spark of electricity and send it skittering onto the metal circle by the door. The doorbell rings.

A few agonizing moments later, Brittany opens the

door. She's dressed nicely for being at home—a short jean skirt and a peach crop top—but there are dark circles under her eyes that her makeup doesn't completely hide. "Hey," she says, and then she stands there like she doesn't know what to do. "Um, come in."

Chapter 36

Brockton Scholar Brittany Cohen has been a member of the
T. K. Anderson Drama Club and the Thespian Honor Society
since her freshman year, and she has been seen starring in many
school plays and musicals since then. Her passion for service can
be seen in her work with the T. K. Anderson Hearts for Arts
program, where she provides free dance and music lessons to
underprivileged children in the local area. She has won the T. K.
Anderson Student Philanthropist Prize, and her performance in
the musical *RENT* won the Cappies Critics Award for Best Lead
Actress in a Musical.

—The Brockton Foundation website

I FOLLOW BRITTANY INSIDE, GLANCING SURREPTITIOUSLY
around me as I do so. The house is strangely empty. There's
almost no furniture in the front room—just one white couch
and a silver lamp in a wide, empty space. Brittany hurries
through the room and down a hallway.

I'm wondering why she's moving so quickly when a
tall white woman comes out of one of the doors in the hall.
Her blond hair is impeccably blown out, and she wears a
full face of elegant makeup. "Brittany, who—" She blinks

twice, smooths her blue blouse, and smiles at me without teeth. "I didn't realize you had a friend over, Brittany."

"Yeah," Brittany says, her face clouding. She stares at the floor and picks at the skin around her nails.

"I'm her mom." The woman looks me up and down. I can feel her judging me, and I'm not sure if she likes what she sees. "You can call me Ms. Shapiro."

"I'm Shay," I say. "I'm in the musical with Brittany."

She considers me again. I fidget uncomfortably under her scrutiny. "Are you one of the leads?"

"Um, yes."

She puts a hand on Brittany's lower back for a moment, and Brittany's posture goes ramrod straight. "Good for you," she says, smiling at me. Her teeth are unnaturally white. "It's so nice to meet a friend of Brittany's. She never brings people over."

I make a sound that's halfway between a polite laugh and a *mm-hmm*. Ms. Shapiro continues talking because I'm obviously not a necessary part of this conversation.

"I've always said that if Brittany just made a little bit more of an effort, she could be so popular," she says. She pats at Brittany's hair, fixing invisible flyaways. Brittany jerks her head out from under her mom's hand and continues to stare murderously at the floor.

"Mom," she says with quiet vehemence. "Stop."

I stand there silently and pretend I'm somewhere else.

Ms. Shapiro gives a long-suffering sigh. "Well, I'll

leave you girls to it. I'm off to the gym." She turns to go, giving me one last polite smile. "And, Shay," she says. "We don't wear shoes inside the house."

I slip off my sneakers, offering an apology to her retreating back. She doesn't respond.

God, no wonder Brittany's so uptight. Her mom has the maternal warmth of an icicle.

"Don't fucking feel sorry for me," Brittany spits at me.

I don't even deny that I was. I follow her silently into a room at the end of the hall, which turns out to be her bedroom.

Brittany's room is like a Target ad. Everything is white or peach, and all the furniture is so artfully placed that it feels like nobody lives in this room or uses the things in it. The only decorations that give a hint at who lives here are the series of framed show posters from our high school's musicals. They're all hung up in one corner of the room, like a decorator's afterthought.

Brittany sits in the chair in front of her desk. I ditch my sneakers by the door and lean against the edge of her bed. She's taken the one chair in the room, so that's my only option.

"I'm not going to, like, beat around the bush," Brittany says, crossing her legs. She starts picking at her cuticles in her lap. "I know I haven't exactly been nice to you," she says. "So you don't owe me anything. But I wanted to ask you not tell anybody what you saw."

I frown. So she's not denying what happened anymore. And she's being relatively polite. Unexpected. "Did he ask you to do this?"

"He's not talking to me." Her forehead wrinkles up. "I think he feels guilty."

"He should."

"I pushed myself on *him*. He doesn't even want me. He just thinks I'm . . ." She waves a hand vaguely in the air. "Some kid."

Because you *are* a kid. I almost say it, but I bite my tongue. If I want to convince her to come forward with me, I need her on my side. "But isn't it weird that you guys spent so much time alone together?" I say, trying to sound as kind as possible. "I mean, why were you in a car alone with him?"

"He was going to give me a ride home because my car was at the shop," she says. "That's it. It wasn't anything weird. He did that for you too."

"But—"

"I was hoping he saw me differently, because I'm eighteen now," she says over me. She leans forward in her chair, not looking at me. "It's sad, isn't it? Being in love with your teacher?"

I don't say anything. I can't believe that she's really in love with him, that he didn't manipulate her emotions.

"You probably think I'm pathetic," she says, flipping her blond hair over her shoulder. "Sure. Whatever. It's just . . .

he was always so nice to me. Like, he thought I was good the way I was." A wistful look crosses her face. "He was the one who encouraged me to try for the scholarship."

"I don't think you're pathetic," I say quietly, because my heart is breaking. She really believes what she's saying. Listening to her talk, I could almost be convinced that he really wanted the best for her. But I have my own experiences with him. He made me feel like I needed him to be successful, even when he was being awful. I can only imagine how brainwashed you would be after three years of him manipulating you.

"Have you ever shared magic with someone you loved?" she asks. "Someone not in your family?"

I'm so shocked by this turn in the conversation that I choke a little. "No. No."

"Don't be a prude. I'm trying to explain something here," she says, rolling her eyes. "Sharing magic—it's, like, the closest you can feel to someone, right? You get that. You're so strong and connected, and you can feel what they're feeling. And with him, all I could feel was this guilt. Like, he hated himself so much." She swallows hard. "I was so excited to be helpful. His asshole dad had cut off his access to his family's magic-sharing pool, so he was going through withdrawals. After everything he's done for me, this was a thing I could do for him."

Oh. That's why he's looked so exhausted lately.

"And I thought he wanted to do it with me," she

continues. "He just kept telling me how special I was, and it felt like he was really seeing me as me. You know? Not as just another one of his students. I know it's ridiculous, thinking he would like *me*."

I sit there, still and unmoving, as the words spill out of her. She's fixating on some point on the wall behind me, like I'm not really here. The more she talks, the more I feel sick to my stomach.

"I told him I liked him a few weeks ago, and he just looked so sad. God, it's pathetic. I know." She laughs, a short and joyless sound. "He told me that it wasn't true, that I didn't like him, but I just couldn't let it go. I acted like such a loser, I couldn't even wait to tell him until after I graduated." She spits the words out with utter disdain. "And then, when he was going to drive me home, I pushed myself on him. I knew he was upset that day because his dad had threatened to never let him access their magic-sharing pool again if he didn't do some work for the family business. But I didn't care, I just—I just wanted him.

"You're going to ruin his life," she says, her focus now on me. I almost flinch under the intensity of her stare. "He just wants to help students. He's such a friggin' bleed-ing heart, he can't leave people alone when he knows they need help. I was always so pissed off that he couldn't see that you were just pretending to be incompetent to get his attention."

I don't know whether to be flattered or insulted by this

bit of paranoia. I settle for a confusing mix of both, topped off with a healthy dose of horror. Meanwhile, my mind is still scrambling to process everything that was just thrown at me. I think she's saying that two days ago was the only time they've shared magic? If that's true, and I don't know how much I trust Brittany to be telling the truth, that means the control he had over her before this point wasn't even magical. That's scarier to me than if they had been sharing magic all along. Even if he has magical influence over Brittany now, who knows if she'll ever be free of him?

"But yeah," Brittany says, fidgeting with a section of her hair. "That's what I wanted to say, mostly. Don't fuck him over because of something that's my fault."

"It's not your fault." Frustration makes its way into my voice, despite my best efforts. "You know, he threatened me with the scholarship to do the show," I say finally. "He made it really clear that doing what he wanted would help me become the Brockton Scholar. I wanted the scholarship, so I dealt with it."

Brittany looks stricken. She shrinks in on herself, her breathing getting faster and shallower. She tries to interject, but I keep going.

"He pulled me out of rehearsal to work alone with him and said stuff that made me really uncomfortable. And when he found out I was a lesbian, he started calling me out in front of everyone and being mean to me. You saw how he acted. You were there."

"I wasn't—I—" She's looking everywhere but at me.

"After that, he made it clear that I had to accept his weird special attention to get the scholarship." I shake my head. "That's fucked up. He shouldn't be able to get away with the stuff he does. We're not the first people he's done this to either. He'll do it again. So please, at least consider saying something about what he did to you."

"He wouldn't do stuff like that," she says, looking hunted.

"He did."

My phone buzzes in my pocket, but I ignore it. I watch Brittany draw herself up, reapply the mean-girl facade that I've always seen on her. "If you say anything, I'll tell everyone about your potions addiction."

"Potions addiction?" Literally what is she talking about?

"I heard Ed talking to Mikey about how you totally OD'd on one of his potions once."

My heart thuds in my ears. I'm going to kill Ed. "I don't have a potions addiction, Brittany," I say. Why was I so stupid to use that energy potion? Of course it came back to bite me. "And why would I even buy one of Ed's potions? I'm a much better apothecary than he is. I could just make it myself."

She frowns. "Well, Ed said you did."

"Whatever. Tell everyone that I'm a potions addict," I say, even though every fiber of my being tells me I'm ruining my future. "You can't threaten me to stay quiet."

"Well, you know you definitely won't get the scholarship," she says, like it's some kind of trump card.

Listening to her speech earlier broke me a little. Is this what I was willing to do for the scholarship? Am I really okay with suffering through anything? Ignoring other people's pain just to get a leg up in the world?

I lace my fingers together, taking my time to muster all my courage before answering. My phone buzzes again. I force myself to make eye contact with Brittany.

"I'm sorry, but I'm going to report Mr. B," I say.

Hearing that come out of my mouth surprises me. It didn't feel completely real until that moment, but that's what I'm going to do. Even if the school doesn't believe me. Even if Brittany spreads rumors about my "potions addiction." Even if it ruins my chance at getting the scholarship and going to Willington.

"This image of him you have, it's not real. He's good at manipulating people. Even if he feels guilty for what happened with you, it doesn't mean he didn't do it."

With that, I stand up. "I'm going to tell the school on Monday. Let me know if you want to do it with me." I take a deep breath. "This is the right thing to do. But, um, I get that this is probably really shitty for you." Brittany stands as well. She looks like someone just kicked her. I shove my feet into my sneakers and walk out of the room.

I'm going to make things hard for her if I come

forward. But I have to. Otherwise, Mr. B will be free to keep manipulating his students.

My phone buzzes again. This time, I check it. I have several missed texts from Lex. I freeze, only a few feet down the hall from Brittany's room, and stare at my screen in horror. My eyes lock on the first text she sent me.

LEX: MAYDAY!!! MR B IS HERE

Chapter 37

This year, the Brockton Scholarship celebrates ten years of helping young witches and wizards achieve new heights.

—The Brockton Foundation website

"YOU SAID HE WASN'T TALKING TO YOU." I TAP OUT A FEW choice words encapsulating my complete internal meltdown to Lex.

"What?" Brittany says, joining me in the hallway.

"Mr. B." I hurry toward the living room, trying to figure out my best move. I wish I had one of those Near Invisible potions. Who cares if they're illegal now? Desperate times call for desperate measures. "He's here."

"He's here?" Brittany lights up and follows after me. I

have a sudden overwhelming urge to yell at her, to tell her to snap out of it. He's a creepy, abusive guy, and there's no reason she should be so obsessed with him. But that probably wouldn't be productive.

I get to the front door with no plan. Lex has sent me more texts.

LEX: he's on the other side of the street, just standing there by his car. should I get out and deal with him???

        SHAY: no don't, I'll deal with him I guess

"I told him you were coming over," Brittany says. She smooths her hair, staring at the front door like she's in a trance. "I thought he would be happy that I was going to try to convince you not to tell. He didn't respond to my message, but I guess he got it."

"Brittany," I say despairingly, rubbing my hands over my face. She looks so genuinely happy. It occurs to me that the only times I've ever seen her happy have been around him. I take her in for a moment—this angry, lonely witch in her strangely empty house with her cold mom—and I'm flooded with rage. My jaw tightens. Mr. B knew she was lonely. He knew she was vulnerable, and he used that to make her dependent on him. He thought I was vulnerable too.

But I'm not. And I won't let him mess with us.

I yank open the door and stride out onto the front side-walk. I am completely and utterly plan-less, and for once I don't give a damn. Brittany follows me like a lost puppy.

There's something so pathetic about seeing him there—just a sad adult man staring at us from across the street. He leans against the front hood of his shiny black sedan, which he's parked on the side of the road. His beard stubble looks more scraggly than usual, and his blue button-down is hopelessly wrinkled. But there's also a healthy glow to his skin that hasn't been there in weeks. I'm guessing it's from sharing magic with Brittany. He still looks tired, but it's nowhere near as exhausted as he's looked recently. I glance at Brittany, who has frozen at the sight of him, and a half-formed idea of how I can protect her crosses my mind.

As I cross the street and approach him, he flashes me that warm Mr. B grin—the one that lets him get away with making mean jokes and touching students too much and being racist.

"Shay—" He pushes himself off the hood of his car, taking a step out into the street to meet me.

"Shut up," I say coldly. I cross my arms and square my shoulders, ready for war. "I'm going to report you. I don't know what kind of twisted satisfaction you get out of manipulating teenage witches, but it's fucked up." I advance toward him. He takes a half step back, off the road and onto the grass. I'm riding high on my burst of rage. He looks about two inches tall to me right now. "Just stay away from Brittany."

"Shay, be reasonable. I came all the way here—just talk to me for a minute." He follows me as I go back across the street. "Just wait."

"You came," Brittany says wonderingly. She's made her way from the front door to the edge of her driveway. He doesn't pay her any attention, just marches past her to follow me.

"I made a mistake. I understand that. But they'll take away Brittany's scholarship for this. That's her future," he says. "I should have waited until she wasn't my student anymore. Trust me, I know. I—I don't know what's wrong with me. I won't make this mistake again!"

This stops me in my tracks. "You won't make this mistake again?" I repeat incredulously, and turn to face him. He comes to a halt and stares at me with a beleaguered expression. "You were already doing the same thing to me!"

His face screws up in confusion. "What? No." He glances behind him at Brittany. "Did Brittany say that? I knew she was jealous of you, but—"

"You pulled me out of rehearsal to be alone with you. More than once. You used the scholarship to make me do things I didn't want to do. You were always touching me!" He stands stock-still, baffled.

"Stop *lying*," Brittany snaps. She steps forward, anger

contorting her features. Mr. B puts a hand on her shoulder for a moment, and the angry lines in her face smooth out. I sense the tiniest magical shift nearby, so small that I could almost think I was imagining it.

"What's wrong with you?" I say, pointing an accusatory finger between Mr. B and Brittany. "You're literally manipulating her magic right in front of me!"

He frowns. "That was . . . unintentional. I'm sorry, Brittany."

"It's okay," she says, looking up at him with wide-eyed trust. "I was totally freaking out."

"No. No, that's not right!" I sputter. "He can't just do that to you!"

"I won't do it again," he says, dripping with sincerity. He turns his attention back to me. "I just wanted to mentor you, Shay," Mr. B says gently. "I'm sorry it turned out like this."

"You don't know anything about me," I snap. "You met me, and you assumed I was some poor Latina charity case. I'm not even Latina!"

"You're . . . not?" he says, his brow furrowing.

"No," I say stonily. "I don't know why you're obsessed with students you think you can, like, save or something. But you're not helping us. And you're sure as hell not mentoring us."

With that, I turn to go back to Lex's car. But before I

can move away, he gestures sharply with his hand, and I sense a major shift in the magic around me. A tingling sensation runs down my body, starting at my shoulders and ending at my ankles. When I try to move my legs, they don't respond. I'm left standing there, immobile, with muscles that feel strangely relaxed.

"You're overreacting," Mr. B says to me, getting even closer to where I stand. "I'm sorry to do this to you, but I can't let you sabotage yourself like this. We can talk about this reasonably."

What is this absurd upper-level magic he's just pulled on me? The closest thing I can think of that would do this is a Partial Paralysis potion. But causing that effect yourself manually? That's truly some higher-level stuff I don't understand.

Brittany comes up behind him and tugs at his shoulder, but he ignores her.

"What are you doing?" Brittany says, staring at him with horror. "You could really hurt her."

A bone-deep fear fills me as I stare at this powerful wizard in front of me. He has this friendly, apologetic expression on his face, like he's sorry that I brought this upon myself. How disconnected from reality is he? He's done something deeply dangerous and frightening to me, and he seems to think that it's something he can play off.

Brittany grasps at his arm, babbling wildly. "Come on,

you don't have to do this. Just—just undo whatever you did. I'm sorry I wasn't more helpful, but—I tried to tell her it wasn't your fault. Really, I really tried. Let me try again!"

He turns to her for a moment, and I sense a third magical shift. Her expression softens into calm. She steps away from him, smiling serenely. I try to clench my fist, wishing I could slam it into his face, but my hand won't move.

My eyes flick to the car, to the back of Lex's head in the driver's seat. From her perspective, it probably looks like nothing is wrong. I'm just standing here talking to Mr. B. Should I have asked Lex to help me handle this?

"You've already won the scholarship, Shay," Mr. B says.

Everything falls away. Brittany, Lex, the slight tingling in my muscles—it's all gone. The only things left are the eerie blue depths of Mr. B's eyes and the roaring in my ears.

"The committee met earlier today. It's yours," he says quietly.

"What?" I manage to choke out.

"I always knew you were special. When I first met you, you were so uncertain, closed off. I knew you would thrive with someone giving you the attention you deserved. That's all it was about—getting you what you deserved. Nothing inappropriate."

His words sound so good. He's painting a version of the world I want to believe in—one where the scholarship is mine, where I get it because I deserve it. It's not hard for me to curve my lips into a smile, to look him in the eye longingly. "Yeah?"

"Yeah," he murmurs, drawing closer to me. "Willington is going to change your life."

I nod, and he continues, emboldened. "It's going to be so much easier for your family if you get into college right away," he says. "But if you make a big fuss about this, that will all go away."

"I know," I say, and I feel the pain of that loss in my soul, jagged and raw.

"So what are you going to do?" he asks. When I don't reply immediately, he leans down, filling my field of vision so all I can focus on is his face. "Are you going to ruin everything for yourself? For Brittany?"

I look down at my feet, then back at him. "No." He keeps looking at me, waiting for more. "No, I won't tell anyone."

His smile is like the sun. "You're making the right choice," he says, stepping away from me. Magic ripples around me. The muscles in my arms and legs all clench, and I'm hit with an intense sensation of pins and needles. Then I can move again, thank god.

"Yeah," I say. I rub my arms, trying to massage away the prickling. "Um, thank you? For helping me?"

"You're welcome," he says, still giving me that radiant smile. "I just made sure you got what you deserved. Thank *you* for helping me. I know I've made some mistakes, but this is a fresh start for all of us."

I nod. Then I stumble toward Lex's car, pull open the car door, and climb in. Lex gives me a concerned look. "What happened?" she asks. "That took a while. I know you said I shouldn't come out, but I was starting—"

"Just go," I say. "Please, please drive."

She blinks at me. "Okay."

As we drive away, I see Mr. B lift a hand to wave at me. Brittany stares at the car, still wearing a tranquil smile as she watches us go.

I don't say anything as we drive, taking the time to compose my thoughts. My heart is still beating a mile a minute, and there's a fog of fear hanging around me that I can't quite dispel. Lex parks in the lot of a nearby Starbucks, then gives me an expectant look. "Well? What happened?"

"Wait a second." I FaceTime in Ana, who's finished with her dance class. Her tiny illusion appears above the phone screen. She has her hair up in a slick bun, and she's still wearing the sweats she likes to warm up in.

With very little preamble, I start spilling the beans on the absurdity of the last hour. Ana closes her eyes when I reach the part about Mr. B telling me that I won the scholarship. I wish, fervently, that she was actually here.

"So you're just fine with that?" Lex interrupts me, bouncing up in her seat. "You're just going to take the scholarship? After everything?"

"No," I say, still watching Ana. "I lied."

"Oh," Lex says, relaxing. "And he believed you?"

"He's the one who taught me how to act," I say grimly. "It's his fault that he fell for it."

It's not that the idea of not getting the scholarship doesn't hurt. It does. But I can't watch Mr. B continue to manipulate the witches he teaches like he has some right to do that to us.

Ana finally opens her eyes, and she looks dejected. "Are you okay, Ana?" I ask.

"I'm upset," she says shortly. "But it is what it is."

"Okay," I say. "I'm really sorry."

"Not your fault."

There's a beat of silence. Then Lex leans back in her seat, blowing out a long breath. "Wow, this is *wild*. So what's the plan?" Lex asks, propping her elbow up on the center console as she leans in toward me.

I look between Lex and Ana, who are both staring at me expectantly. "I won't tell people about Brittany. It'll make things hard for her, and she doesn't deserve that."

Ana raises her thick eyebrows. "So you're not coming forward?"

"No, I will." It takes effort to sound steady as I say this. I'm terrified out of my mind, but I think I'm making the right choice. "I'll just come forward about all the things Mr. B has done to me. And maybe we can get them to pay attention to what happened to Meredith, that other girl he did this to, if we show that he's trying to do the same thing again."

"Will that be enough?" Ana says.

I shrug helplessly. "Maybe not."

"You sure you want to protect Brittany?" Lex asks. "She's horrible."

"I think she's just kind of . . . sad," I say.

"Okay," Lex says doubtfully. "You're a way better person than me. Seriously. I would totally kick her to the curb to take down that creep."

"I think . . . protecting her is the right thing to do," Ana says.

My heart warms. Knowing that Ana supports me makes me more certain that I'm making the right choice. "Okay, I have a plan for how I want to do this," I say, turning to look at the illusion of Ana. "But I don't know if you want to be involved. I won't get the scholarship after this, but I don't want to ruin anything for you."

She bites her lower lip. "I've been thinking," she says hesitantly. "If it's this horrible behind the scenes, this isn't the competition I signed up for."

"You're sure?" I say.

"Yeah," she says, though her eyebrows are knitted together in a look of faint distress. "I'll help you. Whatever you need, I'm yours."

The way those words make me melt is disgusting,

honestly. There's some romance-novel-level swooning going on inside me right now.

"And I'm obviously in," Lex adds.

"Thank you," I say, smiling at Lex and Ana. These witches are amazing. "Seriously. I couldn't have figured out any of this without you two."

Lex practically launches herself across the car at me. "I know you don't like hugs, but this one isn't optional," she says, wrapping her arms around my shoulders. I laugh and accept the affection. She's an exception to my no-hugs policy.

"Also, hi," Lex says, waving over my shoulder at Ana. "It's nice to meet you for real. I'm so glad you two are together now, because I thought Shay was going to actually *die*—like, go to the grave—before she figured out that you two were meant to be together."

Ana snorts. "Me too."

"Please no," I mutter. "Please don't make fun of me. I'm right here."

Lex pulls out of our hug and gives me a catlike smile. "We know."

"Anyway!" I say, because I don't know if I'll survive being thoroughly dragged by both of them combined. My fragile little psyche might just abandon me forever in search of greener pastures. "So I was thinking that on the night of the scholarship ceremony . . ."

Chapter 38

"He told me that doing the musical would be *really good* for my scholarship application," Johnson recalls. "It was obvious what he meant, but I was convinced he was just trying to be nice."

Thus began several weeks of escalating harassment from the drama teacher. Mr. Brockton is a favorite at T. K. Anderson Magical Magnet School. His connections to the Brockton Scholarship, however, allow him unchecked power over students seeking the scholarship.

—Selection from the article "Jeffrey Brockton Grooms Scholarship Candidates," written by Alexandra Evans, Shayna Johnson, and Ana Álvarez

ON THE SATURDAY OF THE SCHOLARSHIP CEREMONY, I WAIT for my parents at the kitchen table. My chest is tingling with nerves. It's time to tell them. It was probably time to tell them long before now, but I can't avoid it anymore.

I spent the whole week dodging my parents, putting off the inevitable. It wasn't hard to avoid them, since I had so much rehearsal. Torturous, never-ending rehearsal. Everywhere I turned, Mr. B was there. If I thought he had favored me before, that was nothing compared to this. His attention was like a spotlight I couldn't escape. He praised me constantly and shot sly grins my way, as if we were both in on some big secret. Even though my body buzzed with nerves every time he approached me, I did my best to fake a smile. Meanwhile, Brittany lingered in the background like a ghost, never quite making eye contact with me.

Restless, I straighten the piece of paper I have in front of me and push one of the midair plants farther away from my head. Then I hear Mom's heavy step coming down the hall. "You're ready already?" she says, clocking my all-black performance outfit as she enters the kitchen. She's still wearing the jeans and blouse she's been in all day.

"Yeah," I say, laughing awkwardly. She tugs at the magic in the stove, turning on one of the burners, and grabs a pot from the cabinet. God, facing Mr. B wasn't as scary as talking to my own mother. "I have something I need to tell you about."

She mm-hmms at me, busy filling the pot with water from the sink.

"Um . . . here." I stand and thrust my paper at her. There are perks to the fact that, as a part of our plan for tonight, Lex, Ana, and I wrote a summary of more or less everything that's happened. She gives me a puzzled look, then puts down the pot and takes it.

Her face goes ashen after scanning a few lines. "Mark!" she bellows. "Get in here!"

Dad appears in the kitchen moments later, half-dressed in his khaki work pants and a nice blue button-down. "What?"

"Read this," Mom says, her expression murderous. She shakes the paper so it makes a loud crinkling sound. He comes up beside her and reads over her shoulder. His jaw clenches, and his eyes flick questioningly between me and the paper.

I sit at the table and watch them read it in silence, visibly charting their blood pressure rising as they get further in. Eventually, I can't take the silence any longer. "Don't be mad," I say timidly.

"Baby, why didn't you tell us?" Mom asks, dropping the paper to her side. Her hazel eyes are filled with hurt.

I stare down at my hands in my lap. "I just—I didn't know what to do," I choke out. "I thought you would freak out, and I wanted to figure it out on my own."

Dad comes to sit beside me, pulling his chair closer to where I sit. "Shay, you take too much on yourself," he says, placing a pale hand on mine. "It's fine to be independent, but we're your parents. You should come to us."

"I know," I say, giving his hand a squeeze. He's right. I could have relied on them for help and advice. But I was afraid of so many things—of not getting the scholarship, of letting them down, of Mom trying to help in a way that would backfire on me. Looking at the hurt on their faces now, I regret hiding everything from them for so long.

"I know we ask a lot of you." His mouth twists wryly. "We probably put too much pressure on you sometimes. But our family is a team. Let us help you."

Mom is studying the article again. "'Mr. Brockton frequently used the scholarship as a tactic to manipulate Johnson, even going so far as to offer to secretly look at her application ahead of time,'" she reads, her lip curling in disgust. I cringe.

"I tried to say no, but he didn't really listen, and then . . . I should have made it clear that I didn't want his special attention, but . . ." I trail off shamefacedly.

Mom comes to sit at the kitchen table on my other side. "Shayna Maree, you look at me," she says. I meet her eyes nervously. She's either going to drop some knowledge or rip me a new one. Maybe both. "Don't you *ever* let anybody make you feel bad for something they did to you." She jabs a finger at me for emphasis. "This man is scum. None of what happened is your fault, so don't let me catch you saying any nonsense like that again."

I swallow the lump that's suddenly appeared in my throat and nod. Dad squeezes my hand comfortingly. "There's one more thing that's not in this," I say. I take a deep breath, and then I tell them about Brittany. Mom and Dad listen to me silently, the lines on their faces growing slowly deeper.

Mom gets to her feet once I'm done. "I'm proud of you, Shay," she says. She shakes her head. "Those poor witches."

"Don't tell anybody about Brittany," I say, looking between her and Dad.

Dad runs a hand over his bald head, his expression troubled. "We need to tell somebody."

"But not the school," Mom says. Dad looks like he's about to argue, but she silences him with a look. "So do you want me to make a fuss at this scholarship shindig tonight? Because I will do that," she says, turning her attention back to me.

"I actually was planning to do it myself," I say, and I explain, briefly, what I have in mind for that evening.

"I'm not sure that's a good idea," Dad says once I've finished.

"It's tamer than what I was thinking," Mom says.

"Denise. What?" Dad gives her a quelling look.

Mom shrugs. "I'm just saying. Look, I know I have a tendency to go in hot to things when it comes to Shay"—Dad scoffs, correctly, at that colossal understatement—"but I'm learning. And I know she can do things by herself. She doesn't have to." She stares at me pointedly. "But she can. So I say we let her go ahead with how she wants to do this. We'll be there the whole time."

A few moments pass, and then he nods reluctantly. "Fine. I just hope this Brockton man doesn't come and talk to me beforehand." He cracks his knuckles. "I'm a patient man, but not that patient."

And with that mildly concerning threat in the air, he

nods and heads off to finish getting dressed. Mom pulls me into a long hug, then goes back to making dinner.

Soon after dinner I'm bundled into the car, and Dad drives us to school, where the scholarship ceremony is being held. In the front seat, Mom keeps shaking her head and muttering vaguely threatening sounding things to herself. I text Ana next to my leg.

> **SHAY: my parents are PISSED**
> **SHAY: I'm worried for the people**
> **who have to deal with them.**
> ANA: yikes. so, not a good time to
> introduce myself?
> **SHAY: lol probably subpar timing**

Once we arrive at the school, Mom sweeps into the auditorium with me and Dad trailing along behind her. There's something odd about coming to the auditorium for a performance instead of a rehearsal. The energy in the space feels completely different. Teachers, family members, and a few reporters mill around the lobby. There are student ushers working the event, and they hand us programs as we approach the main doors. On my way inside, I catch sight of a man who looks exactly like Mr. B but old and grumpy. I avert my eyes quickly and move on, because this day is stressful enough already without being noticed by Mr. B's malevolent dad.

As my parents pick their seats, Lex appears beside me in the aisle. "It's all set," she says in my ear. She passes me two empty potion vials, which I tuck away in the bag I've brought with me. "Ana and I managed to get them all up before anybody else got here."

"Great," I whisper back.

After Mom and Dad sit, I head backstage, which is total chaos since the jazz band and dance team are performing as well. There are dancers and musicians and theater kids warming up and doing their preshow rituals. When I enter the dressing room, Brittany completely avoids my gaze, as she has all week. I sit on the floor next to Ana and try to keep my nerves from showing on my face. Ana pulls out her phone, taps away for a few seconds, and then gestures subtly at my phone in my lap. I flip it over and read the text she's sent me.

ANA: on a scale from 1–10, how much are you freaking out right now?

SHAY: 100000000

ANA: thought so. I know you've got this though.

I nod, trying to internalize the message, and place my hand on the floor in between us. Slyly, she places her hand next to mine so our pinkies touch. We stay like that for a while, just sitting in silence while the chaos of the dressing room swirls around us.

Mr. B calls the whole cast out to huddle in the backstage hallway, evicting several sax players who had colonized the area. He gives us a pep talk, which isn't as much peppy as it is scarily on edge.

"I want you to know how proud I am of all of you. I know we had a rough last rehearsal on Thursday." That's a vast understatement. He gave us a terrifying speech that heavily featured the phrase *you're better than this* after our last run. "But I know you're all going to rise above that here. You know what they say about a bad dress rehearsal." The smile that appears on his face is the least convincing one I've ever seen him wear. "I want you guys to put it all out there on the stage tonight. Make me look good, okay?" He laughs as if this last part is a joke, but it is clearly not a joke at all. I think of his dad in the audience while everyone else nods at him like they've been hypnotized.

When the group huddle breaks up, he pulls me aside. "This is your night, okay?" he says quietly, angling his body away from the nearest group of people.

"Yeah," I say. "Thanks for all your help. I wouldn't be here without you." I almost choke on the words because I'm not *that* good of a liar.

"Wasn't easy, but we got here!" He laughs like we're sharing a private joke.

I laugh and extricate myself from him as quickly as possible.

The ceremony feels excruciatingly long. There are

presentations highlighting each of the scholarship nominees, which alternate with performances from the student groups here. The one about me is last. While the principal talks onstage about my "many artistic achievements" and "notable passion for potionworking," Ed stands next to me in the wings and whisper-chants my name. He manages to rope several people, including Mikey and Ana, in on the chanting. It only stops when Mr. B shoots the entire group a death glare.

Our performance goes right after the presentation finishes. After taking our Light as a Feather potions, we walk onstage in darkness. I try not to hyperventilate. The music starts and the lights flash on, blindingly bright in our eyes.

"It's the Bronxtown Broom Race, baby!" Ed yells, pumping his fist in the air.

The whole cast cheers, and I launch myself toward the broom props in the air above us. Mikey lands on the broom ahead of me, then holds his hand out to catch me. I grab hold, and the two of us execute a spin around the broomstick shaft. Then I boost him up in the air, where he hangs dramatically for a moment before the broomstick prop is pulled upward to meet him.

As we perform the song, I'm so nervous that I'm barely aware of my body moving the entire time. Muscle memory does most of the work for me. The song flashes by like some sort of musical theater fever dream, and it's over almost before I register that it's begun.

Once the music finishes, the other cast members run offstage, leaving me alone at the center. The lights shift from the kaleidoscopic oranges and purples of "Bronxtown Broom Race" to a calm blue. The music for "My Soft Place to Land" starts immediately, cuing me to sing.

"'I remember when that was Nino's bodega, where he sold potions and café con leche,'" I start. "'And he gave you free candy if you got good grades. Those were the days.'"

I make it through most of the verse before I see Ana run up to Mr. B in the wings. Out of the corner of my eye, I watch her gesture frantically, pointing behind her at something. He gives me a glance, then reluctantly jogs off in the direction she was pointing. I wait another few seconds, then stop singing.

"Hi, everyone!" I say. The music continues to play underneath me talking. I'm suddenly very aware of the horrible clamminess of my hands. "Um, this is a little break from our planned performance. I have something really important I want to share, but before that . . . This is me, taking a truth potion." I pull a bottle out of the pouch I've attached around my thigh. After waving it in the air so everyone can see it, I down half the liquid inside. "I'm going to keep the other half in case anybody wants to test whether or not it's real. If anybody is wondering, truth potions don't work exactly how you see it on TV. I'm not going to be literally unable to lie. But this potion will really make it obvious if I do lie. Okay? I would sweat a lot, shake, stuff like that."

The audience stares at me, looking generally confused. Some quiet murmuring has started throughout the auditorium.

Finally, I feel a prickly sensation on my tongue, letting me know that the potion has worked. I take a deep breath and start talking again.

"My name is Shay. You might recognize me as one of the nominees for the scholarship." My voice shakes a little as I say this. Lex gives me a thumbs-up and an encouraging smile from where she sits in the front row. "I auditioned for this musical because Mr. B told me to. I'm usually a choir kid, so I don't really do musicals. I'm sure lots of you know who Mr. B is—he's the drama teacher here, and he runs the scholarship selection committee."

I look out at the sea of people in front of me. No turning back now. "The thing you might not know about Mr. B," I say, "is that he uses the scholarship to manipulate students into having romantic relationships with him."

And then, working in concert, Lex and I both reach for the threads of magic in the air around us and chill the auditorium. Just for a few moments—we can't sustain that effect for longer—the room is noticeably colder. That change in temperature triggers the Unseen Objects potion I brewed earlier this week to stop working.

In an instant, all the copies of the article we wrote,

which Lex and Ana doused in the potion and taped to the backs of the auditorium seats, appear.

Chaos breaks out in the auditorium. People start talking loudly, and I see them grabbing the papers off the backs of the seats.

"Someone get her off the stage!" a man shouts from somewhere off in the darkness. "Are we supposed to sit here and listen to these—these obvious lies?"

"Let her speak!" Mom shouts back.

I continue speaking into the pandemonium, for anybody who's listening. "You'll find the details of what I'm talking about in that article," I say. "The most important thing, though, is that this happened to a witch here at T. K. Anderson years ago, and the school didn't do anything about it when she reported it. Trust me, I wouldn't be doing this publicly if I didn't think that the school would ignore it otherwise."

The lights go out onstage.

"Guess we're having some technical difficulties." My mic has gone off too. I reach into my thigh pouch and retrieve a big pinch of Lightflash powder, which I throw into the air. It forms a cloud above my head and emits a soft light.

Out of the corner of my eye, I see Mr. B appear in the wings off stage right. His brow knits together as he looks at me. Everything slows down for a moment as I stare at his face, lit by my Lightflash powder. I watch as the first inkling of fear creeps into his expression. Then I turn back to the audience.

"Witches should be able to trust that people in power have their backs. It's ridiculous how much stuff wizards can get away with when everyone just accepts that 'that's how things are,'" I say, projecting my voice as much as I can. That guy is still yelling in the corner, and I can see the principal pushing through my castmates in the wings to get onstage with me. "That's all I have to say, really," I say. My gaze flicks back to Mr. B, whose face has sagged into an expression of horror. I deliver the next sentence right to him. "Oh, and I'm bowing out of the competition for the scholarship."

I give a thumbs-up to the crowd—not sure why I do that—and walk off the stage toward my parents.

Twenty minutes later, I'm sitting alone by the school secretary's desk in the reception area. My parents are in the next room over in the principal's office. I can still hear Mom perfectly well through the closed door. "This is a disaster," she says, her voice clear and strong.

I almost feel bad for our principal, who is a mousy man with an unfortunate comb-over. I'm sure he didn't expect to be taken to task by my mother when he showed up for the scholarship ceremony this evening. I can't hear his responses. His voice sounds mumbly through the door, but I can imagine what he's saying based on Mom's responses.

"Look into it?" Mom snaps. "You don't need to look into it. My daughter already did that for you because she had no reason to believe that this school wasn't going to cover their own ass instead of protecting their students. So you are going to remove this man from the campus immediately. I will wait."

A knock comes from behind my left shoulder. When I turn, I see Ana staring at me through the office window. She locks eyes with me for a few long seconds. My heart flutters. It's my girlfriend. In the flesh. She tilts her head to the side, indicating that I should come out to her. I glance at the door to the principal's office, then head into the hall.

Ana's leaning against the wall beside the office door. "Hey."

"Hey," I say.

"You did it," she says, giving me a languid smile.

I go a little weak in the knees, even though I should maybe be used to her facial expressions at this point. "Couldn't have done it without you," I say. "How'd you distract Mr. B?"

"I told him that Brittany was having a crisis."

"Good lie," I say, nodding.

"Wasn't a lie. I iced her into the dressing room with that Enduring Ice potion I took from your collection on Friday." She shrugs. "Two birds, one stone."

"You iced her, like . . ." I say hesitantly, hoping that Ana didn't commit homicide by ice.

She snorts. "Like I iced the dressing room door shut. I didn't kill her, Shay."

"Okay. Good," I say, and I give her a thumbs-up, because I'm apparently on a roll with the strangely timed thumbs-ups today.

She huffs out a laugh and grabs me by my other hand, pulling me closer to her. "I'm going to kiss you now," she says. "Stop giving me a thumbs-up."

"Sorry, I don't know why I'm doing that," I say as her nose brushes mine. And then we're kissing. It tastes like victory.

"Have I told you that you're a good kisser?" I say breathlessly when we break apart.

"You don't need to tell me," she says, grinning at me mischievously. I shove her, because her ego is dangerously large. She breaks away from me, laughing, and peers through the office window. "How's it going in there?"

"I think my mom's ripping him apart," I say cheerfully.

"Good."

I join her in peering through the office window. "I have a good feeling about this," I say, taking her hand. Her palm feels cold on mine. I smile at her, hopeful.

"Me too."

⋄ Epilogue

THE STAGE LIGHTS ARE BLINDING IN MY EYES AS I FACE THE audience. "'On the street where I live, there are people that I love,'" I sing, walking across the stage with Mikey. Out of the corner of my eye, I can see the rest of the cast behind me dancing and singing their harmonies for all they're worth. "'They wave hello as we pass on by.'"

"Fifteen percent off brooms today!" the guy playing my character's dad shouts from stage right.

"'Way uptown, where the people fly,'" Mikey and I sing together. "'You'll find—'"

"'Me,'" Ana sings, stepping toward the front of the stage.

"'Me,'" Ed sings, joining her.

I look over at Mikey at my side. "'Me.'"

Mikey grabs my hand. "'Me.'"

The whole cast joins together for the last lyric, all of us grinning triumphantly. "'On my street!'"

The lights go out. And with that, our opening-night performance is done. The lights come back up, the curtain call music plays, and the audience claps wildly. As we line up to bow, I find my parents and Lex in the front row. They're all absolutely losing it.

Ms. Mooney, dressed up in a blue jumpsuit, comes out onstage with us. "Thank you so much for being here tonight!" she says, and the applause slowly dies down. "This has been a difficult time for our students, as I'm sure you are all aware."

Understatement of the century, Ms. Mooney.

"Even though I didn't have the privilege of working with these students throughout the whole rehearsal process, I am so proud of the show they've put together. They've pushed through all the challenges in their way to make something really impressive." She beams at all of us as she says this. We smile back at her, our stage makeup nearly dripping off our faces after two hours of singing and dancing under hot stage lights.

After everything went down, the school somehow convinced Ms. Mooney to step in as our director, as if she didn't already have enough to do with running the choir. Mr. B never came back to school after the scholarship ceremony. But T. K. Anderson didn't fire him. Instead, he was placed on "administrative leave." Apparently this means he'll be paid not to come to work while they investigate. Which seems like bullshit to me, but whatever. At least he's not here anymore.

"Let's get one last round of applause for the cast!" Ms. Mooney says, and the auditorium erupts in cheers. Then we all run offstage, riding high on the audience's applause.

The cast goes to IHOP after the show, which is some kind of T. K. Anderson theater tradition. We fill up a whole section of the restaurant, and people haphazardly put in orders. Members of our cast sing parts of the show at top volume, dart back and forth between tables, and generally become our waitress's biggest nightmare.

"So we fucking killed it tonight," Ed announces to our table. Ana, Ed, Mikey, and I are all at a booth in the corner.

Mikey nods seriously and continues assembling his floating tower of half-and-half containers. He transfigures his straw wrapper into a tiny flag, which he stabs into one of the top containers.

"Yeah, it was good," Ana says. "It almost sounded like our cast spoke Spanish."

Ed laughs, and then the two of them switch into Spanish. Based on the number of times I hear them quoting lines from the show in slow, exaggerated American accents, I would guess they're still making fun of our castmates' mangling of the Spanish language.

My gaze lands on Brittany, who sits quietly with a group of other senior girls. A sigh escapes me. I'm worried about her. Mom went to meet with Brittany's mom a few weeks ago, because she and Dad agreed it was wrong to keep that kind of secret from someone's parents. Mom came back to the apartment humming with disappointment. When I asked her how it went, she sucked her teeth and looked up to the heavens for patience.

"That woman . . ." she said. "Mm." Then she disappeared into her bedroom and never spoke another word about it.

Should I reach out to Brittany again now that things have settled down? I've made it through all the interviews with the principal and the school counselor without mentioning her, so it must be clear to her that I'm not telling anyone.

Ana flicks me on the wrist. I yelp and swat at her hand. "What the—"

"I know that face," she says, bumping her shoulder against mine. "You're overthinking something."

"Okay, maybe I was," I say, laughing. "But don't call me out like that."

"So did you see the statement the Brockton Foundation released?" Mikey says, and for a moment I'm amazed at this entire normal sentence he's spoken in my presence. Thank god his misplaced anxiety around me is gone.

"Oh yeah," Ana says. "They're doing everything possible to distance themselves from Mr. B. Apparently they'll be bringing the scholarship back next year after some kind of review."

"They should just give you the scholarship," Ed says to me. "Reparations, man."

"Yeah, it's bullshit that they canceled the whole thing for this year," Mikey adds.

"It doesn't matter. I don't want their money," I say.

Ana nudges me with her foot. "You're getting so good at acting. I almost believed that."

I preen a little. "Thank you."

I wasn't completely pretending, though. Yes, I wish that I could have the money and the admission to Willington. But am I willing to sell my soul over it? No. I put too much pressure on myself to get that stupid scholarship anyway.

Our food shows up, greeted by enthusiastic cheers from Ed and Mikey. We all tear into our stacks of pancakes and French toast like ravenous wolves.

"You know that Ken Gardener dude?" Ed says through a mouthful of pancake.

"The CEO from the magic-sharing scandal?" Ana asks.

"Yeah, yeah. That guy," Ed says.

"Are you putting hot sauce on your pancakes?" Mikey asks, staring at Ed.

Ed is, in fact, midway through dousing his whipped-cream-covered pancakes in Cholula. "Don't judge my choices, dude," Ed says. "Okay, so that Gardener guy is going to court now. He could go to jail."

Huh. I thought that rich, powerful wizards were always

fine in the end. Like, no matter what happened, they wouldn't really face consequences for their actions.

"Do you think Mr. B could go to jail?" Ed asks.

Mikey's expression freezes for a second, and then he stuffs a huge chunk of French toast in his mouth. I remember just how close Mikey was to Mr. B. He and Ed have been generally supportive and chill since the scholarship ceremony, but every so often I get flashes of discomfort from him.

The problem is that, like Mikey, lots of people liked Mr. B. But now that he's done something bad, they can't reconcile the Mr. B they liked with the Mr. B who did something wrong. In reality, he's both of those people.

Anyway, I do understand that it's hard to imagine someone you liked going to jail. But I can't field every person's Mr. B–related feelings. They can talk to other people about that.

"Jail? For what?" Ana says. "What Mr. B did was fucked up, but I don't think it's illegal."

"Okay, Mr. B talk is canceled for the day. Thank you," I say, waving my fork in the air for emphasis. "We're celebrating here, aren't we?"

"You're right," Ed says, lifting his hands in surrender. "We did open a show tonight."

"Hell yeah," Mikey says. He turns his attention to me and Ana. "Do you guys think you'll do the show next year?"

"No," Ana and I say in perfect unison.

"Shay doesn't even like acting," Ana adds.

Mikey looks thoughtful. "That makes sense actually."

"Yeah, I hate it," I say. "This will hopefully be the last time I'm ever on a stage."

"Ah, the ice queen cometh," Ed says, his gaze trained at something over my shoulder.

I turn around and make direct eye contact with Brittany. She stops next to our table and frowns down at the laminate floor. "Good show tonight, guys," she says, but she somehow makes it sound like an insult. We all half-heartedly parrot the sentiment back at her. "Shay, can I talk to you for a second?"

"Um." I stare at her, trying to figure out what she could want to say. There's not an obvious answer I can think of. "Sure." Ana touches my arm lightly, and I can sense her rooting for this to go well.

I follow her to an empty part of the restaurant away from our group. Brittany stops between a table and the back wall, then stands there fidgeting with her tank top for a few seconds. "I guess I should thank you," she says quietly, looking as though she would rather swallow her own tongue than thank me.

I blink at her. Did she just . . . ? Wow.

"I read the article." Brittany tightens her ponytail, not making eye contact. "I kept waiting for you to, like, get tired of whatever game you were playing and tell everyone about me," she says. "But I guess you're not going to do that."

"No," I say, glancing around surreptitiously. We're out of earshot from anybody in our group.

"I probably shouldn't have tried to, like, threaten you. I mean, Ed was totally full of shit anyway. You're such a Goody Two-shoes, there's no way you would have OD'd on one of his potions."

I school my expression so I don't show how ironic I find that statement. "It's okay," I say. "Don't worry about it."

"My mom sent me to therapy after your mom went all wacko on her," Brittany says, rolling her eyes.

"That's good," I say. Now I'm interested in what exactly went down when our moms met each other. That's probably a mystery that will remain unsolved, since I very much doubt that Mom is going to tell me about it.

"Yeah, I think it would kill her to actually talk to me without criticizing literally everything, so she brought in a professional."

There isn't a good response to that, so I just nod in a way that I hope looks supportive.

"Um, you were pretty okay in the show tonight," she continues.

"Thanks, Brittany," I say, strangely touched by this half-hearted compliment.

"Yeah," she says. "Okay, bye."

With that, Brittany strides away. I take a few moments

to absorb what just happened and then return to my table. Ed and Mikey are off talking to Mateo at another booth, though I don't doubt Ed will return soon to sniff out any potential new gossip from me.

"That went . . . well?" I say.

"Really?" Ana says, lacing her fingers into mine. "What'd she say?"

"She thanked me for not telling people about her," I say quietly. "And she kind of apologized?"

"Wow. I didn't think that was ever going to happen."

"Me neither."

I turn so I can see Brittany sitting at the senior girls' table. That might have been the nicest she's ever been to me. I still have that image in my head of her pining after Mr. B in her driveway. This moment is a long way from that.

When I turn back to Ana, I catch her staring at me. "Weirdo," I say teasingly.

She shrugs. "I like your face."

"It's a pretty good face." I snag a bite of her blueberry pancakes. "Oh, I forgot to ask you this earlier. Do you want to come with me and Lex to play terraball next weekend? We're going on Saturday after work."

"I don't know if I'm good enough to play with you guys," Ana says, laughing. "You wiped the floor with me last time. It was embarrassing. I don't know if my ego can take that."

"Trust me—your ego can take the hit," I say, shaking my head at her. "And Lex wants you to come."

"Okay. I'll be there." She smiles at me with that adorable dimple of hers.

I lean over to press a kiss against her lips. Then I sit there with Ana, our fingers entwined in her lap. It's nice, for once, to just exist. There's nobody to impress, no scholarship to try to win, no looming sense of failure and inadequacy at my back. I'm just a witch in IHOP having a nice time with my girlfriend. And that feels like a win to me.

ACKNOWLEDGMENTS

FIRST AND FOREMOST, I HAVE TO THANK MY FAMILY. BECAUSE of you, my dreams always felt possible. I hope you got a kick out of this book, especially the parts that play to our family sense of humor.

To my wonderful partner—Jarreth, I love you. You make my heart sing and my dreams prosper.

I want to express my immense gratitude for the incredible teachers I had as a teen, especially Dr. Bassett and Kim Calvi. I was so fortunate to have adults in my life who respected me and nurtured my creativity.

To Gemma Cooper, agent extraordinaire. You're both delightful and frighteningly competent. Having you in my corner is a dream come true. And to the entire team at the Bent Agency—you all do such amazing work!

To Polo Orozco, my intrepid editor. I feel very lucky that my book ended up with you. You are truly a joy to work with. I shout your praises from the rooftops at every opportunity.

Thank you to everyone at Penguin Random House, including but not limited to: Jen Klonsky, Elise LeMassena, Cindy Howle, Misha Kydd, Brian D. Luster, Ariela Rudy Zaltzman, Amanda Cranney, Suki Boynton, and Natalie

Vielkind. I want to send a special shout-out to the publicity, marketing, and sales teams, who make so much of the behind-the-scenes magic happen. And of course, thank you to Alex Cabal and Danielle Ceccolini for creating the cover of my dreams!

To Dr. Effie—I'll always remember the moment I got to tell you I finally sold this book. Your support meant the world to me.

To Ari, for being one of the first people to believe in *How to Succeed in Witchcraft.*

A special thank-you to the Dance Complex. I wrote quite a bit of my first draft on my lunch breaks in Studio 7!

I take particular joy in writing characters who have best friends, largely because I've had the good fortune of having some of the best humans in the world as my friends. Obviously, my acknowledgments wouldn't be complete without thanking some of them. Thank you, Paige, my original partner in crime. You're my blueprint for what a best friend can be; Lex wouldn't exist without you. A massive thank-you to the Three Liquid Girls, my ride-or-dies. Ivy and Tanya, you have the most beautiful souls. And finally, Caro. So much that I admire about you has inspired parts of this book. Thank you for letting me name a character after you!

I would be remiss if I didn't also thank the many, many friends of mine whom I frantically emailed drafts of this book to. Chloè-Rose, Rosie, Casey, Athena, Eden—and other people I'm sure I'm forgetting at the moment—I so appreciate your time and attention. I especially want to thank Emma, because I sent you a truly obscene number of drafts of this book. You were the earliest cheerleader for *How to Succeed in Witchcraft*, and writing my gay little book felt much less lonely because you were there. Thanks for sticking by me all this time.

I have been lucky enough to meet wonderful people in the book world, some of whom have become friends and others who have given me indispensable advice: Ryan Douglass, Jas Hammonds, Namina Forna, Crystal Maldonado, Jessica Lewis, and Alexis Henderson. Thank you for all your support! Building a community during a pandemic is hard, but you all have been so wonderful. I hope to meet more of you in person in the future.

To all the members past and present of my lovely writing groups: Patric, Alyn, Tara, Leyla, Tatiana, Michaela, Vanessa, Peréz, and Jas. You all have nourished my creative spirit in such important ways.

Lastly, I want to send my love to all the survivors out there. You deserve the world.